Hidden Daughter

By the same author

Cells of Knowledge

(Winner of the *Scotsman*/Saltire Society
First Book of the Year Award)

Hidden Daughters

SIAN HAYTON

EDINBURGH

© Sian Hayton 1992

Published by Polygon
22 George Square
Edinburgh

Set in Trump Medieval
by Koinonia Limited, Manchester
and printed and bound in Great Britain
by Redwood Press Ltd, Melksham, Wiltshire

The right of Sian Hayton to be identified
as the author of this work has been asserted
by her in accordance with the Copyright,
Designs and Patents Act 1988.

British Library Cataloguing in Publication Data
Hayton, Sian
   Hidden Daughters
   I. Title
   823.914 [F]

ISBN 0 7486 6136 0

The Publisher acknowledges subsidy
from the Scottish Arts Council towards
the publication of this volume.

The girl-child woke suddenly. There was a light in the tent when there should not be one. Reluctantly, for there was an early frost that night, she sat up and looked over the edge of her bedding. The grandfather had lit a small fire and was huddled over it swaying back and forth and singing quietly. She realised with a shock that he was wearing the cape of office which should have been left for her alone. Then, horrified, she realised that he was taking omens, for on the ground in front of him lay a flat stone, a piece of horn, a length of bark and a roll of skin. He picked them up one by one and scraped a sooty twig over them, then ceremonially spat on each and rubbed it with his thumb. She was terrified and burrowed back into the heaped skins. The firelight threw shifting shadows on the walls and the husky, droning voice of the old man threatened to overpower her with the unfamiliar. In their clan women were the ones to talk to the spirits, but here was a man, of her own family, meddling in the forbidden. His winged shadow that now covered most of the walls showed her an aspect of him she had never seen before. It could only mean disaster.

She tried to hide in the skins so that whatever was nearby would not see her. Before she could seal her mouth a whimper escaped her and she lay rigid with fear. The old women who were training her had told her that when powers were loose it was most important to let nothing in or out of your body. She had been practising for weeks without success and now she failed once again when it mattered most. Something lifted her from the bed with supernatural speed and she closed her eyes

1

so tight a tear was squeezed out. In despair she sobbed aloud and opened her eyes. Her grandfather was looking at her with concern. He put her down beside the fire and she sat up trembling.

'You were not intended to see this,' he said, indicating the tablets at his feet. She did not reply.

'We live in desperate times,' he went on, 'and we need desperate measures. The High-King has set us down here, but the soil is too thin to grow crops. Most of our hunters have been taken away to foreign wars; there are no skins to buy silver; there is no silver to buy spears for hunting; the grazing is worn out since our sheep cannot wander. We will not live through another winter. Since your mother died three winters ago, no woman has appeared with the power to travel in the spirit world and you are still too young for the task. It seemed to me that one of our family might have the power even if he is a man. I am the only one of our blood left but for you. I have to try.' She managed to keep her mouth closed on a groan.

'I am beginning to see something,' he said, 'perhaps if you sit with me you will help.'

He paused for a moment, then draped the Cloak over her, covering her completely. Then he began to sing again. Hidden from his sight she closed her eyes and covered her ears but swayed in rhythm with his voice. Her body might be present, but if she did not know what was said or see what was done she might be spared punishment for this horrible blasphemy. The night wore on and she kept up ceaseless prayers for forgiveness.

She awoke again well into the drizzly morning. The fire was a little heap of ashes and her grandfather was gone. This was not new, for he often went off to hunt in the early morning and left her, but after the events of the night before she felt alarm churning in her stomach. Nevertheless she said nothing to the old woman who came to take her to the caves for training and when she returned she sealed the tent behind her as fast as she could. If they were to discover his absence what could she say? She could never admit the shameful fact that she had been witness to his sins and had done nothing to stop him. What she could have done she did not know, but she knew she should have done something. Their food was left outside the tent as usual. After she had eaten she lay down and waited, her heart knocking against her ribs and her ears straining for every sound. He did not come. Another day passed in the same way and she thanked the spirits that they had not betrayed her secret. On the morning of the third day the old woman who came to fetch her said she was not clean enough and asked what had come over the old man that he had let her get into that state. He knew how important it was for her to be pure, she said, and he had never let her down before. At that the child had coloured and the old woman became suspicious.

'Kigva!'

The child flinched at the sound of her own name. She would have to answer now and she would have to tell the truth.

'Kigva, what has happened to your mother's father?'

'I do not know. He left two nights ago and did not say where he was going. It seemed to me he was going hunting.'

'He went hunting and did not tell you?'

'No. I do not know what he went to do. Perhaps he went hunting.'

Fortunately the old one did not press her further. The child could see that she was not pleased for she pressed her lips together and shook her head. Then, seizing her hand, she took her to the old women's tent where only adults went, and then only when they had broken the law. The child's heart sank further as they walked into the strange-smelling darkness. The three old women who shared this tent were the only ones allowed to keep a fire burning at all times. Flickering shadows surrounded her as they had two nights before and she was sure they must know what her grandfather had done. She peered into the darkness to see if there were any sign of him. Apart from the loom that stood in any woman's house and bunches of herbs which she herself had helped to gather there was nothing to be seen. She was disappointed that the tent where the terrible ones lived should be so commonplace. The caves where they did magic were full of mystery. Magic water dripped from the roof and none knew where it came from. The spirits spoke in strange voices and their breath blew your hair as they passed near you. The likenesses of animals appeared on the walls as the firelight shifted and the great hunting magic made the hair on your back crawl. Here all that could be seen in the firelight was skins.

Ignoring her, the three old ones whispered to each other. Then one of them said angrily,

'There has been too much of this,' and she turned to the child.

'Kigva, come here.' She approached the three and waited for the questions to start. They were bound to find out the truth, for they were the wise ones of the clan to whom everyone came for knowledge. All they said was,

'When your grandfather comes home you are to come and tell us at once. Do you understand?'

She nodded. The terrible one nodded back. This was worse – they must know already what had happened that night.

'Go on up to the cave now,' said the old one, 'and attend to your duties.'

She felt as if her legs were made of stone as she made her way up the hill to the dripping cave. That day, as an offering to the ancestors, she worked very hard and made hardly any mistakes in her reciting, but as she returned to her tent she began to feel the fear again. What if he came home and swore her to silence once again? Whom should she obey – her teachers or her family? All her life she had been told that these were the people to respect, but none had told her who was more important. As it fell out she was spared the agony of this decision, for when her grandfather returned in the pale light of dawn he collapsed on to his bed and lay without moving. He did not even answer her when she spoke his name, so she had no choice but to fetch the old women.

They tended the old man with herbs and chanting until he

4

recovered some days later, then they questioned him. He would not tell them where he had been – not even when they cursed him in the name of every spirit they could name. He lay on his back and stared at the roof of the tent where the smoke escaped, his lips moving silently, and say what they would, he did not budge. At last, saying that there was not much a mere man could do to upset the balance it was their duty to maintain, they left him alone. They did not think to question his granddaughter, for she was just a child, and an unpromising one at that.

Whatever he had done, it was for the good of the tribe. Some days later men came from the other world and brought them flour and salt, and would take nothing in return. Then a smith brought them metal spear-heads and in return took only two sheep-skins. The day he came all the tribe hid in their huts, but grandfather was brave and went to do the bargaining for them. The next spring the smith brought a metal plough and took only a wolf's skin from the men who had used his spears to kill it. The men of the clan began to speak to the old man with respect and asked for his help in finding game and using the new plough. The old women heard nothing of this.

The little girl saw it all and was sure the night her grand-father had put on her Cloak had brought it about, but she did not know how. Months had passed and the fogs of winter had come and gone before she saw that she had better find out the truth. She had got away with silence with the old women, yet there were Others, she knew, who would know what had passed, and they would be expecting her to act. For Them, and in her position as queen of the tribe, she ought to find out where he had gone. She laid her plans carefully, however, for she was in her tenth year and beginning to know wisdom.

The old man continued to go off on his own from time to time. The old women told her to watch him for them, so she continued to pretend that she knew nothing. After a while they lost interest, but she did not. Some mornings when he was gone, he left a heap of ash in the tent. She began to watch for these times and realised that this happened at the time of

5

the full moon. Even now she was cautious and stuck to her plan.

The hunters of the clan found that they had a new apprentice. The queen's daughter had taken to following them around and pestering them with a stream of questions. They were not even good questions. She was not interested in the varieties of footprint or the texture of dung which told the hunters about the size and age of an animal. Her only interest was in following spoor, the qualitiy of terrain and how long a trail would last. Since she was who she was they could not send her home, nor could they ignore her questions, for custom said that a child's questions were sacred, but it was tiresome to have her constantly at their side. To her credit she was light on her feet and as time went by she could move as silently as the best of them. In fact she often scared them badly by appearing on the trail ahead of them without warning, and sometimes made them angry by laying a false trail which deceived the most cunning. After a while she left them alone.

One dawn, before the stags went into rut and falling leaves could make tracking him too hard, the girl-child followed her grandfather into the forest. At first a heavy dew made her task easier than she could ever have wished, but as the sun dried it up she had to look harder for the broken twigs and dented ground that marked his route. Some time after the middle of the day she saw the silvery trunks of many fallen trees leaning on each other like stalks of sickled barley. As she approached she found that the lower branches of these trees were tangled tightly together so that they barred her passage. She started to skirt them but found the barrier wider than she had thought. If she went too far down the hill she might never find her grandfather's trail again. It would be better to see which path her grandfather had taken at the barrier.

She had to cast about for some time to find his trail. Once found it was very difficult to follow, for whereas before the old man had taken a direct route from point to point, now the path twisted like a serpent. Furthermore on the earlier part, as was to be expected from a man of his age, the footprints were deep and even, but now they were shallow and irregular as if he were creeping up on a quarry. She struggled on as the sun sank towards the tree-tops and realised only after some time that the trail was leading, not round the fallen trees, but through them. Then, suddenly, she was standing exposed on the edge of a clearing.

Hastily she drew back into the trees and looked about her. The clearing was very wide and pleasing to the eye, with tall foxgloves and fennel growing abundantly. Below them were poppy, vervain, valerian, nettle and dozens of the other plants for healing and harming which the old ones had showed her. Birds and insects flew in the glade in great numbers and the sun-warmed air was filled with the sound of their voices. In the centre of this busy and colourful glade was her grandfather. He was lying on his back and at first she thought that he was sleeping, or worse. Then his head moved and she realised that he was watching a buzzard as it circled overhead. He looked very calm and cheerful and not at all like a man betraying the customs of his clan. The child was about to hail him when she thought better of it. There might be more to learn by keeping still, so she nestled down in the branches and watched.

The sun dropped below the tree-tops and the clearing grew dark. All at once the old man sat up and looked attentive, as if he had heard an expected sound. Then to her rage he opened his pack, pulled out her Cloak, put it round his shoulders, and walked gravely to a tree-stump on the far side of the glade. The light was changing so that for the first time she could make out a large stone building just inside the forest ahead of him. Grandfather sat on the stump and stared, waiting, into the forest. Twilight fell rapidly, and as the sky flared red with the sunset a light appeared in the building.

With her heart beating in her throat, the girl crept across the clearing towards her grandfather. He had begun to speak loudly into the trees and she wondered if he had lost his senses. Then she heard a voice answer him from the forest. It was a harsh, echoing sound, like the voices of the spirits in the cave and it reminded her also of the sound of the augury stones being tumbled in their metal bowl. The hair on her neck stood up and it took all her hardihood not to leap away through the trees like a hare. Clinging to a clump of grass to keep herself still, terror washed through her time and again. At last she had to lie down, partly for concealment and partly because her legs were too weak to hold her, but once she was on the ground she regained possession of herself and could take in what was happening.

Her grandfather and the other were talking like two old friends – discussing the crops. She would have expected her grandfather to abase himself and cover himself with protecting talismans, but he was as calm and unconcerned as if he had known this spirit all his life. Though she strained her ears mightily for a long time she could not make out a word that was spoken by either. All she got was the impression that the talk was easy and cheerful. Once she even heard her grandfather laugh.

As she lay on the ground a creature, probably an owl, flew overhead. A pause, then it passed her again. She felt uneasy at this attention and watched some time for the bird to come again. When it did not she tried to worm her way through the grass to get nearer and hear what was said, but just as she was getting near enough her grandfather bade the spirit farewell and stood up. She froze like a rabbit and turned her face into the grass, for the hunters had told her that a face would attract notice sooner than any other part of the body. The sound of his footsteps passed, going back to the forest, and to her dismay when she raised her head she could not see where he had gone. She had assumed that he would stay in the clearing for the night which was now drawing on fast. Following him would be impossible and she did not know the way back home.

In panic she scrambled to her feet, ran across the clearing and shouted into the forest.

'Grandfather!'

A chuckle answered her from the blue shadows.

'Grandfather, it's me – I need your help.'

The chuckle came again and with it the rushing sound she had heard before.

'Grandfather,' she cried, 'don't leave me! PLEASE! I don't know the way back. I'm frightened.'

Something tangled in her hair, tugging it painfully. She screamed and fell to the ground. She felt a hand on her arm and she screamed again, squeezing her eyes shut.

'Well now,' said a voice, 'is this the one who will dream the dream for her clan – screeching in terror at a wood-demon?' The hand was hot, hotter than any hand she had ever felt before. She tried to pull away, but the grip was unshakeable. Suddenly it let go and she curled into as small a space as possible.

'It is not that,' came another voice, 'it is a hedgehog.'

She felt a hand on her other arm, but this one was cool and dry. And the voice was familiar. Squinting round she saw that she was right. Her grandfather was stooping over her and he was smiling at her fear.

'Stand up,' he said, 'there is nothing to be afraid of. I will take care of you.'

She got to her feet slowly and looked around. There was no one else.

'Where is the wood-demon?' she asked.

'He has gone back to his home. He knew you were spying on us, but he would not harm you, not as long as I am here.'

'Who is he?' she gasped.

'I may not tell you his name. I only discovered it that night when we sat by the fire. He is very powerful and has great wealth and he lives in the forest. That is all you need to know.'

'Did you ask him for his help? Is that why we got the plough and the spears? From him?'

'He helped me to change the tribe's fortune. He told me where to find some people – powerful people.'

'Then why have you come here today? The tribe is doing much better. The hunting is good and we have enough to eat. Next year we will have trade goods. You did not need to talk to him.'

'It is better to make sure such as he remembers you.'

'But it is dangerous. The terrible ones may follow you, or send someone to follow you.'

'Are you telling me they have not?'

'What do you mean?'

'I was wondering how you came to be here. It is a hard place to find. You must have had help. Admit it, now, the old ones sent you, didn't they?'

'Indeed they did not. I found you my own self. I did not need help. I asked the hunters how to follow spoor and they showed me. I have told the old ones nothing.'

He pulled the Cloak out of his pack and thrust it at her.

'This garment is very old and has much power. If you lie it will hear you, you can be sure.'

'I do not lie. The old ones asked me about you – where you went – what you did – but I have never told them anything – not even about the night you wore the Cloak and looked for the name.'

The old man smiled at her.

'You are a good child and clever. You learned all about trailing from the hunters?'

'Not all. They tried to tell me about hoof-marks and drop-pings, but I did not want that.'

'When we get home you will go and ask them about animal spoor. You must never miss a chance to learn anything.'

He gave her some dried deer meat and they set off up the long trail home.

Once they stopped to rest and she returned to her question.

'If the tribe's fortunes are mended, why did you come to speak to the wood-demon?'

'You will understand one day.'

'Tell me and I may understand now.'

'You are still a child and in our clan children are spoken to. At any time they may speak to an adult and hear the truth. This is necessary for the children to learn everything they need. When the child becomes an adult he does not talk. He may talk to his fellows about work, or join in the chanting at the feasts. But if the talk is not essential it is frowned on. It is very hard.'

'I know that. It is the way we live. It is not so very hard.'

'For members of our family it is hard. We are forbidden to speak to anyone below our station, except the terrible ones, in case we say a word wrong and the world is put out of place. It was said that your mother died only because your father had talked to the High-King about her. We must watch our mouths for the good of the clan. But it is hard. You will find out yourself in time.'

'That is why you come to the wood-demon? So that you can talk?'

'That is why. It is safe to talk to him – he is as powerful as we are, perhaps more so, and the balance is not disturbed when we talk.'

'Will I talk to him when I am an adult?'

'I cannot say. It is more a question of whether he will talk to you. Now come on or we will not be home before moonset.'

Summers passed and she became a woman. Then it was time for her to take her place as the queen of the tribe. The old ones washed her and led her to the biggest cave where she was to fast for nine days and nights. Her course was about to start again and it heightened the sense of doom bearing down on her. They led her far down the cave to the back where she was surprised to find a narrow tunnel she had never known was there. The old ones indicated that she should kneel and crawl through it. Fighting off a choking sensation, she did as she was told and found the tunnel soon widened again into a cave not quite high enough for her to stand up in. No word was spoken as a lamp was pushed through to her then, to her horror, she was left alone.

It was cold and damp in the cave. She was glad she had her skin Cloak to lie on for the chill would have struck her to the bone without it. As the day wore on she kept clutching at this tiny light of comfort – at least she had her Cloak to keep her warm. The old ones had told her water would be supplied and, already thirsty, she heard a dripping in the darkness behind her. On investigating with the uncertain lamp she found a small stone dish on the floor where it caught a runnel *of water – a few mouthfuls a day for her. That was her other comfort.*

She sat down and looked about her. The walls and roof of the cave were painted red. On the red background were painted the animals who would help her through her vigil as they had helped queens before her. The salmon, the hare and the goose had been described to her as particularly powerful, since they moved swiftly and strongly in all the different elements. She did not like the way they had been depicted here and wished she had been given materials so that she could paint them in the glowing colours their power demanded. In her mind she asked their forgiveness for this crude drawing with the eyes too large and the legs too thin, and begged them to continue friendliness towards her in her hour of need. After a while the lamp went out.

The rest of her time of trial passed in a nightmare. At first, since she knew her task was to dream, she lay down and recited the words she had learned over the long years of training. The old women had taught her to calm herself by repeating the words and thinking very carefully about the images that went with them. She soon found her way into the incantations.

'Lying here in the womb of the earth, I await the time of my renewal. Grant, oh mothers, peaceful heart and clear vision as I bind myself to creation. To the fox as he silently hunts to feed his family; to the seal as he traverses the wide minch; to the owl as she flies in darkness; to the wolf as he runs with his brothers; to the sow as she lies in the forest with her litter: to the crow as she searches for the dying; to the trout in the peat-stained water...'

And so through the whole animal kingdom. Once they had all been greeted she went on to the vegetable world and to the rocks and minerals, to the sun and moon, to the earth herself and to the dead. After some hours she felt the ground under her begin to sway and consciousness left her. In her dreams she wandered the forest and the moors rejoicing. Every creature in every kingdom was her friend, and all of them returned her greeting from the pebbles on the shore to the mag-

gots in a carcase. For a long time happiness ran through her in the same way a hive runs with honey. Then she woke up.

She opened her eyes into total darkness. The dark was so strong it pushed down on her eyeballs. She closed her eyes again and there were tiny flashes of light yet when she tried to see again the lights still flashed. She sat up, gasping, and struggled to breathe evenly. With her hands she re-discovered the shape of her body and the cave she sat in. She found the water bowl and refreshed herself. It did not seem very full. How long had she been here? If there was so little water then she must not have been there long. What if she had only been there a few hours? There were still days to go – days in this darkness. Panic swept through her and she found she was gasping once again. She lay down and began her incantations again. She sat up again, choking. In spite of her training and her fast she needed to make water and did so in agony of mind. Her teeth were clattering together uncontrollably and the shaking travelled all through her body. Almost overcome, she moaned aloud, lay down on her Cloak and drew it round her. All around her in the shifting darkness she felt the walls of the cave begin to move rythmically, closing on her little by little until something pressed on her face. She heard her own long scream of terror. And then she was not alone.

She felt a hand on her arm – hot, hotter than human – and steady, comforting her in her despair. The strongest one of all was there, as he had been in the forest and he promised, silently, that he would stay with her for the rest of her vigil. With tears she thanked him and felt herself gathered up in his arms. Together, from then on, they wandered the universe. He showed her things which only he knew. With him she touched the cold, hard moon and walked on the black rind of the sky. She found that stars felt like the taste of blaeberries and the north wind was truly a great river whose source was the mountains of the sun. He gave her jewelled collars and crowns and broke open an oak-tree so that she could feast on the honey. There was no one equal to him.

After nine days and nights the old women had to crawl into the cave and drag out her filthy, wasted body. They thought for a terrible moment that she had died and left her family without issue, but her eyelids quivered and with relief they began slapping her legs to revive her. In a little while she looked out at them and started to weep. This did not trouble them, for people often did strange things after their ordeal. Some never returned to their bodies at all so the signs of Kigva's awareness were all to the good. They washed her hair and her body and she began to talk to them. She told them only what they would expect to hear.

After her inauguration as queen she stopped speaking to anyone in public except the old ones and to them only when necessary. She could not speak to her grandfather while they were in the tent for fear that someone might overhear them. He had taken over the use of the Cloak altogether and she waited in vain for the old women to protest on her behalf. Pehaps they had not seen how much he wore it, or perhaps they no longer felt that far-seeing was important to them. As long as he did not abuse the power in the Cloak, she did not see any need to protest. People often came for his advice, now, leaving the terrible ones alone in their reeking darkness. The advice he gave was sound and the source to her of much prestige. It was not understood how he knew so many things better than the rest of the clan. It could only have come from spirits he held in his control, but the people felt the less they knew about such a source the better. Their intuition was correct, as some of his knowledge had come from the wood-demon. The rest was the wisdom he had acquired over the years which had never been acceptable without some magic to back it. Before this they had relied exclusively on their ancestors.

The secret the two shared about the presence in the forest made a bond between them which no other men and women in their tribe enjoyed. In silence she would lead him off into the forest, and none dared to question them about their comings and goings. Once they were clear of the village they would talk about important matters but when they came to the clearing the grandfather was the only one to speak. She did not complain about this, for even after her ordeal she was *still afraid of the spirit and was happy to leave the old man to carry the burden of talk. If the truth were told she was not experienced enough to have anything to say worth hearing. She only accompanied the old man to ensure that she got her share of the prestige.*

Then the old man had to die. Like his father before him he was killed by the leader of their greatest enemy. She had always known that one day she would put him in his coffin, yet now the time had come, devastating loneliness settled on her shoulders. Who would she talk to? Who would talk to the wood spirit for her and the clan? Most important of all, who would lead the clan in battle?

Her eye fell on the leader of the strangers who had come from the High King. He was very young, as young as herself, yet he carried a lot of prestige as his men deferred to him. With his broad shoulders and muscular legs he was a most promising figure for a battle leader. He had been doing grandfather the courtesy of getting drunk for his wake and was now sagging against the door of the guest-house. The old women were the drunkest of all that night and there was no time to go and ask the wood-demon for his advice. She tried to think carefully about the consequences of her actions as she had been taught to do, but her decision was made almost before she started. In the light summer rain she walked down to the guest-house and sat down in front of the youth.

Along with the clan and the High King's vassal she travelled down the mountain to find a home away from the lands of their enemy. On the third night out they found a wonderful place. A natural clearing in the forest, with plenty of grazing and as much water as they could ever use. There was a level area for building houses and plenty of big timber already fallen to make huts for the clansmen. They had all settled down and made plans to start building when, on their second night there, she had dreamed a power dream. In it she stood in the forest washed with moonlight. A voice she knew almost as well as her grandfather's had spoken to her; the

15

·wood-demon. Trembling with joy, she waited to hear her lord's first words to her since the days of her ordeal.

He said, 'I do not want you to stay in this place. It may seem to you to be a good place now, but if you stay I will visit awful punishments on you. Your sheep will sicken and die with their bellies swollen. Your children will be covered with sores. Your women will fail to conceive and you yourself will be driven from the clan.'

'Why will you do this to us?' she asked him, aghast. 'Our presence here will not harm you.'

'Not now, perhaps, but in the years to come, when the children alive now have children of their own, there will be too many living here. My hall is not far away and, as your tribe spreads out over the land, I will be invaded. I wish to stop this now, before it begins.'

'We would respect your boundaries,' she protested.

'You say so, but who else in your tribe do you speak for? You are not your grandfather and it will be many years, if ever, before your voice has his weight.'

'Already men listen when I speak. I am still the only representative of my family here.'

The answer was a laugh like a gale blowing through the forest. Angry, she said,

'I tell you, if I forbid them to go near your halls they will obey. I might be young, but I speak with the authority of my family.'

'As long as you stayed high on the moorland where life was hard and the forest a dark mystery you would be obeyed. The clan believed that only your mother's kin could walk the forest safe from the spirits that lived there. Now you have brought them far away into the lower lands. Soon the smallest child will walk through the thickets with his head up where before he would stride boldly only on the naked crag. Your voice will mean nothing.'

'How can you be so sure?' she protested. 'You do not know how deep the customs run in our tribe. It is like the bones in our flesh.'

'Some things cannot be avoided, and men's memories are

short. I tell you I have seen much, much more of life than you. As the leaves fall in autumn and the snow melts in spring, the life you led has passed away. With it have gone the customs that sustained it. Your duty now is to follow the hard young man you have joined with your body.'

'Where will he take me?'

'To his father's fortress on the coast. There you and your clan will be treated as nothing much better than slaves, but you will be together. And you will wait for your time to come again.'

Desperate to keep within the circle of his power she asked, 'What about the service I owe you?'

'What service can a poor creature like you offer?'

His answer was a knife in her heart and she replied tearfully,

'You helped my grandfather when poverty laid us as low as our rain-flattened barley. I must repay that debt.'

'I have no demands to make of you. That debt died with your grandfather. All I ask of you is that you should not disturb my peace.'

'Grandfather told me the debt was to have been paid by the whole tribe.'

'Your grandfather had his pride, and offered the service of the tribe in exchange for the favours I did him. I accepted because he would not have taken my help otherwise. It is not good to make people grateful to you. Soon enough such gratitude turns to hate. I have lived long and I know it well. It is wiser to put a price on your generosity.'

Appalled, she said,

'Are you not willing to accept our services?'

'Not I.'

'Then why did you help me at my inauguration?'

'I know nothing about your savage notions.'

'During my vigil there came a time when my strength failed me. I nearly died of horror on that night, but you were by me and walked with me through those dark hours. Do you not remember?'

'You have had a strange dream, child. I never meddle with

17

the rituals of others. You owe me nothing.'

'*There is nothing you wish me to do for you?' she cried.*

'*Nothing except to return to your family and help them to work for their new master.'*

'*I hate him, and I will have nothing to do with him!' she wept.*

'*Then you can do nothing for me,' he answered, 'for that is all I wish.'*

The sound of her sobbing woke her. Her husband had decided to spend that night with his men and she was grateful that he had done so. The grief was uncontrollable and it would have been too shaming for him to see her suffer like this.

She spent the rest of the night in thought and in the morning she summoned the old ones and told them of her decision to leave.

And she was betrayed again. He was planning to discard her – the fine young man with his hair blue and black like the raven's breast. To follow him she had told her people they must leave the forest clearing and abandon for ever all their hopes of a peaceful and independent life. They had come away, but resentfully, and only because she had used her last shred of authority to force them. She knew that from then on any control she may have over them would come from her husband's authority. Now even that was to be taken from her.

The evening she discovered this she had been lying waiting for her man. He was standing outside the tent door talking to one of his men and she could hear nearly everything he said. It was probable that he did not realise she could understand his language or he would not have given himself away so soon. He spoke of the wood-demon and boasted that he had got the better of him in a contest of guile. How he had done this she could not follow, but she was pleased that her husband had made the acquaintance of her master. It would give them equal status.

Then she heard the words,

'The woman I am to marry is young and healthy, and so am I. We will have plenty of children.' She was puzzled. Were they not already married by the fact that he had taken her maidenhead? That night as he lay beside her she unsealed her mouth to ask.

'How do people marry in your land?'

'With a great feast,' he answered ingenuously, 'so that there are very many witnesses. Once the man and the woman have stood up in front of all these people and had their hands bound together everyone will know that they have a contract. Then they go to the bed together and make babies who will be the heirs.'

'Does everybody do this?'

'Only the people who matter – who own cattle and land and forest and shore. When others decide to make children, they just do what is necessary.'

'We are not married, then?'

'What an idea,' he said, laughing uproariously. 'I could not marry you. But do not be afraid. I have been well reared and I will not abandon my concubine. And at the end of the year you may go where you will and your people also.'

When he had sated his lust and slept like an infant beside her, she slipped out of the tent. Beckoning the old one who was on watch they ran silently to the other women. When she told them the shameful truth their eyes glittered in the firelight.

'In his eyes I am nothing,' she said, too wretched to weep, 'and when he marries this other woman I will lose all face before my people. What shall I do? You must advise me.'

'How shall I advise you?' said one, licking her lips, 'I hardly know who you are. You have never found the need to seek our advice before, why do you need us now?'

'Always before you have asked your grandfather for his advice and left us to ourselves,' said another. 'Why do you not ask him now? Go back up the mountain and seek him in his coffin where we left him.'

'We have nothing to say that you would wish to hear,' said

19

the third. The queen was angry at this presumption.

'I never sought advice from my grandfather,' she said. 'Many others did, but not I. I did not need it. I did not need the advice of any of my inferiors, until now. I have every right to ask you for your opinion at any time and I will do what I please with your answer.'

The old ones dropped their gaze. After a pause one of them said,

'You did not ask our advice when you coupled with that youth. Why should we believe you need it now?'

'I do not have to listen to insolence,' she snapped. 'Since you will not give me your words on the matter I will tell you what we will do. I am probably with child by now, and I will not bear the brat in the man's own hall. Therefore we will leave and go back to the forest we know. The rest of the tribe will be under the man's protection, so they will not suffer any more than if I had stayed.'

She paused, seeing that one of them had something to say.

'You will not be revenged on himself?' she said slyly.

'I will not,' she replied warmly.

'The insult to your face must be paid for,' said another.

'True, but it need not be now. My children need the man so I will spare him.'

'There must be a blood payment now, or the spirits will be restless. With a child in the womb it is no time to anger them.'

'Very well,' she sighed. 'I suppose it must be so. Who is suitable?'

'There is one,' said the oldest and again licked her lips. 'His battle chief is a foreigner – one who sells his sword and has no loyalty to clan or king. He fought with Æthelstan against our men, and the blood of one of them could well be on his hands. Let it be him.'

'Do you others agree?' she asked, reluctantly, for the man had not harmed her.

The hooded heads nodded vigorously. She shrugged,

'As you wish,' she said, 'but as soon as it is done we leave this place.'

They were gone as soon as the words left her. Before she might think better of it, they were back, their knives smoking in their hands.

'Now we go,' they said.

In the misty dawn they returned along the track they had travelled. They had taken one horse and the goods they owned of right, nothing more, for they would not steal from the clan, however great the need. As they travelled the old ones talked as eagerly as children about how it would be when they got back to their home. She had to put an end to their hopes.

'How can we go home?' she asked them. 'You forget, our enemies have taken the moorland we worked. We shall have to find other camping grounds.'

'But the caves – our ancestors – everything is there.' They were bemused.

'And everything is in the hands of the Fir Falbh,' she re- peated. 'There is no return for us to that place. Do not be unhappy. The Fir Falbh at least will respect our holy places, not like the dogs who led us away from them. They would only have desecrated the shrines and torn the grave-mounds open for the sake of the treasure they would find there. Treasure! As if any as poor as we could find gold to put with our ancestors.

'We must move on. I only wish I knew where.'

They struggled on in silence along the stony track. The trees on either side leaned down and hung over them without sheltering. The rain had come again – the fine, soaking rain of the hills – and, saturated, they slowed down and finally stopped. The track was proving to be a stream-bed.

'We cannot go on like this,' said the queen through her dripping hair. 'I know the forest is dark and treacherous – paths there twist and turn like adders in the grass – but it would be better to take a chance on losing sight of the road than on everything we own being soaked.'

'True,' said the oldest one promptly, 'and if one of us walks

21

backwards to see that the path we have travelled does not shift as we leave it we should be able to return.'

'Good,' said another, 'over there is a place where the trees part and the ground between them is firm.'

Hand in hand they left the track and made their way up through the trees. As she was the strongest person, Kigva led the horse. The creature seemed uneasy and as there was little underbrush she began to wonder if they had made a mistake. If the way was so clear there might well be people around to clear it, and people in the forest were even more secretive than the moorland tribes. She was opening her mouth to speak when the horse's bridle was snatched from her hand. It whinnied and reared, but whoever held it was strong and determined. She glimpsed a dark-clad form on the other side of the beast, then it was mounted and ridden off into the trees at a speed she would not have thought possible. In its panniers was their tent, their loom and their grind-stones, along with most of their food.

Too shocked to move the four women stared into the forest.

'What shall we do now?' whimpered one of the old ones.

'We must follow them.' said the queen. 'We have no shelter and no food if we do not.'

'Easy to say,' said the old one. 'The wretched creature is nowhere to be seen. Will you risk us all in that wilderness?'

'The horse is gone but its trace is still on the ground. Look!'

'Oh, we know all about your tracking skills,' jeered the old one, 'but what happens when the horse crosses ground that does not take a hoof-print. What shall we do then?'

'If that should happen – and I do not think it likely – we shall turn round and re-trace our footsteps to the road. But let us not run ahead to seek out troubles. We need that horse and what it carried very badly. It is worth risking something to regain it.'

Without waiting for more arguments she made off through the trees and, grumbling, the old women followed her. The horse's tracks were easy enough to follow as long as the rider took it over the soft ground between the trees. They followed on for a long time while the clouds above the tree-tops broke apart to reveal the blue of the sky. It grew hot in the shelter of the trees and the women began to look for water. They came to a fast, clear river and drank their fill, then found the prediction of the oldest was true. The river banks, uphill of them and down, were great slabs of stone. On them no trace of the horse could be seen.

Kigva told her women to rest and wait for her. They moaned and obeyed, gratefully sinking to the ground. She set off downhill with more assurance in her step than she felt. The higher slopes were familiar and she knew the ground was so rough that horses and horse-thieves were less likely. Fortunately she soon saw a hair of the horse's tail tangled in a low branch. She checked that the tracks were indeed visible beyond there and paused to look around. The sun had dried the rocks and the forest was brimming with the sound of birds and insects. She straightened up and threw back her hair with a sigh. The forest was a good place to be, and she would be nearer to her Lord here than if she had gone down to the coast with the youth. Cheerfully she scampered back to her women.

They had fallen asleep on the warm rocks. The pale flesh of their wrinkled faces slumped and pulled their mouths open so that they drooled and snored.

'These were the mighty ones of my tribe,' she thought. 'When they passed everyone looked at the ground and trembled in case they might look at them.'

In that moment she came to a decision. Perhaps the way of life she had grown up in was truly finished – that could be a good thing for her. She was not her mother's daughter nor could she hope to be. Whatever happened, she was sure of one thing. She would not spend her days the way the old ones had done. If she must grow old like them and sag and make nasty noises, she must first see more than a piece of moorland and a few damp caverns.

A noise behind her caught her attention. Turning, she saw four or five men clad in dark, greasy skins. Each held a short, iron-headed spear and a strung bow. The quivers at their

23

waist held small, bone-tipped arrows and the knives at their belts were long and made of blue metal. There would be no escape from such assailants.

'You will come with us,' they said.

They were taken downslope for many miles till they came to a vast level space. There huge beech trees closed out the sky as far as the eye could see. The undergrowth between the trees had been cleared away for miles and in the open space many, many fine pigs were grazing. There were strong wooden houses in the shelter of the trees and yet smoke rose to the high, green canopy of leaves from only a few. This scarcity made Kigva wonder.

'Perhaps it is too warm to build cooking fires,' she thought.

They were ushered silently into one of the houses and found it clean and dry. Good bedding was laid out for them. Food was handed in by one of the men and they ate well. In their clan they valued a full stomach as a means to clear thought and they had had a long fast since morning. After food they began to discuss their situation.

'Do you know these people?' Kigva asked.

'They are strangers to us.'

'They have not offered us harm.'

'There is no reason why they should do us good.'

'Are they the ones who stole the horse?'

'We have no way of knowing, but we have seen no sign of any other people in this country.'

'Many of the houses have no fire.'

'Perhaps none live there.'

'Such fine houses! They must have owners.'

'I have seen no children.'

'I have seen no women.'

'They will be kept apart.'

Their ramblings were interrupted by the arrival of one of the stranger men. On top of his head he had placed a boar's skull so that the fangs jutted forward from his head like horns. A whole boar's skin hung down his back in a cloak except for the pizzle which he held as a staff of office.

'You will all come with me,' he said, quietly.

They allowed him to lead them between the trees towards a great wooden house that stood in the thicket. Kigva noted that the pigs in the clearing were all tethered to the trees by long plaited ropes of pigskin so that they could graze without wandering off. The mast they rooted in was two hands deep and the animals seemed contented. She wondered if the ropes were strong enough to hold them if they were not.

The man led them through the door of the house into darkness. As their eyes got used to the gloom they found themselves confronted by a crowd of men. Their gear lay at their feet and it was obvious that it had been thoroughly examined, for the tent was spread out on the floor and everything else lay on top of it. They heard a whinny from outside the house and were confirmed in their notion that these were also the horse-thieves. The man with the boar's head spoke.

'We are the boar people, now known as the Old Men. No one who comes to this part of the forest may pass without paying us tribute.'

'How may we pay tribute,' said Kigva, bravely, 'when you have stolen everything we own?' She nodded towards their unpacked gear.

'That is ours by right of conquest,' said the man.

'Then so, for that matter, are we,' she replied.

'I like a woman who does not waste time,' said the chief, 'and because I like that I will explain our situation to you.

'For many generations our people worked for a great spirit who lived in the mountains...'

A murmur of assent ran through the assembly. Kigva felt her body tingle at the words. The chief continued,

'His wisdom was our guide and his strength was our shield against dangers. But three generations ago we disobeyed him, and then his wrath was terrible. Since then the fertility of our women has been falling every year. Some cannot conceive, some cannot bring a child into the world alive. Many have died in the attempt.'

A sigh ran through the crowd of men.

'What did you do to bring this punishment on you?' asked Kigva.

'We are not sure. Perhaps it was that we trespassed, unknowing, on his hunting land, or perhaps it was because we killed one of his servants with an arrow. He turned his face from us at the time and would not tell us what our sins were. All we can be sure of is that we are suffering for it.'

'Why are you telling us about it now?'

'You are young and there are many years of child-bearing in you. We will keep you until you have borne us many children. If you do well, at that time we will let you go where you will. If you do not we will kill you because you know our shame.'

Beside her Kigva felt the old ones stiffen with fear. They were long past child-bearing, if they had ever done so. If they had it was never spoken of – nothing they did was ever spoken of.

'What about my women?' she demanded.

'They are no use. We do not need any more mouths to feed which will not do their share of work.'

'We are still strong,' said the oldest, 'we can do our share.'

'I do not think so,' said the chief with a shrug. 'The raising and feeding of pigs takes many years to learn. That is why we want children.'

'We know many things,' said the old woman, 'and we can make potions and charms to help restore your women to fertility. You may well need us more than you think.'

'Do you all know these things?' the chief asked them.

The three nodded eagerly.

'Then we only need one of you,' said the chief and beckoned two of his men to remove the two oldest. The old women began to wail, and the chief looked at them in disgust.

'What is the matter with you?' he said. 'You are old and near to death. Why should you want to clutter the forest floor any longer?'

'Wait,' said Kigva, 'I have something to say.'

'What can you have to say? Be quick, for we are eager to begin.'

'The oldest is a very wise woman. Her charms are potent and she is very powerful in herself.'

The chief rubbed his face and looked at his men.

'What do you think?' he said. 'Shall we keep her for a while longer?'

'It is not good to offend powerful people,' said one voice. 'We know that too well already.'

'She may truly know something useful to us,' said another.

'Old women eat very little. Give her time to prove her worth.'

'Very well,' said the chief, 'let the oldest stay.' The old woman fell at Kigva's feet with a whimper. The soldier started for the door with her junior.

'A moment more, great chief,' said Kigva hastily.

'Do you wish us to spare the other one also? I am afraid this is not possible.'

'You want a fertile woman,' Kigva blurted out. 'Well, here you have one, but I am already with child.'

'You do not look as if you are,' said the chief looking at her flat stomach.

'It is early. A short while ago I was ravished by the son of the High King and I will show my state soon enough.'

'How can you be sure?'

'I told you, my women are very wise. They have certain ways of knowing the truth of these things and they have told me. The second one especially is a very great midwife. Her hands have magic in them and many children of our clan owe their lives to her.'

The chief pulled at his chin for an age while Kigva and the others stood like strung bows waiting for his decision.

'I suppose it will do no harm to believe you. If what you say is true, it would be terrible to destroy such a valuable person.'

'Thank you, oh, thank you, great chief,' said Kigva. 'I am happier than I can say to think that she will be with me in my travail. You will see – her skills are great – I promise you.'

They were restored to the house they had first entered and there they were to live till the child was born. The oldest was taken away daily to show the boar-people's chief all her secrets. Kigva had saved her life for a time, but her heart was broken by her trials and soon the second had to take her place. The youngest of the three was Kigva's personal attendant. This was necessary, for Kigva could not move abroad herself. Like the pigs she was tethered to the house by her ankle and like the pigs also she was contented to stay that way till her delivery. As the days passed and her belly became swollen she knew that her Lord knew of her fate. In time, she was sure, he would come and save her.

We did not send this letter. At first we had the justification that it was too early in the year to send a messenger to Airemagh, but as the weeks went by we left it lying and said nothing. In the end we could not meet each other's eye and by unspoken consent we put it by and left it. I do not know why we betrayed his trust this way. We will surely answer for it when he returns.

To the most learned, pious and venerable Dubdaliethe, successor of Patrick, of Collumbcille and of Adomnan, father of the family of Airemagh, Hw, monk and scholar of Rintsnoc and Rosnat sends greetings.

Most noble father, more than five years have passed since I last spoke to you and your learned sons at Airemagh. With longing I recall the evenings spent in talk to give light to the mind and the mornings devotedly copying the thoughts of men greater even than your self. I was always sorry that we were never able to finish our disputation on the sermon you gave on the Nativity of the Innocents. I left, hoping to follow your line of reasoning but in spite of my efforts I cannot emulate your wisdom, nor encourage the brothers here to search for the illumination you showed me on that day. I realise that I have written to you before to tell how bleak these years have been for me, exiled from the company of cultivated men, and I know how tedious these plaintive cries must be, so I will not repeat them.

The fact is that the quiet and retired nature of my life has done a great deal to improve my health as you, in your wisdom, predicted, and that, coupled with Ælfrid's preparations, has produced one of God's small miracles. I can now walk up the cliff path over to our lookout point at the northern cell without stopping every fifty paces to catch my breath, and I can do my part in the cultivation and harvesting of our few crops. My fellows and I give thanks daily for this wonderful restoration.

Last summer, as you suggested, I ventured to Rosnat with Ælfrid and we spoke to Olvir Brusasson – an unkempt man with skinny shanks and a barrel chest – who now leads the settlement there. It was a not unprofitable journey, and we are in your debt for advising us to make it. As we approached the bay I saw mounds of clay with small chimneys on the beach. They are still baking shells as our founder showed them all those centuries ago, to make lime for mortar. This is the more enraging in view of the stance which Olvir took. He said at the outset that he was paying rent to Jorvik for the use of the land and gave no credence to our claims.

After Osketel died we were in the hands of Weogorne-caster. Oswald was a bad Archbishop to us but when Aldulf succeeded him we were at least left alone. Nevertheless he was happy to take any rents of ours that he could lay hands on with the slightest lawful claim.

Since he has found the fishing there to be particularly good he will not let us move back to Rosnat. We pointed out that the good fishing had been provided for the people of Nynia by the Almighty and that it would not continue if the unbaptised were to use it. He was perplexed when we said this and it was clear he was afraid we might invoke a curse to spoil the catch for him. To err on the side of safety he said that we could sail round once a month to make the offering at the chapel and that will have to suffice.

However he will let us stay at Rintsnoc for as long as he and his heirs survive, and we may keep the orchard, the farming and the fishing, provided that we give him and his allies free use of the harbourage. He has provisioned a guest-house here and we agreed that in these uncertain times it may well be to our advantage to have a friendly group of foreigners wintering with us from time to time. Olvir saw our dismay when he first suggested it, but in compensation he has sent one of his sons to us for learning without expecting us to waive the fee. The lad is slighter than his brothers so he is keen to distinguish himself in study. He talks of restoring the minster at Witrin, and we say nothing to discourage him.

The truth is that Hw pesters him about it every time he sees him, which, as he is the scolog, is every day.

All in all Olvir is making an honest attempt to be civilised and so far has not yielded to the temptation to rob us of our last remaining goods. These years have seen such a flow of people into this country that there is very little territory that has not been claimed. The forest is full of hunters, pig-breeders and charcoal-burners; the beaches are full of fishermen and lime-burners; any land which looks likely to yield is under the plough. Even the high hills have been infested by miners. God will witness that soon there will be no wasteland for the eremite to find His peace.

Were it not for our feelings of rancour at being deprived of our traditional places, we would be very comfortable here. To tell the truth, we are now so depleted that we could not tend the big farm at the Abbey, and in our hands it would soon fall into disrepair. Indeed, were it not for the penitential servants who have attached themselves to us – some pirates who discovered they have immortal souls – we would not be able to survive in this small community. Only three of us can say the most sacred words, myself, Ælfrid and Nuth. Ælfrid's student is not consecrated, nor is he likely to be, since darkness has fallen over his soul and he prefers to continue with his disgusting practices.

I protest at being represented in this manner. I would be consecrated if I could but I think it is important that I should

*help my fellow man by the study of surgery. It is not my fault
that the church considers this unacceptable.*

We have a little hope in that the sons of Nuth's concubines
and other students help to swell our voices at the Hours, and
we have reason to think that some of them may in time
become full members of the congregation. From this you will
see how much we owe to your very great wisdom. Were it not
for your advice we might now still be struggling to gain our
homeland and be attaining nothing. You saw, with a clarity of
vision denied to lesser men, that if we persisted in our strife
with Jorvik and Weogornecaster we would only 'make two
sorrows of one', and more than two, no doubt. In recognition
of our great debt I am sending a copy of the life of our founder.
It is a trifle compared to the vast library of books you hold at
Airemagh, but a shortage of materials has dogged us for years.
Indeed, we are lucky to have our own copy intact, as our
library was raped by Oswald's minions when he took office.

*This pillage by our fellow Christians has meant that we
cannot fill up the empty spaces in our book chests. We no
longer have any books to offer as hostages, so we can get none
to copy. We must depend on gifts from outside – or theft.*

Also as the principle scholar – alas, the only scholar of note
– in the area, my poor health has kept all work to a minimum.
Nevertheless, slight as it is, I offer it now as a 'widow's mite'
that is, the very best offering I can make, to show our apprecia-
tion of your guidance and help. It had been my intention, in
view of my miraculous recovery, to bring the book to you
myself but this would have presented me with a dilemma.
Since we have agreed to accept you as the father of our group
none of us may leave the monastery without your personal
permission, but in order to gain that permission someone
must leave this place. None of our penitents may travel, the
scholars are all too young to be sent on such a mission and
Nuth's concubine is not to be trusted. Unless you should
happen to send an emissary here, a thing which has not hap-

pened for many decades, it seems we are to wait on Godless foreigners before we can get a message to or from yourself. We have spent many hours in prayer over this matter, and we have at last been given an answer in our darkness.

While the letter of our agreement states that you are now the head of our order, it makes no mention of what may happen should we be stricken by one of the many threats which surround us. 'Salus populi suprema est lex' as all will agree. It only remains then, to consider what constitutes the worst threat to us as we wait here, tied to our huts. Now is a loss of communication with the sagacious Father of our order anything other than the worst threat? There can be no doubt that it is. With the Day of Days only a few years away, nothing must be done which might reduce the number of the baptised. Therefore it seems to us that our obligation is to keep in communion with our father even when he has not expressly enjoined us to do so, since not to do so will leave our souls in peril.

This argument is feeble, and he knew it as he made it. The Rule is the Rule and we accepted it freely. It only proves what can be achieved by words. He took a clear month to talk himself into believing it. At times I am glad not to be consecrated.

Bearing all this in mind, last week I had all but resolved to make the journey to you to deliver our thanks-offering and receive any messages from your lips to give our tiny community the heart it needs. Then there arrived a visitor to our settlement, and it became clear to me that my plans would have to be changed. Having found the general principle which allows me to leave the city, I am obliged to act upon it, so that if I am wrong the burden of the error will fall on my soul alone. I have discussed it with Ælfrid and the rest and there seems to be no other road open to us. I will tell you of our problem nor will I leave out any word spoken in my hearing so that you can see that the decision we have made is just. This letter will be delivered by the first one of the community who becomes eligible.

Two weeks ago, on the morning after the Sabbath, we were disturbed at our labours by a commotion near the harbour. When we went to protest we found that two of our boys were the cause. They had been sent to the northern point to tend to the ewes in lamb and check that the watch was keeping the fuel dry in the beacon. While they were on the headland, they had climbed the tower and saw a boat sailing out of the north-east. Now that day there was a fairly fresh wind blowing across the channel from the western sea. People wishing to gain our waters from, let us say, the coast of Cyil would wait for a wind from the north before putting out to sea, unless they had a large crew of brawny men to row them offshore and catch a tide. But this boat, it seemed, was only large enough to carry a tiny crew, and yet it was travelling almost straight across the wind.

For a while we doubted the truth of the lads' words, for youth will often see wonders where none exist. Yet they persisted in their loud protestations, and asked us to come with them and see with our own eyes since we could not trust theirs. At last we agreed and Josia, the youngest and strongest of us and Eclaf, our most steadfast penitent, were sent up the cliff to see what they could of this wondrous navigation. We remained sceptical, as you will imagine, since even the mighty in virtue Tarannon Mac-Oengus of Myrnia would not have ventured south across the head of Sronreamhar with a westerly blowing. One of the servants, Thorstein, who sailed as first oar with Thored Gunnarsson, said that it could be done but only by one who had gained command of a wind demon. After that, rational discourse was abandoned for the day.

Why is it that sailors feel the need to populate the sea and the firmament with a seething crowd of demons? As the only priest in the area I have found myself called on to bless innumerable items concerned with sailing. Trees which have been chosen to provide wood ten years in the future have had to be sanctified; metal for tools to cut the wood has been thrust under my nose before it has even seen the forge; I have raised my arms in supplication to the sea, the sky, and even the harbour wall on behalf of those about to set sail. I cultivate patience, of course, and hope that one day the foreigners will learn to trust God's grace, but in the meantime I am pestered.

That afternoon from the eighth to the ninth hour we were regaled with a ceaseless commentary on the skills of weather makers. Were I to believe in half the entities these old men give credence to I should never cross a beach, let alone set sail in the bosom of the sea. The she-demon Ran and all her kingdom of serpents, finned men and giant fish are enough to dissuade the most hardy soul from making sail. If to that is added the multitudes who inhabit the interiors of gulls and clouds, winds and rivers, there is little room for ordinary mortals to move in safety. Only sorcerers, it seems, can begin to face the perils of the deep and then only after many years of learning which would make our training in grace look like an idle summer's afternoon.

After a very short while I lost interest in their nonsense and went about my business. I am sorry to say Ælfrid stayed and listened closely to every detail, nodding and smiling as if there were nothing else to attend to. He is too patient with everyone and his patience is often abused. I returned to the garden and continued setting up my bean rows but I kept my eye on the cliff path until I saw the men coming back. They came scrambling pell-mell down the steep slope as if there were truly demons after them and we hurried to meet them and hear their report. Both men were agitated and kept interrupting each other as they told the story, but at last we learned that the boat was still making slow progress down the coast towards us. It appeared from their confused account that whoever was steering it was sailing closer to the wind than anyone had ever done before, giving a fresh impetus to the talk of sorcery. When Josia said that the sailor was only using half a sail, I decided that there was nothing for it but to return to the beans. Some of the others made off up the beach to indulge their curiosity.

It was well after Vespers when I was at last able to see for myself what manner of sailor was abroad in this unlikely vessel. The wandering sheep had returned round the headland, had been rebuked for their wanderings and were dispersed to their huts. Ælfrid and I went over to the harbour to pass our time of freedom in a little conversation and saw the boat arrive. We were not privileged at that time to see the wonderful navigation since the navigator had dropped the sail and was rowing in – a wise move with the tide turned and the evening wind blowing offshore. We did, however, see the sailor jump into the water and pull the boat above the sea-wrack before we could get near enough to help. The action was done with such ease that it was clear the sailor was exceedingly strong. Then, all at once I was stricken with fear. My concern increased to alarm when the sailor, having lifted a large bundle from the boat, shook out the skirts of a long tunic and the folds of a long kerchief. The sailor was a woman and my soul warned me that she brought affliction with her.

Ælfrid approached her and asked her if she needed help. She shook her head, 'I need rest,' she said, and we led her to Olvir's great wooden guest-house. There we found that someone had taken it upon themselves to light the fire and lay out food on the bench closest to it.

'We hope you will be comfortable,' said Ælfrid, 'and we must beg you to pardon us, for we must leave you to say the last office of the day.'

'I know that,' said the woman, 'nor will I be offended when no man speaks to me, for I know about your sort of life.'

'Thank you. Your understanding is a comfort to us,' I said, 'but there are servants here who will attend to you if you should need it. You may speak to them.'

'Indeed? I did not expect to find this,' she said, frowning. 'My sister visited your monastery some years ago and the picture she painted for me was very different.'

At the mention of a sister I again felt that chill under my heart, but I kept silent.

'These are troubled times,' said Ælfrid, 'and nothing stays the same for two days together. Since our last Abbot went to sleep with God we have accepted the services of certain men for the good of their souls. We will talk to you in the morning in charity and answer any questions you may have then. For now, God give you rest.'

We left her and turned along the path to our cells. I husbanded my breath and managed to say,

'Ælfrid, I protest.'

'I am sorry, Hw,' he replied, 'am I walking too fast for you?'

'No, brother, I protest at your proposal to talk to this woman in the morning. You know the Rule does not allow it.'

'It is permitted if the person needs to hear the words we say.'

'Yes, but she has no need of us. Thored and the others can help her to launch her boat.'

'If we wait till the permitted time in the evening to speak to her she may leave without hearing from us. The tide will be turned before Vespers tomorrow.'

'What of it if she has? We do not rush with words of wisdom to every guest who happens to lay their head here. Olvir would be angry if we did. The morning comes and they move on about their business. Why should we make an exception here?'

'Why should we not? You are frightened, Hw, I can see sweat on your forehead. You should not allow yourself to become agitated. Think of your health.'

'I am frightened. I admit it freely, and I am dismayed that you should be so calm. You heard her mention her sister, and I think you have guessed as well as I that neither she nor her sister are ordinary mortals. When the morning comes we must let her go and not tangle ourselves in her affairs like cows grazing in a gorse thicket. Like them, we will only come to grief.'

'As Christians we are under certain obligations,' said Ælfrid, 'and in charity we may not deny them whoever may be involved. Surely Selyf taught you that.'

'This one has nothing to learn from us. We are providing a night's resting place for her. It is you who wish to learn from her, Ælfrid. You have always wondered what became of our senior and the family he became involved with, and now you think you see your chance.' Ælfrid looked at me from under his eyebrows.

'Indeed she may be one of that family whose name you are so careful not to pronounce. Whoever she may be, it is clear she has knowledge and skill in sailing which could be of benefit to everyone. The first duty of our order is to collect and disseminate knowledge, or had you forgotten?'

'That is how it was at the outset, but five centuries have passed. We are now concerned to keep our purity and raise our voices in prayer.'

'Not all, Hw. Some of our old Rule remains, or why are we still freezing in stone huts on a rocky beach? Why are we not lying safe in a warm house of Benedict?'

I did not care to join him in argument at that time so I said,

'The first duty of any order is to say the offices, and we are already past our time.' That was the end of it for the night.

The next morning, as we left the chapel after the second hour, I put my hand on Ælfrid's sleeve. He looked at me and, putting his finger to his lips, nodded towards the guest-house. I shook my head and pointed towards the kitchen with a frown. If we were not at refection the lay men would be confused and he knew that as well as I. He smiled and followed me, waiving his seniority, and this show of humility was reassuring.

All that morning I watched the path from the guest-house to the harbour and saw no one. After the sixth hour I realised that the tide was ebbing and that now, if at all, the guest should be heading out to sea. There was no sign of her. I went in search of Ælfrid, but he was alone in the hut where he keeps his herbs and makes his messes. It was in my mind to go to the guest-house and see what had become of her, but I saw that it would be contrary to my vows to even look at her while I still had my duties to attend to. Then, to my dismay, I saw her coming down the path with Josia and no other man near them. I know that young man thinks that he is a law unto himself since he has not taken his final vows. Nevertheless he is a member of the community, and he should make some show of sanctity.

He and the woman were talking animatedly with much incontinent waving of hands. Seeing it as my first duty to supervise this graceless pair, I followed them down to the beach where she had left the boat. She unfurled the sail, and I saw why it had been described as 'half a sail'. It was, in fact, a triangle, that is to say, half of a rectangle, and therefore looked much as if a proper sail had been cut on the diagonal. Also it seemed to be made of a very light cloth.

Because it is smaller the sail does not hold as much wind and such as it holds is easily spilt. With this control the boat does not dance about in the water so much. The sail was made of linen. Since I spoke to her I have been trying to find flax to do the same, but so far I have not been successful.

The woman and her eager student then examined the tiller and again there was much hand waving and they seemed to be describing the movement of the sea. Then Josia noticed me watching them and to his credit he looked abashed, made his apologies and left. The woman shrugged and folded the sail again. She took some time to check the boat and its contents, then set off back to the guest-house. As she passed me on the path she nodded cheerfully and walked on without a word. Shaking, I went back to the garden.

At the evening recreation I attached myself to Ælfrid and dogged his steps as he walked round the city. Finally he stopped and faced me.

'She did not go,' I said at once.

'Perhaps there are things she wishes to speak to us about.'

'Perhaps there are, but I do not think we should speak to her ourselves. She has already found herself a soul friend here.'

'If you mean Josia, I must tell you he had instructions from me.'

'Did he have instructions from you to parade himself in the company of women?'

'His instructions were to find out how the boat managed to sail so close to the wind. He has not enjoyed your rigorous training, Hw, and is disposed to see women as part of God's creation, not as demons waiting to drag his soul off to perdition.'

'I do not deny they are part of God's creation for so is every-thing around us, including all demons which might inhabit the earth. I assert that they all are part of that which is sent to test man's steadfastness.'

'As you wish,' he said, speaking down his long nose more than ever. 'I have no stomach for a debate tonight. It was my notion that her knowledge might be useful and I sent Josia to glean as much as he could before she left, that is all.'

'You sent him into danger. You know she is a woman and she may be worse than that, yet you sent him to her in ignorance.'

'He knew all about your suspicions.'

'You have told him about that? And about Selyf?'

'Naturally. I would be a poor master to keep secrets from my student.'

'You had no right to tell him!' I cried.

Ælfrid raised his hands in dismay and shook his head. I realised I was angry and stopped to bless myself and calm my beating heart. Then I took up another thought which was troubling me.

'Have you spoken to her yourself?'

'I have not. I was waiting for you to discuss it first – and Nuth if he can be persuaded to leave the byre.'

'I doubt if anything he could say would lighten our darkness.'

'That is not the point. According to the Rule all our decisions must be agreed to by the whole congregation. No exceptions are to be made for poverty of intellect.'

'Very well, let us go to Nuth and see what offering he will make to help us in our confusion.'

But at the byre, to my disgust and Ælfrid's amusement, we found that our decision had been pre-empted. Nuth and the creature were already joined in deep discourse about the best time to send our cattle to the shielings. The only mitigation is that they were accompanied by the servants who, incoherent, were adding to the din. Silence fell as we came into the light and Nuth's forehead wrinkled like wind-blown water.

'We are glad to see you still in our company,' said Ælfrid, smirking. 'We were hoping that now we might find out your name and your destination, if you would care to tell us.'

'My name is Barve,' she replied, 'and my father was

Usbathaden, whose name I believe you have heard before.'

All at once a terrible weakness filled me and I had to grip the side of the cows' pen to stop myself from falling. Ælfrid, usually so attentive, did not notice my condition, so rapt was he at the sound of that dreadful name.

'Indeed we have heard of Usbathaden,' he said, 'and we are pleased to greet another of that great family. We have often asked ourselves what could have happened to them... and to one of ours whose life seems to have entangled itself with them.'

The weakness was still upon me or I would have made it clear that Ælfrid spoke only for himself. The woman answered readily,

'I must tell you that I am ignorant of Marighal's fate. Part of my reason for coming here was the hope that you might have more to tell me.'

'Sadly we have not, but let us pool our knowledge and see if we can enlighten each other at least a little.'

'I will be happy to do so. I am in your debt for the hospitality you have shown me and which I cannot repay in kind.'

'The guest-house is not ours.' said Ælfrid. 'It is the property of Olvir Brusasson, and so you are his guest. You need not apologise for being unable to repay him in your own house for he is happy often to shelter landless men. I am only sorry to hear that you have no home of your own.'

Before she could reply, I found a little strength at last and said,

'If she must answer let it be somewhere else, away from the ears of the laymen.'

At that Ælfrid looked up in surprise. He knows no discretion in these matters and would talk exegesis to a farm-hand as easily as to a bishop. Nevertheless he saw that I was inflexible in this and led us monks and the woman to the guest-house. Where, since I would not enter, we sat in the doorway.

Till the day of my death I will remember that evening. The sea-birds left the sky as she spoke and silence settled round us. In the darkening twilight the woman's voice came to us disembodied and it told of things it were better to forget.

41

Gunnhild, Roswitha, Rhiannon, Derdriu, Evabyth, Gwenlieth, Feidhelm, Evir, Ide and Halgerd.

I was one of the twelve of our family who elected to join our friend Kynan at his city on the coast. He gave us a large farmsteading not far away with its own sturdy palisade round it. It was large enough to graze several cattle, even in winter. In exchange for this hospitality we told him how to hide his city from prying eyes. At first, to ensure that his citizens would leave us alone, he put about the rumour that he had founded a religious order of strict seclusion. He made sure that the information passed around as gossip so that if anyone should approach us and find we were not leading a Regular life it would be easy to deny that we had ever claimed to be Christian congregation. Now I realise this was blasphemy on his part, and we should never have permitted him to endanger his soul in this way, but we were still ignorant of many aspects of mortal life. If he was wrong, then it is sure he has paid for it in this life. Who will answer for the next?

Other, virtuous women have set up houses without waiting for a bishop to approve. They will surely be forgiven.

The threat of final extinction had hung over us since my father's death like a black cloud on the horizon at the dawn of every day. It was like the sound of thunder waking us from a nightmare, and we who left the shadow of our father's walls did so only to find company in our newfound mortality. I see now that we were running blindly, like creatures when the stone they have been hiding under is overturned, but at the time we said it was for the sake of virtue.

Marighal and the others were content to stay in my father's hall to watch her growing baby. I do not know what became of them. Two years ago my sister Gwenlieth and I returned to the forest to try and find them. We found most of the road without trouble yet even after all those years, as we approached the hillside where the fortress stood, we began once again to sink into a stupor. Some lingering, baneful power of my father's making still hangs in the air around that hillside and I am sure it will be there on the last day of the world.

We kept each other alert by singing and telling stories about our life on the coast and the people we had seen and by and by we found that we could keep the fog out of our minds. We came upon the fortress almost without noticing it and ran merrily in through the gate, but once inside all we found was a burnt-out shell. The weaving-room, the hall, the kitchen, all were rubble. Even the stone-lined grave where we had placed Grig was empty. Indeed, the only consolation to us was that in all those ashes there was not a trace of bone or tooth, and we concluded that our sisters must have survived the holocaust. Gone also were the metal slaves my father had made. Since his death they had not stirred, but one of our sisters had conceived the unholy thought that she might animate them once more if she studied them long enough. When we left she had not succeeded, but who knows what might have happened. I am sure, however, that fire did not harm them. For a few days we lingered there in the hope that the fortress was only hidden from us in one of Mari's illusions, but if it were, there was no sign of it nor of the family. At last, grieving for those lost to us, we returned to the coast.

In those days, if we had been leading a regular life our conduct would have stood up to scrutiny by the most exacting bishop. Our life in the stronghold had been secluded and silent and we found little hardship in continuing in such a state. Furthermore, in the weeks before we left father's house to set up the steading we had received much instruction from Selyf, the monk who had followed Marighal to our stronghold. He saw it as his duty to bring us to God and to that end he had stayed, and patiently told us about the Laws of Christianity.

He told us that we were fortunate in being virgin and that it would help to mitigate the sinfulness of our condition if we remained in that happy state. We were stricken by his words and with one voice we swore before him that we would live the lives of poverty and chastity which the example of the saints showed us. When he baptised us, he raised his hands over us and blessed us saying,

'Men will tell you that the role of wife is the only one suitable for women,' he said, 'but this is not true. It is only lust and the love of worldly power which drives men to say this. If a man is married he may satisfy his desire whenever he likes, and if his women are fertile he will have many children to work his land and fight his battles. When his sons are due for fostering, they can be sent to the homes of rich families to form potent alliances; when his daughters are ripe for marriage, they can be exchanged for money and land. Thus man increases his grip on this poor world and pays no heed to his status in the next. Soon the Master will come and bring His Host to set up His kingdom here. On that day how much better for a man if he has never known woman. Neither his lands nor his servants, not his strong allies nor his hoarded gold will defend him and he will go naked to his judgement. Then, as he is sent to the darkest pit of punishment, he will lament, too late, his avarice and his luxury.

'But you, wise virgins, can be spared from joining yourselves to such as he. Your father was right when he used his wealth and power to keep you from the necessity of marriage. Consider the position of the wife, imprisoned in this concubinage. She may not leave her house without the permission of her husband, she is subject to his lust, she is condemned to bear children, year after year, and with all this she is less important than a milch-cow in the running of the house. Yet if the baby screams all day, the milk goes sour and the crops are thin in the ear she is blamed for it all as the limb of Satan. Who, given the choice, would chose such painful subjection? Consider, on the other hand, the fate of the virgin. She is safe from the punishment of Eve. She may come and go as she pleases, she may keep her body pure and wholesome and she may stand as an equal to any man. And on the Day of Days she will find her name entered in the ledger of the elect.

'Why should a woman choose the fate of a clod of dung when she might be numbered among the angels?'

This was his message to us, nor were his words wasted. When we arrived at Kynan's city we were sure that no man other than our host and brother would ever approach us, let alone couple with us in sinful acts. Yet in spite of this haranguing, eventually some of us fell from grace, and continued cheerful. Perhaps there are aspects of our nature that make it impossible for us to live the reclusive life needed for virtue; perhaps we are, as others have said, creatures who from before our birth were shaped in evil. He hoped we would be brought to redemption by leading a virtuous life, but it may be that we are beyond redemption. Poor Selyf, our soul friend, I hope he found some reward for his faith in us. I am sure now that we would have been better to stay at his side.

However it may have turned out, when we left my father's stronghold we were prepared for a life of virtue and restraint. We bound our hair under kerchiefs, and some of us even shaved our heads, so that we would not be tempted to vanity and sin, and so that we would not tempt men and angels to lust after us. This was a great sacrifice as our hair is one of the sources of our potency, but we were so terrified of the real death which awaited us that we would have cut off our limbs if Selyf had advised us so to do. We begged him to come with us to act as our guide in this strange new world, but he said our brother Kynan was an honest man well able to show us how to live in the world. He pointed out that it was his duty as a consecrate to stay near the heart of the evil my father had created. He was sure that father would return, he did not know how, and that he would return to the stronghold.

To try and make him come with us, we exhumed our father's body. We knew it would be untouched by corruption since before we had buried it we had cleaned out his fatal wound and packed it with honeycomb and certain herbs to preserve it. We told Selyf we would take the body to the sea with us, as we needed this relic of the past to console us in exile. But we said to each other, 'Since he is so sure of our father's return, he will wish to stay with the corpse to contain the wickedness emanating from his flesh.'

How ignorant we were! Selyf showed no inclination to follow us, and when at last we told him what we expected he said, 'The flesh that God's creatures are clothed in during their span on this earth is not significant. It is like chaff from the threshing or a broken pot which the cook throws on to the midden; it has no value. Your father's soul is what I seek, and I am convinced that it is here, near the centre of his kingdom.'

Nevertheless we took our father's corpse with us. We were still sure that one day Selyf would follow us because of it, and we were not lying when we said that it would console us in our new dwelling. So you may picture us in our farmstead: our clothing as modest as nuns', our activities confined to farming, weaving and prayer as if we had taken perpetual vows. Yet in spite of this appearance, in the middle of the steading, in a windowless house, sat the body of our father on his great chair. He was all decked in his finest clothes and jewels and his great wolf-skin cloak lay over his shoulders. Day and night lights burned at his feet.

This is how we conducted ourselves for the first two or three years. We produced enough food for our stomachs and enough clothing for our backs, and no more than enough. But at the third harvest in that place we found that we had grain from the years before rotting in the granary. When we went to the earth mound where we stored the cheese we found that there was enough for many weeks, yet there were pails of milk still standing in the byre. Also there was cloth lying unused by the looms where we had left it, since we had not worn out many of our clothes. It seemed to us wicked to waste this bounty and we were perplexed for a while as to what to do with it. One day when Kynan made his visit to us we put the matter before him, for at that time we depended completely on his experience in dealing with such issues. He thought for a while and then said,

'If you have more than you need for your daily use, there is only one thing you can do. Most people find that all their surplus goes toward paying tribute to their lord, but this is not the case with you. You are my sisters and my guests in this place and in honour I could never impose on you. If, after paying their dues, people still find that they have stock to dispose of, they usually take it to market and exchange it for silver. In your case I do not think this would be advisable, first because you have chosen not to take on servants. If you were not eremites you might take the goods yourselves or if you had servants they would take it for you – as it is, there is no way to get your goods to the marketplace. Secondly, as your spiritual guide will have taught you, you may not lay up hoards of silver for they will be encumbrance to your souls. My recommendation, therefore, is that you should give what you do not need to the poor.

'Since you have vowed to keep yourselves apart, you cannot approach men directly and give them presents. But I have had an idea which may answer your needs. I will build a hostel near here and provide you with a manservant whom I know to be honest. You can give your surplus to him by putting it outside the gate in a sack every week on a particular day. That way you need never speak to him. He can prepare food which will be given to the poor every evening and in the morning, after they have rested, he can give them clothing if they should need it.'

This seemed to us an excellent idea, well in keeping with our vows of poverty, and we agreed at once to do as Kynan said. For the first year, since he had appointed a good man and his wife to run it, the guest-house ran very well. Then Kynan found that they had been selling some of the honey and the cheese for coin at the market. Then it transpired that the money they made had been spent on things like knives and a metal spade for the hostel. We were not angry and told Kynan we did not wish him to dismiss our hospitaller. Indeed, we were chastened by the thought that we could have supplied such things to them ourselves if we had known that they needed them.

'Perhaps this seclusion is not such a good thing,' we said, 'if it keeps us from finding out the things people need. We have so much to give them.'

But our older sisters knew what was proper. 'Our main purpose in coming here is to prepare ourselves for God's kingdom,' they reminded us. 'In order to do this we must remain seperate from human kind. Have you forgotten everything we were taught? Good works are only a part of what we must do to prepare ourselves, and they are a small part at that.'

I must confess some of us were wearying of our life apart. From time to time we talked among ourselves about the people we were helping.

'Do you think they wonder about us?' asked Rhiannon, one morning. 'I must confess I get great pleasure from thinking about how grateful they must be, the poor things.'

But Gunnhild, the oldest among us, rebuked her.

'Shame on you, Rhiannon. Do you think the Almighty created the weak and the poor so that you might find gratification. I am sure that Selyf would not be pleased to hear you speak like that.'

'The days are slow passing,' I answered, 'and there is little pleasure in this life of ours. If my sister finds some joy in thinking that others are grateful to her, what is the harm in that?'

'It means that she is not thinking of her immortal soul, but of the effect she is having in this life. Does not the Gospel say that when you make a charitable offering you should wish to go unobserved: "let not your right hand know what your left hand is doing"?'

I had no answer, but I reflected to myself on the ease with which one of our number was quoting Holy Writ.

Then one summer a great black cloud rose out of the western sea. It spread greedily over the land and rain fell like a river for days which turned into weeks then into months. At the end of the rain the crops lay stinking in the fields and pestilence rose from the earth, with the stench to kill men and cattle and bees alike. At first it did not affect us, for we never suffer from the diseases of men, but in the end it brought great alteration to our lives.

We were so cut off from the world that the first intimation we had of trouble was when the food we put out of the gate was not collected. Up to that time our only knowledge of diseases was from the books we read and when we saw the food lying mouldering at our gate we had no notion what had happened. I and my closest sister, Derdriu, volunteered to go down to the guest-house to find out the cause of this absence. At first my sisters were reluctant to send us on what might be a perilous mission, but we pointed out that we had a responsibility and must live up to it.

'We took up this burden cheerfully,' said Derdriu, 'nor did any man force us to help those in need. Over the last months there must be a large number of people who have come to depend on our services for their survival. If, as it now seems, we have lost the custodian, we must take steps ourselves to see that no one suffers.'

Our elders had to agree to that but not before they had voiced their deepest doubt. We consulted together and it was agreed that if we must go on this reckless mission we should go heavily veiled. So it was that early the next morning, for the first time since we left our father's hall, we walked through the gate into the world of men.

I recall this pestilence myself. It was a flying venom and it destroyed everything in its path. I know this because some of those who were feverish saw the demons at the heart of the evil.

It was now late in that terrible year. Mist hung in the trees around the palisade and heavy dew muffled our footsteps. The guest-house was near the shore and sheltered from the sea winds by a few trees. I am sure the tree-tops moved as we came near, yet that morning there was not the slightest breeze. We called out first to see if there were anyone near, but got no reply. This silence dismayed us, for we had hoped to be spared close contact with the humans, but now all we could do was go up to the door. The guest-house was empty so we hurried over to the hospitaller's hut, which stood a little apart. The door was open and from the hut there came a foul, foul smell. I took Derdriu by the elbow and we walked in, reluctant to take our first look at the dissolution of flesh.

The custodian and his wife lay in their bed. We could be sure they had died of disease and not at the hand of man for they lay at peace. They had died some days before and within a short time of each other for they lay face to face and each clasped the dead hand of the other. The eyes had disappeared from the sockets and the lips were shrivelling, pulling back from the teeth. The smell of their rotting bodies filled the hut and must have warned anyone who came by that there would be no service in the guest-house. Fear of the murrain must have stopped passers-by from looting.

'Look, sister, how they cling to each other, even in their last minutes,' said Derdriu. 'Is that how humans always die?'

'Indeed, I cannot say. These people had been together for many years and I suppose there must have been affection between them. It is my understanding that in spite of lust man and woman can be gentle with each other in some ways, as a mother is with a child.'

'Have you seen a mortal mother and child?'

'I have, once or twice,' I answered, leading the way out of the hut. 'And I have read that there is much tenderness in that and in many other human partnerships.'

'I should like to see for myself. It must be a comfort to face death knowing there is one to stay beside you through the bitter hours.'

'Perhaps it is, but it is idle for us to speculate on such matters. We have vowed to live as virgins and it would endanger us to come close to that experience in others, let alone to go through it ourselves.'

'Sometimes I wonder why we left our father's hall if we are to spend the rest of our days avoiding human kind like this.'

'We left to escape the baneful influence of our father's spirit. You must remember that.'

'You and the others may have done so, but I wished only for a change of scene,' said Derdriu. 'The only other person we have seen since we came here is Kynan and although he is precious to me I am sure I would be pleased to see another in his place.'

'I will not listen to another word,' I said, and began to collect kindling. She helped me to stack it around the hut, then we took the fuel from the lamps – a nasty animal fat – and put it on top of the kindling. I took out my crystal and began to make fire when she stopped me.

'Should we not say a prayer for them?' she said.

'Indeed, it does seem right to say something,' I agreed, 'but to my great regret I do not know what prayer to say.'

'I know one,' she said, and began, '"O Lord God of my salvation, I have cried day and night before You, listen to me now for my soul is full of troubles and my life is coming to the grave. I am counted with them that go down into the pit, I am like a man with no strength. Free among the dead, like the slain that lie in the grave whom You remember no more, and they are cut off from Your hand. You have laid me in the lowest pit, in darkness, in the deeps. Your wrath lies hard upon me..."'

'Forgive me, sister,' I interrupted her, 'but I do not think that is right. It is a psalm, is it not? I am sure there is a separate collect to be said for the dead, and it does not include that.'

'I am ignorant, it is true,' said Derdriu, 'but I learned that psalm a long time ago when we had just learned we were going to die. It matched my feelings and I have never forgotten it.'

'However that may be, it would not meet with approval from those who know better than we. I propose that we should say a prayer for the start of the night and leave it at that.'

'Oh, very well,' said Derdriu, 'but I think we should learn some suitable prayers as soon as possible.' She began to mutter, 'Noctis tempus exigimus...' with little sign of grace. Then we threw lighted kindling against the hut and watched till the fire took a hold. The seasoned timbers of the walls burned quickly but clouds of smoke issued from the inside, choking us and driving us down to the beach. Derdriu pulled her veil aside to wipe her streaming eyes and it seemed to me she took a long time about it. I shall never know whether it was the smoke or some strange pity for the humans that brought the tears to her cheeks.

'Cover your face, sister,' I said hastily, 'you know what we agreed with the others.'

She paid no attention to me but stared out over the sea. The sun had broken through the mist and turned the water from grey to dark blue; sea birds had taken wing and were calling out over the bay.

'If you put to sea and sailed on beyond the island, what do you think you would find?' she said.

Reluctantly I answered,

'I have heard many stories, but I do not know which to believe. The oldest story I recall from the days of my first childhood says that you will find the land of the dead – the land of eternal youth – where nothing troubles mankind. In that land all labours are finished and all sufferings at an end. When men come to live there their bodies are so airy they have little need for food and such little as they need is laid in the meadows at their feet. Rivers run with ale and wine so that all you need to quench your thirst is to dip your cup into the stream beside you. The days are never colder than a gentle day in May, and the nights are short and mild. Music comes from the throats of silver birds who sing in golden trees by day and by night. Human voices are never heard raised in anger and fear. Only quiet talk and quiet laughter fill the halls.

'The Land of Heart's Desire where all your sins will leave you – enter and be forever blessed.'

I looked up at Derdriu and saw her tears were flowing again. I went on rapidly,

'It is also said that if you travel far enough you will come to a great waterfall where the sea runs off the earth into a great basin beneath, but since no man has seen any of these things I cannot say which is true. All I know is that we should not be troubling ourselves about this world, for it will soon be carried away by the hosts of God. Come away now, sister, and cover your face.'

'I will not cover my face, for there is no one to see it, and the breeze off the sea is pleasant.'

'We agreed with our sisters that we would stay veiled, and it is showing too much love for the flesh to let the sun and the breeze pleasure it.'

'I like my flesh,' she answered, 'and since I will not have it for much longer I should like to enjoy it while I can. As long as we were in our father's house, I could not feel things keenly in this way.'

I was dismayed at these words, for I realised that there was much temptation in them. I hoped that she would not talk so among the others, especially the younger ones, and disturb the smooth running of our lives. Poor creature, by now she will know for herself what lies on the farthest shore of the sea.

They have not heard tell of Vinland. That is strange, for they know so many things.

'We must go back and tell the others what we have found,' I said, and without giving her a chance to argue I walked up the beach. She followed me and we went to make sure that the hut was burning safely. It had burnt to the ground, but the bed was still whole and on it the two charred corpses still lay side by side.

'We will have to bury them,' said Derdriu.

'Yes, but not now,' I answered, taking her sleeve. 'The others will have seen the smoke and will be wondering at our absence.'

Derdriu replaced her veil and we hurried back to the farm-stead without further argument. Our sisters were indeed worried about us, and opened the gates with eager faces. We told them everything we had seen and we discussed what we should do, but could not agree on any course of action. We had not yet realised that the disease was as widespread as it was and thought only of the future of our hostel. Some said that one of us should wait till dark and go to Kynan, so that he could arrange a replacement; some – the ones who wished to see more of the world – said that we should try to run the hostel ourselves and not trouble Kynan; some – the older ones – said that we should not trouble ourselves with any of it, but wait for God's will to manifest itself. In the event that is what we had to do for we were obliged to attend to the tasks allocated to us. We retired without making a decision.

The next morning there came a terrible knocking at the gate. Gunnhild climbed the ladder next to it and looked over the palisade. Voices came over the fence as soon as her head reached the top and she scrambled down again in haste. We were under silence again so Rhiannon pulled a kerchief over her head and went to look for herself. She sprang down and, deciding that this situation was an emergency she spoke and told us what was going on.

'There are more than ten people waiting at the gate. Their clothes are ragged and their feet are wrapped in cloth. There are men and women and one has a baby tied to her. They must be the poor who used the hostel and have come to need it.'

We agreed that they must be and tried to decide what to do about them. We could not in charity leave them to starve at the gate, but we could not allow them to come within our walls.

'I knew no good would come of this guest-house,' Gunnhild muttered and took herself off.

At that the rest of us felt free to make our own decisions and we elected to fill a basket with food and drop it over the wall. This was done as rapidly as we could, and when Rhiannon looked over the wall again she reported that the people had gone away. Very much relieved we went back to our daily duties, but as night began to fall we were once again disturbed by the knocking. Once again we dropped food over the wall to the people and once again they dispersed.

The disease was manifested in a bloody flux, which Ælfrid called 'scitta'. Those who died of it, died rapidly. It was as if they melted away. It was not a disease that any of us had seen before and the best we could do for any of them was to give them water to drink. It was preceded by a terrible wind which destroyed many buildings and houses and I think that the population took ill from lack of shelter as much as from the venom of the demons. At all events the wind blew and the pestilence appeared. If it should come again I will try to eliminate it with a great exorcism and give the local people as much food as we can spare for their own stomachs. They will persist in eating barley with mildew on it and badly salted meat even though we tell them it is bad for them.

We agreed they must have gone to the hostel for the night. The next morning the knocking started once more. This time it was more orderly and there was no shouting. Confident that we were doing right, we prepared the baskets and Roswitha climbed the ladder to pass them over. She looked out and quickly dropped to the ground again.

'There are more of them,' she cried, 'many more.'

Gunnhild pressed her fingers to her lips and shook her head, but in vain. We crowded round Roswitha.

'How many people?' I asked her. 'Where have they come from?'

'A crowd – I cannot be sure how many – more than twenty, more than thirty, perhaps.'

Derdriu climbed up to see for herself and her head nodded as she numbered them.

'There are forty and three,' she reported, 'and twenty of them are children. There are eleven women and the rest are men. All of them are young.'

'We shall need to put out more food than we have done so far,' said Evabyth, the second in seniority.

We began to consider how much food we would need, but Feidhelm raised her voice in protest.

'This has gone too far,' she said, 'we have already compromised our vows in front of Selyf by contact with these people.'

'Not so,' said Rhiannon, 'we have not spoken a word to them, and we keep our faces covered. This is not contact as humans would call it.'

'Yes, but we have broken away from our pattern, and having started where will it end? Yesterday there were barely more than a handful, today there are four times that. If the crowd continues to increase like this who can say what will happen.'

'Feidhelm,' said Roswitha, 'you are one of the oldest among us and therefore closer to dissolution. You are frightened of the future and death and so cling to the rules Selyf gave us for our salvation. This is not to be wondered at nor do I blame you, but it seems to me that fear has made your judgement faulty. Did not Selyf tell us it is good to give to those in need?'

'Indeed, Roswitha,' said Feidhelm, 'you are right to say I am afraid and I am horrified by any turning away from the paths we take for the safety of our souls. But when Selyf said that gifts were a blessing to the giver I felt some of the old, wicked paganism in his notions. My father was celebrated for his generosity to those who served him, yet Selyf never praised him.

'We are in a situation which has never arisen before within our long memories and I am sure that we must, therefore, take up a new pattern of life. I have decided, then, that seclusion is more important to us than charity.'

'You are a fool,' said Evabyth, 'we have spent most of our lives in seclusion. There is nothing new in it for us any more than there is in generosity. Neither of these notions is new to us therefore I think that not everything we thought and felt and did in our former life was wicked.'

Gunnhild was pale with rage, but she kept herself well in hand. She said,

'The seclusion we endured in our father's hall was not of our choosing. It bears no comparison with our state here. Like the holy virgins of the past we have made a free choice to come here to escape the baneful influence of our parent. We should not allow any temptation to move us off the narrow road. How can we be sure that these creatures are not sent by some devil to confuse us?'

Before we could warm to this debate there came a knocking at the gate again. This time the knocking was fierce and it was accompanied by angry shouting. This made Gunnhild also shake her head, saying,

'I knew nothing but evil could come from Kynan's hostel.'

'That is folly, sister,' said Derdriu. 'How can providing food and shelter for a few helpless humans be evil?'

'You must remember how our father tried to help these people. Year after year he offered them the benefit of his knowledge and the strength of his arm, but they turned their backs on him.'

'That was only because they feared his stature and his strangeness,' Gwenlieth told her. 'If they had known him longer they would have learned that he was not all wicked.'

'She is right,' I said. 'They will see us only as weak women. There will be no fear to corrupt our dealings with them.'

Then from the gate there came a truly ferocious knocking and we all flinched. For a moment I feared they might break the wooden maul, so loud was the din, and a man's voice called out savagely,

'We know you are inside. Where is our food? The custodian has died of the plague and his house has been burnt over his body. Must we stand here and starve?'

He was joined by a clamour of voices all raised in fear and anger. We looked at each other in dismay when we heard his words, for in our simplicity we had not paused to wonder why the custodians had died together like that. Plague could not affect us, we knew, but it could mean a lot to the humans we wished to help. For now we ceased debating and fetched more bread, cheese and honey to be handed over the wall. I took my turn up the ladder this time and looked at the crowd who had come to beg from us. Some of them had been to our hostel before, I could see, since their clothes were made of the good green and blue cloth we wove. Another group clearly had come far, for they sat with their heads drooping or leaned on each other with great weariness. The local people were shunning them and pushed them aside from the growing mound of food. So weary were the strangers that they were easily removed and did not try to hold their ground. I was angry at this ungenerous behaviour.

'Stop jostling your brothers like that,' I cried, 'and let them take their turn. There is enough for everyone.'

'They are no brothers of ours,' one of them replied, and I shouted in anger,

'All men in need are brothers,' and they left them their portion. Behind me Gunnhild gave a shriek and other voices joined her, this time. I descended the ladder slowly and faced her with a sinking heart. Rage made her voice tremble as she said,

'Barve, you must do a penance for that terrible lapse. And you must never go up that ladder again. I am your senior and I have the right to tell you that.'

'Is not our life enough of a penance?'

With that I turned away and stalked off to the weaving

shed. Once there I was too distracted to continue with my work and my thread kept tangling and slipping out of the shuttle. With my mind's eye I kept seeing the faces of the new arrivals as they sat slumped on the ground, too weary to raise a hand in their defence as the others pushed them away. I thanked God that in all my life I had never known such abjection. For the first time in many months I began to think that there might be some virtue in being one of our detested family.

The day passed without incident. Towards nightfall Derdriu mounted the ladder to see what manner of crowd were waiting for us that evening and said that there were adults in the group, but she could not say how many. All I know is that we seemed to be handing out food to them for longer.

After refection we talked about our dependants. Some of us were troubled in case the bread should run out. We checked our supplies and found a mountain of grain in the granary. Now that the beggars were fed and rested they would be able to use the quern and the oven by the hostel for themselves.

'That is true,' said Roswitha, 'but even that grain is not of an infinite amount. What if the number doubles once again, or even multiplies by three? Can we find enough then?'

'It is not probable that the number will increase by that much,' I said. 'We must continue what we have started.'

'We have gathered that there has been a plague,' said Rhiannon. 'But we do not know how great the mortality has been. Clearly the harvest has failed, but we must find out whether it was because of pestilence or lack of hands to bring in the harvest. There are other things about the populace we need to know also if we are to do the task that has been put on us.

'Let us assume that there are two thousand people within a day's journey, including both those who travel on foot and by boat. If out of each hundred of these only one person has died, the numbers would not be diminished enough to fail to gather the harvest. In this case I conclude that the harvest has failed due to a blight and we will be visited by one thousand and eighty beggars in a very short time. If, on the other hand, eighty people have died out of that hundred the harvest will have failed for lack of harvesters and the largest number of visitors we can expect is five hundred. Finally we must consider the fact that some of the people may have died, not of plague but of eating rotted grain.'

Hw was very angry at all this numbering. He said it was presumptuous, like trying to see into the mind of God. I could not understand his point of view, for I think that numbers are the very way in which God has chosen to speak to us of his mind. I am not alone in this, but Hw has no patience with any idea of mine.

'Listen, Rhiannon,' said Evabyth, 'we have known you and your love of reckoning for all our lives. Sometimes it has been of use to us, but in this case, I fear you are no help. If five hundred beggars come to our gate we shall not be able to feed them until Advent, let alone through the winter.'

'I did not say that we would. It was my aim to show you all how important it is for us to have more information. We must know how many people do live within a short distance of us; how many have been dying in each settlement, and of what; and what state the harvest is in. We may then decide what our next action should be.'

Gunnhild was quick to notice the threat.

'How, please tell us, do you intend to get this knowledge? Are you saying that we must leave the steading to find out more about the beggars?'

'That would seem inevitable.'

'Nothing is inevitable,' said Gunnhild, her big pale eyes starting from her head with rage, 'except God's will. We can stop this wickedness at once and be free of this crowd of wasters. We have grain to spare, it is true, but this is because we work hard at raising our crops, nor do we let ourselves be turned aside from our task by idle fancies. If these humans have no food it is because they have been distracted by their folly and laziness; if they have children who are starving the fault is their own for yielding to lust in spite of holy exhortation. Accordingly God has punished them for their wickedness by sending them this plague. It has not troubled us because we have done our duty. Our course is clear: we must close the gate, ignore their importuning and wait for our our protector to come and drive them off.'

I saw that one or two were nodding at these words. It began to look as if she might prevail.

'That is a shameful way to speak,' cried Roswitha; 'even the thrifty can be afflicted by ill-fortune. Why have we been allowed to produce grain to spare if it is not to help others?'

'And what of the children,' said Evabyth, 'whose only fault is that they have been born at this time? Must they pay for their parents' sins in suffering and death?'

'They must,' said Gunnhild, 'for it says in the Psalms that the children of the wicked man should be fatherless and that they should be vagabonds and go begging their bread.'

But Evabyth had studied the scripture as well. She replied, 'In the book of Deuteronomy it says "neither shall the children be put to death for the fathers; every man shall be put to death for his own sin".'

Gunnhild had no answer, so she turned to Roswitha.

'You must not talk of ill-fortune, Roswitha, you must talk of God's plan for them.'

'None of this is to the point,' Rhiannon said quietly, 'though we could debate the issue all night long. They know we are here and that we have food. If we do not give it to them, in time they will come and take it.'

'They may try,' said Gwenlieth, 'but they could not succeed against us. Not if it came to a battle.'

'We could protect ourselves, it is true, but at what price?' I asked her. 'Remember, we made another vow to Selyf that we would not use our infernal powers. It always seemed to me he thought this the most important of our self-denials. He said it would be an evil to use it because the world would then know what we are. But – more significant by far – if we did we would be yielding to the demonic side of our nature.'

'Then we shall not protect ourselves,' said Gunnhild, 'but if death should come, we must accept it like the martyrs that

60

Selyf told us about.'

'Then we shall have tempted these people into greater wickedness,' I said, 'and we shall have done it because we had more care for our own immortality than for them. That is not charitable.'

'It is very difficult to live as a human being,' said Derdriu.

The debate lasted for many hours and we did not all agree. Nevertheless, in the morning some of us went out to the people and found out what we needed to know to provide for them. So it was that our vows of seclusion were brought to nothing, but I am sure Selyf would not have criticised us. In the end, only Gunnhild continued to keep herself apart, but there were enough of us to do the work without her. We could not deny her the right to live as an eremite if that was her wish.

At this point Ælfrid raised his hand to silence her. He explained that it was time for us to say our office and retire. Then he asked her if she wished to leave on the tide the next day. She said she would like to tell us more and that she wished also to ask us questions. He agreed that we should return the next evening.

I left the guest-house with shaking legs. My heart was pounding furiously against my ribs as if it wished to escape from its pale of flesh. We should not have spent so much as the blink of an eye in listening to these whoredoms yet we had just passed an hour on them; an hour, furthermore, which should have been spent in edifying discussion, not in mendacious gossip. The incomplete account of what befell Selyf shows us that these are wicked people, and not to be trusted to tell the truth. Her account of their emulation of a coenobitic life was sheerest blasphemy; their pretensions to theological debate made the hair stand up on my head, and the erroneous conclusions they reached caused me to grind my teeth in rage. Yet the silence was on us and I could say nothing, nor could I have lowered myself to answer their ignorant ramblings. That night I did not sleep, but watched from hour to hour, wondering what action I should take. The others seemed pleased to let her finish her story and I was obliged to join them, indeed it would have been wrong of me to leave them alone with her, so seductive were her lies.

Eventually I prayed, 'Father, I must leave my ears open to this endless wickedness, for the Enemy is clever. Keep my heart clean, I beg you, and do not let the honey of this woman's words seal up my eyes so that I do not see Your truth. Who reigns...'.

The following evening Barve came out to meet us at the door of the guest-house. I was happy to note that she had kept to herself during the day and when she appeared that evening her eyes were reddened with much weeping. I hoped that it was a sign of contrition, but I was prepared to be disappointed. Ælfrid began and, as always, he had questions at the tip of his tongue.

'We have been on this site for many years and many of the people who travel between Galwythel and Eirinn stop here, yet we have never heard any speak of your hostel. Why is this?'

She answered slowly, and, it seemed to me, guardedly.

'After the year of the plague we found ourselves once again with a few clients who returned often. We told all those who depended on us that our presence was to be kept a secret and that if we were found we would be removed. To such weak people the idea that we might be lost to them was a source of great fear, and so keen were they that we should go on providing we were completely safe.'

'Did they realise that you were not true nuns?'

'If they did, they said nothing to us. Some of them suspected we were not, I am sure, but they did not ask questions. Life had taught them it would be unwise to do so. Our way of life was in danger, although we did not know it, but the threat was never from the simple ones who needed us. They knew how to be silent.'

'I fear you are right,' I said, 'there are many baneful forces that govern their lives. They are full of shame and deal furtively with us when we try to help them.'

'I do not doubt it. I have often thought that if you and the priests were less inclined to describe their actions as sinful they might talk to you more freely.'

'Wretched creature,' I cried, 'this Law is not of our making, nor may we change it as our whims move us. This Law is given to us by our Holy Father in heaven who knows how easily we are removed from righteousness. It is not for us to redefine sin with each change of the tide!' Once again my heart was pounding and I could not find the breath to continue. Ælfrid tugged at my sleeve.

'Calm yourself, Hw, you know you must stay calm. Remember the misery of demons and restore yourself to cheerfulness.'

I turned away and said prayers for my peace of mind. Ælfrid told the woman,

'His health was broken when he went in search of Selyf. Since he returned from that long and fruitless journey he has not been able to find the strength he knew before. Rage, always his greatest weakness, leaves him weakest of all.'

I thanked my brother for restoring my humility. The woman apologised for provoking me, though nothing she could say would soothe the raging in my heart. I sat on the step, and as the conversation continued around me I struggled to regain the calm which had been mine before she came.

'Did no one ever uncover your secret?' Ælfrid asked the woman.

'Only once did we suspect that someone had told the outside world about us, but by the time there was any evidence of it all those involved were dead and we could never be sure who was the betrayer. I can be sure of one thing, however, and it is that Marighal did more harm than she knew when she produced that abomination.'

'Do you mean Kynan's queen?' asked Ælfrid.

'Her and no other. Kynan brought her to visit us once with the bishop she kept always at her side. We sat modestly veiled and answered his questions with single words. She did not speak either, but simpered and wriggled as the bishop whispered in her ear. They never came again, and as he left the Bishop gave us all a long, studying gaze. He did not wish us well, but now I know there were many like him. We were surrounded by spies and we never knew it, and Marighal's monster paid for many of them. One even lived in our farmstead for a while.'

I had a longing to find a name for this noble bishop but I could not yet trust myself to speak to the creature.

'You said that there were questions you wished to ask us,' said Nuth, before I could collect myself. 'Do you wish to ask them now?'

I looked up and saw Ælfrid nodding his agreement.

'Thank you,' said the creature. 'There are some matters which do not agree with the description of your community as we had it from Marighal and Selyf. Why, for instance, do you not do the farm work yourselves? I had thought that your Rule forbade this.'

I ground my teeth at the insolence of the woman, but Ælfrid was not perturbed.

'In general they do, and it is this observance of true poverty which sets us apart from other monks. However, after our visit from your sister and the disappearance of Selyf, the older brothers were afraid. They found our isolated position was no longer a chance to free the soul from worldly considerations and when the Bishop at Brychan gave them the chance to join the large house there they were pleased to go.

Not so pleased to stay. They are crowded together in a shed outside the walls of the Abbey. They are not even treated as regular clerks, but may only call themselves canons of the cathedral. This, in itself is a mockery, for they are really no more than the worst pensioners imaginable. They may not sing in the congregation; they may not observe the hours and decisions about their lives are made about them in Chapter meetings where they are allowed no representation. They are not allowed to read during refection and may only read during sewing on one day of the week. They are never allowed to perform any of the penances they have found seemly for all their adult lives. Altogether their invitation from Brychan was a disgrace. I have been to the city for business with the Bishop and I spend my journey home with tears in my eyes for the shame of it. I wish we might restore the Minster only to provide these poor old men with a refuge.

'This left the farm here undermanned and for a while we lived entirely on the charity of the gentiles. This could not continue indefinitely, so Hw and I went to Eirinn and asked the Abbots to send us penitents seeking holy labour. That is why you see so many laymen in the community today.'

'And were the Abbots pleased to help you? Marighal told me that the men here were surrounded by enemies in the church.'

'To our everlasting sorrow we are,' said Ælfrid, 'but it is how we have lived for more generations than we can count and, which is more important, we are at peace with ourselves. Our brother, Hw, has struggled to reconcile us with other Christians since he has the learning for it, and in spite of his poor health he has succeeded in bringing a measure of peace and harmony to our lives.'

'Why did you elect to stay here when your brothers left for Brychan?' she asked.

'I was not here when the others decided to go,' answered Nuth, the innocent fornicator, 'but I am glad I came back here, for I can keep my woman and her sons nearby.'

To her credit the woman looked shocked and stared at him.

'Not all of us have taken vows of celibacy,' Ælfrid explained, 'and we have often found it necessary to replenish our numbers within the community. Not for us are the flocks of students who came to hear the teaching of our founders.'

'But you, why are you here?' asked the woman, 'You are not keeping a concubine. You are one of the men of learning, whom Marighal talked of.'

'I have some learning, but it is not wide, as you will find in the case of Hw. I am no scholar of scripture like him, nor have I studied theology in the monasteries across the sea. That which keeps me here I grub for in the ground and my work is all for the flesh of man.'

The woman was confused by this.

'Ælfrid is an apothecary,' I told her, 'and he has a herb garden here which contains many strange plants. He will leave it only when the last trumpet sounds, not before.'

'Ah, I see why you have remained,' she said, and at once her eyes were filled with tears – pure tears of water – and she continued, 'I wish you could have spoken with two of my sisters. They, too, grew plants with healing qualities and collected them from the wild. You would doubtless have thought such a meeting improper.'

'Indeed, I would not,' said Ælfrid, 'though I cannot answer for my brothers. It is not scandalous to exchange knowledge for the healing of mankind.'

But the woman was weeping now and could no longer speak. We waited for her to become calm, but she was beside herself with grief. Darkness was beginning to settle round us when Ælfrid said at last,

'We will leave you for now, sister, and come again tomorrow when your grief has passed. Will you stay here another night?'

She nodded without a word and we left her.

'What is this terrible sorrow that wracks her?' Ælfrid asked me, but I could only voice speculations,

'Let us hope it is contrition for her sinful state, brother,' I said, 'if not for her own sake, then for ourselves.'

'Why should I wish such terrible grief on anyone?' he cried. 'It is of no service to me that she should be tormented.'

'If she has not repented of her former state we are knowingly consorting with a liar and a blasphemer,' I told him. 'She and her sisters pretended to be consecrates when they could not be. She is sure to have been a harlot also and our ardent wish should be that her heart is clean of this wickedness or else we are polluted ourselves.'

Ælfrid said nothing, but sometimes he is very obtuse.

The next evening we gathered at the feet of our Babylon and she began at once to speak.

I must beg you to forgive my lapse yesterday. I had been thinking all day of my sisters and it had come to me then, for the first time, that I might never see any of them again. It was terrible to think that they have been destroyed, and also, I must confess, I was feeling pity for myself that I am the last of my family and alone in the world. Today I am calmer, since I have told myself that this may not be so and I must persevere in my search for them. I will tell you what happened to us and it is possible you may have some advice for me.

We stayed in our farmstead for some years and we were able to help a great number of the people. This was a joy to us, for our knowledge, though great, was futile without new minds to share it. It was as if we had taken a new, unspoken, vow that if it were in our power we would help any who asked. Kynan sent us many students to learn skills from us that his own people had forgotten.

Gunnhild very soon went to sleep with her God and we were happy for her as we buried her mortal remains. She had lived as an anchoress among us, but she had taken her part in our life together and at the last she died serene and smiling. Indeed in all that time most of us partook of that cheerfulness, and it is a testimony to the good we did that we passed most of the days in harmony with each other and the world. I know that some among your faith deny that working in the service of others is good for the soul, but in our long lives we have found nothing more satisfying. If we were wrong, then what happened to us was just and we have paid in full. If Gunnhild was right and grace alone is the right way to God, she will be safe in His love. Whichever is the truth many of my sisters will know it by now, but they have not yet found a way to tell me.

Destruction came on the feast of St Martin. I had travelled inland to find a family of charcoal-burners for Kynan. They do not stay in one part of the forest for more than two years. I thought I knew where they would stay that year, but I was wrong. I must confess I enjoyed these excursions away from

67

my sisters, for there were times when a great deal of talk and little action became tedious. I spent some time looking for the charcoal-burners with no success and returned on the evening of the second day of the feast.

I was by now looking forward with pleasure to joining my sisters in a meal to mark the day. Back at the settlement I was uneasy when I found the gate hanging open and no one to greet me. There was a strong smell of smoke, which I thought at first had come from the steading. I made my way towards the kitchen and the sound of weeping met me at the door. Inside I found Evabyth, Roswitha and Rhiannon sitting beside the wall. Roswitha had covered her head and wept aloud, swaying backwards and forwards as I have seen mortal women do in deepest distress. The others were silent. Evabyth did not know that I was there and Rhiannon shook her head at me, struck dumb by whatever she had seen. I realised that the smell of smoke had not come from here. I ran outside, but could not see the source around the farmstead. I fled through the gate again and down to the beach. I looked across the bay to Kynan's city and saw a column of black smoke climbing from its heart. Then I knew the gentiles had come.

I fell to my knees and wept. I prayed that I was deceived by what I saw. The great stone walls which Kynan had built had not served him. Somehow the pagans had learned of the city and its riches, and their greed had spurred them to invasion. The thickness of the walls had not daunted those who came against them with fire. The trees planted on them and the illusions painted on them had not hidden the innocents from malicious eyes. The last stones of the minster were to have been put in place at the offering that Sabbath. People had come from miles around to the feast – parents to show their children how great stones could be raised aloft – others return- ing, eager to refresh their memory of the sights – young men bringing their new wives – old men, eyes shining with pride to think that they had lived in such times – all had come to their destruction.

After a long while, Rhiannon came up and lifted me to my feet. I found I was weak and had to lean on her. Together we took the road to the city and the ache in my heart grew with each step. There was a voice crying in my head, protesting that this calamity could not have happened – that it fitted no pattern that we had learned of God's justice or loving kindness – that there was nothing but deception and when we got there we would find our mistake. But Rhiannon began to speak.

'We saw the first sails at dawn, heading due north. They must have waited overnight at the inlet of the gorge. There were two big longships – one about a hundred feet long carried about one hundred and twenty men, then another five smaller ships bringing about one hundred and fifty – and any number of little crafts in amongst them. I would estimate a score more than three hundred came against us. Somebody put a lot of silver into this adventure. We thought at first they would sail on up the coast, but all of a sudden they dropped sail, ran out the oars and pulled for the shore. We realised that, after all these years of safety, it was our turn to suffer.

'Derdriu and the rest took up weapons and made for the city. They called to me to come, saying that pirates could not prevail against us if we united with the citizens. I cannot speak for the others, but I could not break my vow to shed no human blood. Tell me I did right. Please tell me I did right. I have been thinking of nothing else for hours and I cannot come to a conclusion. You must be my judge.'

'I am no fit judge. Where was I when I was needed? I was wandering in the forest, enjoying the fiery colour of dead leaves when my friends were burning. Do not ask me to judge your actions.

'This I will say, if our seven sisters have been destroyed, it is unlikely that adding your hand to the force would have turned defeat to victory. Console yourself with that if you can.'

'I have been trying to do so. I have not succeeded.'

We walked on in silence till we reached the landward gate. The bodies of the guards lay all about us and I saw that many of them had not had time to draw their swords. One who was lying at the edge of the ditch seemed to move, but when I approached him he shuddered and breathed his last. A movement back along the beach caught my eye and I saw Evabyth and Roswitha hurrying along to catch us. We waited for them, reluctant to face the inside of the city, and even after they had joined us we paused before entering. Evabyth had cut off her hair and now held her braids, two in each fist, as if they were swords. Roswitha covered her head again and her shoulders shook with sobs; Rhiannon was as rigid as a bowstring and as pale as milk. I had bitten the inside of my cheek and kept wiping blood on to the back of my hand. We could not look each other in the face.

What manner of creatures are we?

I turned along the main road through the city. There was the body of a man at the end of every lane and alley. Every house gate had been burst in and every hall stood open. Fire which had been started at the King's keep in the centre was spreading outwards. As I looked at one carved roof, yellow fire blossomed in the thatch and in an instant had covered the house. Somewhere down the alley beside it we heard a child crying. Before we could stop her Evabyth darted away and returned with the child in her arms. It was only a few years old at the most. Evabyth clung to it and it struggled and shrieked.

'You are crushing the creature,' said Roswitha, 'be more gentle or you will kill it also.'

'Why do you say "kill it also"?' said Evabyth. 'I have not killed anyone.'

'I meant that it, also, will be dead if you are not careful. Give it to me.' Roswitha took the child and pushed back her kerchief to let it see her face. He calmed down.

'We have accomplished something,' I said, 'thanks be to God.'

'Keep your thanks,' said Evabyth. 'It had been hidden in the crib under an older child. That one had been run through with a spear where it lay. This one was nearly impaled on the same shaft.'

'Thanks be to God,' I repeated, 'we have witnessed a miracle.'

A call from Rhiannon silenced us and we hastened to her. She said she had seen movement over by the church and we ran towards it without hesitation. The fluttering of cloth caught our eye and we turned into the orchard beside the Bishop's house. The Bishop hung in one of the trees. His silk and gold-embroidered vestis hung in bloody rags about him and his right eye had been gouged out. Blood soaked his right side. At the foot of the tree lay the body of the monster Marighal had created. She had been stripped and raped and sent to join her master. Her fine clothes and shoes had gone and all we could find to cover her blood-streaked body was a piece of blanket. All the Bishop's household had vanished, including his wife and sons.

'This is strange,' said Roswitha staring at the Bishop, 'the gold threads there could be saved and used again. Why should someone destroy fine work when it could be sold? And would not the woman creature have been worth taking for ransom?'

'She was old and had never borne children; and there are none left to ransom her,' said Rhiannon. 'Further, I am beginning to think that there is more to this raid than simple gain.'

Then there came a sound over by the minster and we hurried to find out the cause. Yet though we scattered and searched all about it we could not find anyone, friend or foe. The door hung open and we blessed ourselves and went inside. We found Kynan there. He had been tied to the cross behind the altar and the gentiles had slit his back to make a blood-eagle of him. The westering sun shone on him through the window and it seemed, strangely, that there was a smile on his lips. His lungs draped on the cross behind him gave him the look of a fiery angel. I sank to my knees as I looked at this horror and ice formed again in my veins.

At last my sisters and I found the strength to approach the body of our beloved brother and lord. We lifted his broken corpse down with tenderness we had never showed him in life, and we wrapped him in the fine cloth he had brought for the altar. We found that an arrow had been shot through his spine, just below his skull.

'This is one of Gwenlieth's arrows,' said Evabyth. 'I recognise the fledging, and she is the only one I know who could shoot as well as that.'

'Why should she kill our dear brother? He did not deserve such treachery!' exclaimed Roswitha.

'This was not treachery,' I said. 'It was the last service she could do for him.'

She still did not understand. Evabyth explained,

'It takes a while to die in that manner. She shot him to spare him pain.'

'Then the killing of humans is not always an evil,' said Rhiannon, and she swayed where she stood. I knew that she was near losing possession of herself so I went and struck her in the face very hard. She reeled under the blow and began to sob.

'We can talk of morals when we have leisure,' I said, 'but now the only thing of importance is that we should find out what has happened here. Where are our sisters? All the bodies we have found have been of warriors or of old people or of very young. Of women, children and craftsmen there is no trace. Do you understand? You, whose mind is the keenest among us, must see what this means.'

'Slavery!' cried Rhiannon. 'They have been taken into slavery. They are not dead.'

'Indeed they are not, but we must find out where they have gone.'

'This is not possible,' said Evabyth. 'No mortal man could defeat any of us in combat when the invocations have been made.'

'There were over three hundred of the gentiles here this morning,' Rhiannon said, 'no seven of us could defeat that many, though we fought all together, side by side.'

'And you know that there are ways of weakening us even when we have made the invocation,' I reminded her.

'True, but this is not known by any mortal.'

Roswitha had walked away from us to soothe the baby. Suddenly she called and we went to her. She had found Gwenlieth – that is, the mortal remnant of her. What we saw made us tremble with horror. The gentiles had been robbed of their sport in Kynan, but there had been no one to help Gwenlieth when they took their revenge.

'I had never thought that mortals could do such foul things,' said Evabyth, 'and I believed the monks when they told us we were irredeemably wicked. How could they dare!'

'They will tell you that this is the work of men who have given themselves to demons,' Roswitha answered her, 'and then they will say that this is God's judgement on our wicked clan.'

'Gwenlieth never raised her hand against any creature,' Evabyth protested. 'She was quiet and kind and even the mortals loved her.'

'Not her own actions, but her inherited sin have brought her to this.' said Roswitha.

'I am not going to listen to any more of this muddle,' I said. 'We have duties to do. The dead must be buried; the living, if any, must be found, and the stolen must be retrieved. I will not listen to prating on sin for another instant.'

My sisters sighed and came to my assistance. They would have spent the next year debating the chances of their damnation if I had not rallied them. The three of us left with the power to do so called on our father's strength and dug a pit in the graveyard beyond the city walls. Evabyth searched for corpses in the ruins and left them where we would find them. After a brief debate we threw the bodies into the pit without any attempt at ceremony. Only Kynan and Gwenlieth were wrapped in grave clothes we brought from our farmstead. Then we laid them in the church for the night.

All the time we were digging and collecting the corpses I was sure that someone was watching us, but I said nothing to my sisters for they would have wished to stop and look for the intruders. All I could think was that night was falling and the job in hand must be finished if the buzzards, gulls and ravens were not to feed on the flesh of our friends. I must confess that our vigil was not strict since we were exhausted. We slept from sunset to sunrise on the tainted stones of the church. Roswitha went to the farmstead to feed the child and tend to our livestock. It was beyond our strength to think about our situation.

The next morning we prepared to send the dead on the start

of their long journey. As the oldest, Evabyth was elected to say a blessing, but as she raised her hands to pray a clod of earth hit her. A voice cried,

'Demons, demons! Get away from our dead!'

We looked about us, but could see nothing. Evabyth turned to the grave again and was struck full in the back by a rock. Angry, she turned and ran over to the bushes where it seemed to have come from. Again a voice cried,

'Demons! Whores! Have you not had your fill of our young men?'

Evabyth had found nothing and returned to us with a frown. I saw a movement under the walls and indicated to Evabyth that she should start the prayer again. This time, as she raised her hands, two turfs flew through the air, but we saw where they came from and all of us ran to the spot. There, cowering behind a stone fallen from the wall, we found an old man and an old woman. When they saw us they blessed themselves, spat at us and made other warding signs we did not recognise.

'Keep away from us!' they shrieked. 'We are old and our flesh is dried up. You will not like the taste of us at all. Leave us alone!'

'What nonsense is this?' roared Evabyth. 'Do you think we have a taste for mortal flesh?'

'We know you do,' said the old man. 'We have heard about the ceremonies you hold in that farm of yours. You eat babies and copulate with dozens of young men at a time and you drink human blood in golden chalices. You even took one of our babies away yesterday. We know all about it. The Bishop told us.'

'The Bishop lied,' said Roswitha. 'We have never eaten human flesh of any kind, nor do we drink blood. Why should we? We have plenty to eat in our hall without it. Besides, there is not much to feast on in a baby. It has had no time to grow anything but fat.'

'You do not understand,' I told her. 'Bishops tell these lies to frighten mankind. They are not talking about our daily diet. It is something to do with their own superstition.'

The old man's answer came pat.

'The Bishop told us and he cannot lie. He is a holy man. He told us that you do all these vile things when you worship demons. Demons are only happy when mortals are being wicked and miserable, so you do all that filthiness to please them.'

'I understand now,' said Roswitha. 'Well, old man, I must tell you you have been cheated. The Bishop was talking in ignorance and I think that was a great dereliction of his duty. He is taken to be the authority on sin and the enemies of mankind, but in this case he is mistaken.'

'His first error was to tell you that we are mortal,' said Rhiannon, and ignored my gestures to her to be silent. 'We are only semi-mortal, but up to now we have tried to live as mortals since we thought it was the path of salvation for us.

Bishop Ailbhe Ua-Robocain – it must be he. I heard that this undistinguished man of an undistinguished family had been bundled off to Kyil by the coarb of Cunotegernos. It seems he was embarrassing his fellows by his ignorant perse-cution of 'heretics' in Lothene. These idiotic accusations are typical of the kind that he would make against his victims. They are the same accusations that were made against our ancestors in the faith, against Jews, against Saracens and against heretics. So over-used are they that I doubt very much if they have ever been true.

'In the second place he was wrong to tell you that we eat human substance. It would be most disagreeable to us to do so since we eat only the flesh of cattle. God himself will witness we have not even taken part in your Communion meal. As to the mass copulations, while it is true that some of us took lovers among mortal men, they were only one at a time. I think copulation with many people at one time would not be pleasing.'

The old man stared at her with his mouth open, but the old woman croaked,

'Whoredoms. You admit to whoredoms.'

'I do not – not for myself, that is. My sisters had their warmer moments, as do most humans.'

75

'Yes,' skirled the old man, 'and now a judgement is come upon them. The gentiles have murdered them or carried them off into slavery. You are all demons. Demons and whores as the Bishop said.'

'The Bishop is offal and we are still standing,' I said. 'What judgement has come upon him and missed us?'

'He said it would come to this. We should have burned you out months ago, he said, but you were doing charitable work so the townsmen said you should be left. But look what it has brought them. It is a judgement upon our laziness. The pagans are God's justice!'

It was clear that this talking was pointless, but before I could bring it to a close Evabyth rushed on the old man. She lifted him up by the front of his tunic and shook him like a rat saying,

'You know what has happened to our sisters. Tell us.'

The old man was choking and could only shake his head so she dropped him and turned on the woman.

'Who took my sisters away?' she cried. 'Tell me, or I will build a fire and hang you over it and peel you inch by inch till you tell me.'

'How is it that Evabyth's strength is restored?' murmured Rhiannon.

'It is the rage,' said Roswitha. 'Sometimes it works that way in us.'

'That is a thing worth remembering,' mused Rhiannon.

I went to Evabyth who had thrown the old man and the old woman in a heap and was preparing to beat them. In that state of mind she would have killed them with the first blow, so I seized her upraised hand.

'This is not the way to the truth,' I said to her. 'We hate the men who destroyed Gwenlieth's flesh and carried off the others. Why, therefore, should we set them up as our teachers? We have vowed to help humanity, nor should we stint now, when everyone is suffering.'

'They call us whores and demons. Let them see but once how a demon can work and they will not insult our family again.'

76

'I understand your anger, sister, but it is futile. Fear is only making these poor creatures weaker in the mind than they were before. Go and calm yourself. I will ask them what you wish to know and I am sure I will find answers.'

She walked some distance apart to stop herself from shaking. I sat on the ground beside the old ones and waited. The old woman stopped sobbing with fear after a while and they began whispering to each other. My sisters moved closer and I waved them away. The old ones fell silent and stared ahead with glazed eyes. Finally I began to speak to the humans, saying,

'You have angered my sister greatly and, you now know, her wrath is terrible. I am sorry that she has frightened you in this way, but you must see she is worried about our sisters. Do you not have family who cause you concern?'

The old ones looked at me but their eyes were only blank pools that reflected the sky. I continued,

'I have never woken to a day when I did not worry about my sisters, especially the younger ones. They are so restless and yet in these times of trouble there is no safety. I could not have them wandering alone on the roads, but if they were too confined I was always afraid they would run off. Has this not happened to every adult?'

The old woman nodded and I paused. She said,

'Yes, we have ... had a son. He was always staying out overnight. I said nothing good would come of it, but who listens to a woman? My husband beat him regularly, but he could have saved his sweat. The boy ran off and we never heard of him again. The girls, now they were good girls, and knew their duty. Thanks be to God they are all married on to good men and went away. They will have been spared this raiding.'

'That is a blessing,' I said, and sighed. 'I wish that I could say the same of my kindred,' and I wept in real sorrow.

'I am sorry for your trouble,' said the old one, while her man pulled at her arm.

'Tell her nothing,' he hissed, 'once you have told her she will kill us both,' but the woman did not seem to have heard him.

'I don't know for sure what happened to them,' she said, 'but I know that another one was killed. They put her in a sack with stones to see how long she would take to drown. We watched from the bushes along the shore there. The rest were taken with the others to where the pagans came from.'

Behind me I heard my sisters' gasps of horror and Roswitha cried aloud. She is afraid of water and this death would strike her heart. I turned and frowned at them all to keep them silent.

'Did you know anything about the foreigners?' I asked. 'Where they came from?'

Again the old man tried to silence his wife, but she was eager to speak.

'I did not know their faces yet I am sure they were not all foreigners. Some of them spoke to each other in Scottish and British tongues. They said they were going south.'

'Did they carry a banner or anything to mark them out?'

The old man stared at the sky but the woman said,

'They had a banner on the biggest longboat. I am not sure because my eyes are weak, but I thought it had a cat on it, or maybe even a ... I thought it was a rat. Most likely I saw it wrong.'

'I did not see that,' said the man, but his eyes were too wide.

'It is no great matter,' I said, 'please do not be concerned. If it is God's will we shall find our sisters again. If not, we must hope that they have found a good ending to their adventures.

'Now let us finish this burial and send our companions on their way.'

They joined us in that and then came to our farmstead for food and a night's rest. They told us that the child was called Guaire son of Skeggi son of Marcan, and that his mother had been taken alive to the longships. We told them they could stay with us as long as they wished and it seemed to me that the old woman would have liked to take up our invitation. However, the next morning they were gone. The fear that had been planted in the old man's heart could not be uprooted by a little kindness. I doubt if they survived the season in the forest.

Winter came on us suddenly last year. We had so few hands to do the work that we could only attend to the necessities. In addition to our regular duties we went to Kynan's city each day and burnt the remaining houses or pulled stones from the walls. We had decided that no foul pagan would defile the place by living there. At least the boy thrived, so closely did Roswitha attend to him, and if the loss of his mother troubled his young soul there was no sign of it. When the ice left the pools and spring was wakening in the soil the time came to consider our position. We sat in the kitchen and talked for many hours before we came to any agreement. Evabyth began and she said that above all she wanted nothing more to do with humanity.

'Marighal told us that we would find nothing but pain from mixing with mortals. She warned us that their ways are strange and that they set themselves rules for living which they do not follow. I do not wish to have anything more to do with such creatures. They insult us and drive us away, and accuse us of crimes without producing witnesses. Yet the fruits of their wickedness lie all around and they do not see them.'

'Remember you are half-mortal yourself,' said Rhiannon. 'You cannot shun that part of your nature.'

'I do not shun it, but I wish to see it used properly; not put to the destruction of its fellows.'

'I feel the same way,' said Roswitha. 'We have the child and we will raise him to live like the best of mortals. We would serve him better if we do not let him meet the ruck and come to follow their ways. I say let humanity take its own road to hell and we will follow ours. We shall see who gets there sooner.'

'What of our sisters,' I cried, 'surely we must try and find them again? We swore to live together in peace and charity. Surely we cannot leave them in slavery?'

'They are in God's hands,' said Roswitha.

'They are in the hands of men,' I said, 'and that is not a good place for them to be. Have you forgotten so soon how they butchered one of us and drowned another?'

'I have not forgotten it,' said Roswitha, shuddering, 'and I only wish I could.'

'I see it now,' I cried, 'I see it all. You are afraid. You were afraid when the raiders came. You did not go and fight for our friends because you feared to share their fate. You were not thinking of your vows to avoid combat, you thought only of the survival of your own flesh.'

'You are right,' said Roswitha, and tears ran down her face. 'I was afraid then, and I am afraid now. And even though I waken each morning to my shame, I do not want to die the final death. Is that strange?'

'It is not,' broke in Rhiannon, 'it is only part of your human heritage. Do not be ashamed. Even as I took my first vows in front of Selyf, I was afraid of what lay ahead. I shall never be sure if I stayed here out of piety or dread, but I begin to think that it is not important.'

'How could you say such a thing?' I asked her. 'You suspect that you and these others sent our sisters to death and probable damnation. You watched as they picked up their weapons and ran to battle to help their friends and you did not make a move to help them. You admit that you are a craven wretch yet you do not think that it is important?'

'What we have done is finished with. I might ask you what you were doing to linger in the forest all that time, but I will not. I know the reasons for what we did will be revealed to us when God's kingdom comes. What matters is what we will do now.'

'We can redress the wrongs we have done by rescuing the captives.'

'This will only cause us grief,' said Rhiannon. 'We may be forced to kill, or to hurt, or we may face the same dilemma we have just discussed.'

'I kept my vows,' said Evabyth, 'no more. And I say let the ingrate mortals rot.'

'I have no desire to hear myself called a whore or a demon ever again,' said Roswitha. 'I wish to rear a man who will see us for what we are, loving, generous and wise.'

'Such was our father's plan for Kynan and those who came

before him,' I replied. 'You will recall how little success he had.'

'Not all of them were failures,' Evabyth said. 'Kynan was a good friend to us.'

'The more reason to try and rescue his people for him.'

'I have another notion,' said Rhiannon. 'I do not think it would be practical for us to stay here. Strong as we are, the steading is too big for us to manage on our own, and from what we have heard it is clear we could not hire human servants to assist us. Whatever happens we must leave.

'It has long been a desire of mine to travel across the sea. I yearn to see the land where the birds go to when they leave at sunset or in the autumn. I might even find the place where the sun rests at the end of the day. There is a vast world beyond these shores and I long to see some of it before I leave this flesh for the last time. I propose, therefore, that we should take one of the boats that we have used for fishing and set sail for another land.'

For once we did not fall to loud argument. I think that we had all thought of such a course of action at some time, but had never spoken of it to anyone. We were silent for many minutes, then Evabyth said,

'I will go with you.'

'What about the boy?' said Roswitha. 'How will he fare on a long sea voyage?'

'He has grown fast over the winter and he is sturdy and has all his teeth. I have heard that settlers have taken ship for cold northern lands taking children and livestock and everything you could need to set up a village. We could do the same.'

'That was in a bigger boat than either of ours,' I said.

'Not so,' said Rhiannon. 'Maedbh and her servants went to the Ice Land in a four-oar and the larger of our boats is nearly thirty feet long.'

She was more stirred than I had ever seen her before. Her cheeks were red and her eyes were shining. It was sure that she was hungry to make this voyage. We debated the issue far into the night, but I knew all the time that she would prevail.

She always had more wit than any of us and her arguments were well thought out. Every argument I put up she answered easily, as if she had thought of it for a long time herself. Her plans were all made, down the storage of the cheese in cloth in a tin-lined box. In the end I felt myself to be the betrayer because I would not join them. I still wished to find any members of our family I could, and the others saw at last that I would not be budged.

During the winter we had slaughtered and salted most of our livestock. We had done this because we had not enough hands to care for them all, but it served another purpose now, and my sisters were able to pack their boat with enough food for many months. We placed our father in his chair amidships and his blind face stared ahead into the unknown. When they made landfall he would take his place in their midst to support them through the uncertain times.

We were like Adam and Eve, driven from our quiet paradise. As I watched my sisters set sail for the lands of the west, I wept for the tranquillity that could have been ours. A tiny pebble rolls down a hill and disturbs others which in turn set others in motion. This process continues until a terrible land-slide sweeps down the valley destroying crops and cattle and killing people. In the same way, leaving our father's house had been the first move that had led to all our calamity. Yet I could not see how we could have done otherwise.

I returned to the farmsteading and set a torch to it, and waited till nothing of it was left.

'Master of the Universe,' I said, 'whom mankind in his folly has called Almighty and Merciful, in this pyre I send to you the last mortal remains of our hopes and good wishes for humanity. Take them and reflect that you have brought to destruction those who wished for nothing but peace of mind. When the time comes for me to leave this flesh, I will meet you at deathgate, and when that happens you will need to have many witnesses prepared.'

On this bitter note I set sail. And the God will testify I wish with all my heart it could have been otherwise. Now I am alone and I will not give up searching for my kindred until the last breath leaves my body.

The time had come to leave the woman again for the night. With a heavy heart I retired to my cell and considered all that I had heard. By the first hour I had realised that there was no help for me. I must finish the task my father had failed to finish. There is no one else to attend to it. Of all the meagre congregation I am the least fit for the tasks of maintaining our livelihood. The little bit of garden that I keep will be easily taken over by any other in the household. Similarly, my students are not so advanced that one of the older students cannot teach the rudiments to the younger ones. When I return I will make up for the time lost by greater endeavour.

My reasons for this sad conclusion are as follows: only two of us are consecrate and consequently safe from the actions of the demons – I have already proved this when I went to fast against Othin and I know that I will hold my ground whatever temptation is thrust at me – Ælfrid cannot be spared from his duties as a leech to the local people. Unhappy to relate, it is his ministrations alone that keep many of them within the fold. They do not speak to me if they can avoid it since my piety is the greatest here and I remind them that they are backsliders and sinners. Furthermore, I am afraid that despite his vows as a Christian Ælfrid still persists in collecting his herbs with pagan observations. He studies the movements of the stars before he goes out to fetch them, and I am sure I hear him making invocations as he goes about it. He denied this when I confronted him with it. Nevertheless I see him as in danger of sinking into the mire when pollution surrounds him.

I spoke to him of my decision at recreation time the next day – the woman's departure being again delayed by adverse winds. He was reluctant to let me go, of course, but he soon saw that there was no help for it and gave me all the medicine I would need for two months' journey.

Foxglove – for the heartbeat – the second year's growth of leaves, but do not let the liquor on to your skin when you are plucking them for you will be sick perhaps to death with headache and spots on the skin. Do not boil the plant or you will destroy the benefit. Infuse gently in spirits of wine.

Elder – for the water-ill – the shoots and the young leaves alone must be used for the berries will make headache and sickness. Pour boiling water over the fresh plant and remove it once the water has cooled.

Buckthorn – for the same – the dried ripe berries may be eaten or infused.

Mullein – for the coughing – the leaves in boiling water will help you to spit.

He has also promised that the community will pray for me at every hour. It will comfort me to think of my brothers joining me in their hearts at every psalm and the Almighty will perhaps hear the voices of his humblest followers.

When I informed the woman that I would accompany her, she smiled and shrugged.

'I hope you are a good sailor,' was all she said.

On being told that I was one of the best on that coast she nodded and told me at what hour she would be leaving the next day. We will be going in search of her sister Olwen at first, for she was married to a landowner and battle leader and may be able to assist us in any attempt to rescue the people of Kynan. This will take us southward to Dyfed, and perhaps further. The last word Barve heard of them was that they were in Rhos, but they have moved on. The man killed their father when he carried Olwen off with him, and it seems to me that he could well be the man to make an ally of in my struggles with the unnatural ones.

This sense of urgency about our task will not leave me. Who can doubt that the last years are upon us? I have seen the corruption among the great men of the world where bishops are no more than the servants of the king. They are puffed up with pride and wealth and ride into battle as if consecrating hands had never been set upon them.

Consider the fate of Rome herself. The Emperor is a child; his father consorted openly with sorcerers who even now hang round the Imperial court like wasps round a midden. The mother is 'arrayed in purple and scarlet colour, and decked with gold and precious stones and pearls...' I saw her myself, you remember, and that was when her husband was alive to contain her limitless pride. I truly believe that this child may prove to be the anti-christ, for as a result of wickedness his father died young and left the Empire to struggle in the grip of the puling babe. At once he was carried off by his uncle but the abominable woman enchanted prince and bishop alike until the child was returned to her. At her death her vile mother-in-law took her place and in the child's name has encouraged abominations everywhere. Who can doubt that this child – by every account a decadent Greek in all but name – will be the last Emperor? His fall will mean the end of every creature on earth and the purification of the world before the Son of Man appears in glory.

The long-haired star has been seen; pestilence covers the land; and the afflictions of the gentiles on our shores, though not new, have been becoming worse of late. Whereas before they skulked in forest and marsh, now they walk the streets of every city with their faces uncovered.

These therefore are undoubtedly the days of trouble when God sends his demons against man to test him in the final test. I must not let this woman escape me. Her evil endeavours must not be allowed to succeed, and all she comes into contact with must be protected against the temptation she brings. There is so little time to convert the last of the heathen. Not a soul must be left in danger. This, and this alone is my reason for going with her. I do not go out of vain curiosity.

Forgive me, father, for presuming upon your permission to leave, but the woman has said that she will be gone in the morning whatever the weather. She is impatient, for she sees the year as wearing away even though we pointed out to her that it is not yet Lent. Ælfrid will send this letter to you by messenger as soon as one can be spared. I beg for your prayers on this perilous journey that I will be given the chance to confront the wickedness in this woman and her kindred before my failing body betrays me.

Valete.

Ælfrid, monk and apothecary at Rintsnoc, Hw, monk, his graceless brother and gyrovagus sends greetings.

Dear brother in Christ, before I left our community you and I talked about the approaching Day of Days. It seemed to me that you did not agree with me that the day is almost upon us, but there was not time enough for me to set your mind at rest about the facts. You have not travelled as much as I, therefore you have not had the chance to weigh the evidence I have seen. If you had, there is no doubt in my mind that you would be at one with me.

We have never differed over the fact that we should be slow to believe in miracles. The direct intervention of the Almighty in natural processes is not to be expected or even hoped for, as it is evidence of hopeless disruption in God's Universe, both before and after the fact. Equally we have agreed that it is unacceptable to ascribe actions to the Enemy of God and man without unequivocal proof of the agency. On the other hand, you must remember what you saw with your own eyes, and what your brother Selyf has described. The family of Usbathaden have strange powers, and while this, in itself is not sufficient reason to doubt their virtue, they themselves have admitted that they are at odds with the Father of All. There can be no doubt that their very existence itself is unlawful, and that it is our plain duty to contain their powers.

As you will recall, the day we left was most auspicious. There was a good fresh wind from the north and as we cleared the harbour it caught us and took us briskly southwards. I began to think that we would make the coast of Powys before two Sabbaths had passed, as the woman said. It being Thursday, I fasted and sat quietly in the middle section of the boat reading the Psalter and reciting the hours. As I completed the sixth hour with the lines blessing God for his blessings to man she laughed aloud, but when I came to the words, 'The dead do not praise the Lord nor do any that go down into silence' she nodded and said,

'That is true, after a long life and much learning who could find it in his heart to praise God?'

I was not free to answer her but I resolved to do so as soon as it was permitted. Then the woman's temptation came upon me and I looked into her face and I saw that she was beautiful. The braids of hair that hung below her kerchief were the black of a raven's wing; her skin was pale with only a little colour on the cheeks and not a single blemish; her teeth were white and even; her hands long, smooth and well fleshed, and by some unholy skill without scar or callous. The eyes that stared so insolently at me were very dark blue, almost the colour of sea at night when the moon shines on it. Then I knew how much I had been mistaken to think that I was proof against her female wiles. I blessed myself against her and said a short prayer for protection. A smile twisted her face and she covered it with her kerchief.

'I will not trouble your weak flesh,' she said.

As we crossed the estuary the tide drove us up river. She saw me gazing back toward the open sea and said,

'This turning aside cannot be avoided. I have calculated for it and it will not take long.'

This proved at least that you were right, brother, when you said she has no supernatural power over tide and current. It was getting late by now so I answered,

'I hope it will not be long. We must soon make landfall or we will be left sailing in the dark.'

'Be patient,' she said, 'the tide will slacken soon and we will win across to Skimi's fortress well before darkness falls.'

'We might land at the sainted Nynia's island,' I ventured. 'We would be safe there.'

'Indeed we might, but we would still have to find ourselves slack water tomorrow to cross the estuary. I know there will be slack water soon today so I shall go on.'

Now that I had thought of it, I longed for the Founder's island as a lamb longs for the ewe. I pressed my case.

'If we get carried too far up the river we may find ourselves on a sandbank. The land here is treacherous and constantly changes shape.'

'You have not seen many years,' she said, 'even by the standards of your kind. If you had lived as long as I you would know that the land everywhere is treacherous and constantly changes shape. Rivers run in different beds, lakes leave their valleys and beaches grow and shrink from decade to decade. Only the tides do not change their pattern, as Rhiannon found out. She tabulated their movements over the centuries and discovered the order of their coming and going. This knowledge she has shared with me so that when I say we are safe, you may believe me.'

'I know that the tides are regular in their courses,' I replied, 'although I know no-one who has charted them, but I cannot believe that the land changes the way you have said.'

'It is not important whether you believe me or not. I have found that much of what mankind takes as immutable is subject to change, but the smallness of their vision prevents them from seeing it. It is there none the less.'

I had no desire to bandy words with her so I said merely, 'I must believe you. We are taught that nothing but God is immutable, so when you say the land changes shape you may well be right. Everything in the world comes to decay.'

'You are exceedingly kind,' she said, but I could see her mouth did not agree with her heart. 'You must forgive me if I indulge in some scepticism about your own belief. You say that only God is immutable, yet I see no reason to think that this is so. It is said that God created man in his own image and it is surely true that man himself grows from baby to child then to man before he finally ceases to exist. It would follow from this that God is ageing also.'

'Ignorant wretch!' I answered her at once. 'This is as foolish as it is damnable. When we say God created man in His image we mean his spiritual dimension – his soul – we do not refer to man's sodden, fleshly being. This is only a vehicle for use on this earth and bears no relationship to God's being.'

'I see that you have studied the matter and sincerely believe that God is unchanging. It will not be easy, then, for you to believe what I say. However, my sisters and I have debated the matter and we have concluded that probably He is changing over the course of time. If we who were immortal can find ourselves breaking the habits of centuries, why should not He also? It seems to us that even if God does not grow old as man grows old, He must change in some way or else what was the purpose in creating this world? Here men and women know so much suffering that I wonder that they do not all kill themselves or become permanently demented.'

'This perpetual misery is a result of man's sinful nature, nothing more. God has sent them His messengers to show them the truth and yet they choose to follow on their wicked path.'

She did not appear to have understood for she went on,

'Yes, they continue to live with it and, worse, they continue to make the same mistakes as their ancestors, when they could easily change their ways. The deity, if He is omnipotent as you say, might easily intervene to prevent all this, but He does not. Thus suffering goes on from generation to generation when a moment's reason might prevent it, nor can I detect the slightest purpose in it. The only justification for it is that it is the means by which God teaches Himself something. What He is learning I cannot guess, so all this is idle. Undoubtedly I will find out the truth on the other side of the grave.'

She fell silent and turned to watch the wind and the tide. It was good that she did for it gave me time to recover the breath that this appalling heresy had driven from my body. I knew at once that she had said these things in a demonic effort to remove me from grace so I refrained from making any reply to her absurd remarks. After a while she went on,

'There are those who think that change is essential to everything. They say that all matter comes out of four elements, fire and earth and air and water. Everything that can be seen under the sun is composed out of these substances and everything that happens arises from these materials changing their state. Fire makes itself into the moving air of wind which then gives birth to rain. When rain has fallen it forms the earth then the process is reversed and earth produces moisture which melts into air. The air moves and becomes fire once more. Thus everything is in a constant state of change and this would include the Deity. Do you have any notion as to the truth of this theory?'

He should have answered as follows: if everything changes beyond recognition, what existed before can no longer exist. Yet simple observation shows us that it does exist. The earth does not fade from before our eyes when the winds blow violently out of heaven. It follows, then, that while things interchange substance, that substance must itself be made of something immutable and which changes only in the order of its composition. In the same way, letters are always the same, but in different sequences make different words. It is a pity Hw did not lower himself to spend more time with us in our debate.

I did not descend to answer her. I decided that if she should embark on her blasphemous course I will put my hands over my ears and block out her voice. So far she has not provoked me to this.

She had been speaking the truth about the tides, at least, for soon I felt the change under the keel as the current slackened off. Then we made rapid headway west and south once more till we saw our destination. The massive, ancient stones of the harbour soon rose above us; we quickly beached the boat and took our goods ashore. I was glad to see that they have just built a small wooden oratory on the headland beside the cross. As yet there is no presbyter living here, so I made the offering for the company. There were baptisms to be performed also since the steading has grown in population. Skimi's men were surprised to see me after so many years, and with a woman, but they forbore from making ribald comments. Whether this was from respect for my piety or because she had the grace to veil herself I shall never be sure. When it was clear we would not seek to enter the mead hall we were conducted to a tiny hostel at the back of the settlement. They told us that there was no other space available that night, but I suspect they wished to keep us away from them.

The guest-house could not have slept more than two or three at the most and I was therefore forced to spend the night in closer proximity to the woman than I should. By God's mercy I was able to resist her temptations even though we lay with only the reed partition between us. For a while we listened to the din from the mead hall then the woman spoke to me through the wall.

'Do men always pass the night in such drunken revelry?' she asked.

'Not always, so far as I know, but it will soon be Lent, and I suppose they will be making the most of their last couple of Sabbaths before it starts.'

The sound of shrill laughter came to us on the breeze.

'Is that a woman's voice?' she said. 'Is she what you call a harlot?'

'Be silent,' I answered, and I heard no more from her that night.

In the morning I awoke to recite the second hour and found that we were surrounded by thick, white fog. Silence engulfed the small hostel as if a sheepskin had been thrown over it and every blade of grass was hung with shining drops. I spoke to the woman, but receiving no reply I thought she was asleep until I went to wake her, then I found she had gone out. Her bundle was still there, all packed up, and I took the chance to unroll it and see what demonolatry it contained. There was some clothing made of fine linen and soft wool – luxurious but not extraordinary. Some books in a leather case gave me a momentary pause until I found that they were a psalter and a testament. What the creature was doing with them I could not think.

The plates of metal we saw in her hands at our home were

packed underneath them and I studied them closely. They seemed to be laid out in tables like a calendar but there were holes in them whose purpose I could not fathom; also there was some illegible writing scratched on the surface. It looked somewhat like Hebrew to me, or perhaps the scrawl used by Saracens, and there were rows of circles. I decided to challenge her with them some time when it would suit me. Further down there was a small piece of metal wrapped in a cloth. It was dull and grey, and looked totally worthless to me but I wrapped it again and put it back. There was nothing else of note. No amulets, dried plants, parts of animals, writing materials or other paraphernalia of wizards. It was very suspicious.

I tied up the bundle again and replaced it beside the woman's pallet just as I had found it. I rekindled the fire and sat beside it with my psalter until she returned, swishing through the grass with her long, immodest stride. She bade me good morning and I replied before I could stop myself. Smiling she went on,

'This fog will not clear until well into the day, and we will not be able to travel. I think we will have to keep your Sabbath and wait to move on Sunday evening, when the tide will be in our favour.

I said in very few words that I was of her opinion and that it had pleased God keep us, since the souls there had much need of my ministration. If ever I needed proof of her evil intent this would be enough, for she takes every opportunity to make me speak and break the Rule.

She walked past me to her bed alcove. After a moment she came back and sat down in front of me. She said,

'There is no purpose to be served in looking in my pack as I keep everything I value highly about my person. Now, since you wish to see my few worldly goods, be so kind as to look at this.'

'How do you know what I did?' I said swiftly, as she pulled her scrip from her belt.

'The knots I use to tie my pack are known only to myself. Your meddling was clear to me as soon as I saw the strange knots you used retying it.'

I must confess my chagrin made my colour change. How could I have hoped to deceive those who have spent centuries studying deception? As she tipped the contents of her purse out in front of her I showed no interest.

'Look here,' she said, 'I will show you everything. You will see that I have no means of harming you.'

'Since the Words of God are in your pack I must conclude that you place no value on them,' I told her.

'No, I do not, except insofar as those are the only books I have left, and I value all books. But do not be afraid, I may not be what you would wish me to be but I bear you no ill-will.'

'I am not afraid of you,' I replied. 'You have no power to harm one whose faith is as firm as my own. I need to know what manner of spirits you command, that is all.'

'I command no spirits, foolish man; look at all the power I command. A comb for my hair, a glass for making fire and smoothing linen and a jewelled box containing mementoes of my family.'

'They are all the means of conjuration women need to keep men enslaved. A comb drawn through your hair will summon spirits. I have seen them and heard them when my mother combed her hair, but she was a good Christian and at once prayed for their departure.'

'If it will please you, then teach me the prayers and I will drive them off also. They are of no concern to me.'

'What, then, about the burning glass? That brings down the spirits of fire. Only a holy bishop should use such as that, for only he will contain enough sanctity in his person to control them.'

'I know nothing about such spirits. I have never heard tell of any and I have never seen anything of them myself. But if it will please you I shall not use it and you shall kindle the fire from now on.'

'Why do you persist in tempting me into your sinful ways!'

She shrugged her shoulders and looked at me insultingly.

'What about this?' she said after a moment, and opened the jewelled box. Inside I saw three locks of hair, one fair, one black and one reddish-gold.

'Surely you cannot believe that a few strands of hair will lead you astray?' she sneered.

'I do not, but the ways of your family are so strange that I have no way of being sure.'

'I am sorry to hear that, monk, for your journey with me will be most miserable if you think like this. I will promise to keep them out of your sight while you are with me and use them only after you have had a chance to say prayers for our safety. Will that content you?'

'It will not. If you were to act in good faith you would take them at once to the oratory and leave them to be destroyed by the bishop when he comes.'

'You are asking too much, monk. It was no wish of mine that you came with me on this journey. I admit that I am glad of your silent company but remember that I never requested it. Now you must take your chances with whatever evil spirits you fancy throng round you. What is mine I keep. It is little enough, God knows.'

She put the things back into her purse, hung it on her belt and left the house. I went to the oratory and prayed for the rest of the morning. While I was there more people came to me with requests for baptism and instruction in the faith, and in the evening there was another mass to be held. The woman returned after it and sat eating in silence.

'Where have you been all day?' I asked her.

'You are not the only one whose services are needed,' she replied. 'Some of the farmers have asked my advice about the stock and the state of the fields before sowing starts.'

'Why should they do that? How could they know you would help them?'

'I have said before that you and your kind do not know everything about the simple people who live near you.'

'Do you mean to tell me that you have been known to them?'

'Yes, I and my sisters also,' she answered, smiling. 'We were known to many people for our knowledge and skill.'

'Knowledge of what? Skill in what? In idolatry and whoredoms?'

'I have told you, and Marighal told your brothers, we know no religion but that which Selyf taught us. Your word "idolatry" means nothing to us but a vague notion of images, singing old songs and dancing. I will not deny that we have done these things but it was for nothing other than our amusement.'

'What was it, then that you could offer these men, if it were not coitus?'

'I shall try and put a stop to your raillery, although I doubt if it is within my power to do so,' she said, sighing.

'You are welcome to make the attempt,' I told her, 'but you are right in thinking it will be fruitless.'

'I am sure my sister Marighal must have told your kindred how she went abroad and learned about metal-working and many other arts. What she did not know then was that this happened to many of us in our early lives. It was our misfortune that as long as we lived with our father, our memory of these events faded and was at last forgotten. I, for instance, spent my third or fourth incarnation in the home of a woman called Finnavair. It was said she raised cattle by spitting in the dust and moulding the mud into calves, but that was just one of the silly stories peasants like to tell. If they fail at something where another succeeds they pass off the success as wizardry. So to make themselves feel less foolish, you see, they practise greater folly.

'Finnavair knew the ways of all animals, wild and domestic. For instance she bought fat bulls from the Frisians to improve the meat on her beasts. She also taught men how to use their hunting dogs to herd cattle and sheep. Even though she was of farming people, she knew how to read and would learn from books and from any other source that might have a new idea to offer. My years with her were filled with learning and discovery, but after two more incarnations at my father's hall dust settled on my soul so that I lost all recollection of them. When I left there, my mind was reawakened.

'Others of my sisters went to the small men when they all yet lived in the valley of the miners. And others joined the forest workers and learned how to live by hunting and by the husbandry of pigs and bees. They also learned the craft of growing trees for special purposes such as are needed for boat-building. With our long existence we are well suited to this sort of harvest, but it all came to nothing when our life in the fortress stupefied us. There were those who learned the arts of war, those who studied medicine and others who added to our oldest skills of weaving and sewing.

If this is so then their death is a source of nothing but grief to mankind. Hw should not condemn them. I say no more.

'You see, then, that we had much to offer the people of Kynan once we left our bondage. We were not always success-ful teachers, but most of our students returned to us daily.'

She paused at this recollection of her former life and stared past me with unseeing eyes. Sadly she went on,

'Some students came to learn only one set of skills and went about their business once they thought they had mas-tered what they needed. Others came to learn all that they could from us and returned often until they had spent some time with each sister. Some of these, of course, had other motives.' She fell silent.

'Are you talking about the sisters who committed fornica-tion?' I asked. 'You have indicated that you knew of some sins of this kind among them. If it is true, you are party to it.'

'I was not party to it. I argued violently against it, but lust prevailed.'

'Which of your sisters were involved and what kind of acts did they commit?'

She looked at me through narrowed eyes saying,

'It cannot be of any matter to you which of my sisters fell from grace. Your curiosity is unseemly.'

'You are wrong to set yourself in judgement over me. I have every right to enquire to what depths of iniquity your kin could sink. I may have to call for help from higher authority.'

At this she laughed a long, loud laugh. In that incontinent laughter I saw her demonic nature for the first time and I was at once reassured and filled with fear. I grasped my psalter firmly as her hilarity subsided and she went on with a shrug.

'There was no harm intended in my sisters' actions. Nor, now that I look back on it, do I see any harm in fact. My only regret is that I did not take the opportunity to share the pleasures of the flesh when it came my way.'

'Why did you resist when the others did not?'

'I believed what Selyf had taught me – that chastity was the only road to heaven.'

'Do you no longer hold this to be true? Can you be such a backslider?'

'I held it to be true, but now I have seen too many things and I am not sure.'

'There are few things to be sure of in this life, but I have not the faintest doubt that there is no sin equal to coitus. In the first place it weakens the body so that it is less fit to do the work which God has given us. In men it drains his vital spirits into his manly parts so that his vigour is impaired. In women it distracts them from the contemplation of their duty to God, for it is well known that once a woman has experienced copulation she can think of nothing else. If proof were needed of this, consider how women dress. Even the most modest woman whose clothes are coarse in texture and sombre in colour walks so that her ankle peeps in and out beneath her hem. Her hair, trapped under a kerchief, slips out to attract lustful glances. The tying of her shift at the neck draws the eyes of men to her bosom. It would be better if women were locked up and never stepped into the daylight once they have committed fornication.'

My heart was thundering from rage as I contemplated this horror. I took some of the tincture to control the beating.

'I see that you are very troubled by this matter,' she said.

She walked to the door of the hostel. The last of the fog had gone and it was a fine evening with a blue sky and small clouds.

'Skimi has arrived,' she said, 'you had better go and hear his confession for he has travelled far and waited long to make it. At least he will be glad to bare his heart to you.'

When I returned she had taken the metal plates from her pack and was sliding them between her fingers. She curled her lip when I blessed myself.

'You had better go to sleep at once,' she said, 'you will have much to do in the morning.'

I smothered the fire and we both lay down. The day had been a busy and demanding one for me, more so than for many months, and I was tired, yet I could not sleep. From the rustling in the alcove I decided that the woman was restless also. At last she spoke to me.

'You were asking about my sisters' amorous activities.'

'I wish that you would not talk about them,' I said, keen to avoid such a distracting topic. 'I am not pleased to dwell on such matters unless it is in my capacity as presbyter.'

'I am sorry to hear that, but I was not about to burden you with sins of the flesh. I was going to explain that my sisters had sound motives for accepting men's embraces – they gave the matter much thought and did not fling themselves heedlessly into lust. Even when the strange old woman told us that mortal men were always wicked, they continued their liaisons. They said that what they enjoyed was an exchange of gifts, not an invasion of one by the other.'

'Tell me about the old woman,' I said, shuddering. 'It seems to me that she had good advice. Why did she not stay with you and continue to show you her worthy example?'

'She left for her own reasons, and she did not tell them to us. Now I look back on it, she told us very little about her present life, but she described at length the many wrongs that had been done to her in the past.

'I have often found that this is the way with mortals. Once, long ago in the past, someone commits some crime against them and it becomes the only matter of any interest. All their time and all their strength are spent on this one act, and proper revenge for it is the only goal they know. Often they will take their revenge even if it means their own death. I am curious about this strange way of life. Perhaps one day I will find something important enough for me to wish to surrender my life. I do not think it likely.

'Hers was not a new story. Like many women who are not

taught to defend themselves, she had been raped by a conquering warrior and left pregnant. He had lied his way into her bed saying he would take her to his father's court and marry her but once there he laughed at the hopes he had aroused and taken her by force. Following this she said that there was no good to be found in any human man. Since she was the only woman outsider that we had ever talked with we were impressed by her words.

'My sisters thought about what she said but concluded that it would be wrong to judge all men by the experience of one woman. Kynan had proved in the past that men could be loyal, honest and courageous, and if we found that only a few lived up to this standard it was not enough reason to abandon all faith in them.'

'Why did the old woman stay with you if you would not join her party?'

'She did not come to us to win allies. If we were foolish enough to attach ourselves to menfolk, she saw no reason to interfere. Her chief concern, as we found out, was to bend our father to her will – a foolish aim.'

'What happened to her?' I asked, thoroughly awake.

I moved over to the hearth and stirred up the fire. After a few moments she joined me and told me this strange story.

She arrived one day in autumn when the frosts had started. She came all alone in a cart drawn by an ox with gold tips on its horns. We heard a knocking at the gate and looked out to find a little woman, heavily veiled, begging us for shelter. We took her in and she stayed for a while before she told us the story as I have just told to you. I think that if she had had her choice, she would have kept it to herself. We only got it out of her because we caught her in a criminal act.

It happened this way. Since she had no retinue we let her stay with us in the farmstead. In the later days we kept a small house by the wall for women travelling alone. We thought she would move on after a few days' rest, but weeks passed and she was still with us. At first she kept quiet but was always pleased to help with the work about the farm, and indeed she was very good with the livestock. The only clothes she had were of fine materials, yet she would bundle up her skirts and take her turn with us cleaning the byre and though she was small she was strong. In all that time she never took the veil from her face, though it must have been uncomfortable when she was working, and when Roswitha pointed out that we were all women in that place and it would not be unseemly to remove it, she shook her head. One day I found her staring at the wall-hangings in the main hall. They were a few we had saved from my father's hall and they showed scenes of our past lives. She asked me about them but I was no weaver and told her to go and talk to Feidhelm and Gunnhild. Later I saw her go into the kitchen where Feidhelm spent most of her time and when I went in they were talking merrily about the events the wall hangings recorded. I took my sister aside and said,

'I do not think that this is well done. Those hangings tell stories about our past that mortals find dismaying. She might report our activities to the ignorant.'

She only laughed at me and said,

'Do not be alarmed, sister. I have not told her that the stories concern us. I have put it to her that they are legends known to us, no more.'

'I hope that will be enough to keep our secret,' I said, and that was the end of it for the time being.

Winter came upon us with rain and gales and we were confined to the houses. The weather was too bad for visitors and the days were dark and we began to argue among ourselves or withdraw to our own bed alcoves. One afternoon I grew tired of the smoke and the voices in the kitchen and stepped outside to draw a clean breath. I saw the small one flitting among the houses and looking in through the cracks in the doors. I hailed her and she turned round and stared at me for a moment. Then she collected herself and came to me saying,

'I was wondering where to find you. I could not see you in the kitchen. I am worried about one of the cows that had a late calf.'

She took me to the byre, and it was true that the cow had a

swollen leg. But I could not forget that I had been in the kitchen just before I saw her and had been there for some time. Why did she peer into our houses like that, and why did she try to conceal the fact? I said nothing to my sisters for I knew they would say they had nothing to hide that was not already well hidden and that I should not concern myself with her. It was true that the only thing we wished to conceal in the steading was my father's corpse. The house he was enthroned in had no windows and the walls were lined with black cloth. Anyone spying through chinks in the timber would see nothing. Nevertheless I was uneasy at the way the woman had been searching our stockade, not like the idly curious, but as if she were looking for something she knew would be there. I began to watch her, but as the days shortened it became harder to trace her movements.

Midwinter day came and with it the first snow. I was in my bed carving a piece of wood when a shout went up outside, and I ran to the door of the house. Ide, Rhiannon and Feidhelm were calling and pointing to a row of tracks in the snow. I fetched my shawl and joined them and the others who were gathering round. The tracks led straight to the house where my father was kept. Silently we ran to the house and rushed in. The stranger was kneeling at my father's feet, weeping and crying,

'I cannot do it. I have tried everything I know and everything has failed. I am defeated.'

We looked at the corpse of our father as it towered over her and saw that it had been horribly used. The foolish creature had painted open eyes over his closed eyelids. She had stuffed his mouth with food and his hands with weapons, and had lit a fire in the middle of the floor. His fine clothing had been daubed with crude pictures of animals, but the worst thing of all was what she had done to his flesh. She had pushed back his sleeves and cut long wounds into his arms so that the dried blood had trickled out, and into these cuts she had driven slivers of metal and pieces of root. His tunic had been ripped open across the front to expose his fatal wound, and this had been emptied of the preservatives we had put there and refilled with the guts of an animal. Now the desecrator raised her bloody hands to her veiled eyes and wiped at the tears. Streaks of red soiled the cloth.

Evabyth was the first to move. She stalked over to the little one and dragged her away from the corpse.

'What have you done?' she cried. 'You wretched creature, why have you been meddling with our poor father's remains? Was his life not long and miserable enough that he may not rest peacefully in death? What idiot scheme have you been hatching?'

Evir went to her and disentangled her fingers from the folds of the woman's clothing and hair. The creature was wailing and sobbing and the noise in the death house was appalling.

'Calm yourself, sister,' said Rhiannon, but for the first time in her life I saw her pale with rage.

'Take that thing away. Barve and I will clean away her abominations and remove that rubbish. Keep the wretch in her house until we can get to the bottom of this matter.'

Over the next few days we questioned the woman. She was distressed by her experience and at first she would say nothing, but sat and sobbed. At last her natural hardihood reappeared and she calmed down. It was then that she told us her history and what her intentions had been with regard to my father. It seems there was an old custom of her tribe whereby the people kept the bodies of their dead in a great cavern. Once a year, on the longest night, the elder women of the tribe would journey to the cave to ensure that the ancestors were comfortable. If the tribe were in trouble the dead would be consulted and their advice was always taken and always proved to be correct. When the woman heard of the death of our father she was sure that she could revive him in the same way and would thus have access to all the power the demon had had in life. It was nonsense, of course, but to one such as her it would seem the right thing to do.

After a while our rage subsided. We told the woman she could stay with us as long as she needed to and until the spring came she did, although she never left her house. Then, one morning when a haze covered the forest, her cart was gone and her with it. We were not displeased, for since midwinter we had not felt warmly towards her, but some of us felt uneasy that she had gone so secretly. Gwenlieth and I agreed that there had been some truth in what the woman said about reviving my father for we were sure something of him survived. Furthermore, she told us that the first day she went into his house he had spoken to her.

The next day, as soon as the tide was in our favour, we rowed away from land. The wind was no longer as good as it had been and I was not hopeful when she raised the sail. I was preparing to take up my oar again when I learned for myself why the sail was such a strange shape. The wind was coming in from the west, yet we seemed to take a tack which barely headed us back to land. Even when we swung out to sea we were still heading nearly due south, for her half sail could swing right round the mast. I was fascinated by this procedure and tried to commit what I was seeing to memory so that I might tell the brothers. As the day wore on we took a long reach out to sea and the woman began to talk again.

'I wish I could be sure that my father is departed. I know this is foolishness, and at all events my sisters will have taken his body far away by now. Nevertheless I am alone, and my future is uncertain. I wish I could have spoken to the old woman again before she left.'

I decided that there was no further purpose in observing silence. The woman would always seek ways to make me talk and it will be better to thwart her by responding blithely than to frown and struggle for silence. I will accept any penance the Bishop places on me on my return, but I am sure that he will see that I had no choice but to relax the Rule in this case. I said,

'Surely you must see that this notion was a result of her deluded upbringing. She and her kindred doubtless worshipped demons, for it is most unlikely that the Word of God would have reached up to their savage mountains. When it became apparent that the people were about to leave their habitation, the demons would become enraged to think that their servants were to be removed. Since the woman was a leader, and more than likely some kind of priestess to the spirits, she would be the first one they would choose to possess. They would follow her into the forest and wait till she was in child-bed, which is known to be a time when women are open to invasion by demons. Then, seizing their chance, they would squeeze her soul and force themselves into the space. After that she would have no more control over her body and they could make her do whatever they wished, be it never so foul.'

'I am glad you have told me this. My sisters and I have often wondered what took place in a mortal when dementia set in. We have heard people speak of it but have had no chance to study it. I had concluded that it was the product of the great misery humans know for most of their lives.'

'The misery itself is a sign that men have been wicked. A truly good man is happy in the same manner as virtuous monks who have lived the life of virtue all their lives. God is always just.'

'I do not doubt your word, but I see that while you are a virtuous man, you do not seem to be a happy one.'

'I am not yet perfectly happy,' I told her, 'for I have sinned in thought, even though my actions are beyond reproach.'

'I think I understand you. Selyf was good and he was the happiest man I have ever seen. His thoughts were all of how he might serve others.'

'Selyf was not virtuous,' I protested. 'He disobeyed the Rule by harbouring his concubine after she should have been a stranger to him; also he stayed away from the family far too long and in the end died without returning. There is no virtue in that.'

'Do you believe that he is dead?'

'Better for him if he were, for his long absence is inexcusable. Do you have more news of him?'

'I know nothing new,' was her answer; then she said,

'I do not yet understand why you say you are not happy. You do nothing but serve your fellow men and that is the greatest happiness I have ever known. How can you continue to be miserable?'

'When you say that service is a good way for man to be happy you are right, but this happiness is as nothing to the rapture known to the saints who have passed into the eternal presence of God. That is what we should aim for, and it is attained sometimes on earth by the most holy of our saints. I am not one.

'In my own case my poor health is proof enough that I am a sinner. God would not be punishing me otherwise.'

'God gave Ælfrid the knowledge to relieve your suffering.'

'It is alleviated but not removed. I have no strength and I must not be distressed or the breath leaves my body and will not return.'

'How will you know when you are becoming happy?'

'The saints all report that the first sign is a deep interior struggle. The conscience awakens and the sinner begins to know that his way of life offends the Almighty, whether it is through unchastity or through greed for possessions. As this struggle continues, the sinner becomes restless and dissatisfied and he is drawn from side to side, now throwing himself at the feet of a saint, now haunting the brothels and taverns. On one side salvation beckons, on the other debauchery. He begins to weep and the tears flow for days as he battles with his flesh. Then the moment comes when the truth fills him and he is drawn at last to the light for the rest of his earthly existence.'

'I understand now, and I think you have answered my next question before I have even asked it.

'My sister, Olwen, puzzled us mightily. Some of us said that she was once left with one of our mothers when she was young and vulnerable. This poor mother suffered one of the worst and bitterest labours of the many we have seen and the midwife of the day foolishly tried to make a potion to save her life. Olwen was left alone to watch her and it turned her mind. In the tenth year of this, her last incarnation, she was suddenly given to long days of watching on the fellside. She would return with her eyes blank, and would not speak to anyone for days. At other times she would throw herself furiously into activity; sometimes weaving for hours until she had completed a piece of cloth, which always had to be the finest weave; sometimes she would take a sword and work for hours with our training machines until the sweat ran from her body and she was pale with tiredness, but she would not stop until she had beaten the machine.

'One of us, concerned, spoke to father about it. She was summoned to his hall and we heard their voices raised in long argument – first his voice harsh with rage, then hers, quiet and cold as melt-water. We will never know what was said, but when Olwen came out her eyes were blazing with cold fire.

'"I hate father," she said. "I cannot find the words to describe my hatred, it goes so deep. Every drop of blood in my body burns with hatred for him; every hair on my head crawls with loathing for him; if a sea of fire were to engulf this fortress today I would not be satisfied to watch him burn in it, I would have to find a weapon and fight my way to his side through the heat so that I could wound him and watch him die."

'We were terrified by this. None of us had dared to defy him to his face before, and though many of us felt stirrings of hatred, we never would have said a word to each other about it. After that day Olwen became truly secretive about her movements, and where she went we could not follow. Some days we might come upon her in the passages and she would sweep past us as if we were invisible; another day we might find her in her bed lying and weeping inconsolably. She never came to the kitchen, and heaven alone knew when and what she ate.

'"Come along, Olwen," I said one time, "why should you spend so much time in tears? Life is not so bad for us here. Father is not kind, it is true, but we have each other and if we care for each other we may be happy enough."

'But I might have wasted less time trying to blot up the ocean with a kerchief.

'"I am a sinner," she cried, "born into such a wallow of sin that I will never be clean of it. What shall I do to clear myself of this dreadful guilt?"

'"Olwen," I answered, "if you are a sinner, then there is no one here who is free of guilt. What do you want? Do you think that there is a special burden lying on your shoulders that has been kept from us? Do not be so foolish. We have all been born by the same route, and though none of us would surrender our lives, we would all give our most precious possessions, the treasure of many lifetimes, if we could have been made otherwise."

'I could have saved my breath, for all she said was,

'"You may have come into the world by the same method as I, but you have been spared the understanding of what a terrible thing it is to live like this. Think about it, only think of the poor, foolish woman who gave her life so that you might live. Our family is sunk in guilt beyond the sight of all safety!"

'And she fell to weeping again. In vain I pointed out that the fate of every creature was to live at the expense of another, from birth to death, but she would not listen. Instead she shut the doors of her bed on me and carried on sobbing until the dark. She stopped eating, and at night she would not sleep, but lay moaning, or walked about the yard of the fortress until dawn stained the sky. We were soon out of patience with her for we had enough to fill out our days without trying to tend to a madwoman.

'After some years of this, one day she disappeared. We were troubled at first, but when we went to father he said that she was safe enough and that we were not to look for her. When she returned, and he seemed sure she would return, it would be in her own time. We were satisfied with that and went about our business. Olwen had not done much work of value about the fortress, so she was not missed for that and we were not sorry to miss the nights broken by the sound of her sobbing.

'Finally she did return, with her head shaved and a kerchief over it, a great wooden cross tied to her belt and a smile on her face. She told us that she had found a way to lift the guilt from her back and told us that we should do the same for the sake of our souls. We did not know what she meant by "soul" and, while we were grateful for her advice, we should not like to disturb our way of life. Then she showed us this terrible garment she wore next to her skin and the iron belt which caused her constant pain and said that she had never known such happiness since she started to wear them.

'What could we say? There was no more sobbing, no more agony over the burden of guilt, no more restless prowling. Instead she was as calm as a summer dawn and as happy as a bird on the nest. If this constant torture helped our sister to face her life why should we stop her? Our father laughed at her when he found out, but that did not discourage her. She simply resolved to go and live in the convent with others of her kind, and would have done so if that strange warrior had not come and changed her mind. Do you think it is possible that she would have returned to the convent if she had been free to do so?'

'If her conversion was genuine then she most certainly would.'

'Is this how it was with you?' she asked.

'No, God in His wisdom has had me born into the true Faith, and I have not had this struggle. This is how holy men and women like St Bega whose shrine lies on the coast just beside us was called to God's service. To this you can add St Gregory, St Augustine, St Padraig and many of the fathers of our church.'

'Do you wish it could have been this way for you?'

'No, I most surely do not!' I replied swiftly. 'It has pleased God to send me into this world enlightened, and I thank Him for it every day.'

'Do you not wish to be tested in your faith?'

'I have been tested in the fire already many times. When I went to search for Selyf at your father's stronghold I was prepared to fight with evil spirits, and found both my body and my spirit taxed almost beyond endurance. When I went to the Orcades I was tested in battle with a mighty demon called Othinn and I prevailed.'

'What do they look like, these demons? In my long life I have never seen them. I know you call my father demon, and it is sure he was unhappy, but he always denied that he was any kin to them.'

I was pleased to see this interest.

'I have only seen one once and it was not a new manifestation. Only the holiest of our saints are allowed to discover new demons and it is from their accounts that we know of them. When I went up against Othinn I fasted for many days until I received a vision of him and because he had been described by the saints of our order and I knew him when I saw him.'

'How did he appear to you?'

'He was tall – half as tall again as myself. He was dressed in black and the hair of his head was black. One eye had been torn from his head but the other one stared at me like a dart of ice aimed at my soul. His face bore the marks of many years of suffering and the voice came as it were from the depths of a cavern.'

'His hands, what were they like?' she asked eagerly.

'They were big and covered with black hair and the fingers were furnished with long claws of steel.'

'Ah, you have disappointed me,' she cried. 'I thought at first that you were describing my father.'

'Then you consider that your father is a demon?'

'I do not know what I should think, although I long to know the truth. Just now I thought you began to describe him, but his hands were not as you said. They were large but they were in all other ways the hands of a human warrior – calloused from their weapons and the skin brown from the weather, and his nails were like any other man's. It was not father you saw. Tell me how you defeated this Othinn.'

'I found him in his homeland. It is a terrible place where rivers of ice stand still for ever and never melt. Nothing grows there, although once there were trees, for their dead trunks rise out of the frozen land. The wind is so strong it blows flakes of ice into your skin, cutting till it bleeds. There are no other beings than the demon himself, and his loneliness is terrible. I stood waiting for a while, then I summoned him with a great shout.

'When he saw me in his territory he flung himself on me with a howl of rage. I wrestled with him and pinned him to the ground. The breath from his mouth scorched my face so that it

110

turned black and split open. The pain was terrible, but I hung on to him. His shoulders heaved as he tried to rise and horns like long knives sprang out of his chest and plunged into my throat. I did not yield to him. Even when his steel claws tore the skin off my back I kept him pinned under me and at last he admitted that I was the superior.

'You must understand I was given strength by my faith, and although my body suffered pain which would have killed other men I was filled with the knowledge that it was only my flesh that was troubled and a great radiance surrounded me. The demon saw the light and had to go away from that place. And when I left, I found that my wounds had been miraculously healed.'

'Do you know where he went?'

'He went into the outer darkness, which is where all demons dwell.'

'Why do they leave this outer darkness if it is their home?'

'They come to earth to test man's faith.'

'Who tells them to do this?'

'Their master, the great Adversary. He is known as the Devil and his servants do his bidding without question.'

'What does he tell them to do?'

'He tells them to test men with temptations. If they fall into sin then they will be shown up as devoid of grace.'

'Who bestows grace?'

'God the Father.'

'Why does the Devil want to know which men are devoid of grace?'

'So that he can claim them for his kingdom when eternity dawns.'

'He must be a very powerful entity, this Devil.'

'He is, indeed, but not as powerful as God, who is Master of all.'

'If God is Master of all, then he will give orders to the Devil.'

'Correct. He sends the Devil to tempt man, for the Devil has no mind or will of his own. He is only created to test man's grace.'

111

'But if God has bestowed grace, why should He wish men to be tempted to find out which one has it? He must know who receives his own gifts.'

I am shocked that Hw allowed himself to get caught in this old conundrum. I am sure the woman is not as simple as she seems to be. Or, if she is telling the truth about her age, she has spent much time debating this issue to have the arguments so well prepared.

If it were not for my fear of exile from my brothers and from my place of work I would give the woman the answer she is looking for. God is all powerful, the creator of all things and there is no Creator but him. He at once contains and brings into being both good and evil and He has placed both of these in His creation so that they may struggle. Man was created only to be happy through enjoying God but the evil in creation has drawn him from his only true vocation – to make up the number of the Elect who will live in the blessed City.

To question why God, who is perfect, has brought evil into being is to fail to understand His Nature. God is not trammelled in any way in the universe as man apprehends it with his senses or his intellect. God is beyond the grasp of man. If we are to limit ourselves to claiming that that which is, is only that which can be grasped by the senses and the intellect then we might say that God does not exist. I prefer to say, along with Johan of Eirinn, that God's being is more than being and at the same time less than that. He belongs in the same order of entities as the essences of things.

But if I said all that, I would be punished. Therefore I do not commit the words to the travelling air where the wickedness of my mouth would be carried abroad, I write them. On paper my thoughts are contained and no miasma of doubt is produced to contaminate the world. It is the truth that if in my life I had been given access to much paper, I would be a virtuous man. My thoughts would have been committed to a place where they could be scrutinised, criticised and dismissed. Since it has been my fate to be paperless my thoughts have been allowed to breed inside my head, unhindered. And

*this is the result. Whenever I find a scrap of paper I reproduce
my thoughts and bring despair to my teachers, who see in me
the failure of their teaching.*

Before I could answer she looked towards the land and her
eyes grew great with surprise. I turned landward to see where
she looked. We were approaching the dunes that protect the
harbour of Glaunna. The pagans have called it the raven's sea,
and there have been rumours of pirates using it of late, so that
I should have been on my guard. My heart sank within me as I
looked and saw a boat pulling away from the shore.

'Do you think they have seen us?' asked Barve. 'We are well
out to sea.'

'It is almost sure that they have,' I answered. 'I have travelled a great deal and I have learned that those who get their
living from the sea are most keen sighted. They can see a ship
hours before a land-dwelling man will make it out. Can we not
outrun them? We have plenty of sea between us.'

'We shall try, but the wind is weaker than it was. Do you
know how to row quickly, you who are so wise?'

'I have done so often, but that was in the days before my
sickness came upon me. Now, we would not get far before
I fell panting over my oar. Can you not row and use your
father's power?'

'I might but I will not. It is not sure that boat is coming for
us and even if it is, it may not mean to harm us. Remember I
took an oath before Selyf that I would never use that power
again, except to save another life. Also, I have other means to
protect us if they should prove to be unfriendly. We will have
to trust ourselves to the wind and hope they will not trouble
us.'

I knew before she spoke that her hope was vain. The boat
gained on us and as it grew nearer we could see that it was
rowed by six oarsmen. They were very skilled and drew the
small boat over the water so fast that we were barely level
with the estuary before they hailed us. Barve brought the boat
about but the sail emptied and hung limp against the mast. At
that she sighed, furled the sail, covered her face and sat down

113

with her hands in her lap. The other boat pulled up to us as we lay dead in the water and I saw the faces of the crew as they twisted round to look at us. They were as ugly a gang as I should ever wish to see.

'What have we netted here?' said the helmsman, a runt of a man with bowed legs. He stood holding the steering oar and squinted down at us while his free hand picked at scabs in his beard.

'A white monk,' said the man at first-oar, grey and toothless but still powerful in build. 'We would do well to throw him back – his kind bring bad luck.'

The crew laughed at this drollery and spat into the sea. Then they began all to speak at once in that revolting patois that pirates use – a mix of British, Scottish and pagan tongues. I listened to them and made out what I could without letting them see that I could understand. It seemed they were hoping to impress someone with this catch, but who that someone was I could not discern. The man at second oar stepped across to our boat. His face was red as a rose-hip and the skin across his nose and forehead was peeling off. It was plain that he was one of those pale-haired types to whom the sun and wind are no friend. If he had the brains of a dog he would seek occupation within doors or at least wear a wide hat. But he did not have the brains, even of a dog. He reached over with a meaty hand and pulled Barve's veil aside.

'A lady,' he gasped, in mock surprise, 'and a fine young one, at that! What sort of a ransom will she fetch, do you think?'

'I am a lady,' said Barve in British, 'and you should remember that. But as to ransom, you are wasting your time. To the best of my knowledge I have no living relatives who would pay for me. Of this I can be sure – if you detain me without my wish you will pay, and dearly.'

I spoke up in haste before she might tell them how vulnerable we were.

'The lady and I are on our way to find her kindred in Gwynedd. She has not seen them for many years, but you may believe that they do not like being crossed.'

'If she has a powerful family, why is she travelling without a retinue?' asked the first-oar.

'She has been on religious retreat for a long time,' I answered him, 'but news came that her mother is dying so we set off without waiting for an escort. We are in God's hands.'

Someone sniggered and said,

'Greasy fingers has this god of yours.'

Barve was frowning at me but she kept silent.

'Why was she on retreat?' said second-oar. 'Has she been a wicked little girl, then?'

'That is no concern of yours,' I told the godless one, 'and, since you seem to know about Christian ways, you must also know that I could never tell you.'

'Christians!' he said, and spat into the sea again.

The man at first-oar called,

'Bring them inboard here and tie that boat onto our stern. It is too good to give to the sea.'

'You will not keep us!' cried the woman. 'We have no business with such as you. We only wish to go on our journey. Take your hands off me.'

Her protests were ignored. Our hands were tied behind us and we were tossed onto the bottom of the sexæring like bales of hay. Barve said something unseemly.

'Why are you letting them do this?' I whispered. 'You could free us in the blinking of an eye.'

'I am curious,' she replied. 'I have not seen men like these since we went to the fair at Gobhan.'

'Be silent,' first-oar said, and kicked me as I lay at his feet.

I was silent. Barve attempted to sit up, but second oar put his foot on her neck. She lay still, smiled at me and received another kick. I lay with my ribs grinding against those of the boat and wondered who might be the leader of this miserable crew. Whoever he was, he had a powerful hold on these pagans, for I gathered from their talk that he had gone away and left them to take care of his business for him. It is not wise for a war leader to go from home and leave his merchandise with a gang of soldiers unless they farm his land or are otherwise dependent on him. As far as I could gather, these men were nothing but traders and warriors and stayed loyal to their master out of fear. From their reluctance to use his name he might have been the Adversary himself.

After a long time made longer by pain, the keel grounded on shingle. The oars were shipped and we were dropped onto the beach with our feet in the water. Then we were carried up to the grass and dumped there with our luggage while they pulled the boats ashore and made them fast above the tide-line. Barve managed to sit up and then helped me to do the same.

'Do not think that we might escape,' I said.

'I am not so deluded,' she answered. 'Look at the estuary. The gathering of the rivers has piled sandbanks all around. That reach will be as treacherous as the waters of the Sul Wath and you know how few men can sail there. I see now why they would not let us sit up on the way to the shore. They did not wish us to learn their route through the channels.'

'I had no hope of escape that way. Moreover it would be worse if we were to run inland for we would soon be lost. The mountains behind us are free of forest, but that is only because they are rocky and steep. I know this from others who have travelled here.'

'Did these others tell you also who is the leader of this pack?'

'I do not know, but his men describe him as a merchant.'

'Can you understand them? I can scarcely follow the main burden of their speech.'

'Yes, I know their tongue, but I beg you do not let them know it. It may mean our safety that we have this knowledge and keep it secret.'

Our captors came towards us up the beach. As they approached they argued with each other and what they said boded ill.

'Our master does not like us to spoil the goods,' said first-oar.

'How will he know of it?' said last-oar, whose face was sunk in about the nose as if it had been broken with an iron bar.

'The woman will tell,' said the helmsman.

'She will not tell of her shame,' said another.

'Then the monk will tell.'

116

'He is her escort. He will not tell of his failure,' said second-oar. 'I have been staring at those nether parts all the way in. I will not wait any longer.'

'Then we must all be party to it,' said first-oar, 'so that one will not tell on the others.'

'We agree,' said all the others. They picked up the woman, untied her hands and laid her on the grass. I turned away and stared out over the dunes, as it was not fitting for me to witness what was about to happen. I searched through my mind for a suitable prayer to distract me from the screams I knew would come. All I could recall was the eighty-second psalm, but my protection was not needed, for as I came to the line, 'Defend the poor and the fatherless,' I heard one of the men cry out in pain.

'Thor's curse on you, woman, submit!' said another.

Bent-face passed me staggering backwards at speed and fell on to the sand. A laugh came from his companions and I looked round to see that Barve was standing upright and the men were scattered around her. Her kerchief had been pulled off but otherwise she seemed unsullied. Second-oar lay on the ground groaning and holding a badly twisted arm. Another had covered his face with his hands while a third was bent double, vomiting into the grass.

First-oar came over to me, sniggering. 'You must be grateful to your lady, monk. You may be sure that if they had succeeded with her you would have been next. As it is, I doubt if those four will look at slit for many days. I am glad I am old and my heat has faded.'

'What kind of men have we fallen amongst!' I cried.

'Men. The common kind. Two arms, two legs, two eyes, one cock.'

Barve came over and picked up her pack, using her kerchief to brush the dust off her hands.

'Did they harm you?' she asked me – out of habit, not because she cared to hear my answer. I said,

'My body is as well as it might be, but my soul is troubled and I cannot speak freely in front of these men. I must ask you, though, why have you hurt them?'

She stared at me for a moment then said,

'They are not badly hurt. I have only used some arts of wrestling that all my family know. There is no damage to them that will not heal.'

She walked down the beach and dropped her kerchief into the water, pulled it out and shook it. Then she went to second oar and looked carefully at his arm. He could not raise it and it looked to me so badly twisted that it would never be used again. Placing one hand on his shoulder and another on his elbow the woman wrenched at it. The man gave a scream like one who sees the Pit for the first time. I covered my ears at the sound, but then I saw that he was moving his arm. To be sure he was swinging it slowly and I doubt if he would be using plough or sword for a long time, but he could move it.

'My father always taught us it is a poor warrior that cannot heal the hurt he makes,' said the woman, and she wrapped her sodden kerchief round his shoulder.

'You must keep that kerchief wet and cold and your arm will be healed by morning,' she told him and dried her hands on her skirt.

'I do not have a kerchief for you,' she said to the other two men, 'but my advice is the same – keep the damaged parts cold.'

Both men stood up groaning and staggered off to the waterside.

Second-oar's scream had been heard elsewhere. A horseman came round the headland at a gallop and halted with some difficulty beside our group. He spoke to the men in the pure tongue of the black foreigners which I cannot follow. He was almost young and still vigorous and his black eyebrows hung over his eye sockets like thatching. The woman stared at him in her bold fashion and when our captors gestured towards her he looked up and caught her gaze. I think he must have realised that his underlings were concealing something for his eyes narrowed and he began to question them rapidly. They answered him one word at a time and their reluctance added to his suspicion. At last his patience was worn out and he turned to me and spoke in bad Scottish.

'On your honour as a monk, tell me the truth what happened here. Did the sailors rape the woman?'

'No, sir,' I said, 'to tell the truth, she would not let them.'

He scowled at me, then said, 'How did she stop seven men from doing their will?'

Barve stepped forward and put her hand on the horse's neck.

'I have some skills,' she said. 'If you wish I will show them to you. I have done nothing a mortal could not learn if he cared to.'

The horseman looked at her, swallowed and spoke to me again.

'Is this the truth?'

'It is, sir,' I answered. 'She has come from a foreign land and can do many things that seem strange to us.'

The woman stamped her foot.

'Do not speak about me as if I were not here!' she cried incontinently. 'What do you think I am – a pebble from the beach?'

The horseman looked at her again and again he swallowed. He gave an order to our captors and those who could walk led us off around the headland; then he rode off towards the beach. Our captors grumbled as we walked, for it seemed that they had been about to take us to another place, but now they would have to do as he had told them whatever that might be. Then the man with the sore eyes made a suggestion which seemed to please them all and we marched off in haste. We walked a little way inland where the river ran into a valley formed on either side by steep slopes. We turned off the main track and up a path which led close under the overhanging rocks. Our destination proved to be a small house at the side of a big, empty stockade. Barve and I were pushed in without ceremony and the door bolted behind us.

'We are on our guard against you, now,' they shouted through the door. 'Do not try to trick us again.'

They went away and everything was silent. I cursed them in my heart as they had not done us the small courtesy of letting us wash our feet. Many animals had been kept in the stockade recently. I opened my satchel to take out my psalter

119

and found that it was wet. Searching further I pulled out the skin that contains my medication and discovered that the rough handling the sailors had given my luggage had made a leak. I swallowed some of the vile tasting stuff and tried to find a way to seal the hole. At last I pinched it shut and sewed the crease down. It is not the best repair but it will suffice. We must pray that there was not much medicine lost.

We pray for it most urgently. Since Hw does not tell us which of the three bottles we made for him is damaged we cannot say how well he will do. If it is the foxglove he will soon find out when his heart starts to beat like a rabbit's. If it is the others it will take longer for signs to manifest themselves.

While I was occupied, Barve ranged the dim interior of our hut. She found a set of chains in one corner and a little firewood in another. The firewood was damp but the day was growing cold so she began to make a fire. She pushed a corner of the roof up to let out the smoke and looked out at the yard, then she said,

'Until now I have not felt any haste to finish my journey. Today I have seen how vile men can be and I begin to think with dismay about the fate of Olwen. I had always felt that she was foolish to surrender herself, but that she would be well treated because the man she had chosen was besotted with her. Certainly she was sure that he would be a loyal husband, and she a devoted wife, and though we all had our doubts about her future, she paid no attention to them. Now I am concerned that she may have fallen into the hands of others who are ill-disposed to her. In these circumstances I fear that her foolishness has led her into danger.'

She turned to me.

'You are a close student of human kind. Tell me, why do men wish to violate women?'

'There are two reasons why men do this,' I answered, 'and since you seem so concerned I will tell you what they are.'

I paused before continuing. All our talk seemed to lead to

the topic of lust and it always left me in distress. I looked at her to see if she was at some wicked scheme, but the gaze she held on me was mild enough. I dealt with the subject as swiftly as I could.

'The first cause is the perniciousness of women themselves. They tempt men to lust by the clothes they wear and the sweet perfumes they use on their skin. I have told you before of the tricks they play to drive men into frenzy, and I will not repeat myself. But believe me, when they employ these subterfuges they must not be surprised when their victims – the men – respond with violent craving.'

'I have not employed subterfuges,' she said. 'I do not know where to find them.'

'There is another occasion when men are driven to rape by an evil other than that which dwells in women. That is when a holy virgin appears before them and the Adversary intervenes to drive them to violation. In this case the woman may have taken great pains to lose her feminine wiles. The clothes she wears will be of the coarsest, roughest cloth; she will not wash herself; she will have fasted hard so that her breasts and other soft, womanly parts have disappeared; she may even have managed to grow a beard. She will have done this because she wishes to serve Christ rather than the world, and has ceased to be a daughter of Eve. This is the perfect woman, almost a man.'

She looked at me with astonishment. 'Have you seen such a woman?' she asked.

'I have not seen one with my own eyes, for such women shun the sight of men and lock themselves away, but the history of our church is full of these examples. We call it one of the white martyrdoms and hold them in reverence.'

Then I told her the history of St Thenew and St Thecla, explaining carefully as I went on,

'The Synod held at Ver recognised that it is not permissible for women to pass themselves off as men. Nevertheless it is important that woman should shed her femaleness on her road to sanctity. Now, if she wishes to set herself apart for Christ, she must not cut her hair nor wear men's apparel.'

'What you have said is very close to my own thoughts,' said Barve. 'Tell me, now, when those men wished to violate St Thecla, was it because they thought that her virginity gave her power?'

'They were physicians, and they were jealous of her skill as a healer. They knew that her skill came from God and that she had dedicated her life to Him. They thought, therefore, that if they forced her they would make her more like a woman, then she would lose her special favour with God.'

'So a virgin state will give power to a woman?'

'It is often said so. That is why I have taken such a vow.'

'That agrees with my findings. I have often wondered what it is that produces our special powers. Selyf said that they removed us from God and made us take a vow not to use them, but I think he was in error.'

'Is that why you broke your vow this afternoon?'

'I have told you that I did not break my vow. I used tricks of combat against the men. If I had used my full strength they would have been dead, you must believe me.'

She turned and poked at the fire.

'I do not know why I care what you may think, for surely you are an ungenerous man. Perhaps it is for the sake of your father, Selyf, that I still wish to find a way to virtue.'

She rubbed at her eyes then said,

'Listen and I will put myself in your hands completely. Our strength can be removed from us in three ways; first by using a particular kind of singing, this effect will only last as long as the singer is within hearing distance. Secondly if we cut our hair, our bodies will be like those of ordinary mortals, but our strength will grow again as our hair grows, and when it is at its longest we will be restored to our status. In this we are like the one in the scripture they call Samson.'

I raised my voice in protest.

'That is not the same thing. Samson was the champion of the people of Israel and a man. The Almighty Himself had told him to keep his hair long, nor would he have cut it to save his own life until God told him that he should. You have had no divine instructions so you cannot claim parity.'

'If I said I had, you could not deny it,' said the wicked creature, and her eyes gleamed. I blessed myself and she laughed, but quietly this time.

'Finally – and I have not tested the truth of this – if we lose our virginity, our strength will go, never to return. In this we are just like the virgins of your church; if we are removed from grace we are removed from power.'

'This is not the same as holy virginity,' I answered straight away, 'the church tells women they must not cut their hair to stop them presuming to be men. A vow of virginity is taken to deny fleshly longings, not to maintain power. The power comes from acquired holiness, it is not within us from birth.'

'It is no matter to me,' said the woman, 'for I shall keep my virginity for my own reasons, not yours. My reflection was all about my sister Olwen. She was a very virtuous creature. Her first ambition in life was to be a holy virgin like those you spoke of, but the man who became her husband took her away from that.'

'When her clotted flesh called to her, she gave in to it. There is no virtue in that.'

'You must understand – when she surrendered her body to him she gave away her defences.'

'That is as it should be. It is God's will that the man is the defender of the woman's body in the same way as he is the guardian of her soul.'

In her agitation the woman was striding up and down the little hut. This brought the hem of her tunic far too close to my face. She said,

'So, you tell me it is God's will that you should surrender one virtuous state in order to gain another.'

I pondered on this for a while for fear she had laid a trap for me, then I said,

'It is not that God wishes us to surrender virtue, but rather that He wishes us to chose between evils. It is not always clear which is the greater evil, yet in this case there is no doubt that your sister should have kept her virginity and stayed closer to virtue. Her unnatural strength is sinful only if she uses it to bring hurt to mankind.'

123

'Even if she might save her own life?'

'Particularly if she might save her own life, for that would be to put the survival of her flesh before the laws of God.'

'Again I hear it,' said the woman and sighed, 'that death is not the ultimate evil. Why, then, am I to blame if I kill another when I am the means of sending them to a better life?'

'That is not for you to judge. It is as God wills it.'

'How am I to learn God's will?'

'Through prayer and study.'

'And if my prayer and study tell me to do something which a Christian would not approve, which course of action do I follow?'

'You must do as I say, for I have studied God's laws and am closer to virtue than you.'

'Not even you are the final authority. I know Christians differ from each other, for I have heard different words from your father's mouth.'

'I must ask you not to refer to Selyf as my father. He is nothing more to me than a brother monk. My father is the Abbot of our community.'

'You are avoiding my question. Tell me the truth, monk, do all Christian men agree with each other about God's law?'

'Not all Christians think alike, but they who dissent are vile heretics who do not enjoy the protection of the church. They will be damned when God's kingdom comes.'

'I shall go and talk to the heretics next time I have leisure,' she said and, sitting down at last, she fell to brooding. I had nothing to say to this unabashed wickedness and began to calculate if it were time to say the office for nightfall. Then the woman spoke again,

'I wonder if they will give us food?'

'It is no matter if they do not,' I told her. 'I am used to fasting and you must learn to do so if you wish to conquer your flesh.'

'If I fast too much my flesh will be conquered by others,' she said, and stirred up the fire. She went on,

'You have left me baffled as to whether to think of this as a good thing or not. I told you, many of my sisters had associations with the men of Kynan's city, and this is why, when the raiders came, they did not pause but picked up their weapons and ran to help their menfolk. Yet if they surrendered their power with their virginity they would have been no more use than any other warrior in defending the ones they loved. They will have died for nothing.'

'If they died, and that is not yet sure, it was not for nothing,' I said, for I suddenly wished to end her perplexity. 'The end of every mundane creature is death and there is no help for that, nor should we seek to change it. The issue is rather how the short life of the flesh is lived – whether it is sanctified, or whether it is corrupted by the actions of the will. Your sisters died in an attempt to save others. This is sacrifice and such is never in vain.'

'Are you telling me that my sisters may find a place with the elect?' she asked, and I saw that her face was alight with hope.

'I cannot say. It will depend on how much the wickedness of their other actions outweighed the good.'

The woman stared into the smoke and bit her lip.

'Most of their actions were such that they might be described as virtuous by one of you Christians, if not all. Nevertheless, there was something they did which I am sure none of you would hesitate to condemn.'

'What was this thing which was so truly wicked even you cannot defend it?'

'In our steading we had very many skills and many apt pupils to learn them. The women students were few since girls were not encouraged to learn away from home, but those few were very keen. The men students were more abundant yet less able. The Bishop let it be known that he did not approve the students coming, though he could not forbid them outright as the King was our protector. As I have often noted in the affairs of men, when he spoke forbidding a thing outright, his design failed. In fact he did us, his enemies, a service, since when word of his disapproval reached them the craven and the stupid were afraid to return. The few who chose to defy the Bishop and came back to us for lessons were the best. We warned them it would be better if it were not known that they still came to us. So the conspiracy was born.

'I do not know if my sisters and their students were joined in the flesh before the conspiracy. I am sure that some were, after, for I often saw the twining of hands and rubbing of limbs that showed their intimacy to the world. While I did not disapprove of this, I did not join it, and preferred to keep apart from those who indulged themselves. To tell the truth this was simply because the urge never took me. I may claim that I rejected it out of virtue but this would be false. Since my teaching was mostly of the breeding of cattle, coitus had no mystery for me and promised no joy – nothing more than that kept my virginity whole.'

I felt my heart pounding rapidly and my breath was almost stifled as it struggled past it. With eyes fixed on my psalter I offered up my usual clamorous pleas for the strength to cleave to the Rule and keep silent.

The clouds overhead had gone and a few flakes of snow fell through the gap in the roof, so the woman closed it. We sat in the gloom and I took my chance to say the office, adding a penance for previous omissions. After a while it grew dark outside and we lay down to sleep, but in my case without success. I lay until the first hour wide awake, for though I am well accustomed to a hard couch and rejoice in my discomforts, as I must, tonight something kept me watching. The sad truth is that it was a long time since I had slept so far from the sea and the silence of that place, buried deep among trees and mountains, oppressed my spirit. Furthermore, an owl was hunting nearby and its dismal cries echoed around us for all the hours of darkness. May I be forgiven, but I could not find it in my heart to be grateful for this test. I prayed perpetually that my soul would quiet itself and meekly accept its ordeal, but all that rose to my lips was a lamentation for my confinement. When at last the grey of dawn lit up the sky I gave thanks for the end of a bitter night. I hoped that the next one would show me more steadfast.

At dawn, after I had read the hour, the woman stood and stretched. She took a twig of heather from her bedding and chewed at it, but it did not ease her hunger and she threw it aside with a grunt. Then she took the chain from the corner, wrapped it round one of the withies beside the door and, bracing her feet, she heaved at it. The withy broke off at the foot and a section of wall lifted, leaving a gap beside the doorpost large enough for us to crawl through. To keep the hole open she hooked the chain on a protruding branch at the top of the wall.

'I saw this weakness last night,' she said, pointing to the rotten withy, 'but I thought it better to wait till daylight to use it.'

I did not answer her. She waited for my reply then shrugged.

'Be silent if you wish. I am going to look for food. Do you wish to come with me?'

I answered in charity, 'It would be better for us to be patient and endure our imprisonment with rejoicing, for this is the sort of test of your virtue you should wish to make.'

'I do not wish to test my virtue, monk, and you tell me yours is beyond question. Let us, in the name of health, go and find some thing to break our fast.'

So saying, she thrust her pack out of the hut and scrambled after it. I was obliged to follow. The snow clouds of the night before had gone, leaving us a morning bright but very cold. We hurried across the stockade and tried the gate. It was barred from the outside, but in a poor state of repair. Together we pushed as hard as we could and it swung outward and almost opened. It took only a couple of swings then with a mighty crack the rotted bars outside gave and the gate flew open. I was glad I had not tried to keep beasts in such a place. We hastened down the path to the track which followed the course of the river. On the left it led back to the shore where we had arrived, but after a brief pause the woman led the way in the opposite direction, inland. Soon the river curved away and the track went on into the trees. A little way on we came to a clearing where another stockade stood with its gate open. This place was well kept and the timbers were in good repair.

'I hope we are not kept prisoner here,' said Barve, and in my heart I agreed with her.

127

The river seemed to have curved round to the rear of the stockade for through the trees we could see women drawing water. Inside we found a large, stave built house and few mean huts. Sheep grazed in the open space between the buildings and a few hens picked round the door of the big house. There was a smell of baking. The woman sniffed and said,

'I am going to find the source of that.'

She made off towards the large house without a backward glance. The house was surrounded by a wattle fence and a path of planks led to the door. She strode up the path without waiting for an invitation. A dog set up a barking from the rear of the house and as she approached it the door swung open. The horseman we had met the day before stood in the opening wearing only shirt and leggings. He looked amazed to see the woman and myself.

'The shore watch said you ran off,' he told me in his clumsy Scottish. 'I went to the place I had told them to put you and you were not there. They planned to use you for their self, no?'

'I could not know what they planned,' I said, 'since they did not tell me. Your honour almost certainly has the right of it.'

I still did not wish to let him know I spoke their language. I said to the woman,

'It good that we left that place. I do not think we would have fared so well this morning.'

She shrugged and stared unwinking at the gentile.

'They will be sorry for it when my master comes back,' he said.

'Why do you not punish them yourself?' asked Barve. 'You must be in command here. This is a fine house.'

'The Master likes to do his own punishment,' he answered, still looking at me. 'I have not the power. I am only here to watch.'

'I am hungry,' said Barve, frowning. 'What can you offer me to eat? Or must we go elsewhere?'

The man looked at her from the side of his eye and muttered,

'Yes, we have bread, of course, for the guest. Come.'

We followed him as he led the way into the house. At the

far end a table had been set up with a cloth and a woman was putting food out on it. When she saw us she ran through the door beyond the table and we heard her calling to her companions. Barve walked up to the table, pulled out her knife and sat down. The gentile hastened and pushed the bowls toward her, but he kept looking back to make sure I would join them. I took my place on the bench and said the blessing before food.

'You are most generous, sir. May I be so bold as to ask the name of our benefactor?'

'My name is Merthun son of Rhonabuy, daughter of Malloluch, and son of Valgard son of Umar Sufyan of Itil. Who are you?'

'I am Hw of Rintsnoc, and this is the lady Barve...'

There was a pause as the woman reached for a plate of broiled fish then she said, '... daughter of Usbathaden.'

I trembled to hear that terrible name and my spirit quailed, but Merthun clearly knew nothing of the giant for he went on, speaking as if by rote,

'My father's mother was a gift to my grandfather, and when he died she was sent back to the family at Birka. She was pregnant when they set her aside, yet she said nothing of it for the fear that they might keep her for the child. I have travelled far into the lands of the Rus. I have never met my grandfather's family. My mother was from Mona and she chose my name.'

Barve had stopped eating. She stared into his face as if she had seen the Angel Michael.

'Have you been so far?' she asked him, and for once he looked at her as he replied,

'I have travelled much. West to Vinland, south to Cadiz, and North to the land of the everlasting night.'

'This land to the west, what is it? Is it truly the land where the sun sleeps? I do not ask out of idle curiosity. My sisters have set off to go there and I dearly wish to know. Is it a difficult voyage? Will they have made landfall in safety.'

'When did they sail?' he asked.

'Perhaps two weeks ago. They were sailing northwards first.'

'That is the route all must take. Are their husbands lucky sailors and well learned in the ways of the sea?'

'They do not go with husbands – they are alone.'

He turned his gaze on me.

'Then you must make a death offering for them. You have seen their last.'

'I do not think so,' I said.

'He wishes it were so,' Barve said.

The gentile passed his mournful gaze over her and back to me.

'The currents are very bad and the cold in these days is straight from the mouth of Ymir. But that one is very cunning,' he said, pointing at Barve with his chin, 'and perhaps her sisters are also wælcyrgies. They may yet live.'

Barve turned to me.

'What is a wælcyrgie?' she asked.

'I do not know for sure, but I surmise that it is a female demon.'

Merthun covered his ears and shook his head.

'Bad people to anger. If they not like you they wait till the battle and trip you up or fetter your spirit.'

'You say I am like them?' she asked.

'You are a battle woman. You have hurt men badly.'

'The men I hurt wished to violate me. There was no doubt of that. Do you say I was wrong to stop them?'

'Wrong? What is that?'

I told him the word 'harm' in his own tongue and he frowned.

Silence fell for a while and I ate a little bread. The woman suddenly stopped eating and sat and stared at the table-cloth without moving. The serving-woman came in with more cheese, bread and porridge and placed them on the table in front of me. I shook my head to show that I had no more need of food, but she, in turn shook her head and pushed the bowls even closer. I took a little more to show that I was grateful for their hospitality. She smiled a wide, brown-toothed smile at me and wiped the sweat from her head. Her cheeks and her pebble of a nose shone red from the oven.

'I am Frakokk,' she said, 'my mother baptised me Yestin. She was Thora of Magh Aodh.'

'Then I may have known her,' I said, delighted to find a simple soul. The woman smiled into my face again, straightened and waved to her colleagues who were lurking by the door. Four women appeared, smiling shyly, one of them carrying an infant which she thrust at me.

'This is Erlend,' she said, 'bless him, father.'

Before I could protest Frakokk slapped her away.

'Let him eat,' she said in the foreigner's tongue.

The women stepped back, bowed and sat on the bench against the wall. As I ate I could feel their eyes on my back, but this is not new to me so I finished my meal, washed my hands and blessed myself. My audience kept a respectful silence till I had said a small prayer then they crowded round me once again with innumerable questions. They seemed to think that a man of my calling knew every ruffian who sailed between Powys and Trondheim. I gave them what news I could and even blessed the child, then at last I begged for a moment to sit at the wall and read my psalter. They released me and Frakkok sent them about their tasks, but all the time they kept peeking round the door to see if I was at leisure once more. As I read I could hear Barve and Merthun talking in low voices. I could not make out what they said, but they would have found it hard to understand each other. Nevertheless the woman persisted and I heard her laugh and then the man joined her. This sudden intimacy alarmed me, so I cut short my office and joined them.

'He is going to the Master's hall soon,' Barve told me. 'I think we should join him. The people there may have news of my family.'

'I do not think that we are far south enough to have contact with them,' I said doubtingly, then added, 'but if your sister's husband is a great warrior, his name may have been heard here.'

'What name is this?' asked Merthun, but before I could reply there came a commotion at the door behind us. Into the hall tumbled the men of the shore watch; first-oar, second-oar, bent-face, sore-eyes and all. They paused when they saw Merthun sitting with us and spoke to each other, looking at us through the tail of their eye. After a moment they all nodded and came towards us and I could see they were not in a kindly mood. First-oar was the spokesman and he addressed Merthun in piratese saying,

'So you have found our prisoners. Well, it will do you no good, for we have come to take them back. They are ours by right of conquest and we can keep them in our own place until we decide just what to do with them.'

'What are they saying?' Barve asked me, but I shook my head at her.

'You did not conquer them,' said Merthun calmly, 'and you know the Master claims the first part of every profit you make. It is his right as long as you eat his bread and live on his land.'

'Perhaps we will not be living on his land much longer. If we can make a little profit of our own we could be independent, and you are not man enough to stand in our way.'

'I am not going to stand in your way, but I do not think you can keep the Master in ignorance. He has his watchers in many places, and he hates to be cheated of his right.'

First-oar strode menacingly up the hall and stood at the end of the table. His followers straggled after him.

'With the two boats we have now we can be well away before he hears anything of this. Unless you tell him.'

'I will tell him nothing. I am not paid to spy on you. I only record the stocks. But think, first you have to find the family of both these people and get negotiations under way; then you have to decide terms; in the meantime you have to make sure that your prey are taken care of, for if they die before you conclude the ransoming you will never see your profit. And since the woman is of noble stock she must be fed and clothed according to her station. All this takes time and costs money, and you will have to pay those who negotiate for you even if there is no conclusion.'

'We will not waste time trying to ransom the monk. His tribe are vowed to poverty, but the woman should be worth something. Even you can see her linen is of a fine quality. We'll take the monk to Gobhan with us.'

Suddenly there was a great shout from the rear door and in marched the women. One was carrying a harness bow, another a wood-axe, a third brandished her loom sword. Frakokk was in the van and as they walked over the plank floor their feet in their pattens made a terrible din. They stopped and their leader shook her fist at first-oar.

'You shall do no such thing!' she shouted. 'You leave the good father alone. He blessed the bairn Erlend and that puts him under our protection. He is not to be one of your poor creatures.'

'Mind your business, woman!' shouted the man.

'It is our business when you take meek, wise and holy men as prisoners. The father's kind have always been good to us and I will not stand aside and see him ill-used by such as you.'

At this the women shouted agreement and shook their weapons at the men. The men retreated a pace.

'What of the woman?' pleaded first-oar. 'She will fetch good money however we deal with her. Look at her fine linen, and the ring on her left hand. If we sold that we would have enough to set up where the land is kind and the sun visits more often.'

Frakokk scratched her head, then said,

'She is a fine young woman, true, but she is under the father's protection. That puts her under ours also. So go and see to your duties. While you stand here, the Dublin men could be half way up the dale.'

'Thor protect us all when women take to battle,' said first-oar and his cronies nodded. They all made for the door, but bent-face turned to say to us,

'This is not the end of it. We will not be cheated. We will find you empty-handed one day.'

The women cackled like geese and gestured at him with their weapons. The men ran out.

Barve pulled at my sleeve saying,

'What has happened? I cannot understand what went on. Did those women chase the men?'

133

I decided that there was no future in pretending to ignorance and I explained,

'The men wished to take us again, you for ransom or worse, me perhaps for slavery. The women, on the other hand, are grateful enough to my kindred to oppose them. We are safe, for the time being, thanks to the fact that my order are well thought of.'

'Did I hear you say that the women opposed them?'

'That is correct.'

At that Barve laughed for a long time and clapped her hands.

'That is good to know,' she said. 'Thus shall the meek inherit the earth – with a harness bow for a club. I am truly indebted to your order for its protection,' and she laughed again. Then she stopped and said,

'What happens to a man kept in slavery? I have heard it talked of but I have not yet found out what takes place.'

'It means that one man owns another as he would own his horse and his sheep. He may at any time sell the man for money or geld him or put him to death if he is too restive. The Church has tried many times to put an end to the practice, but there is so much profit to be made that our efforts are futile.'

'I do not understand all of this, but if the Christians are against it, then so must I be also.'

Merthun spoke up then saying, 'The men have gone for now, but they have long memories. I fear they will be back and this time the women will need more than harness bows to protect you. It is plain you must leave this place. Come with me up the dale to my master's fortress and you will be safe.'

'That is good advice,' I said, 'for the mean-spirited such as they will not forget their spite. They have been humiliated before us twice and they will wish to remove that slur as soon as possible.'

'I am pleased to go with you to the fortress,' said Barve, 'but what will happen to the women who have defended us? Will they not suffer for their actions?'

'No doubt when they return and find you gone they will beat the women,' he answered, 'if so, it is no more than they have done many times before. The women knew that when they stood against them.'

For the first time I saw the woman hesitate.

'We cannot go and leave the women to suffer,' she said. 'They came to protect us in full knowledge that they would be made to pay for it. It would be vile indeed to leave them to be beaten by their menfolk.'

'They have been beaten before,' I said. 'You were asking about the nature of sacrifice and here you have an example of it. It is their duty to support the church and as they are only simple women this is as much as they can do. If we stay we will be taken captive again. Do you wish to deny them the good of their actions?'

'The men will not beat them too bad,' said Merthun. 'They will need the women to do the work and if they break bones the work will not be done. The women are strong, but you must go, soon.'

Barve covered her face and sat swaying in her perplexity. Finally she roused herself and said,

'I must accept that. Women have been beaten times without number, and alone I cannot change the world. But tell me, Merthun, why do you not act against those vermin?'

'I have told you. I am not commander here. I am only here to watch. If I give orders my master will be angry.'

'But they insulted your person. Why did you not defend your honour?' the woman persisted.

Merthun hung his head and his face was the colour of the rising sun as he said,

'I have no honour to defend. Years ago I offended a spæ-wife and she put battle-fetter on me. I am no warrior, now. I only carry news. The men do not talk to me.'

'Was it one of your wælcyrgies that did it?'

'No, it was only a bad old woman.'

'How did she do this thing?'

'There were some words said. I cannot recall. They struck into my spirit like elf shot.' He stood up suddenly saying,

'I must go now. There are things I must do. I will be back at nightfall. Do not go out of sight of the women.'

With that he disappeared through the rear door and returned

wearing a cloak, tunic and shoes. With no word of farewell he left the house and disappeared, to reappear a moment later leading a horse. We were left to our own devisings again. Barve turned to me.

'What is this thing, a spæ-wife?' she asked, as I knew she would.

'It is the sort of woman we monks have been taught to guard ourselves against from our earliest days. Women who have no place to stay where they might be decent, but who wander from farm to town and back and make their living by claiming to tell the future and other vile deceits. There are very few of them now.'

'Can they prophesy, indeed?'

'Some of them can.'

'Then why do you call them deceits if they can do what they say?'

'The deception lies in telling men that their power is legitimate. Some are even so bold as to say that God has given them the gift of prophecy when the truth is that their powers come from the Devil.'

Barve frowned but said nothing more.

'I am going now to meditate,' I told her. 'You must find your own way to pass the time.'

She walked through the rear door and spoke to the women. Some time later I found that she had asked them for water so that she might use the bath house. I took myself to the river bank to avoid the sight of such things and took with me my pen, ink and this palimpsest I am writing on now.

As I was writing, a gull glided overhead crying its desolate cry and I suddenly was striken by a terrible longing. I recalled as clearly as if I were living it that day when we stood on the beach at Rintsnoc and you told me of your love of God. Dear brother, it was the only time you ever spoke of such things to me. You said,

'Nothing man does, or will ever do is equal to the miracles God produces for us every day. The whiteness of a gull's breast, the wings with which it flies, the feathers that compose those wings – these are all evidence of the great Love which has produced the universe. That Love is all that stands between ourselves and chaos and if we turn our backs on it, we will surely die. I hope you follow me, for I see dangers before you which you do not understand.'

I did not understand you then, and even now I can only glimpse a meaning in your words. Yet for a moment, as the gull mewed overhead, I could smell the sea and I am sure you were beside me. I hope all goes well with you, brother. The medicines you gave me are still plentiful and tomorrow we go to a great hall where I may meet with those who can renew my supply. If not, I am sure that I have enough to sustain me for many days yet.

Merthun has said that there is a lad who will bring this to you so I finish in haste,

Valete.

Ælfrid was not a scholar and he often wished to say things for which he could not find the words. When he spoke to me of the pattern he saw in nature he often left me baffled and struggling to follow him. One day, however, he was able to say something clearly. We had been collecting plants for the cure of a rheum that was going about. He lifted up a leaf and asked me,

'Why do we pick the flowers when we do? Why do we spend so much time watching the state of the stars and the moon before we bring them out of the field? Why do we not run to the bush the first instant we need them?'

'I had not thought about it,' I answered.

'I wish that you would,' he said, 'for it is most important. I will say only this for now: the power of a plant to heal is not always present. It arises only when the virtue of the plant is at its greatest and this virtue is only to be found when outside and inside the plant the conditions are right. This is true of man and of all living creatures. That at a point in their lives their internal state and the external conditions produce their greatest moment of virtue. If God is kind, He will take them

137

to his bosom at that moment – when they are closest to perfection – but all too often the creature will elude Him and live on only to deteriorate.

'I do not dispute the creature's right to live on. If it is possible to improve on the virtue of that moment, they should be given the chance to do so. Once dead it is not possible to improve.

'We must imitate the merciful God. We must try to cull our plants at that time when they are closest to perfection and preserve that perfection contained in their dead flesh. If we leave them the virtue may well sink once more, never to rise again in its life.'

I hope this record does not lead to accusations of blasphemy against Ælfrid. He did not mean to compare us directly to God, but only to demonstrate that if you wish to cull plants, some times are better than others.

Ælfrid, monk and apothecary at Rintsnoc, Hw monk and presbyter, greetings.

My dear brother, for the last two days I have been hearing a chronicle of what claims to be terrible injustice. If it had not been borne out by the testimony of others here I might not have believed a word of the story, still less felt pity for the victim. As it is, I will require many days of reflection and prayer before I can give my judgement on the events which have taken place. I will lay it before you as it was recounted and when we meet again we can compare our opinions.

Whatever the man Merthun did with his time I cannot guess. All I know is, in spite of his insisting that we should waste no time, he delayed our departure until the next day, and well into the morning at that. I fretted all the time between the hours in case the men of the shore watch should come back while he was absent. Barve was unconcerned and passed the whole time in talk with the farm women, as if there had never been an attempt on her honour. She said that she was keen to learn their language but I think she was no more than idle. At last our escort's errands were finished and he said we could go. I read the third hour, and never have I said with more fervour the lines, 'You have given us like sheep appointed for meat and have scattered us among the heathen.'

Then Merthun appeared, leading horses for us and a string of mules laden with covered packs. We returned past the compound where we had spent our first night then climbed a narrow, tree-hung pass behind it. Merthun said we should avoid the shore watch that way but it was a very steep descent and I feared that the horses would fall. I am a poor horseman and would have been happier on a humble but surer-footed mule. At the foot of the hill we turned to our right and travelled for about three miles in the shadow of a steep, high crag. The soil in that dank forest is very shallow, for everywhere as I looked I saw slopes littered with fallen trees, their roots turned up and exposed to the sky; their trunks broken as they leaned against their fellows. Merthun was a poor sort of travelling companion, being as silent as the forest around us, and the patter of the animals' feet was muffled by the lingering mould. The stillness unnerved me once again.

At last we reached the end of the escarpment and the sun shone on us. Ahead of us lay a wide cultivated valley, the sky was blue and a fresh wind blew at our backs. Merthun now told us to keep close to him and travel in single file, as this part of the way led through marsh and was very narrow. I followed him as rapidly as I could for the next hour was almost upon me but the woman, who rode ahead, was more concerned about the road we had travelled and kept looking back over her shoulder. Once we were again on high, dry ground she pulled up and rode beside me saying,

'There is some mystery here. Why did we ride through that rocky defile where the horses may have been injured? Surely we could have come here along the valley of the river that ran by the steading? It would have been easier riding on the other side of that crag.'

'It is no matter,' I answered, 'we are here safe now. It may be that the river valley is too swampy to pass through at the head, even though it is kind at the place we stayed. Do not be alarmed.'

She shook her head, but held her peace as I read my office.

At the middle of the day the others rested and ate a little. Barve, seated on a rock on the river bank above us, looked at the way ahead and said,

'We are well set on the road, and it may seem ridiculous to ask this, when we are so far along, but I have not yet heard the name of the man who is to be our host at this fortress. Is it one we should know?'

'Your host there will be the same man whose guests you have been for the last two nights. You must not wonder that you have not heard his name. These valleys as far as the eye can see are in his hand yet his name is known by very few men beyond them. I do not understand it, nor would I ever ask him why, but he is one of the few men of his state who shuns fame in his own country. He is known from Iberia to Rus as a great trader and a mighty warrior but in this valley he is known as the Master and no more. However there is no harm in your knowing him now that you are here. He is called Culhuch.'

'A blessing on the mouth that tells me this!' cried Barve springing to her feet. 'That is the man whom I seek – the man who took my sister in marriage all those years ago. I do not understand how this can be, for I was told that my sister had been taken to a land far to the south. What has happened?'

'That is my master's secret way,' said Merthun. 'He will have left false news of himself. What was your sister's name? We will see if we are both speaking of the same.'

'My sister's name is Olwen, and she is the most beautiful of all my family. She has skin as white as the drifting snow and her hair is white-gold like the sun at noon. Her eyes are as grey as the ice on the river and she carries herself as proudly as a swan.'

'That was her likeness,' cried Merthun, 'at the time she came to us. Though I fear dark days in her life have dimmed her brightness.'

'Then this is the happiest day I have had for many, many months. Soon I shall see my sister's face again – when I had almost given up hope.'

'Do not think so,' said the man, and to our shame we saw tears in his eyes, 'you will be sore disappointed. Your sister, if it is truly she, has gone from this place.'

'What are you telling me?' said Barve.

He said nothing but turned to her and clung to her knees. She started to draw back, but paused and with an awkward hand began to stroke his hair. After a while the fury of his grief abated so that Barve could free herself. She knelt beside him and he looked into her face. He said,

'I see a likeness of you and her. You are beautiful also.'

The vain creature smiled and nodded.

'We are all alike, my sisters and I. But please, I beg you tell me what became of Olwen. Many of my family have been killed and I am most eager to find the few that are left to me.'

Merthun looked at the sky and sighed.

'We do not have far to go and the weather is fair for the time of year. I think it is best I should take time now and tell you what I know so that you will not be surprised by what you find at my master's hall. This will not be easy, for I loved your sister like the monks love the Blessed Virgin.'

I was shocked but soon forgave him for his simple blasphemy, for he was as miserable as a dog that has lost his master. I reproached him a little, saying,

'No regard for a fleshly woman could ever equal the pure worship of the Mother of Heaven. You are only a pagan and could not understand what is known to monks, but I see that you mean no lack of respect. Please continue.'

'The love I knew for Olwen could not be purer. Listen to my story.'

I remember how she was when she first came to us. I was myself a whole man still and I had spent a few summers raiding with Culhuch.

It was my first experience of raiding with the men of the sea-lochs and I was rejoicing in it. My childhood and youth at Kaupang with my mother's people had been spent in study, for it was my mother's wish that I should be a scholar. My father had been killed when he was young and she wished that I should not be taken away to die by the sword. Many books I had from my father's family and for some years I was happy to study them in my solitude. I made friends among the sailors at the harbour and from them I learned a little of every language spoken under the sun. After a while word got around that I was very learned and merchants who wished their sons to learn trading sent them to me. I taught them about the foreign lands they would be seeing before they sailed. They thought that safety lay in knowledge, and they were partly right. I made a good living from my teaching but as the time went by I felt myself being drawn to the foreign places I spoke of. It was no longer enough that I could speak something of the tongues of all these places – I wanted to see for myself the sunlight on the ochre sands of Iberia – I wanted to taste the sun-warmed wine of the Levant – indeed I longed for a change, in any shape it might come. But my mother counselled patience.

At last the day came when I was driven beyond the limits of patience. Culhuch had arrived at Kaupang with his fleet. They were fine-looking warriors with white teeth gleaming in sun-browned faces. They wore much gold on their arms, and some wore it in their ears. You will see them at the fortress for yourself. They told us of their voyage to Byzantium where they had bought silk, gold, wine and spices. One of them handed me a little black fruit that I took for a sloe, but when I bit into it I was amazed to find that it was not sweet. Its oily, bitter taste called up the spirits of my ancestors and they spoke through me when I went to my mother. I said,

'I have done your bidding for all these years. You cannot say I am a son who does not know his duty. I have served the people here willingly as a teacher, but they do not think of me as one of them because I live among books. The time has come for me to go and fight for my living like a man. Do not grieve for me. I shall leave provision for you and I will return a rich man so that you will spend your last days in luxury.'

My mother sighed and said,

'I knew this day would come. I have been dreading it ever since you were born, but my fear has not stopped it from happening. Go, if you must, but it will be without my bless-ing. I do not want you to return rich, all I want is that you should return soon. Until then, I shall think of you as dead.'

She turned away from me at that moment and said not another word to me until the day I sailed. Three years after I left, I heard that she had married again, so I do not need to concern myself with her. Culhuch laughed at me when I asked him for a place on one of his benches. He showed me my soft hands beside one of his own men's, calloused and leathery, and pointed out my narrow shoulders and skinny arms. I said,

'The hands and arms will soon change with use. Every man who starts to live as a sailor is weak because he is a child. At first I will be of little use as an oarsman until I grow stronger. In the meantime I have knowledge which could be useful to you. I can speak to many people in their own tongues. In a foreign port you will not have to pay a foreigner to translate for you, and then worry in case he has not told you the truth. I can talk for you and I will put you on your guard if any should try to dupe you.'

Culhuch saw the truth of my words, for he is a most cunning man. I sailed with them a month later. First we went to the place in the Orcades where my master kept his longships, and moored the deep-water boats safely. Then we went raiding along the west coast of Eirinn.

I was delighted by everything in my new life. The smell of the freshly cut wood where the boat had been repaired was a source of joy to me as great as the sight of a new port appearing ahead. Every day I took time to learn about swordplay with one of the crew as a teacher, and though I was not the stuff heroes are made of, I was a fair sort of warrior. And all this pleasure I kept in spite of the hardships I had to endure.

For the first time in my life I slept on a hard bench. The blisters on my soft hands broke and bled many times until someone showed me how to cover them with fat and wrap them in rags. The other sailors treated me badly. They thought that a stranger like myself should not have tried to change his way of life. Culhuch told them that I would play my part when the time came, and I must be treated as one of them. They were careful not to let him see when they made water in my beer cup or smeared my bench with filth. I always knew what was happening, but I knew that to complain to the Master would be to lose all chance of their respecting me. I threw away the beer and scrubbed the soiled bench and kept my lips fast.

The morning of our first raid I was told to stay at the

longship. It was the custom to leave a small crew on guard, and I was left with one old man and one man whose leg was bent sideways at the knee from injury. I climbed up the forestem of the ship to watch so that I would know what to do when it was my turn. From this I learned what to do, but nothing could tell me how I would feel when the morning came for me to fight.

We had been told that this township would be easy prey, so I was allowed to join the raiders. In the silence of a grey dawn we beached the warships. The sea washing the shingle was like strands of tangled silk. The people of the steading had just started the day and a few threads of smoke were wandering towards the sky. Beyond the village lay the blue mountains where we would soon see the sun rise, and the world seemed to hold its breath. I was with the second ship and we had been told to attack from the landward side. We crept round the outer fence in silence and split into two groups, one for each side of the rear gate. We heard the sound of cows' feet coming and prepared for action. The gate swung open and the herd trotted out followed by a dog and two boys. The ship leader snatched the children from the road and we rushed in through the gates. The dog had started barking and we heard a cry go up from the shore side.

Suddenly there were men rushing towards me. I hurled myself at them and shouted a challenge. The two younger men ran forward, swinging their short swords. I swung my axe at the one on my left and felt the blade jar on bone. The man called out in pain and his brother cut at my belly. I avoided the blow easily and thrust at his guts with my sword. This time the blade sank in deep and as I watched his eyes grow dull I knew the satisfaction of a successful kill. At once I saw that the long days spent at the oar had turned me from a man in a boy's body to a man indeed. I felt that I could live forever.

I ran to the centre of the steading and found the men putting up a fierce fight. Our spies had been wrong and there was a real danger that our raid might miscarry. I leapt into the fray and set about me with sword and axe as if I had known no life but the slaughter of men. Time and again my axe swung and hacked through muscle and bone, and blood flew. The only danger I recognised was that the blood was making my hands slippery, but I dared not stop to clean them. The men of the steading were not weaklings and every hut seemed to contain a crowd of them. It came to me that rowing had made my arms very strong, for the constant hewing was only beginning to tire them. I felt very proud.

For all their brave resistance the men of the town were not equal to us. Soon there was silence but for the wailing of women and the roaring of fire in the thatch. Our haul that day was not great, but for me it was a fine day for I had won my share with my own hands, and no one could deny it to me. After all my years as a scholar, leaning on the strength of other men, I was now the equal of any. My only regret was that it had all happened so swiftly that I could not recall every moment.

But I am like an old man who sits by the fire telling and retelling all his days of valour. You asked me how it was the lady Olwen came to the fortress.

One morning Culhuch came out of his bed and called us together. He said a terrible dream had visited him that night and he could not rest until he had seen its prophecy fulfilled. He had seen the face of a woman whose beauty was greater than any in the world. She had looked at him sadly as he lay sleeping and told him that she would be his wife if he could rescue her. Her father was a fierce lord who lived in the mountains of the north and she was kept a prisoner by him because of his terrible jealousy. Soon she would be forced to become his concubine, and she was living in terror of the moment. She begged Culhuch to come and save her before she became the victim of this polluting lust.

'We must now move with the greatest speed to save the lady Olwen. Who will come with me on this mission? I must warn you that this man is very dangerous and some of you will not return, but I can promise you that if we prevail, those who return will be remembered as the mightiest warriors of the age.'

Every man there wished to go with him but he took only those closest to him and most experienced. They set off inland early one morning and disappeared from sight. As time passed we began to wonder if we would ever see Culhuch or the lady he had dreamed of, and after months of waiting some families left the valley. Then one day, as the year was drawing to a close, we saw them coming over the pass.

It had been cloudy until late in the morning and massive black clouds lay heaped over the mountains. Around the middle of the day, a band of blue appeared over the sea. After that many pieces of blue appeared and by the afternoon the sun blazed over all the valley. The master and his men rode down to the fortress with his banner waving over their heads.

She sat in the midst of the troop as quiet as a flower in bud. We all ran out to meet them and Culhuch lifted her from her horse as you would lift a bird with a broken wing. From the first sighting women had been preparing the hall according to the instructions Culhuch had left them. The walls had been hung with fine weavings from the eastern lands; the tables were put out and all were laid with fine clean linen, and the gifts that Culhuch had been collecting for years were placed on them. There was a golden silk robe as soft as her skin, embroidered with purple and red flowers and gold threads twined in at the neck and hem. To wear over that there was a silken shawl woven in every colour of a rainbow and it was so long that it would trail on the ground behind her. There were heaps of linen and wool all bleached to the purest white, shoes of soft leather dyed every colour you can think of and embroidered with silk and beads. There were many, many golden arm rings and many pairs of golden brooches. These fine clothes and jewellery were all laid out on the tables before her arrival and everyone was brought in to see the display.

When my lady saw them all she smiled at my master and said they were too fine for her. She said that such clothes belonged to a princess of high birth and that she was only a maiden from the forest. He told her that her modesty was very pretty, but that she would decorate the clothes, not they her, and that nothing was too good for the wife of Culhuch. After the exchange of more such courtesies he began to frown with real anger, and she kissed him and said a very pretty thanks.

Then she was taken into the small house that my master keeps for his own and decked out in all the silks. She reappeared, blushing like the pimpernel, and everyone called out their praise. Then we sat down to a feast that went on for days. Yet my master had found so many spices in so many lands to season the dishes that no matter how long the feast lasted each dish tasted different. It is remembered here and in all the lands of Eirinn and Alban to this very day.

After the feast none left empty-handed. Some were even given silver coins, and I still see them being worn as jewellery by the ignorant ones who do not know how to use them. I received a silver bowl with a gilt rim. There was no doubt in any mind that this was the greatest wedding feast since the King himself was married. Then we went raiding in the Sudreys, but it was the only voyage that year for, as Culhuch kept reminding us, there was more treasure to be had at home. That was true for him, if not for us, but he was a generous master so we stayed with him.

Soon enough my lady bloomed with child. That winter we sat in the hall and feasted while she grew large. Those were pleasant days and we were young enough to be carefree. Outside the storm raged and the snow built up drifts higher than a man, but we were warm within our thick stone walls. We could not know the storm was about to break through the doors and seep through the thatch. I thought once that it was unkind of the Gentle ones not to give us warning of how things would go with us, but now I see that ignorance is a blessing. I wish often that I were still like one of the sailors who sail with Culhuch. Nothing troubles them but hunger and tiredness, and they sleep long at night. If you have ever watched terns fishing you will understand me. They fly fast above the water many times the height of a man, and as fast as the eye can follow yet still they can note their prey. As soon as they see a victim they fold their wings and dive. They neither pause nor reflect, and pass from sighting to attack in one movement. That is the only kind of man that is happy.

The lady Olwen was like the sun to us. We followed every move she made and wondered every day at our master's luck in winning her. A weaker leader might have found himself challenged for the attentions of such a sweet woman but Culhuch would not let that happen. He let everyone see he was besotted with love for his lady. He took his food only from her hand; he would not go out of her sight. When visitors came to the hall, no matter how great they were in dignity, he would not let her carry the cup to them more than once. At our daily feasting he would not let her retire without him, and when, in spite of herself, her eyes began to close, he would rail at us for tiring her. She would smile at all this and kiss him on the cheek and the feast would go on, but we became careful to watch her, and if she showed signs of tiredness we would seem to fall asleep at the table so that she could go and rest. None of us would have seen her come to any harm, and we were happy to cut our drinking short so that she could be spared.

When the raiding season started, Culhuch was slow to leave. Olwen was growing ripe and he was dismayed at the thought of leaving her alone to bring the child into the world. You may think that this is not the usual way for a man to go on when others leave women to the business of rearing babies, but there are two things you must bear in mind. First, my master is a foundling and has no brothers to take over his possessions. If he died, there would be nothing left unless he had a son either by adoption or by birth. Secondly, Culhuch is not a young man, and he had almost given up the hope of seeing the fruit of his loins growing to take his place.

When he gave voice to his doubts Olwen patted his cheek. She reminded him that she was about to do something which women had done for all the generations of man, and that she was in God's hands and His will would be done whether Culhuch were there or not. Finally she said that if her lord would not go about his business there would be nothing to support her and the child. After this had been said many times for many days we left, but the Master's heart was at home and he took no satisfaction from raiding. We returned before the child was born. The only time that year he warmed to his task was when he saw some treasure that he thought would please his lady. Once I saw him cut the finger off a woman so that he might take the ring she wore on it. She was a fine woman, but he maimed her without a thought for the crystal on her hand. When Olwen saw the ring she was dismayed at the blood on it, and said she did not like it. For the first time, then, he raged at her and told her that she was an ungrateful wretch.

'Did I not come to your father's hall when you called me? I brought my best men and two of them died for your sake. It might have been myself that died that day, and you would now be bound to your father's side forever. If it were not for me your child would be the monster of an incestuous union.'

We were all well used to his anger, and I have seen two of our fellows die on his sword for a moment's insolence, but we trembled when he raised his hand to her. This time, however, the blow did not fall, for she took the ring from the table at once and put it on her finger. She was not the sort of woman to set herself against her lord.

After that they were as kind to each other as mating swans. Then came the birth of their son, and Culhuch was so pleased you might think it had never been done before. He put the boy on his shield and brought him through to show all of us like a trophy of war, which in a way he was. We complimented him on the child, but there were those who spat after they had done it saying that it was ill-luck to praise a child in front of its face. It is sad, but as it came to pass they spoke the truth. Three nights later there came a terrible shriek from the women's house where Olwen was lying, and Culhuch rushed from the hall. When he returned his face was pale as a corpse and his eyes were sunk into his head. Staring blindly into the midst of us, he told us that the child was dead.

From that night his kindness to my lady ceased. We knew he did not leave her alone, for soon she grew with child again, but there were no more nights spent feasting under her gentle gaze. Instead we were all men together, and some said none the worse for it. We were never told what had killed the child, but there was no grave made for it and we did not dare to ask. We saw little of Olwen after that, for she kept to the women's side of the hall, but from time to time we would see her crossing the yard. When we saw her we greeted her with pleasure for she was still our lady, but all she did was smile and hurry past. Sometimes we would hear Culhuch shouting at her in their house, saying that she had forced him to go on a raiding trip to get him out of the way. He said she was a witch and that she had killed the child; he said that she had tried to turn the child into a monster. She did not reply, but we could hear her weeping. After this, most of the men stopped talking to her.

In the summer we raided with Grim and Olaf Trygvasson who is now king in Lochlann. We kept clear of Glaunna and overwintered in Athcliath. Word came in the spring that Olwen had borne another son and Culhuch was filled with delight. He became impatient to return home and we could see that he was as pleased with his lady as he had ever been. When we came into the harbour he stood staring inland as if he could see the fortress just by wishing. He leapt onshore as soon as we came near it and started demanding horses to be brought at once, before we had made the cargo safe. We might have attended to it ourselves and let him hurry off, but he insisted that we should ride with him to his hall in a troop. At last we set off and hoped that the cargo would be safe. Someone had taken word to the fortress that we had arrived, and, almost at this very place, Olwen and her women appeared riding to meet us. Culhuch jumped to the ground and pulled her from her horse with a shout. He threw his arms round her and embraced her warmly and we cheered to see them united again. Then he went back to his own horse and put her on the saddle in front of him. She sat smiling there as they rode back to the fortress, and everyone from the dale came out to give their greetings as they passed. At the hall the infant was held up to his father on his shield once more, and this time we did not say what a fine boy he was.

We did little raiding that year. My master was reluctant to leave his new son and rode about the dales with the child on one arm to show him to all his people. He even took him up to Æt Eamotum to show to his lord. When they were out of hearing of their lord the women said that such a small child should not be travelling so far, and on horseback also, but my lady was complacent as ever. She smiled at her lord and son as they stood beside the gate together and wished them farewell saying cheerfully,

'Take care of our son, my lord, and bring both of you back to me as soon as the lord Grim has done with you. I do not say this out of fear for the child, for I know you will cherish him. Furthermore, he is of a mighty stock and will not take ill from hardships that would destroy other children. I commend him to you now with a light heart, and commend you both to God.'

With that they rode out of the gate and over the pass. She turned indoors as calm as if they were going for an afternoon's outing. Some of the women who were Christians blessed themselves and murmured that nothing good could come to a child from such wanderings, and they called the fate of the first infant a dire warning. They might have saved their breath, for a month later Culhuch and his men came back laden with gifts for my lady, and the infant was as rosy as if he had just woken from a night's sleep. Grim had given the child the name of Asgrim, and his wife, being a Christian, had called him Jon and Olwen was pleased to accept the names. This was the faith Olwen had in Culhuch, even though he was not as loving as he had been.

Winter came and with it desolation. The wind blew mild and wet from the sea for day after day. Our feet were never dry and the days were warm so the sweat soaking our bodies made our clothes stick to us like a second skin. The rain soaking the outside met the wet inside and kept us constantly chilled. We spoke longingly of the bright days of winters past when the frozen ground rang under our feet and the stars filled the sky at night. Now heavy clouds made the days dark and the nights long, and they brought with them a bloody flux. One by one we started sweating and then came the fluid from the gut for days. Even the men and women who lived through it lay in their beds too weak to raise a hand. In the byres the cattle sweated and died unattended.

Of all people in the fortress who were stricken I recovered the fastest. I woke one morning shivering and with pains as if iron nails were being driven into my knees and elbows. As soon as I could move I reached into my mattress for the herbs I kept there and chewed some willow bark. Then I found some clean water and drank as if to empty the well. I had learned to do this from one of my grandfather's books on physic. It was the right thing to do, for the sweats and the flux only lasted for two days and on the third I was able to move about. It was well I did, for there was much work to be done in the fortress. Others who had passed through the murrain without harm were working, but with the sick to be tended as well as the regular tasks there had been little time spent on either. Culhuch was down at the harbour making sure that the downpour had not waterlogged the boats. So, even though weakness made the ground tilt under my feet, I left my bed.

The lady Olwen had been spared from any sickness and she was going from bed to bed giving out healing drinks and washing fevered bodies with warm water. The fire in the kitchen was kept going at her orders so that there should be a constant supply of water and pottage for the sick. We were lucky to have her services at such a time, for many lived who would have died without her. I found her in the kitchen and offered to do as much as weakness would let me. She asked me to look in on the cattle to see how many were left alive.

I went out to the byre at the rear of the fortress. There I found one of the company dragging out the bodies of dead cows, for all had died but three. He was weak, not from disease, only from tiredness. I told him to rest and he at once lay down on a heap of straw and went to sleep. He had dug a ditch on the far side of the fortress for the bodies and I went on carrying out the corpses. My way took me past Culhuch's own house, and as I went by the door I heard a woman sobbing.

For a moment I hesitated. I knew my master was not inside, for I had seen him leave. Yet we had never been allowed to cross the threshold and I was not easy in my mind about changing such a habit. Then I realised the plague had changed the order of our lives and that the inside of the house was dry and pleasant, and I pushed the door open. At first I saw no one and I thought I had been mistaken about the source of the sound. Then I stepped in and saw into the dark corner beyond the fire. There was Olwen, bent over the cradle, weeping sorely.

At once I thought that the child had died. When there is a great mortality the children are the earliest to die. I said,

'Poor woman, is it not enough that you have lost your firstborn? Has the plague taken off your latest child also?'

At the sound of my voice Olwen straightened quickly and put her body between me and the cradle.

'Have pity on a grieving woman, Merthun,' she said, 'and leave me alone with my dead. I have lost both my boys and they will never be replaced, though I bring a thousand children into the world.'

'I will leave you, Olwen, if that is what you wish, but please, I beg you, let me take one last look at the child's face. For so many months he has been the bright centre of all our lives that I cannot believe he has gone. I must see for myself that he is dead or I will continue to look for him round the corner of every house.'

When I said this Olwen covered her face and sank to the ground with a groan. I stepped forward and looked to see the child with his eyes closed in the last sleep. The cradle was empty.

'What has happened here? Have you buried the child already? Could you not wait until his father returned to take a last look at the boy?'

'Ah, Merthun, I must confess to you. It is not the plague that has carried off my poor son?'

'Then where is he?'

For a moment she looked at me as if she would like to see into my soul. Where is the man who could enjoy such a scrutiny? I stood under that powerful, sad gaze, wishing I could hide from it, until at last she spoke.

'Merthun, I have noticed that you are not like the other men of this company. You have spent much of your youth in study, is this not so?'

I nodded my assent.

'I believe that this has set you apart from your fellows. While you are in no way lacking the courage that marks the

154

warrior, you have other qualities as well.'

I drew breath intending vigorously to deny this but I saw that now was no time to tamper with the truth.

'It was not my wish that this should be so, but fate never consults our wishes. I am as you say – set apart.'

'Then I may hope that fate has made you a man who will hear things another would find too strange to apprehend.'

'Tell me what you wish, my lady. I will not promise to understand everything, but I will swear not to tell anyone else what you have said.'

'That will be enough,' she said and bowed her head. 'The child may not be dead. I came here from attending in the women's house. I had been away for perhaps an hour. Like all mortal children Asgrim is never still and needs to sleep during the day, so I put him to bed. He was not sick. When I came back to see if he was awake I found the cradle empty. I have looked for him in every house, store and bed in the fortress, but I cannot find him. I am sure he has been taken away.'

'Who would do such a thing?' I cried. 'Perhaps he has left the fortress. He is a very strong child and can crawl very fast. Did you look for him outside.'

'I have looked for him outside. I ran half-way down the dale, and half-way up the pass. There is no chance that I can have missed him. He is a warm-blooded child and has no love for the rain falling on him. If he had the chance he would have returned here. That is why I am sure that he has been taken from me.'

Once more she sat down and gave way to despair.

'You seem to me most sure that your child has been stolen. Have you any other reason to think this is what has happened?'

'I am afraid to say it, but I have,' she said. 'It was put about that the last infant I bore died in its first days, do you recall?'

'I recall that sad day too well. I thought the master would die of grief he was so pale.'

'He was pale, indeed, but not with grief. It was rage that made his face the colour of ash.'

'Not against you, lady, surely?'

155

'Against me, yes, for he believed that I killed the child myself,' and here she wept again, 'and he believes I burned the body to forestall his rage. He said that many women have overlaid their infants in their sleep and that I had done so but would not admit it. I could not have done such a thing. My poor child – I knew every breath he took. I will never forget the smell of his mouth.'

She paused again for tears had choked her voice. I recall that she was holding the doll her child had always carried with him. It was carved out of a single piece of wood with a round head and a stump for a body. It had no arms or legs but the face and clothing were painted on with a deep purple dye. The patterns painted on the body were such that I have only seen in the country near Constantinopolis. I suppose that the Master collected it on one of his journeys there. Olwen held it against her forearm and stroked it as she took herself in hand. She went on,

'I must tell you, there is a mystery here I cannot fathom. The child, my firstborn, was not found dead, but like his brother was taken from his cradle. I begin to think my father has stolen them both.'

'Surely your father was killed by your husband?'

'There is no certainty of that. My father was wounded, that is true, and with a wound that would kill most men. Yet his strength is great, and his knowledge of healing arts un-equalled. It is possible that he survived.'

'How was he wounded and where?' I asked, thinking to reassure her.

'My husband threw a short spear at him and it stuck in his belly.'

'Had he fallen to the ground?'

'No, he was still standing as I left his fortress.'

'Then you may be right. A thrown spear may have done no more than cut through fat and muscle. Had Culhuch driven the spear in with his hand, it is more likely that he had given a fatal blow.'

'Then this is my father's work. It is very like him to do such a thing. He did not want me to leave him and his resentment would be deep. I cannot think of a better way for him to punish me than by stealing my children. With one act he deprives me of the fruit of my body and brings on me the hatred of my husband.'

'But since your husband took you from him, nothing has been heard of him. Culhuch sent messengers to find the burial place and they came back saying that though there was no grave neither was there the least sign of him in the forest.'

'True, but my father's ways are as devious as they are cruel. He could find a way to hide himself from the eyes of men, if he wished.'

'I have thought, from time to time, that Culhuch made very little of his slaughter of your father. Such a deed would have brought him much esteem in the country, but he says nothing when he is in the company of strangers. Perhaps he shares your doubts.'

'If he does, he has said nothing of it to me. Indeed when he has wished to taunt me he has said that I should be ashamed to sleep with my father's killer. He said that a woman of spirit should be planning revenge on him, not bearing his children.

'But this is not to the point. What I wish to say is that if my father took them, they may yet be alive. I am sure my father would not kill them. It was always his dearest wish to have a son of his own loins, but his offspring were all daughters. Now there are two grandsons of his line and if he has them I know he will cherish them. I may yet see them again.'

'Then, my lady, I must hope that you are right, and that one day we will all see their bright faces.'

'I can find no other explanation. Let us pray that I am right. In the meantime I have to face their father with the news, and that will not be easy. He will swear that the child has died of plague because I did not watch him closely enough.'

'Do not alarm yourself, my lady. Culhuch will be angry that his son has been taken, but when his rage is cooled you may tell him what you think and he will go and rescue them, just as he did to you.'

'I do not think so,' she answered, 'for when the first child went I told him of my thoughts about my father. He would not hear me, and swore that he had killed my father with that single blow. He said the spear had some power that was sure to destroy my father though he could not tell me what. I think the truth is that he has no wish to be robbed of his triumph. This is folly, for even to stand against my father alone took more courage than any other man alive could muster. Sadly, Culhuch does not see it in that light and persists in saying that he is dead. But my father is not easily destroyed, even by those as strong as himself.'

She rose and put the doll into the cradle. I was sure she was lying to herself with these tales of her father. People laden with unbearable grief will believe many things before the truth of their loss. Weary as I was, I saw that it would be cruel to kill her hope so I said nothing and took my leave. She tried to smile at me, and said,

'I know you will tell no one what has been said here. I must find my own way to face my husband's wrath. One day, God willing, we will go together to find our children.'

I assured her of my silence. As I learned later, she was concerned for the wrong reason. When Culhuch was told of his son's loss he was not angry, nor did he rage against my lady for her neglect. Instead he spoke to her with the greatest courtesy as if she had been a visiting lady of high rank. That is how he treated her for nearly all the rest of their time together. They might have been strangers, not the loving bed-mates of the past. I thought that Olwen would be sick at heart. I feel she would have liked it better if he had raged at her and beaten her near to death.

That summer we raided on the coast of Eirinn. The plague had left very little for us to find but Culhuch set about it with such ferocity that we were successful. Soon the sight of his banner at the top of his mast was all that was needed to make people surrender without question. We overwintered in Cleveland and raided among the southern Sæxons the summer after. We were very successful there, for the plague had not visited them. That winter we feasted well in Orcades and in the spring we set off for the city of Constantinopolis. I was filled with pleasure at the thought of this voyage, so that I could not rest at nights. The men laughed at me for this childishness, but I could not hide my excitement. I gave very little thought to what might be happening back in this dale.

After nearly four years we returned. As we pulled into the harbour a fine drizzle washed my face and for the first time I knew what it was to be glad to be home. This time we made the ships safe and stored the cargo properly before we made for the fortress. Neither Olwen nor any woman came to meet us on the road, but this was because the Master had forbidden the lady to leave the fortress. I did not know this at the time. All I knew was the feeling that this was a bleak homecoming.

Culhuch had brought her fine silks and jewels, as was fitting. He showed them to her in the mead hall when we were all gathered there, and she spoke her thanks gracefully. Yet there was no charm in their meeting and when they retired together we were sure that he would soon return. He did not, and for many nights after that he must have laid with Olwen and it was no surprise when word went round that she was with child once more. After that, when her lord spoke to her there was a little softening of his manner, but no more. She seemed contented enough when I saw her, but we never mentioned our talk at the time of the plague.

That summer we raided in the usual way and returned to the dale at the start of winter. My lady had given birth to a fine little girl, and though my master was surely disappointed that there was no son, he smiled warmly at the infant when she was brought to him. However things may have stood between them, I saw very little of Olwen as the winter drew on and Culhuch spent every night with us in the main hall. I found out the truth of it when I was told to take a special guard duty and found myself sent to the door of Olwen's house. At the doorway I was told that I must not let the lady out on pain of death, and that all visitors were to be reported to Culhuch in the morning. He was making sure that his daughter was not going to be lost as her brothers were. Even the window had been sealed with planks.

I called through the door to Olwen and asked if she was well. She replied that she was well enough, but tired by her day's work. Then she said she was sorry but she could not talk to me, and silence fell. I sat down in the doorway and spent the night fighting off sleep by recalling, page by page, the contents of my grandfather's books. I am sure now that sleep lives in a cloud like the plague, and if a man must watch at night he must be on his guard against it or it will overcome him when his vigilance flags. Then it flings itself over his head, smothers his eyes and blanks out thought, so that he is helpless underneath it. I hate sleep for this, though many call it a comfort.

The next day I slept until sunset then joined the others for the meal. They asked me, with many ribald suggestions, where I had spent the night before, but one of the house-carls told them where I had been. They fell silent and one said,

'I do not envy you your watch. Even if you should be so foolish as to try and heat your bones against the witch I doubt if you could find steel in your knife with the old one looking on.'

'I did not see any old one. What are you talking about?'

'Merthun Head-in-the-clouds,' jeered the house-carl, 'did you not know who you were guarding?'

'I knew I guarded the lady Olwen's door. No more than that.'

'Then you spend too much of your time with your precious books. How could you not know that the Master went away to fetch his mother? You must have been sleeping.'

'I did not sleep. The Master often goes away on his own business.'

'You are the only man in the dale who does not know what this business was. The old one is to stay with Olwen every moment to make sure she does not kill this child as she did the others. She is not to take her eyes off her. I am sure I could not make the beast with two backs with my mother looking on, but the Master is a man of great vigour, and there she sits, by the fire in his house, and neither woman goes out of the door except to the privy.'

That night I tried to find another man to take the watch, but no one wished to share the task with me. The third night I took the makings of a fire with me. I sat in front of it as it crackled and hissed, and rejoiced in the distraction for my mind. Unhappily I found that watching the fire dropped my guard against the monster sleep, and my head kept nodding until I almost fell over. The next evening Culhuch spoke to me.

'I am not pleased that you lit a fire at my lady's door. The place beside my house is not to be treated like a campsite. The nights are not so cold that you need a fire to warm you – put on a heavier cloak. I will make sure you have one.'

'Sir,' I replied boldly, 'you are right that the fire is not needed in these nights, but it is not for warmth that I lit it. I was trying to find myself some way to occupy the time since I have no companion on my watch.'

I waited for him to begin shouting at me, but he did not. Instead he said,

'I gather from the other men that you still pass your time with books. They say you have a solitary nature and do not join them when you are all at leisure. This was why I gave the task to you, because I thought that a man who likes his own company would find it easy.'

I was surprised to find that he had made such a close study of my habits, but I merely said,

'You are right, sir. I do spend much of my time alone, although it is as much because the others shun me as because I prefer my own company. Nevertheless, I need something to pass the time away. I am not a horse, that can stand awake all night motionless.'

Culhuch sighed and pulled at his moustache.

'I am displeased that you are shunned by your companions. I wish my men all to find pleasure in each other's company and spend their leisure together. This way I can be sure that they will fight together when the time comes. Your not joining them makes me uneasy in my mind. You are no more than adequate as a warrior and a man who stands apart threatens the unity of the whole troop. In the last batch of captives I found another interpreter who knows more of most tongues than you. If you refuse this duty I have no use for you, yet I will not have it said of me that I turn men off for no good reason. Have you any wish to return to Kaupang?'

'I have not, sir, but at the same time I am a warrior and I have no wish to stay where I am not seen to play my part. I will go as soon as you wish.'

'No, you will stay. I will not have you wandering the country saying that I am ungenerous.' He thought for a while, then said,

'Can you find a way to carry a light with you without the light spilling all over the ground?'

'Yes, sir, I can make a screen out of animal skin. I have often used one on draughty nights to stop the wind from blowing out my lamp.'

'Very good. If you can do this and it will satisfy your busy mind, you may read while you are on watch.'

And so it was. I had many books to chose from by that time, for on my trips I had acquired plenty to add to my grandfather's supply. Some books I had not had time to study. I began work on my lantern the next day, and on watch that night it was a relief just to think how it would be when it was finished. I wondered also about the new interpreter Culhuch had spoken of. All the people in the fortress were known to me and I could think of none that could speak as many tongues as me. Then I thought of the black-haired, black-eyed concubine that the master had brought back from the last trip to the East. She shared his couch in the mead hall and I had thought her no more than the usual kind of slut men use for that purpose. Now I thought about the keen-eyed way she looked about her sometimes, and I realised that she was cleverer than any of us had known. All at once I was afraid for golden-haired, ivory-skinned Olwen. It is a well known fact that a cunning concubine is never happy about the presence of her rivals in the master's hall. This one might be tempted to try and remove the old stuff to the midden where she fancied it belonged. It was sure she would find allies easily enough, for a number of the warriors were suspicious of Olwen by now, thanks to Culhuch's talk of witches. For the first time I noted that the house I guarded contained two weak women as well as the child. And for myself, I realised I was still in the fortress only thanks to Culhuch's pride.

Once I had my light the nights passed easily. I did not always read, nor was I always thinking deeply. Sometimes it was a pleasure to sit in my little pool of light and listen to the sounds of the night hunters. The scream of a vixen, the baying of a wolf, the shriek of an owl – why do they strike us to the heart? Why do the hunters call and the victims stay silent till the moment of death? I wondered about these things on my vigil. I never heard a sound from inside the house I was guarding.

Soon I felt myself to be a stranger in the mead hall. The other warriors went about their business in the day and our lives touched only at the evening meal. Then, as I ate, I might have the chance to hear news of the dale and plans for the summer. It seemed there was to be a long voyage east to the land of the Rus and perhaps a land-crossing. Culhuch had gone to the Orcades that month to enlist the hands and make other arrangements. I was enthralled by the thought that I might see the land of my grandfather, but I was still guarding the women's house and there was no word of Culhuch's plans for his wife. For all I knew I may have had to guard them for the rest of my life, and the master was not a man to you could ask about his intentions. I did my duty and waited.

As it happened, a change in my life was brought about by my ward, herself. One night as I approached the house, I saw a dim yellow light coming from the doorway. When I got there I called out,

'You had best close the door, mistress.'

To my surprise she appeared in the doorway and smiled at me.

'The evenings are warmer now,' she said, 'and my husband in his kindness has allowed me to open the door for a while.'

'Yes, but it would be better to wait until I am here to guard your door before you open it. There are many creatures waiting in the twilight for darkness to fall. And some of them watch this door.'

'What do you mean by this? Are you telling me that you know who is threatening to carry off my daughter?'

'No, I do not know, and if I did I would take action. I am not a man to mutter and stare from under his brows, and leave an enemy to guess when I might strike.'

'I am glad to hear it, Merthun,' she said, 'I need the arm of a man of action in my party.'

'Is it come to parties, then, Olwen,' I asked, 'for I have not heard tell of a division in the fortress.'

'It has not been spoken of to my face,' she said, 'but my husband is cold to me, and when the women come to attend to us they will not speak a word, when before they would tell me something about the world outside.'

I realised that this talk of rupture between himself and his wife would be reported to Culhuch by his mother. It would not increase my favour with him. I distracted her with,

'How is the child, my lady?'

'She is well, thank you. Do you wish to see her? She is asleep, but if you are quiet you might come in for a moment.'

She pulled the door all the way open. Out of courtesy I stepped inside and went to the cradle where I saw the beautiful child for the first time. Her hair was the colour that touches the clouds after sunset and her skin was blue-white like the snow, with a slight flush of red on her cheeks.

'She is beautiful, my lady,' I said.

A movement behind the cradle caught my eye. One of the doors of the bed opened a little to reveal a dim figure watching us. Olwen did not notice at first, then she saw where I was looking.

'That is my husband's mother,' she said, 'who has come to help me keep watch over the child. She will not talk to you and it would be better if you would not look at her as she is not used to strangers near her. My lord has told me I am very lucky that she has agreed to come and help. She watches by night and I watch by day.'

I looked at Olwen and saw she was not dismayed by the presence of the old one in her house. To change the course of the conversation once more I said,

'Do you have a name for your daughter.'

'I have not given her a name yet, as it may be a means for

some other creature to summon her away.'

The doors of the bed flew open and the old one climbed out. Her face was hidden by a long black veil but I saw her eyes glittering behind it as she walked to the door. Olwen said,

'She is better pleased to go out when there is someone here to help me guard the child.'

Now I had a chance to say a word of warning and I seized it without hesitation, saying softly,

'My lady, already they say in the mead hall that you are my concubine. You must take care to guard your honour better than you have. Forgive me for speaking this way, but you do not see how many enemies you have.'

'I thank you for your concern, but it is not necessary. My husband may have cooled towards me, but it will not last. He will turn his face to me again, and when he does, I will remember my friends.'

'I am your friend, lady, but not because of future hope. You need advice if you are to survive.'

'I have done no harm to anyone here so I cannot have enemies. The best guard of my honour is my honesty. If my husband's mother sees for herself that we talk easily and openly, she can witness that there is nothing between us.'

I wondered at her simplicity.

'My lady, anyone in a powerful position will always have enemies. Envy will breed hatred whether you do harm or no.'

'Who would envy me?' she asked. 'I have lost two children and with every day that passes my chance to find them again shrinks. I live in daily fear of the loss of my daughter, and because of it I may not walk in the light of day. My lord despises me and shares his bed with another woman. I live only in the hope that one day things will be better. Is this a life to envy?'

'It is not, my lady, but misery such as yours is the lot of many who have power over their fellows. The envy people feel is of that power itself and they account the unhappiness that accompanies it as nothing.

'Consider your state. You are still acknowledged as Culhuch's wife...'

165

Before I could open her eyes to her position the door opened and the old one returned. It seemed to me that as she came in her gleaming eyes studied us closely from behind the veil. Olwen, in the cause of honesty, said,

'I see your meaning, Merthun, but I have faith in my lord's great wisdom. He will see at once the falseness in any accusations against me, I am sure of that.'

After that night Olwen spoke to me whenever I arrived. As the days went by I spent more and more time inside the house talking with her. She assured me that the old one would bear witness that our talk was innocent and after a while I believed her. The three of us often shared our supper and afterwards Olwen and I would talk far into the night. She asked me about the voyages I had made with Culhuch, and I told her everything I could. Her eyes shone when I told her about the foreign places we had seen and I was glad to be able to bring some light into the darkness of her prison. Sometimes the child was awake when I was there and I would bounce her on my knee as people do to make children laugh.

So it is that men trammel themselves.

The blow fell when we were at our easiest together. Olwen withdrew to bed and I sat down at the table with my book as usual. There was a hard frost that night and Culhuch's mother silently offered me a cup of hot wine. I thought that the old one had come to enjoy my tales and nonsense as much as Olwen, and accepted the cup as I had so many before. I emptied it with one draught then, as I read on, I was stricken by an overwhelming drowsiness. Nothing I could do would keep me awake, neither pinching myself, nor pulling my hair, nor biting my tongue. Soon my head struck the table and I was sound asleep.

I awoke later to the sound of crying. I tried to lift my head, but found it as heavy as if it were made of lead. At last I twisted it round enough to see most of the room. The doors of the bed stayed closed in spite of the crying and the door to the outside hung open. I tried with every atom of my will to get to my feet, but it was useless. My limbs were of the same substance as my head, and any attempt to move them was met by giddiness and a terrible desire to vomit. I stayed still and kept my eyes on the cradle, and that took all my strength.

Something was standing in the doorway. To this day I cannot say what it was, for in my bewitched state I could not even say if the creature were large or small. The harder I looked at it the more its shape wavered as if the impact of my sight on it made it change. A groan came from my slackened mouth. I closed my eyes. When I opened them again I saw something standing beside the cradle with the child in its arms. The child's bright head was lifted up and scanning the room. I think she was crying but the noise in my head was too loud for me to be sure. The dark figure holding her towered to the rooftree one minute, and the next seemed lower than the edge of the crib. I drove all my will into my arm and managed to lift it from the table. It fell to my side. The figure turned towards me and I saw something black and rainbow shimmering like the skin of a beetle. Again I groaned and darkness overwhelmed me.

For hours after that I lay between waking and dreaming. Now I thought that the child was in the crib and being lifted once more; now the house was in darkness and I could see nothing. Sometimes I thought I saw the thief and it was Culhuch's mother, then I saw the thief as a man with his face covered. Sometimes the thief was Olwen. Until daybreak stood grey in the doorway I struggled to distinguish dream from truth with no success. And then at last I slept.

I was awakened by a rough hand shaking me. I found that I was lying on the floor at the side of the bed and the old one was standing shrieking by the fire. My clothes were sodden and I looked down to find that I was drenched in wine. Above me the doors of the bed hung open and I dragged myself to my feet to look inside. There lay the lady Olwen, her body naked and her mouth open and snoring. There was a reek of wine about her and her hands were covered in blood.

The child's body was never found, though the search went on all that day and the next. Olwen's circumstances did not change, for she was still confined to her house with her husband's mother watching her. Indeed, very little in my own life changed, since I was not restrained in any way and I still ate in the hall with the warriors, but now no one spoke even a single word to me. Then Culhuch returned and no one would look at me either.

The morning after his return I found I was followed by a guard no matter where I went. Even when I went to the privy he stood outside and waited for me. When I returned to the hall I found the warriors ranged round the walls and Culhuch seated at the high table. His mother, veiled in black as always, sat at his right hand and his concubine stood at his back. Olwen knelt in the straw in front of him. I expected to be made to kneel beside her, but instead I was led to one side and made to stand facing the table. I saw that Olwen was pale and hollow-cheeked and that her hands were still stained with her child's blood.

Culhuch started to speak and at once silence fell. He said, 'Everyone here knows by now that my daughter is dead – murdered by her mother. I will not tell you how this has wounded me. That I, trusting and openhanded, have been betrayed by this poisonous leech of a woman who shared my bed. I should have seen all those years ago when she visited me in my dreams that no good could come of it. Who but a vile, calculating witch would have come to me that way? An honest woman would have sent a messenger – a trusted servant who would bring me to her. It is clear that this woman could not find a servant as foul as herself to do her bidding so she appeared to me in my sleep like a succubus. Being no more than a foolish man I was charmed by her and thought that she was beautiful beyond all other women. As if bleached eyes and flax-coloured hair could ever be lovely to me! And in my enchanted state I went to her father's hall in the forest and took her away before he glutted himself on her in incestuous union. Two of my finest men, my oldest companions, died that day for this ingrate. And how am I repaid?

'I will tell you. One: she has maligned the venerable old woman who bore me and called her a liar and a witch. Two: she has seduced and destroyed a most valued member of this company by stupefying him with wine and offering him her body.'

At this all faces in the hall save Olwen's turned to me. I felt my cheeks burning with shame at being the centre of this audience. I tried to speak, but Culhuch waved me to silence saying,

'You will have a chance to tell your story later, Merthun. For now we have come to the worst crime this monster has committed. She has murdered the three children she bore me. I do not know what infamous rites she practises but I have heard of rituals where they drink the blood of children as joyfully as if it were fine wine. All shame is forgotten, indeed by that time they are so removed from human virtue that even copulation between brother and sister, and parent and child is encouraged. I do not wish to think about such things. But there she stands, herself the living evidence that this vileness exists. Let us hear what she has to say.'

A man stepped forward and pulled Olwen to her feet. She stood swaying slightly in front of the table, and did not seem to know what was taking place. Then all at once she appeared to shake off her stupor and pulled herself erect.

'I have not killed my children,' she said.

Culhuch gave a mighty roar of laughter.

'Foolish lies,' he cried, 'the witness of the deed is still on your hands.'

Olwen looked at her hands as if she had never seen them before. Then she held them to her nose and shuddered at what she smelled there.

'That blood is not my child's blood,' she said, quietly, 'it is the blood of a sheep or a lamb. If you would but smell my hands for yourself...' and she held her hands out to her husband.

He recoiled, saying,

'How can you do such a thing, woman? To ask a grieving father to smell the blood of his dead child – what depravity have we here?'

A murmur of outrage went round the hall.

'Am I not a grieving mother?' asked Olwen, 'And have I not lost all my little ones as you have? My grief is so great I feel bands of iron crushing the heart inside me, but this does not blind me to the truth. I tell you this is not even the blood of a human being,' and once more she offered her hands to him.

'Bring water and wash her hands,' cried Culhuch. 'I can no longer bear to see the trace of my lovely child's murder.'

Women rushed to obey him and he turned his attention to me.

'And you, Merthun, do you deny the truth of this terrible accusation?'

I stepped forward and said,

'Culhuch, you may be right that the woman killed your child. It is sure I was bewitched by something that night, for what I saw remains only as a tangle in my mind, therefore I cannot argue with any man who says he knows what happened. But there are two things I saw which I clearly remember. When the child was taken from her cradle the door to Olwen's bed was closed. Whether she was within or without I cannot say, but the door was not opened until the morning, when I was found. The other thing I am sure of is that I did not copulate with her. Those who discovered us will witness the truth that I was not in the bed with her and that I was fully clothed even though she was naked. Also I was drunk on wine and, being only a simple man, my manhood was gone from me. I could not have done it.'

I saw men nodding at this and I was greatly relieved. I felt bold enough to add,

'As to the murder – whenever I saw her with the child, Olwen seemed to be a most loving and tender mother. I cannot believe that she would kill her own offspring.'

'Did you see mother and child together often?' asked Culhuch.

'Almost every day I was on guard there at the house.'

Culhuch turned to Olwen.

'So my mother was right. She said that you had been planning the seduction of this poor man for weeks. It was not the impulse of the night that made you try to ensnare him.'

Olwen was shaking the water off her hands. She sighed and said,

'I will not say any more. Any words I speak can be like a

knife in my hand that twists itself and strikes against me. Those who wish to bring about my destruction have me in their power for the present. I deny that I seduced him or wished to do so, that is all.'

Culhuch was enraged by her calm and his face became red and swollen.

'Do you deny giving him wine to make him foolish so that he would do your bidding?'

She smiled at him and shook her head. I said,

'Sir, I was given wine that night, but it was not she who gave it to me. Your lady mother handed me the cup.'

With a terrible scream the old one leapt to her feet. Everyone looked in terror at her as her dreadful cry echoed from the sky to the sides of the dale. She raised her right hand and seemed to grasp at the air then she lowered it and pointed at me with the two outer fingers of her fist. I felt a blow in the middle of my body and my knees turned to water so that I sank to the ground. There was a foul writhing sensation in my loins. I tried to fold myself up to protect my soft parts and found I could not straighten my back. Every muscle locked in agonising cramp. Suddenly the sensations left me and I was left with a need to vomit.

When the horror subsided I looked up to see the old one whispering in her son's ear. He nodded sagely at what she said and spoke to me.

'The lady, my mother, tells me that you must be excused. You were the victim of enchantment and it is still working in you as your collapse has just proved. You may sit down if you wish to.'

I stumbled to the bench at the wall and fell on to it. Culhuch turned his attention to Olwen.

'No man has stood up to champion you, indeed only one man has spoken a word on your behalf, and since you have clearly bewitched him his word does not count. In most cases of this kind your wronged husband would have you executed at once for your foul deeds and your body would be burned to remove the taint of it from the land.

'But you are a very fortunate woman, as I am not made of

171

such unforgiving stuff. I believe that even the worst sinner must be given the chance to make some reparation for their crime before they die. Therefore I will not kill you at once, but I will give you a penance to perform.'

'I must thank my husband for his clemency,' said Olwen. 'I know it comes from the kindness he once felt for me, even though it has been destroyed by those close to him now.'

Culhuch started to speak then closed his mouth and began again.

'At the foot of the dale there are three rivers to cross. One runs over firm shale and is easy to ford, one runs under a good stone bridge which I caused to be built, but the third runs through slime and mud. At high tide those wishing to cross may swim over with their horses, but at low tide the water is shallow and the mud is deep. Then horses must be dismounted to stop them sinking in mud to the neck, and their riders become soiled in the mud. You will live in the hut beside the road there, and when the tide is low you will carry the riders on your back through the mud and over the river. You will do this service for them at any time of the day or night that they may choose and you will do it until I say you may stop. On that day you will no longer be my wife.

'So that you may be protected against footpads or any revenge my loyal followers may wish to visit on you on my behalf, I will give you as concubine to the man you lusted after.'

I found all eyes on me again. I searched for my voice.

'Sir, I am not worthy of this kind attention,' I said. 'I have confessed that I was lax when I guarded the woman. Perhaps I did not lie with her, but I did talk to her and was idle with her when I should have been guarding the door. I do not deserve any woman in reward for such poor service, let alone the Lady Olwen.'

'Believe me, you will not have an easy task,' said Culhuch. 'Resisting the wicked schemes of this woman will take great strength. You will find that I am not kind.'

'But, sir, to give me a house and a woman when I have been a poor servant to you – it is too much!'

Culhuch grew impatient.

'Will you take the wretched creature, or no? I tell you, if you will not have her I will give her to my warriors to do with as their fancy takes them.'

I could not leave the woman I had spent so many pleasant hours with to such a fate. I stepped forward and took her hand. Then Culhuch turned to Olwen and asked her if she had anything to say.

'I must thank my lord and husband for sparing my life,' she answered. 'I promise to make my penance with all of my strength, and I hope that one day I will see him and his children smiling at me once more.'

This was not what my master had expected, I could see. Most women would have wept and wailed and begged for another chance. This dignity also made an impression on the onlookers and they stepped aside to let us leave. Olwen's kist had been packed and left ready for her at the door. I collected my horses and we set off down to the sea, and only when we were among the trees did she give way to her grief. I consoled her the best I could, saying,

'We are alive, Olwen, and yesterday I expected us both to be ashes by this hour. We must make the best of the time ahead of us, and perhaps you will see your children again, as you said.'

'This is true,' she answered, 'but if I am to stay tending the ford at my husband's pleasure, I do not see how I am to go to find them.'

'If fate will have it so, then the chance will come. In the meantime it is best to take each day as a gift. I have found the truth of this myself, for I chafed for many years at my mother's side until fate brought Culhuch across my path.'

'I will do my best to be patient as you advise,' she said, 'although God will witness I will not find it easy.'

And so we began our life together. There was a little hut beside the ford where we were to live. Part of the roof was missing and I went to fetch reeds to mend it. I had nothing to cut the reeds with but my sword and I was angry that I had to spoil my fine blade on this chore.

That evening she made the one small bed up and we lay down together. I felt a stirring begin in my loins, but at once it was followed by violent sickness and I turned my back to her. After a while I heard her weeping.

'Do not despair, Olwen,' I said, 'your children will be returned to you.'

'I am sure of that,' she answered, 'the cause of my tears now is that you have turned your back on me. It is clear that even you believe the tales of my wickedness, though you have spent many pleasant hours with me.'

'Olwen,' I cried, 'I am only a man, and the truth about your wickedness is between you and the God you worship. I do not fathom it. I turned my back on you tonight, and will do so every night because you are another man's wife.'

Olwen took my hand and covered it with her tears. She said,

'You are an honourable man, Merthun. I have been very lucky to find such a guardian and I ask you to forgive me for not seeing that before now. It is only that I long to find just one mortal who will believe in my innocence.'

She raised her hands to her face then offered them to me.

'The smell of sheep's blood is still there. But who has done this thing, and why?'

She spoke the truth about the blood. The smell of slaughtered sheep was as strong as if it were freshly killed. But who could say who had killed the sheep and dipped her hands into its carcase? It could have been done to her or she, if she were guilty, could have done it herself. The only evidence I could trust was the woman I had known for the last two months. She could not have done it. I shook my head to clear the fog out. This much was sure, we were going to have to live together for a long time. I said,

'I am as puzzled as you are, Olwen, but one day we will find out. In the meantime I am sure that you did not kill your children. Your loving nature would not let you do such a terrible act.'

She threw her arms about my neck and hung there sobbing.

'Thank you, Merthun. God in his mercy has sent me one

mortal who believes in my innocence. I pray that others will soon follow your example.'

I wished I did not feel so sick.

The trading season started and Culhuch did not send for me. That year we were perhaps to have gone near the home of my ancestors and I was sorely disappointed not to be with him. I told myself that he was making sure of Olwen's obedience and that the next season he went out I would be with him, but I did not believe it.

Olwen did her penitential task with patience. It was fortunate that she did not need to do the task often in those first weeks, for it left her exhausted and covered in filth. When she came out of the mud after taking a traveller across she would run through the trees to a pool she had found there and strip off her clothes. With shaking hands she would scrape the mud and worms and rotting slime from her thighs and wash herself from head to toe in the stream. Then she would throw the clothes in also and pummel them and trample on them as if she would drive them into the gravel on the bottom. I have never seen anyone so appalled by a little mud.

I asked her once why she was so horrified. She said,

'I was reared in my father's fortress which is high in the clean air of the mountains. I am unused to this muck.'

'Yet I recall that when the plague was here you tended the sick. Then you often had to clean sweat, ordure and spittle from round their bodies and you did not flinch. Here you have only mud to deal with and you shudder as if you would die.'

'The service I performed during the plague was to restore life to the suffering and to bring comfort to the dying. This mud is made up of nothing but dead matter. It is composed of the bodies of dead trees and plants; it is the dead flesh of the mountains; it is the rotting remains of birds and animals and humans, and all are being carried off to their graveyard in the sea. Nothing about it but speaks to me of mortality. It smells of death, it is the colour of death and the only life in it is the worms who eat the dead.'

'Why should this dismay you so? Death is the end of life as everyone past childhood knows. Everything that lives will one day die. That is the brotherhood we share with each other and with the living things around us. It is a source of joy to me that when my time comes I will not be alone. I will be in company with the whole fabric of the world.'

'You seem to think you will be extinguished like the flame on a taper. Are you not afraid?' she asked me, astonished.

'I am not afraid. Indeed I will be sorry to leave the pleasures of life, but for a man in my station of life these pleasures are few. If I grow old – and if your husband does not restore me to the war band I will – they will leave me altogether and be replaced by pains which outnumber them by far. Then I shall not be sorry to depart. Who would wish to live forever?'

'Do you not believe in a God of any kind?'

'I have met men from every quarter of the world and talked to them in the long nights of winter about the God they worship. I have read my father's books which list each demon that inhabits the crevices of the world, but none of these agree about the nature of God. I have yet to find a religion which is anything other than a way to calm the fears of frightened children.'

'About death?'

'About death and plague and war and famine and ageing and giving birth and losing money and all the other fears that beset humankind.'

'I must consider what you say,' said Olwen and for many days she did not speak much to me. Then one night as we lay down to sleep she said,

'When I was young I sickened of my father and my family. It seemed to me that the way we lived was wrong and that one day I would find the one, true way to live and think. I studied with Christians and I even thought of becoming an anchoress, so deep was my longing to change my way of life. Then Culhuch came and talked to me of my beauty and his wisdom, and how together we would build a kingdom that would last for a thousand years. I was still young and foolish, and I believed him, but look what it has brought me.

'When my husband began to make my life miserable, I thought I deserved it because I had betrayed the Christian

176

sisterhood at Caerluel to go with him. Now you say another thing altogether. What am I to think?'

'You ask a question I would be foolish to answer. All I can say to you is this – many men have found their own way to their own truth, and died with a smile on their lips. Who had the right answers I cannot say, but of this I am sure, they did not come to it overnight, nor even in the course of a short year. Each one has taken a long time to study the matter and has not rushed to an answer. My advice to you is not to hurry. You have some time ahead of you before you die, therefore use it and do not try to fly before you can walk. Above all learn to enjoy each hour as it comes. That way you will learn without pain.'

'I think that is good advice,' she said, 'but I doubt if I can take it. My life here is wretched. Every day I fear my strength will give out as I am carrying a passenger and I will sink with them into the mud. When that happens Culhuch's final wrath will be visited on me and there will be no more chances to learn. Also I think my penance here is deserved, not because I killed my children, but because by consorting with Culhuch I brought about my father's death and left my sisters unprotected.'

'Forgive me, but I thought that your father was a wicked man who forced you all into incest with him. Surely you have protected your sisters from that.'

'This is a cursed lie,' she cried, 'my father would not have used any of us in that way. All that talk of incest was a story Culhuch made up so that his men would follow him willingly and I, wretch that I am, did not deny it. To do so would have showed the world that our love was less than perfect, and my pride would not let me do so. That is why I take my punishment now, and sometimes I wish it were harder.'

I had no argument for her, but I wished I had. Her misery in those days was terrible. The summer was at its height and some days she had more than twenty passengers to carry in either direction. Some of them took pity on her for her state and gave her gifts of money to recompense her. Others delighted in her humiliation and as she carried them across would use her worse than they would their oldest mule. I would have liked to stop them, but I was sure that it would not please my master if I did. At least Olwen seemed less disgusted by the muck she waded in, and one day I heard her speaking to a worm she found on her thigh as 'brother'.

Autumn came and the traffic crossing the river grew less. In the mornings the grass was laden with grey frost and leaves hung lifeless waiting for the gale to carry them off. As I went about my duties in the valley, I felt that I was being watched. This puzzled me, as I knew Culhuch and the trading party were still in the east and would be so till the next year. Then one evening as I rode back to the house I saw three horses tethered to a tree beside the track. I heard men's voices coming muffled through the trees. I retreated back down the track and hid my horse before creeping towards the sound.

Three men stood at the edge of the trees looking at our house. I did not recognise them, but as I came nearer to them I heard the name of Culhuch. One of them was saying,

'If we do it now we can be sure that we have done what he wanted.'

'Leave it too long and someone else will do it and get all the reward,' said another.

'What if it is not what he wanted?' asked the third.

'Who could doubt it? You heard what was said. 'If anyone should wish to visit my revenge on her.' He's sure to do well by us – might even give us a place in his hall.'

'What about the guard?' said the doubter.

'He is up at the pens doing his counting. You saw him there yourself.'

'What if he should return?'

'What if he does? There is only one of him.'

'Very well,' said the reluctant one, 'but we must go and get the horses. I will not begin if we cannot make a speedy escape.'

Grudgingly the others went back with him for the horses and I was alone. Clearly they were planning to kill Olwen. I should have been on my feet and running to the house with my sword drawn, but I lay still in the dead bracken. I heard them returning on horseback. I saw the blue line of smoke rising from the roof of my house as Olwen prepared the evening meal and, as happened before, my limbs and head became so heavy I could not lift them. Somewhere, someone was working enchantment on me so that I could not help and to my shame I lay in the forest, a log among logs. One day I may forget that dreadful time; for now it still grieves me beyond healing that I left her alone in that hour.

The assassins rode on to the green in front of the house and reined their horses. I heard them call to Olwen and she came out knotting up her skirts ready to do her duty. One of them said something to her and pulled his sword out of its sheath. She shook her head and stepped forward.

Her actions then were so swift and so violent I believe she had been possessed. She seized the reins of one horse in one hand and the two others in the other and forced their heads back. The horses reared and the men had to struggle to keep their seats – they were probably only pikemen and unused to moving on horseback. Olwen continued to move forward, backing the horses towards the river. The horses shook their heads to rid themselves of her grip but she hauled on the reins and kept all three on the line she had chosen. The tide was almost full and the river was swollen with rain from the mountains so that they soon came to the margin. With a mighty shout Olwen released the reins and the horses reared high, throwing their riders down into the greedy mud.

Moving with great speed Olwen caught the horses again and dragged them along. She pulled them in such a line that the terrified creatures trampled on the fallen men. Backwards and forwards she led them over the slippery mud where the men struggled to stand in vain. Time after time the men rose from the mire, and each time they were struck down by a horse passing by. Finally the men rose no more, but Olwen kept dragging the horses over the place where they fell. Soon they were wading through a sea of churned red. Back and forth, back and forth in the foaming red slime she led them till nothing moved and only a broken bundle of rags tangled the feet of the horses. At last she released them and they fled, white-eyed, to the sea.

As soon as I could move my feeble limbs I crawled back through the trees to my horse. I sat on the ground beside it shaking like a man in fever and my teeth clashed together. I clenched them to keep them still and waited for the shivering to subside. When it left me I had to fight off a terrible tiredness that made me want only to lie in the grass and sleep until the last days of the world. Then my horse nuzzled me and I woke enough to pull myself on.

When I returned to the house, twilight had washed forest, sea and beach the same colour of blue. Inside the house it was dark and the only sign of Olwen was a high-pitched moaning. I found her lying in the bed with her kerchief pulled over her face. Lighting the taper I bent over and whispered her name. She sat up at once and clung to me and I thought she was weeping, but when she looked up her face was dry. Her hands were pieces of ice.

'Men came to kill me,' she whispered, in a voice like the dead leaves rustling outside the window.

'What happened?' I asked. The falsehood came easily.

'I killed them with the horses and the mud. The means of my penance became my weapon for murder. What will become of me? What will become of me?'

'I saw no sign of this. You must be mistaken.'

'The tide is at flood, when it ebbs we will see the evidence of my crime.'

'It was no crime if they came to kill you. You had to defend yourself, for I was not there to help you as I should have been.'

'But I killed them with neither fear nor rage. It was as if I were a rock or a tangle of seaweed.'

'The fear has come late, little one. You are trembling now like a leaf in a high wind. It is often like this for warriors, especially when they go into combat for the first time.'

'I killed these men, but I did not kill my children. You must believe that.'

'I believe it. Three foolish men came to kill you for a reward. They believed that your husband wanted your death, but they were deceived. Your husband will believe that you were only defending yourself. Never fear, they were kinless men and you will not need to pay recompense for them.'

So great was her misery she did not ask how I could know this. The shuddering ceased at last but the skin of her face was burning hot. I built the fire up and warmed some beer to put her to sleep. When I heard her breathing become shallow and regular I lay beside her and wondered what would become of both of us. The hopeless grey of dawn lit the house and at last I slept for a while.

No more travellers came to trouble her that season. There was heavy rain early in the winter and that must have taken the dead out to sea for they never rose to accuse her. The river banks became solid with ice and once or twice the road through the dale was blocked with snow so that our supplies ran low. Olwen was so wrapped up in her guilt this hardship passed her unnoticed. Yet as the thaw set in and the earth smells surrounded us again, we began to laugh together as we had done in the spring before. News came that the concubine up at the fortress was great with child and would soon be delivered. Olwen shrugged when I told her and said that she would wait until the child was safe before she decided what to do. We sat under our ice-hung eaves and watched the drops of melt water falling.

The thaw was complete and the river swollen to its greatest when we got news of the birth. It was a boy and a sturdy one at that. Olwen sat in the corner for a long time, brooding. Then once more horsemen came to our door saying,

'Olwen, come out and speak to us.'

'You had better go,' I said, 'I will come at your back in case it is another assassin.'

Outside we were met by the two thegns Culhuch had left to watch the fortress. The elder spoke to Olwen, saying,

'You must give us the gold silk dress and the rainbow shawl your husband gave you on the first day of the wedding feast. The lady Teleri has given my master a son to replace those you foully murdered, and his mother says that the clothes are now her due.'

'The clothes you speak of were given to me as a bridal gift by my husband, and are due to no other woman.'

181

'My master brought that dress and that shawl from the farthest lands of the world. He risked his life and his men to bring it to this valley and it belongs to his true mistress. You are not she. She is in the fortress now with her son and she grieves that she is being slighted by your keeping these garments.'

Olwen tapped her foot on the ground and frowned. For one fearful moment I thought she would defy them, but she turned to me and said,

'Merthun, please be so generous as to fetch the chest of wedding gifts from my lord.'

I did so and she took it from me. She pulled the dress and shawl out and said,

'Is this the dress of which you speak? This shawl – is it the one for which Teleri mourns? There must be no doubt that these are the ones.'

'They are the same. Give them to us at once.'

Olwen held up her hand,

'One moment,' she said, and my blood ran cold in my veins. 'Was there nothing said about the jewellery my husband gave me? Does not the lady – if such she may be called – Teleri grieve for that also? Do not her poor eyes rain with tears when she thinks of the linen and the sweet white wool that should be gracing her kist at this time?'

The thegn shifted in his saddle.

'They did speak of it,' he said, staring at his hands, 'but I was told to come back tomorrow and seize the jewellery.'

'I am sure you were also told to come the day after that and make off with the linen.'

The man did not look up and his companion said something to him which I could not hear.

'The intention was to make me suffer longer by taking one thing at a time,' said Olwen and slammed the lid. 'You had best take it now and save yourself a journey. You can tell them you took my dowry from my clutching fingers, piece by piece, if you so wish.'

The chest was large, being about the length of my arm and half as wide. It was made of oak wood and bound with iron. I am not a weakling, but when I brought it with her it had cost me effort to lift it. Now Olwen took it in her two hands and raised it over her head like a bundle of bracken.

'Take it, if you can,' she cried.

The men flinched as she swung it and threw it far over their heads into the mud of the river bank. Again I was amazed at the power of her arms.

'I have no use for the cursed stuff,' she cried, 'and believe me cursed is what it truly is. I wish your mistress joy to wear it, but warn her of my fate. Tell her that from the first day she wears that finery her destruction will be in sight.'

'What sorcery are you threatening us with now, Olwen?'

'No sorcery, Gwyar. You were there when my husband took me from my father's hall. What sorcery did he use against my father then?'

'None,' said Gwyar, his face as still as a stone, 'you were taken in fair combat.'

'Then none is used now. Only the hand of mortal man will work against Teleri, nothing more, and I am trying to warn her as I was warned. No doubt she will pay as little heed as I did myself.

'She thinks that she will please my husband with a child of his body, but you must tell her that there are powers abroad that will prevent her joy.'

'The lady will not heed your foolish threats,' said Gwyar, 'and I warn you that if you are seen near the fortress, you will be killed outright.'

Olwen laughed,

'I do not need to stir a foot, nor lift a hand. The fate that comes against her is not my will. It was written in the hour she first cast her greedy eyes over my man.'

Gwyar looked at her sombrely for a long while, then shook his head as if waking from a dream.

'We are going now,' he said, 'before you say any more and trap us with your cunning.'

'Fare well,' said Olwen, and she turned away at once. The men scrambled off after the chest to catch it before it sank into the mud. I watched them struggle to retrieve it then followed the lady indoors. I found her at the table packing her last clothes into a bundle. She also packed the doll I remembered had belonged to her infant.

'Are you going to leave me, Olwen?' I cried.

'I must, Merthun, for now my marriage is ended. I did not care about the clothing nor the jewellery. In my father's hall I had that and much, much more. It was the fact that my husband had given them to me as a bridal gift that made me cherish them. Now that the old one and the one she protects have taken them I no longer feel I am Culhuch's bride.'

'But this may not be Culhuch's wish. The concubine was not well born, and I do not think that he would call her bride if he were here, even though she has a son of him.'

'Perhaps you are right, but my lord is not here, nor will he be for many months. In the meantime I am unprotected but for yourself, and what will you do if they send a troop to dispose of me?'

'I admit I am only a poor sort of guardian, Olwen, but I am answerable for your life. What shall I say to them when they come to claim you?'

'Tell them that I used sorcery on you. You will be believed readily enough, as you know.'

'How will you get out of the valley? You know there are sentinels on every peak.'

'It will be dark soon and fog is rising from the river. It will be easy enough.'

'Where will you go?'

'First I shall go to my father's hall. It is a long and difficult journey, overland, but it is possible I may find my children there. Finding them is now the only thing that I care about.

'Ah, Merthun, believe me, this is the happiest day I have known for many years. I am rid of my obligations to this people for freeing me from my father; I am free of the shackle of marriage to a tyrant. I can take the road through the hills and follow my desires. You should envy me.'

'The year is yet young and the hills are full of dangers. I should go with you, but I must give an account of my actions to Culhuch.'

'I do not wish you to come with me. I shall be safe enough on my own. And even if the wolves do take me, what of it? You have said yourself that everything dies.'

In this sudden manner she said goodbye and I have not seen her since. Culhuch made a great show of rage when he returned two years later, but I think he was glad to be rid of a complication. Teleri, the concubine, died with the next child she bore him and his mother is rearing his son.

I have stayed on in the house we shared, waiting for Olwen to return. It was not until she left, with head up and a free swinging stride, that I saw how much she meant to me.

There were tears in his eyes as he spoke. We stayed silent while he shook his head and rubbed his face, then he said,

'It is late. We must hurry on to the fortress to make ourselves known before it gets dark. Culhuch will not let strangers stay overnight until he knows all about them. I fear he may not take kindly to a monk in the hall. You will have to take care not to provoke him.'

I smiled at Merthun and said,

'Men of my order have spent years studying humility. I will not offend him with a loud voice or a strutting gait as others have done. Indeed I am anxious to meet him if he is a tyrant, since our family have always taken it as their first duty to convert pagan rulers.'

'Culhuch is no pagan. He was converted many years ago before he took his wife. He is a Christian tyrant.'

'Has he built churches? Has he raised crosses? Has he endowed land for the support of monasteries?'

'There is a cross on the far side of the dale, which he paid masons to make for him. There is a chapel in a corner of the fortress where he spends a night in vigil before we leave on a long voyage. He has not set up a monastery as yet and I do not think he plans to do so.'

'If he has done what you say he may safely claim to be a Christian ruler. I will do what I can to persuade him over the monastery while I am here.'

'I hope you will not. You will only rouse his anger. He is nearly sure that Olwen has taken herself to one. He thinks of them as his enemy.'

'It is my sworn duty to try, nevertheless. Do not alarm yourself, Merthun, he is in God's hands, as we all are, and He will shine the light of His grace into this man's soul.'

Merthun grunted and Barve looked at me with her hand shading her eyes. They spent the rest of the journey to the fortress talking to each other, pagan to pagan. I was content to let this go on, for I was reading the office and praying for the wisdom to show them their error.

The fortress was visible miles ahead. It was built on a rocky outcrop and hung high above the road that wound past it up the pass. In that bleak valley it stood out clearly, built as it was of white stone. The walls around it were higher than two men, but they were in a bad state of repair. The iron staples had been taken out of the corners and they were out of alignment. On arrival we found that the fortress was full of square stone buildings which had stood for centuries and were beginning to decay. I concluded that it must have been built by the conquering Romans at the time they were in this country. Once someone had tried to repair the walls with free stone, but without success, and the rest of the gaps had been filled with pieces of wood. A lookout had been posted at every corner of the fort and we heard the call that said we had been seen on the road. The sun passed behind a cloud and a chilly wind sprang up and buffeted us as we climbed towards the walls. As the gates came in view the rain began. Barve pulled her veils over her head.

Our horses were taken from us as we entered. Merthun was spoken to with something like deference and it was clear that we were not in the company of a disgraced man. Nevertheless he was not addressed as an honoured member of the company and as we entered the main hall he stepped aside to leave his goods at a lowly bench. There was no sign of the master of the hall but Merthun led us through the door at the back out to a smaller house. There we found a man seated at a table. His hair was nearly all white and only his heavy black brows testified to the fact that he had once been swarthy as a raven. The table was littered with tally sticks and indented papers and there was a heap of silver coin which he rapidly covered with a piece of cloth. He frowned at Merthun and said,

'What are you doing here? You were not due to come back until the day after tomorrow. Have you lost track of time?'

'I brought these two strangers to you.'

'What is wrong with you? They could have found their own way here once you had set them on the road.'

'There was trouble with the shore watch. The lady is nobly born.'

'If she is nobly born what is she doing her with nothing but a scruffy monk and a bundle under her arm?'

Merthun stared at the wall behind his head.

'There was trouble with the shore watch,' he repeated, and looked towards the woman. There was a short pause then,

'I understand,' said Culhuch. 'Get back to your place.'

Merthun left with neither word nor glance at any of us. There was silence while we all looked at each other. The master's frowning gaze did not bode well. I had drawn a breath to begin my speech when Barve suddenly let out a moan, dropped her face into her hands and slumped against me. The man got hastily to his feet and came round the table to her side.

'Sweet lady,' he said, and put his arm round her to support her. 'I have been a poor host to one gently raised as you are. Please forgive my lack of courtesy. I assure you that the scum who have given you this trouble will be punished at once. I will have them hung up by their wrists and flayed for their vileness to your person and your property.'

He took her hand but she kept her face turned away from him.

'I pray you will do no such thing,' she murmured. 'The men were deceived by my lack of display. We arrived in a small boat, unannounced. I am sure they meant no discourtesy.'

She continued to bow her head and seemed close to fainting and I saw the man smile secretly into his beard. I prayed urgently that he would not make the same mistake as his men. He led her over to a bench and helped her to sit, but held on to her hand. Kneeling before her he said,

'My name is Culhuch, and I am lord of this dale and commander of the fleet owned by Jarl Grim. May I know the name of her whom I am privileged to call guest?'

She held her veil close in front of her mouth and said,

'My name is Barve, and my father holds much land in the heart of Alban. I am on my way to visit my sister who is married to a great lord in Gwynedd, but my father is opposed to my trip, so would not provide servants for me. He wished me to marry this year – a very sound connection for the family – but I am not ready to lose my ... maiden state.'

God preserve my eyes for what I saw then, for above the veil the bitch flushed red as if she were a shrinking virgin. Culhuch leered and put his lips to her hand.

'You are safe here with me.'

She pointed at myself. 'My chaplain also – he is my truest friend. You will take care of him?'

He turned and stared at me, and I knew at once why the men of the dale all obeyed him. I said swiftly,

'Sir, by your leave, I need nothing from you but a small shelter.'

'You shall have it,' he said.

He rose, went to the door and summoned two men. When they came into the room he spoke to them in the language of Lochlann. He told them to secure me and to fetch his mother to watch over the woman. I rejoiced then that we had been discreet and caught Barve's eye. She shook her head at me and continued to lean against the wall. I followed her gaze and saw a small child peering round the door jamb. It was a thin-faced, yellow-skinned, squint-eyed brat and it was watching everything that went on. When it saw it was observed, it walked into the room and adressed Culhuch in the British tongue.

'Grandmother has gone down to the pens. She said I was to stay with you.'

'Why has she done that and left you alone?'

'She heard that there was a man there who can make horses

out of wood. They say they are as good as life and I want one.'

'Your grandmother is too kind, but she should not have gone herself.'

'She said she was the only one who could persuade him to do it.'

'Your life does not depend on a carved horse. Go to your house and stay there.'

'I never go out. Why must I always stay at home?' wailed the child.

'Do as I tell you,' said his father as mild as milk, and.the child ran off.

The two warriors led me to a lean-to beside the wall. They pushed me in and when I heard them bar the door behind me, I sat down and resigned myself to another night in confinement. Somewhere outside I heard a wailing and I assumed it was the wretched child. After a while the door was unbarred and I was taken to a small stone house in the compound where I found Barve sitting sobbing. When I stumbled through the door she ran to me and hung about my neck as if I were her lover, not her chaplain. She whispered in my ear,

'Stroke my head and comfort me, you fool. Never mind your vows, or we will both die.'

I did as she said, promising to do penance for it later. One of the guards said in poor Scottish,

'She call for her chaplain and cried until we fetch you. You stop that fussing before Culhuch comes and asks why.'

They hurried off. Barve went to the door and looked outside before closing it and fastening it tight. She pressed her mouth against my ear and said,

'That man, Culhuch, is indeed the one who carried off my sister. I thought for one moment he might recognise me, though we met a long time ago and I still wore the body of a child. We must be very careful not to let him know me.'

'What of Merthun? Will he not tell him what he knows?'

'He will not. As we rode here he said to me that we could find trouble here. He would not tell me exactly what sort of trouble, but he seemed to think it would be best for us to say as little as possible. For the sake of my poor sister he will keep silent, I think. I will try to keep you with me all the time, though this may be difficult.'

'We are in God's hands,' I reminded her.

'I do not like this place,' she said, 'it is too much like my father's fortress. The walls are so thick and the windows so small – I feel trapped.'

'It was built many centuries ago by men who came from Rome,' I told her. 'It was then that the truth of the Anointed One was learned in this country, and the founder of our order was shown the path of grace. Once we had the knowledge to build walls as strong as these for he brought masons from the Holy City. Our first church was built in this fashion.'

'Perhaps this is a comfort to you, monk, but for myself, I must say that this fortress seems to me a prison, and from what I have heard of Culhuch, he shares my point of view.'

Just then, as if at a summons, there came a violent knocking at the door. The woman picked up the psalter that had been lying on the floor beside her and pulled mine out of my satchel. She pushed it into my hand and then pointed at the door. While I went to unbolt it she arranged her veils to hide her face and opened her book. Culhuch was at the threshold, and he frowned terribly when he saw me.

'Why are you here?' he shouted.

'My lady sent for me,' I answered, and the tremor in my voice was not a deception.

'She should not have done so,' he said, 'my mother will be here soon to be the guardian of her honour.'

'Is your lady mother baptised into the Christian faith?' I asked. He glared at me, then took command of himself again.

'Alas, she is not,' he said, and looked almost pitiful, 'and it is a great source of sorrow to me. She is a most wilful and assertive woman and takes a great deal more on herself than I would wish. It has been my hope for many years that she would one day meet a Christian lady to give her an example of gentleness and compliance. When that day comes, I am sure my mother will join me in my faith.'

'Poor man,' cried Barve, 'do you not have a wife to lead your people into the faith?'

'I had a Christian wife,' he answered, 'but to my everlasting sorrow, when our children were taken from us she was lost also. The mother of my only living son was a pagan, and I am sorry to say she died in her error. Who knows but God may now have sent me a helpmeet without my willing it?'

He smiled at Barve who made the appropriate simpering. I grew sick of this blasphemy and opened my psalter. I saw 'Deliver me, o Lord, from the evil man; preserve me from the violent men who imagine mischiefs in their heart; continually are they gathered together for war. They have sharpened their tongues like a serpent; adders' poison is under their tongues.'

Culhuch was watching me again, and when I looked up at him he said,

'Will you retire for the night?'

'My lady has asked me to watch tonight with her. She and I have travelled together for many days now, and she has learned to trust me as she would her own sister.'

For a moment he was silent, and I saw he bit his lip. Then he said,

'It must be as she wishes. She is a guest in my house and I will not deny her anything. Tomorrow my mother will be here.'

He turned on his heel and left us. Barve pushed her shawl back with a shaking hand.

'What shall we do tomorrow?' I asked.

'I think it would be best if we find materials and write to your family of what has befallen us. We may be given the chance to send a message to them, and find a little safety. If not, then at least it will keep you occupied. You may not be noticed writing away in the corner and they may forget to remove you. I will find some pious nonsense to trouble the old one when she comes.'

'I would remind you that this "pious nonsense" has kept you alive. I must ask you not be so discourteous.'

'Forgive me, Hw, I have abused your kindness. Without your help my foolishness would have betrayed me many times before now. I shall always be in your debt, and one day my family will repay yours, I swear it.'

191

I did not see what the creature might have that I could accept as payment but I said nothing. The night went by without incident and in the morning I began the account which I hope you are reading now.

Whatever faults her kindred may have, there is no doubt in my heart that the woman Olwen tried hard to become a gentle, pious woman. Her husband has not treated her well and is so far from grace that he will use our faith to forward his scheme to debauch her sister. I am sure she is not the first to have been so abused. He is one of those men we know too well who will have his way and will use any method in his power to attain it.

His mother has been installed with us. She does nothing but sit by the fire all day, with her veil over her face. Barve's 'pious nonsense' so far has consisted in joining me in saying all the hours, except the first one of the day. She insists that there are still secrets here that must be uncovered. One matter that she pointed out to me is that Culhuch claims to be a foundling, yet his 'mother' lives with him. This, and other things have her questing like a hound on a scent. She may be right, but our task is to find her sister. I wish only to follow her route as rapidly as possible so that I might return to my beloved family, but I must live with disappointment a little longer. Culhuch describes us as his guests but the truth is we are his prisoners and escape is impossible for the time being. Nevertheless, I am sure we will be delivered before long.

My fingers are swollen in the morning when I come to lift my pen. I hope and pray that it is not a return to my water ailment. Tears fill my eyes at the slightest provocation and threaten to reveal my weaknesses. The medicines you gave me are running out but I have put my faith in God's love. I am his servant and he may do with me as he wishes.

Merthun has returned and has proved to be more of a friend than I had hoped. His life with Olwen has turned his heart toward God and I begin to have hopes for his conversion. He promised to deliver this letter by the hand of a friend. It may be that you are reading it, my dear brother, and know now what difficulties I live in. If so, I beg you to pray for me and for the souls of those I am trying to help.

Valete.

Ælfrid of Rintsnoc, Hw, monk and presbyter sends greetings,

Dearly beloved brother in Christ, son of holiness, the events of this Lent will live in my memory for ever as one of the keenest deprivation. I write this letter now, sure that you will never receive it unless we are favoured with a miracle. Our only contact with the outside, Merthun, has not been seen here for nearly two weeks and I fear he has been forbidden to see us. Nevertheless I have vowed that I will make every effort to send news back to the community so I will continue to record events and pray the Almighty will grant me the sight of your face once more.

The woman and I have been confined in this house in the fortress. This has been a great trial to Barve who is accustomed to move freely about the countryside. I counsel patience every day and, to be just, she can be a model of piety and humility, as long as she knows she is observed. I can believe now that she and her terrible sisters could deceive men into thinking they were members of a holy community. I accept the days of tedium as yet another chance to prove that my love of God endures in all circumstances. Furthermore He has given me the grace to suffer now that the medicine is all but finished and the disease is manifesting itself once more. At night my heart thunders so rapidly in my breast that I think it will burst; my feet and ankles have started swelling again so that some mornings I cannot fasten my shoes. My fingers have waxed fat and I fear they will become so large I will not be able to hold a pen. Other than this I am not severely afflicted as I have no duties other than to say the offices which can be done as well by a cripple as by a whole man. Sickness is only a curse when it impedes the execution of our duty to God. For himself a man can only give thanks that he has been tested in the fire.

In particular this experience has given me an opportunity to exercise control over my rage. I recall your words to me that the best way to imagine rage is as a fire which, if it is not fuelled, will not burn. Therefore if I turn away from those things which will ignite the fire I will be safe. At all times I avoid looking into the faces of men and women; I rarely seek to correct error when I find it, and above all I remove myself from conversation. Mercifully Barve and I cannot speak to each other in the house for Culhuch has installed his mother with us as our overseer. When she leaves us for brief intervals to report on us, we have a chance to exchange words as we were wont. We have concluded that Culhuch has put the old one in with us to find out the name of Barve's father. We assume that he wishes to negotiate a ransom for her, and that once he finds out who she is our lives will be forfeit. Consequently any talk in front of his mother is all of piety and exegesis, not our worldly concerns.

By a mixture of cajoling and threats, Barve has managed to keep me at her side. Using the deceptions she employs so easily she indicated to Culhuch that she was prepared to consider coitus with him and at the same time threatened him with the might of her nameless father. All this is done with her eyes lowered and her face turned so that her veil hides it. I am styled her 'consolation' and, fearing to be recognised as a godless lout, he lets me stay with her. I do not complain, as the accomodation is better in her house than it would have been in my cell. Happily this is the man's busiest time of year so we have seen little of him. When he has more leisure, we may find persecutions beginning.

Now our days pass in the following fashion – I sleep by the fire on the trestle boards and the women sleep in the bed together – that is to say the old one lies down beside Barve, but I doubt if she sleeps. We have remarked to each other that it must have been a severe trial for her sister Olwen when she was confined with the old woman. In addition to her ceaseless vigil, even though she accompanies Barve to the bath-house, she never bathes herself, and so stinks like a fox. Her face she keeps covered with a dingy veil and from under it utters the occasional word of instruction as, 'Come', 'Sit', 'Eat'. From there also comes the rattle of bones and teeth and other amulets and I see that any notion of converting her to the true faith is futile. She wears a sleeveless tunic on the coldest day and when her arms appear from under her mantle, as when she tends the kettle, the brown flesh of her upper arm flaps loose. At least she provides us with a little diversion when – may God forgive us – we mock her behind her back.

Just like a great lady, Barve joins me for the third hour. She has a pleasing voice, mellow and clear like a boy's before manhood, and she learned the offices quickly – thus proving that her wiles are numberless. After that the women break their fast on food brought from the kitchen. Barve says that it is always cold, and on a rainy morning the bread is sodden, but the cheese is well enough. I join them in a mixt, as my illness demands it, after the middle of the day. In the afternoon we may be allowed a brief recreational walk in the company of a guard while the old one visits elsewhere. Then we may talk a little about our situation, but since nothing changes there is less and less to discuss. Nevertheless it is good to be away from the old one for a while.

As long as her presence makes our lives unwholesome we have devised a means of conversing under her gaze. You must understand, to the outsider our methods may seem close to blasphemy, but it is necessary that we resort to it from time to time. It happens as follows; while we sit or kneel at prayer after the sixth hour the woman overlooks her copy of the scripture and may discover something relevant as for instance, Jeremiah – 'Why do we sit still? Assemble yourselves, and let us enter into the defended cities, and let us be silent there.'

I will reply with Isaiah, 'And it shall come to pass in that day, that the Lord shall punish the host of the high ones.'

To that she quoted Nehemiah, 'And I went out by night by the gate of the valley, before the dragon well, and to the dung port, and viewed the walls of Jerusalem, which were broken down, and the gates thereof were consumed with fire.'

She was telling me that we could escape out by the midden where the stones of the wall have fallen out unheeded. I counselled patience thus from Job:

'And the Lord turned the captivity of Job when he prayed for his friends.'

I am sure she looks on it as no more than a diversion. It may prove to be a way to get her to attend to the Word of God, and I hope we may be forgiven if our actions are blasphemous. We must find what light we can in our affliction.

The evening refection is occasionally taken with the rest of the household in the main hall. Then we are stared at by many pairs of eyes rather than one. Barve has more hardihood than myself at these times, since she has spent all her long life in a great household, but I find it hard to eat under scrutiny and when I swallow sometimes I think I may choke. Then we are returned to our confinement.

Merthun has managed to come and speak with us once or twice. He has brought his precious books for us to study to beguile the time. I cannot read most of them for they are written in a foreign script, but Barve has some knowledge of the language and has told me all I wish to know. From what she has said, I gather that they are filled with blasphemy and heresy and should not be studied by a man of God. Those in Latin are finely written and are the works of the Greek fathers of our faith. I study them as much as I can but I find it difficult to keep my thoughts under control in our present situation. Merthun has told us that Culhuch is spending a great deal of time with the fleet in preparation for a great trading voyage, and, thanks be to God, he has not found anyone to deal for us. It is probable that we will be kept here for a long time until he decides how to dispose of us. Do not despair for us for we are not desperate in ourselves.

Valete.

It is now the feast of the Annunciation, and I have been contemplating the theme. It is not a feast which is celebrated in our community, but it seems to me that we might profit from a meditation on the event. I re-open the letter so that I may send you my thoughts on the matter in the hope that one day they may help to illumine the hardened hearts of the unregenerate.

When I was younger I often questioned the wisdom of the Almighty Father. Why did he chose to enter this kingdom in polluted flesh just like any swineherd through the body of a woman? Why should the Saviour of the City enter it through the drains? Why should one of the sex least likely to appreciate it be the first to know of the redemption of mankind? These questions so troubled me that in my thoughts I often came close to heresy. Perhaps it was true that God did not beget the man Jesus but that He chose one of those already begotten to be His Son on earth. Perhaps His Son was made out of His breath in the same way as He made Adam. Yet the illustrious fathers of former times had said not so, and I could not set my heart against their judgement. Then one day God's great wisdom and mercy were shown to me and I understood the enigma.

Propagation from the Virgin is not subject to the law of nature. As we have agreed on previous occasions, there are three orders of events: the miraculous, which are attained by God's will alone; the natural, which are accomplished by created nature and the voluntary, which are accomplished by the will of a created being. Those of the first order, being accomplished by the will of God alone, are uncontaminated in any way by the will of a created being. If they are willed by man they will immediately become corrupted because of the original sin of Adam and Eve. Therefore it was absolutely necessary that the birth of Jesus, in order to be free of contamination, should be miraculous. Thus he was conceived in the womb of a woman who had never known man. As a result of this Jesus himself was perfect. He was happy and free and just as all men should be and would have been if Eve had not listened to the Serpent. As a result of this perfection he alone was a fitting sacrifice to redeem us from the sin of our first parents.

Consider also the vessel He chose. She was not the sort of wretch whom we usually see running about the roads. Not for her the vanity that expresses itself in ornament; not for her the perfumes, the jewellery, the sleekly bound hair; not for her the seductions of the feasting hall. No, from her very first days she felt her fate upon her. She lived apart, speaking with no one, not even, after her early years, her venerable father. Her mother alone attended her, bringing her the little food she ate and praying beside her through the night when the pain of her destiny would not let her rest. On the days when she left the house to attend the temple she was covered from the top of her head to the toe of her foot with the garments of modesty.

When her heavenly Father visited her to engender His great Gift on her, she had not yet fallen into the way of women and the courses had not yet come to her. Thus she was not contaminated by the slightest sensation of lust which we know does not visit women until after they have menstruated. After the birth of her only Son, her virtue was so great that she was able to persuade her husband that they should live thereafter in complete continence as the heroes of the Church did in earliest times.

Consider now the vessel of our undoing. Eve, the devil's gateway, the first deserter of divine law, destroyer of God's image, man, on account of whose desert even the Son of God had to die. Eve, who spends her time wondering how best she might make herself the focus of man's lust and envy. Eve, the mother of sin. Only by spending her life in pain and mourning might she hope to make restitution for her loathsome crime. The two women stand together like winter and spring. It is no accident of nature that we celebrate the Annunciation at this time of the year. The ram is in the heavens and the black winter is gone. The winter is the mourning time of Eve; the spring is the bright hope of Mary. Winter itself is the very model of the fallen one. It is dangerous to man for darkness falls on him before he has finished his work. If he travels the road it is made treacherous and slimy under his feet. Even if he stays within doors, winter, like the harlot, will seek him out and, if his vigilance lapses, will destroy him in his very home.

Spring comes and once again man is free to move about. He is peaceful, happy, and caring towards his fellows. Mary is the spring, fresh and uncontaminated, bringing him renewed hope and healing and faith in the mercy of his Creator. As the one is dry and dark, cold and dejected the other is moist and mild, light and mirthful. Is not this wonderful evidence of the goodness of the Creator, that after Eve he gave us Mary? Is not this a sign of his mercy to womankind that though one of their number destroys us an Other will heal?

Who reigns.

Culhuch has returned from the coast. Something has happened which has changed his mind towards us and no longer does he smile fawningly or seem to defer to Barve's wishes. Now he smiles as a wolf who has scented a lamb, and he looks at her from under his brows as if he had already possessed her. The old one has been away from us for a long time today, as if he feels no more need of her. In our time alone together we conferred and agreed that we had no notion what had caused the change. We were taken to refection at the main hall yesterday evening. There was a scandalous amount of food served for Lent, but I was told that the expedition would be leaving soon.

'Then we will have Lent enough for any monk,' said my neighbour and shouted with laughter. These sailors are proud of their powers of endurance.

Culhuch made much of Barve, as if she were a visiting noble. She was well able to play the part he put on her and sat scowling with pride at his right hand. I was shown to a place about half-way down the side as if I were her chaplain. Of the old one there was no sign, and when I questioned my neighbour he said only that there was trouble in the valley. When I asked him what manner of trouble could take the old one from her son, he fell silent. Culhuch stood up and addressed the company saying,

'In a few short days, after the feast of Easter has been celebrated, we will be leaving on a long voyage. As you know, it is not my custom to tell anyone of our destinations in case pirates pursue us. Yet you may be sure we will travel far and not all of it by sea.

'The dangers we will face will be many, but not more than we have faced in previous voyages, so let us have no long faces or tearful farewells when we embark. A sailor has nothing but memories of home to console him when he is away at sea therefore, you women, let his memories be of cheerfulness and ease.

'The food and ale are plentiful tonight, though there are many here who will witness that in this fortress this has not always been so. Enjoy them, now, for who knows what tomorrow will bring? Man's life changes as the wheel of fate turns, and even the farmer cannot be sure if he will die near his homesteading. Forget the perils of tomorrow, for they will come on you no matter what you do today, and only the coward tries to run ahead of his destiny. Let us enjoy tonight.'

The gathering cheered him then as if his meagre rod of philosophy had lifted the veil of wisdom. Even Barve smiled at him and did not flinch when he took her hand. To my amazement we were returned to our house together. Not even the old woman's absence signalled our separation. We sat and stared at each other over the fire and I said,

'Do you think you are safe?'

'I do not think you would have been sent here with me if he intended to make assault on my virtue.'

'Something is being planned for us, I am sure. If it is not that, then what can he be doing?'

'Perhaps he wishes to lull us from our watchfulness.'

'Most likely.' I replied, 'but I have another thought that must be considered. Perhaps by leaving us alone together he wishes to join our name to scandal and destroy us that way.'

'If this is true, then you should leave before anyone comes to witness our liaison.'

'But I cannot leave you undefended against him.'

'If he comes with his warriors what will you do? I wonder only that if he intends to debauch me in this manner why has

201

he not done so before? Or are we being unjust to him?'

'You heard of his treatment of your sister. Do you doubt his cruelty?'

'I do not, but I am confused. He may have been deceived as much as anyone else about her guilt.'

'Guilty or not, her birth entitled her to better treatment. I do not doubt that he is a savage.'

'Let us spend the night in prayer,' I exhorted her, 'so that if we should be surprised, it will be in an act beyond any chance of reproach.'

'Very well,' she answered, and together we passed a perfect night. By the light of the taper we kept our vigil over the Scripture and this time the woman, I am sure, found comfort in it. Nevertheless our fears were groundless for none came to our door, neither to perform wickedness nor to witness it.

O, God, have mercy upon me, that I may soon forget what my eyes have seen today. Preserve me from my own memory. I know that too much reflection can turn thoughts from tame cage-birds to ravening eagles. Grant me, O Lord, the grace to lose myself in prayer as one who sinks into a healing spring.

At dawn Culhuch sent a man for us. He led us to the hall and told the women to give us food. As far as I could judge, most of the household were there breaking their fast, and when we arrived all of them avoided looking at us. Barve was still eating when the master strode in with a wide smile on his face. At once I noticed that the others there were watching us from the tail of their eye. He came directly to us and addressed the woman courteously.

'Lady, I ask your forgiveness for my long neglect of you. Believe me, please, when I tell you it was not from choice.'

'Please believe me,' she replied, 'if I say there is no offence to forgive. It would have been presumptuous of me to expect any more attention than I received. Your duties to your people will be very demanding and I could by no means expect you to neglect them for me.'

'On the contrary, a lady of your nobility has the right to

demand precedence over anything else. I can only express my profound regret that you have not had your due before now.'

'Dismiss the thought,' said Barve, and her eyes grew wary. 'I do not feel in any way neglected.'

'Your modesty is as great as your virtue,' he said, 'but I have now some information that will contradict you. At least now let me make amends, if I can for my negligence. Today is declared a feast in this domain. I hope you will give me the pleasure of joining me on an excursion through my lands as I say farewell to my people.'

So saying, he ordered horses to be brought for us and even, at a hint from Barve, changed mine for a good mule. There was no chance for us to talk before we set off but we looked at each other and her lips formed the word 'Merthun?'. I replied with a shrug and a frown to warn her to be watchful.

We set off from the fortress with no delay and took the road to the sea. It was one of those blustery days in spring which make banners fly and horses caper. Sunlight glinted off the helmets of men and the harness of horses. Sun, blue sky and the pure white of clouds, O Lord, why did you not warn us? What we found should have been presaged by black rain and hail. Instead flowers nodded at our feet and memories of winter were banished.

Culhuch never left Barve's side for a moment. I was parted from them by two of his house-carls and could only follow like a loyal hound. He seemed very much at his ease and talked all the time. I was sure that Barve had the presence of mind to keep her own counsel, but this cheerfulness was disarming in a grim warrior leader and I hoped that she would remember to keep her tongue hedged by her teeth.

We did not follow the road to the sea I had expected. Instead we took a southerly fork about an hour after we left the fortress. I realised then that we were going towards the half of the dale which Merthun had avoided on our way here. As I jolted along I pondered on what wonders we might see. The treasure of a lifetime piled on high, perhaps? Culhuch may have thought that my lady would be so impressed by his wealth that she would succumb to his blandishments. If so, I thought, he would be sorely disappointed. If he knew her as I did he would know that wealth at least meant nothing to her. Idly I looked ahead at them as they rode in the van. He seemed to be amusing Barve for she laughed often and had grown careless about keeping her veil close round her. I hoped this slovenliness would not find her out. Beyond them rose the steep side of the glen and I noticed that it was cleft in two by a mighty waterfall. I attended to the hours and did not concern myself with things around me.

Like a hunting party we paused for a while to eat in a glade. Sheltered from the wind the sun warmed us and a stream nearby gave us clear, clean water. Now that the sounds of our motion were stilled I could hear the roaring of the waterfall even though we were now too low to see it. I refused to eat and sat apart. Barve came to speak to me.

'Have you found anything out?' she asked.

'I have had no chance,' I replied, 'since I am riding alone. Furthermore my nearest neighbours are warriors and prefer to ride stern and silent. Have you no news?'

'Not I. The man is genial, and the talk flows like a stream, but it is all gossip from the castle of his master. It means nothing to me.'

'Has he told you what we are going to see out here?'

'Nothing other than it is his "Empire" as it amuses him to call it. I wish he would be quiet for a little. I would like to study the road we are on.'

'You might tell him that you wish to ride with me for a while to read a psalm.'

'I dare not try. If he felt slighted his anger might be kindled against you, and I cannot put you in such danger.'

'I am not in danger if I am loyal to my vocation.' I answered, but added, 'I thank for your concern. I will take the time to look around me and if God is merciful I may see a route that the guardians of this dale would not observe.'

'I hope that you succeed, though I am afraid you will not. From what I have seen the hill-posts on this side of the dale are even more numerous.'

'We are in God's hands.'

She walked back to Culhuch, and I saw that he was frowning at us.

The rest of the journey was short and I could see nothing beyond the surrounding trees. It is possible I may have slept a little as I rode for I can recall nothing of that part of the journey. The first thing I remember is that I looked up and my heart leapt in gratitude as I saw a palisade ahead. I was sure this was our destination, nor was I wrong. It was certainly one of the highest walls I have ever seen. The greatest timber in the forest must have gone into it for it stood three times the height of a man. There was a barbican over the gate and the watchmen there must have seen our approach for the great doors swung open ahead of us. The guards who had accompanied us dropped behind and followed us as we rode straight in. I wish we had not.

The inside seemed to be made up of nothing but small compounds. Each had a palisade of its own and from behind them came a terrible stench of humanity. Such things as bathhouses and latrines seemed to be unknown here. Every small palisade had a hole in it and Culhuch, dismounted, went over to look through one. He beckoned Barve to do the same. I could see she had no taste for it but she obeyed his summons and went across to look. She looked for a long time, saying nothing, and her silence said much. After a while she pushed herself away from the wall and went to another one, then another and another. I got down and limped over to her.

'What is it?' I asked, but she answered only by pointing to one of the windows. I looked in and soon I was doing as she had done, almost running from one to another. Inside each compound was a yard of hardened earth and a small house. And a group of prisoners with gyves on their legs.

Not all the compounds contained the same sort of prisoner. Some were young men in the fulness of their strength; some were young women; some were families, the mothers feeding their children while the fathers sat staring at the ground. Most of the men wore short gray tunics with sleeves and the women wore short skirts, which told me they were British. One of the compounds contained older men who were, I think, craftsmen.

Their legs were free of shackles and one or two of them occupied themselves by carving wood with a small knife. Even this early in the year, every compound had a crowd of flies hanging over the latrine pit. Their buzzing was the only sound in the village. There were no children other than the babies. None of the prisoners spoke to each other, nor did any of them look at the other. The shame of their condition had stopped their mouths with clay and silence lay over the village like the earth over a grave.

Culhuch watched us as we hurried from one window to another. Then he mounted his horse and came after us. He caught me by the hood and dragged me after him to Barve. He took her by the arm, and she did not resist for she was too occupied with furiously looking about her.

'What do you think of my empire?' he asked. Now the sneer on his face could not have been mistaken for a smile.

'Is that your merchandise – slaves?' I cried, 'Do you deal in anything else?'

'Yes, of course. These are just some of the first goods I will take out to trade with. There is little effort required to find them, then I take them to Frankland, or to the Saracens in Iberia if they are particularly fine. I have always used them to make coin for trading expeditions.'

He answered me, but his eyes were on Barve. She was still swinging on his arm like a distracted child. Culhuch shook her and she looked up at him. Too late I realised her face was naked under his eyes.

'Why are you showing us these things?' she asked quietly. 'Did you think that you would frighten me into submission?'

'Why should I wish to frighten you?' he asked.

'You know who I am,' she replied.

'I do not,' he answered, and something in his voice made me think he told the truth. 'I wish to know your family so that I might ransom you, but if you do not wish to tell me I am not perturbed. I will find out when I have the time, you may be sure.'

'Until then I am to be your prisoner – perhaps for years?'

'I had another proposition to make and that is why I

brought you here.'

'What is this proposition?'

'That you should become my contracted wife. I wished to show you how I make the wealth to keep you, for it is said the last woman died after the shock of the discovery. I do not understand why.

'Your monk can stay with you. He will be a credible witness to our vows.'

'But what about my... your first wife?'

'She is dead. If she is not, it is certain she will not return.'

'But I have no property,' replied the woman, and I was alarmed to hear hilarity in her voice.

'You do not need it. I have enough for both of us, and more. You have good teeth and your skin is fine. This is sign enough for me that you are of good stock.'

'Indeed, you must be skilled in judging human stock,' she said and the laughter threatened to break out. I stepped in hastily saying,

'Why do you deal in human lives? You know it offends the church.'

'It does not offend the church so much that it will not take my gifts. It was pleased to have me to set up a cross. I pay my dues in silver, not in virtue.'

'It is not possible to buy your way into heaven,' I told him.

'This is not how it seems to me,' he said, scowling. 'The bishop at Grim's court has said that if there is no time for a man to pray, the monks will do it for him. Therefore after the next voyage I will set up an oratory. All the other leaders do the same.'

Barve had herself in hand again, but her next question set my heart pounding and cut off my breath.

'Are all tyrants as simple and as generous as yourself?' she said. To my surprise he replied calmly.

'Tyrants do not need to be subtle. Our strength commands men. I was born before my time and I nearly died soon after. My mother commanded her followers to slaughter a young pig, a sow and a boar, one after the other. As each one died I was dipped into the smoking carcase and bathed in the blood.

Now most of my followers believe I have the strength of a boar and follow me because of it. I would be a fool to tell them I have only a man's strength and I am sure they would not believe me.'

'That is subtle indeed,' I said, 'but did you not also kill a demon to prove your strength?'

'There was a demon, yes,' he answered, not looking at me. 'He kept my first wife captive until I rescued her. But as I did not have the corpse to show the world, I have been careful how I used that story.'

'But why must such a powerful leader deal in human flesh?' I asked.

'My mother advised me it would be my best course, and she is never wrong. God will witness that it is not an easy trade but my reputation for miraculous strength serves me well in it. People hear that my boats have been sighted and the terror that strikes them makes them foolish. For instance, they will run to the church for sanctuary, thinking that the Saviour will protect them from us. They tell each other we are the servants of the Devil and the only safe place is in the house of his Enemy. This only makes my task easier, for when we land I send my men straight away to the building with a cross outside it. There they find the captives gathered and all they have to do is lead them to the boats.'

'This is iniquitous!' I cried, 'These captives are human souls. You must not treat them in this fashion.'

'Why not?' asked Barve, and Culhuch looked at her. 'I have read your scripture as thoroughly as any and I have found nowhere a line which says "You must not keep slaves". Indeed I have often found that the fathers of the church kept slaves. Every one of them led me to think that slavery was a just punishment for some form of sin.'

'Surely charity must tell you it is wrong. Men should not be treated in the same manner as cattle. It is an affront to human dignity.'

Culhuch shrugged.

'How else are some men to free themselves of debt? A year of raiding and a year of famine and it may be that the only way he can see his wife and children fed is by selling them.'

'But a slave is not free to chose his courses of action. Slavery impedes the operation of grace.'

'I do not understand why slave trading should be considered less acceptable than any other. Consider this, slaves do not breed as fast as free men, and if they are taken as children they may soon pass into heaven.'

'How can they survive when you have left them no hope?' I said, 'Why should they make children when they will not see them grow to manhood?'

'Is this a bad thing?' he replied. 'Our presbyter tells us that making children is wrong, and that life on earth is only preparation for heaven. It seems to me that slavery should please you for this.'

'What man is free to chose what he does?' said Barve. 'Unless he lives as a beast, without companionship and without artefacts, his life is constrained.'

'This is why the holiest of our saints chose to live in the desert. To find this freedom and this humility was their goal, and ours.'

'But you bind yourselves by your Rule. You are not free.'

'Our Rule is a gift of grace to help us to heavenly purity.'

Barve was ready for me.

'Then why may not slavery be a help to another man to find heaven? It may be voluntary and it may be by capture; whichever route is taken, it may lead to precious humility.'

'I have no answer for you,' I said, and I sank to the ground gasping for breath. The tears had started to run from my eyes, nor could I do anything to stop them but cover my face with my hands. Barve dropped to her knees beside me.

'My kind Hw,' she said and embraced me. 'You should not heed me. I know nothing of virtue. You must forgive your poor student for her folly, but reason was my only friend until God sent me to you.'

'Reason is not always man's friend,' I said, sobbing, 'but it must be mitigated by love. I am happy you have found that out.'

Culhuch looked at us with curiosity.

'One thing I know, you cannot say that the slaves have no hope. One of the reasons I came here today was to see a new sight here. A woman has appeared among the slaves whom they say is the reborn St Brigid. It appears that she is sleeping under a cloak and has been for a long time, but the slaves claim that when she wakes she will lead them to a new freedom.

'It is ridiculous, of course. They are too well guarded and we will be leaving soon. I have come to see if the woman could be a danger, for my mother recommends that she should be removed. I wish to draw my own conclusions before taking such a step. Slaves sometimes die if you make them too unhappy.'

With these words he led the way through the village. I saw that our destination was the largest compound at the centre. The guards rode ahead of us to the gate and dismounted there ready to open it for us. Culhuch nodded to them as he approached and they swung the gates wide. I followed close on his heels and found the misery and the stench were at their worst. Children were huddled against the walls in countless numbers. They sat, as silent as the adults, and they did not look up as we arrived. I cannot count the times I have walked into a crowd of scholars. Every time they chatter like starlings until I arrive, then they fall silent in respect and their eyes follow me with avid curiosity. That is how children should be. They should not be numb, dear God, from apathy.

I also caught sight of a man who sat against the wall with crutches leaning beside him. Like the children he did not look up as we walked in, but I thought I recognised him. Before I could study him I heard a sound behind me where Barve was following us. I turned to see what had happened and and what I saw made my blood freeze.

Barve had one hand round the throat of one of the guards, and had lifted him off the ground. Her veil and kerchief had fallen off and her hair writhed in its braiding like serpents. She shook the man like a puppy and dashed him against the gatepost while her other hand seized his arm.

'This ring,' she shrieked, 'where did you get it? It is not yours. I gave it to my sister Derdriu before your alfather was born.'

I rushed to her side with Culhuch close behind me. The other guards stood gaping at the sight.

'Barve,' I cried, 'let the man go. You are choking the life out of him,' but she did not hear me.

'Listen to me, woman!' said Culhuch, more calmly, and his voice was strong enough for her to hear in her rage. 'You asked the man a question, let him answer.'

She turned a blind face to him, then looked at her victim. She released him and he fell against the gate.

'A raid,' he gasped through his crushed throat, 'last Martinmas.'

There was a long silence while I realised what he had told us. Then Barve spoke and her voice had changed. It seemed to come from far beneath us and I will swear till God's kingdom come, she did not move her lips.

'My father's helpers made that ring. Themselves they took the yellow gold from the ground and smelted it. When it was cool they drew the fine metal into a rod and beat it into shape. They chased it with the portaits of creatures whose like no longer walk the earth; they studded it with jewels they brought from distant mountains; weeks it was in the making. And this was all before men raised cities in Alban or Eirinn.

'My father gave the ring to me the day I won my name. In turn I gave it to my sister when once she saved my life. We were hunting when my horse stumbled and threw me into a chasm. My sister, braver than any warrior, caught me as I fell and risked her own life to preserve mine. This ring then was given in gratitude, and in love it was received. And now it lies in the mud, no more than loot torn from its rightful owner, and on the arm of stinking offal! I ask again, black-souled villain, where did you find it?'

Before she might vent her rage on the man, Culhuch's voice rang out. 'I gave it to the man as a reward for courage. The woman we took it from fought like a demon, and the wounds he received in subduing her nearly killed him. He earned his prize, and none shall deny it to him.'

Slowly, slowly Barve turned and looked at him. Then, I think, for the first time he knew whose kin she was and his face became corpse white. She said nothing but bent down and took the ring, breaking it off the man's arm as if it were flax. In her strange voice she asked,

'And the woman you took it from? What of her.'

'She was too much trouble,' said Culhuch and his voice quavered like an old man's. 'We killed her to stop the other slaves from struggling.'

'How was she killed?'

'She was drowned.'

'Drowned?' cried Barve. 'Drowned! Cursed be the mouth that tells me so. Nothing she did in all her life merited such a punishment. Of all of us she feared drowning the most.'

She began to keen, but a keening like that was never heard before. Her screaming filled the air around us, swelled to fill the valley and erupted to the sky. Yet the woman scarcely moved. Then, suddenly, she raised her clenched fist high over her head and brought it down on Culhuch's head. His helmet split from the back to the nasal and he fell like a polled ox at her feet. Again she raised her fist and this time by some foul enchantment it held a knife, but before it could find its mark the woman gasped and dropped it. She reeled and put her hands over her ears and looked about her as if searching. Her eyes fell on the doorway of the house ahead of us.

There stood the black garbed figure of the old one. Now, however, her veil was lifted and we could see her mouth was opened wide as if she, too, were keening. Yet no sound could we hear even though the dogs snarled and the horses pulled at the rein. Whatever strange, silent incantation the old one used it struck Barve like a sword. Her knees gave way and she sank to the ground beside Culhuch. At a signal from the old one the guards ran to Barve and bound her wrist and ankle with heavy slave chains. The horror on her face told me that she had at last seen her destruction. I went to her and said,

'Barve, wretched woman, what has done this to you? You are as weak as a new colt. You cannot save yourself from what will happen now. They will take their revenge on you, you may be sure. Is there nothing to be done?'

'There is nothing, Hw,' she said in a whisper. 'The old one,

God knows how, has learned the secret of our weakness. I am as helpless as your Samson was in Gaza. It is all over for me, as it was for my poor sisters.

'But what will they do to you?' she asked. 'I have put your life in jeopardy. Can you ever forgive me?'

'We are in God's hands. If it is His will that I should die here then I will be happy to do so. The church will have another martyr. I should be grateful to you for this.'

'I will never understand this joy you take in death,' she said, and looked across at her victim. 'It is sure my sister's murderer will not survive. When I think of what he has done to my family, I could wish him a thousand lives so that I might kill him again and again. One death cannot pay for all their suffering. Not every mote of gold he owns could pay the blood-fine, though he went raiding every year.'

Culhuch lay with his head in a pool of his own blood. Gently, as a woman with a babe, one of his men lifted the helmet from his head. He shuddered at what he saw. The mother knelt by her son and her small white face was grim but she summoned others and told them to make a pallet for him. Once it was arranged she watched them lift him on to it and hissed and snarled at every sudden move. When she was satisfied that her son was bound safely on to his bed she told the guards where to take him then turned her attention to us. Barve was thrown onto the back of a horse so that the chains hurt her cruelly. She managed to turn her head and smile at me as the horse was led off. I may have been mistaken – it may have been splashes from her victim – but on her face I saw streaks of blood. Nevertheless we had seen many things together and so I raised my arms and prayed for her. I felt the hot tears running down my face.

'Almighty Father,' I prayed, 'I have been but a poor instrument of Your will. I have failed to bring this creature from the wilderness of sin which has been her home. I have failed to shine the light of knowledge into the darkness of her soul and like a pagan she exults in her revenge. Nevertheless I pray that you will not turn your face away from her now throughout the trial that lies ahead of her. Who reigns.'

The old one gave her instructions for me.

I was pushed into the slave compound and the gates were shut and bolted behind me.

Save me, O God; for the waters have come into my soul. I sink in deep mire where there is no standing; I have come into deep waters where the floods overflow me.

I am weary of my crying; my throat is dry; my eyes fail while I wait for my God.

They that hate me without cause are more numerous than the hairs of my head; they who would destroy me being my enemies wrongfully are mighty; then I restored that which I did not take away.

There was no help for it. I walked into the house and waited for my eyes to accustom themselves to the gloom. The stink of unwashed bodies made the air thick, and on seeing the dirt on the floor I elected to keep my shoes on my feet. After a while I could see that the house was about fifty paces long. Most of the space was filled with trestles and benches and soiled clothing but there was a small crowd at the far end. I made my way through the house towards them and as I approached, one of the children looked up and saw me. I paused then to greet them, but the child turned away again and none other paid me any attention. It was as if I were invisible. The attention of the whole crowd was bent on a trestle that stood in the midst of them. I could not see what lay on the trestle that thus held their interest. I studied them and saw that while most of them were children, there was a number of adults in the group. None of the adults, however, were whole. All were crippled in some way or another. There was a woman who was so covered in sores that I might swear she had leprosy; there was a man who had lost both his legs, the one from below the other from above the knee. With such lowly creatures was I imprisoned.

By now I could see as much as I ever would in the dimness of the house. On the trestle which formed the centre of their world I could at last make out some details of what lay there.

It was a human but the creature was so old and so gaunt that it scarcely raised a mound under the foul blanket. There was so little flesh on the bones the gender was impossible to determine. The skull-like face was bearded with a fine down and the head was swathed in soiled linen. The closed eyes were sunk deep into the sockets; the neck was a twig. I reached over to feel if there was a pulse beating. My hand was pushed away but the cripples were so packed around the body that I could not make out who had done so. I looked at the silent, watching faces one by one. None returned my gaze.

'Is there breath in the body?' I asked.

'There is breath in the body,' came the reply and a clawed hand held a feather before the sleeper's lips. Indeed as I studied it the feather moved, but with such a slight motion that it was hard to be sure if it was breath that stirred it or a draught from the door. Again I reached for the neck but my hand was put by without comment and without violence.

'Give me leave,' I begged.

'Let him,' said a voice, 'he's a monk.'

'What is it to him?' came a reply.

'They make good witnesses. People believe them.'

'The wonder belongs to us alone.'

'What good is a wonder if no one knows about it.'

My hand was taken and placed on the neck. The skin was cold as a serpent, yet dry and almost firm, unlike a corpse. I could feel a slight flutter at the pulse point.

'She's been like that since Christmas,' said a voice, 'not dead, but not alive.'

'How do you know it is a woman?' I asked.

'She was not like this when she came,' said the one with sores. 'She was already thin but she was able-bodied. And she could talk better than any preacher. It was then she told us we would be free one day.'

'Where did they capture such a creature?'

'They did not capture her. She came here of her own free will to save us.'

'Did the guards let her in?'

'Aye, they let her in.'

215

'They thought it was a great joke when she knocked at the gate. They all took her and then they threw her into the compound with us – the dross of the hoard.'

'Why have you been allowed to live?' I asked, 'It is clear Culhuch will not have any profit of you.'

One of the adults fixed me with a wall-eyed stare and answered,

'The other slaves need to know there is someone whose life is worse than theirs. We are the ones. The rest can look at us and rejoice that they do not share our lot. Without that joy they would sicken and die.'

One of the women added,

'Child slaves are weakest. If they can find a way to stay alive and grow up here they will make strong and cunning men. If not, it is no matter.'

'The food is always scanty and full of mould,' said another. 'It costs nothing to keep us.'

'So you see, we have our uses.'

Several of them uttered a rattling in the lungs that I took to be a laugh.

'But what will happen to you after the feast?' I cried. 'Then the trading fleet will leave with the able-bodied and your usefulness will be at an end.'

There was no answer. All the eyes turned away from me, and silence fell. The man whom I had seen outside with the children was standing in the doorway. He said,

'They think the woman will rescue them before that time comes, but they dare not say so in case they are wrong.'

The others scowled at him.

'Do you not think so?' I asked. He did not answer but turned and left the house. On his crutches he moved slowly and it was easy for me to follow him. He lowered himself to the ground beside the palisade and looked up at me. At last I recognised our friend Merthun. His right hand had been cut off above the wrist and his knees shattered. I stared at him and the power of speech left me. He said only,

'It would be a kindness if you would not stand there. I have smoothed the ground so that I can write in the dust and you are packing it down again.'

'Forgive me, I did not see.' I said and sat down beside him.

'Why did they do this to you?' I asked. He did not answer. I said,

'We wondered when we had not seen you for such a long time but we had no idea that this had happened.'

He stared across the compound and kept silent. I pressed on;

'Did they ask you about us?' but it was to no avail for he was fixed in silence. I changed the topic just to hear his voice.

'What do you think of the woman's state?'

He sighed and at last he said, 'I think she has passed over beyond returning, but there is little curiosity left in my heart. Perhaps she will. All I know is that she has brought hope to these poor fellows of mine.'

'Then this is a blessing,' I said.

'Truly I wish I could think as you,' he replied, 'but I do not see it so. Hope in this place is vain – it mocks the truth of our situation. Yet who am I to deny this comfort to my companions? They have a right to find what solace they can.'

'Do they believe the woman is sent from God to help them?'

'No, indeed,' he said, 'the one you call God has turned his back on this place. Or so they think.'

'Are you relapsed into your Godless state? I had hoped you might repent one day and be baptised.'

'I cannot say. I have given over praying, that is sure.'

'But you told us Olwen had drawn you to the true faith.'

'I do not deny the good of your faith, Hw. It is just that I know there are parts of the world which God has forgotten. He has made the pit of Hell to punish the wicked and to purify the blest. This place is neither to punish nor to purify. It is a place where men are forgotten – their prayers rise toward heaven and fall back. When God's kingdom comes it will sink unnoticed into the sea and the names of all who have lived here will be forgotten.

'Better for me to have stayed a true pagan, for if I could believe as the others I would be able to see my Goddess face to face.'

'Do they believe the woman in there is divine?'

'She, and others. Look behind us up the mountain. Do you see it – the waterfall? They have given it many names – Tower of Milk, Moon-hair, White Skirts, White Feet. And there to the right of it there is a great fell which used to be one of the holy places of these people. When Culhuch built the slave pens in this valley here it was his intention that the sight of the fell would throw the prisoners into dismay. He said they would be so shamed in front of their holy places that they would lose all heart and never try to escape. It was nearly true. They are shamed in front of their divinity but at least they could reach out and touch it if they wished.'

One of the boys came over to us and spoke to Merthun, then he took a twig and drew in the dust at our feet. The man replied by taking the twig in his left hand and drawing another word. Then for some time they both wrote in the dust, and other children came to watch. I seemed to be witnessing a lesson, though when I went to read what was written the children stared at me and looked away. I looked at the sun and took out my psalter.

After a while a guard opened the gate and pushed in a kettle of food. The children ran away and took it indoors. One of them reappeared and brought a mess to us. I was surprised at their discipline and said so to their scolog. He replied,

'Once they would have fought over the dish, it is true. I showed them that they must help one another or they will not survive here.'

'A Christian message, indeed,' I said, smiling, in spite of myself. 'And the writing lessons? What of them?'

'My concern is to teach the children what I can. If they have some learning they may have a little cash value. They will be spared.'

'What do you teach them?'

'To read and to write, that is all I can. The trivium and quadrivium would take too long.'

Then he smiled a smile like a puckered scar, and said,

'I have to ask, now, why are you here? I assumed when I saw you both that Culhuch had decided to dispose of you and not wait for ransom for the woman. How did she come by that miraculous strength? With that power she could have freed you long since.'

'Do not call it miraculous!' I cried, 'for it is the gift of the Devil. I always prayed that she would not use it, but at the last her hunger for revenge overcame my efforts.'

I told him all my story then, and as I unburdened my soul I wept with relief like rain after a drought. It had been so long since I had spoken to a sympathetic hearer. He listened quietly, then said,

'It is nearly dark now, and we will soon be told to sleep. If we talk after that we will be punished severely. We will speak more about this in the morning.'

That night was one of the strangest of my life. At first it seemed as if silence fell in the house even deeper than before. This was no hardship, but I was deeply troubled by the thick press of my fellow humans around me. With habituation I had ceased to notice the smell, and the number of bodies had the advantage of keeping us all warm – there was no question of a fire for us – but I am used to a solitary cell. It always surprises me how much noise men make when sleeping. The night is filled with grunts and snores and rustlings as if a whole army was there. Above this constant stirring there came the sound of the forest beyond the walls. I heard an owl shriek and could not prevent myself from wondering if it were the same I had heard two weeks before when we were first captured. And then I wondered what had happened to Barve. I was sure it could be nothing good.

The owl shrieked again and thankfully I turned my thoughts to the forest outside. The wind shook the trees and branches creaked. I heard a distant laugh from the guard house, then I noticed once more the deep troubled roar of the great waterfall in the hills. Such a terrible sound it made it was like the moaning of a captured demon, I could not turn my mind away from it. The pagans thought it was divine, and as such reverenced it, and from its persistence and power I began to think like them. Is this the anguish of God's love – a ceaseless din grinding at the senses? Are we who call ourselves

His friends merely those who have accidentally heard the voice once, and having done so, will never cease to hear it?

I slept only a little. When I judged it to be the time, I left the house and went to recite the hours beside the wall. Each time I woke I looked across to the trestle where the woman lay in her coma, and by the faint light I would see at least one follower watching at her side. Beside me the former pirate stirred and muttered in his sleep.

I am the man that has seen affliction by the rod of His wrath. He has led me, and brought me into darkness, but not into light. Surely He has turned against me all the day. My flesh and my skin He has made old; He has broken my bones. He has built around me and surrounded me with gall and travail. He has set me in dark places like the dead. He has planted a hedge round me so that I cannot get out; He has made my chain heavy.

Perhaps Merthun is right and authority is a tree which can be bent. A constant wind or the will of man can both turn the trunk and shape it for their purposes. Then where shall we look for our salvation? The day is drawing close when we will both be carried off to exile or, more probably, to death. Once men turned to us for wisdom and counsel, and now we lie together in the hall of the damned.

It appears that I will never find out for sure what destiny overtook Selyf, my father. Did he fulfil his promise to our Abbot? The Lord gave us a task, why then did he not give us the time and the strength to fulfil it? Shall we witness the coming of the kingdom in the flesh as a farmer looks at his harvest? Or shall we die, no more than a hand half raised in blessing?

The slaves continue to wait for their own millennium, but the sleeper sleeps on. Whenever I approach her the watchers stir and shift like a flock of sleeping birds.

Tears are never far from my eyes, and when I lie down I feel as if a great stone had been laid on my chest. What is to become

220

of me, O Lord? If I were a pagan I might say I am about to become converted to the true faith. Yet I am already baptised and have lived a life of unswerving devotion to my God. Why, therefore, should I feel this despondency? Why do I weep to think of the misery of the children here when I should rejoice that their sufferings will soon pass them into Heaven. I have contemplated the death of my Saviour for days every Easter, yet have never shed a single tear when around me my brothers wept and moaned. I have rebuked them, saying – 'Why should you sigh and grieve like this for the death of the Anointed? His death is no more than a passage through darkness; His resurrection is a triumph over the flesh. We should rejoice and give thanks for this day.'

For answer they would shake their heads at me and turn their eyes to the cross. Now I am condemned to weep for the unworthy.

The Lord is my portion, says my soul; therefore I will hope in Him. The Lord is good to those that wait for Him, to the soul that seeks Him. It is good that a man should both hope and quietly wait for the salvation of the Lord.

But though He cause grief, yet He will have compassion according to the multitude of his mercies. For He does not willingly afflict or grieve the children of men. To crush under his feet all the prisoners of the earth, to turn aside the right of a man before the face of the most High.

These words have always caused me dismay and confusion, for they seem to say that the Almighty himself is the source of evil. We are taught that the agent of evil is the Serpent. I wish, now that I have time lying on my hands, that I might be able to resolve this confusion and, like Boethius in his prison, console myself with philosophy. Unhappily I find I cannot think about a subject for the length of time necessary. My mind wanders from one matter to another like a grazing sheep.

I start from the point that just as there is a difference of degree between men, there is a difference of degree in the goodness of things. From this it follows that there must be a sovereign Good which is God, and at the foot of the mountain, so to speak, is the greatest evil. The criticism of this is that the Good of one thing may not be compared with the Good of another. Is the good of a warming fire in any way to be placed on a scale with the Good of prayer? One warms the flesh and the other the everlasting soul. Again we find ourselves left with no other scale to weigh the Good than the degree to which it has been polluted by the flesh. Have we no other way to recognise the Supreme Good?

Of all the faculties we possess, reason is the only one which separates us from the beasts. Nevertheless it is only a human faculty and as such is contaminated by its association with the flesh. God stands beyond reason. In the world of human experience wisdom alone is the means by which we may approach God. As long as we are in the flesh we will never be able to perceive Him, but out of His mercy He will send us wisdom so that we may be elevated out of our sunken state. It is possible a revelation is close to me.

It is possible I will not have the faith to perceive it.

My eyes have wandered from the page once again. I stare at the body of the sleeper and wonder if that which preserves it is a force for Good or for evil. Is the inspiration of hope it has brought a Good? Will the sleeper wake, and if she does will those hopes be destroyed or fulfilled? I cannot find the answer. All I am good for is to weep and pray.

One question has been answered at last. This morning Merthun and I stood talking beside the sleeper's trestle.

'The face of this woman recalls something to me,' I said. He nodded.

'It reminds me of a newborn child,' he said. 'I have often been asked to tend to one because its mother fancied it was near to death. The down on the cheeks, and the deep furrows in the skin are very like those infants.'

'Indeed, I had not thought of such a likeness until you brought it to my attention. What I had in mind was the description of St Pelagia. "A face haggard with fasting – her eyes like trenches in her face" – surely you must have come upon it

222

in your reading?'

He was puzzled for a moment, then I explained.

'I am speaking the words of Father Cassian. He was one of the guides for those who follow an eremitic life. He commends the most rigorous fasting and subjugation of the flesh as the only road to sanctity. I do not mean to say that this woman is an example of holiness – this is not possible, since the pagans believe she embodies one of their demons.'

'Did not she tell them that she would free them?' he asked. 'Surely this could mean she will lead them into your faith?'

'I cannot say. All I know is that Barve had lived a life of chastity and abstinence yet I could not say that she had attained holiness. She would not join the church and we know there is no salvation outside it.'

'Truly,' said Merthun, 'there is very little salvation within it for any but the strongest.'

I was shocked by his bitterness and came close to rebuking him but the shameful tears fell again at my disappointment. I turned away to dry my face, then all at once the old woman who sat watching at the sleeper's head began to skirl,

'She is waking! She is waking! Look, I saw her eyelids move. Look!'

She set up such a shriek that the others came scrambling in as fast as they could. Merthun looked down and shook his head.

'I see nothing,' he said.

'She is waking, I tell you,' said the woman. 'Look where there is a slit between her eyelids.'

Miraculously someone produced a cup of clean water and a rag. The old woman began to wash the grisly face with it and wiped around inside the lips. The upper lip folded back and caught on the teeth and I saw that they were firm and white. Again the old woman drew the rag over the dead face and the body shuddered. There was a gasp from everyone in the house.

'Her time has come, at last,' said Merthun. 'It often happens that one in a coma will seem to revive just as death strikes.'

'Hush you, now!' said the old one. Merthun recoiled as if she had struck him.

My eyes, and everyone's, fixed on the closed lids. They trembled, relaxed then trembled again and again – and finally they parted. Everyone in the house held their breath as if they feared their exhalation would blow out the last flicker of life. The sleeper's eyes opened wide; the scanty chest heaved, the lips moved and yet no word came out. There was a movement under the cloak and a hand was drawn out. The flesh was wasted from the hand so that the knuckles seemed gigantic. A clawed finger beckoned the old woman who at once wiped the mouth with water and squeezed a few drops from the rag between the teeth. This operation was repeated several times then came the faintest of whispers.

'Ale,' said the sleeper.

She was lifted up and propped against a heap of clothing. The chest and shoulders which now appeared were little more than a skeleton with skin drawn over them. There were no breasts under the shift, and the cloth on the head slipped off to reveal that the creature was completely bald. It was difficult to believe that the person before me was indeed female. She was as repulsive as death itself. Her followers seemed to know what to do to help her wakening. A pot of warm ale appeared at her side and one of the women spooned the liquid between her lips. After that came a quantity of a green slime which smelled pleasantly of herbs, then, God knows from where, came milk. This sequence of beverages was repeated several times.

After a while the knobbed hand waved away the attendants. The eyes closed and the sleeper slept once more. This time, however, the rising and falling of the chest was more pronounced and there was animation in the skin of the face. For the rest of the day the creature slept or was fed by her attendants. Merthun took the children away to continue their studies. Their time of departure was drawing near so, once I was satisfied that there would be nothing new from the sleeper's house, I went to play my small part in the school. I have used up much of my ink and scraps of vellum to do so, but I am sure this is a better use for them than any I could find.

Throughout the night the attendants waited on the waking

and sleeping of their charge. Every time I rose to read the hour there was a faint light and a whispering beside her trestle. Still she did not speak, and some of her followers began to grumble.

What her first words might have been I will never know, for soon after dawn guards came into the house demanding to talk to 'the confessor'. Someone directed them to me and they came and said,

'The murderess has been given a hearing and her fate has been decided. She has asked for you to hear her last confession before she is taken out to punishment.'

'You called her 'murderess'. Is Culhuch dead?' asked Merthun.

'Not yet,' replied the guard, 'but it will not be long. He is lying in a deadly sleep and the honoured lady, his mother, is sure he will not waken.'

'Why, then, did you try Barve for a thing that has not happened?' I asked.

Every shoulder in the house turned away from me. The guard struck me and knocked me against the wall.

'Will you come?' he said.

'I will come,' I said, and took up my scrip and satchel. I looked around the house and none would meet my eye. It is only what I deserve. I have looked the other way too often and my protesting voice has been silent when it should have been raised. In that house all that matters is to stay alive with as little pain as possible.

At the fortress I was returned to the house we had lived in before. This time I found Barve sitting shackled to the fireside by a short chain. I went to her side and embraced her and our tears mixed as they fell to the ground.

'Ah, Hw,' she cried, 'what will become of you?'

'Comfort yourself, Barve,' I said, 'death is not far from me, nor has it ever been.' I showed her the swelling of my limbs. 'My heart is racing as if it would jump out of my body, and I cannot lie down to sleep. It will not be long before I face my Judge. But what has befallen you? They told me you will die tomorrow but I cannot believe they would be so harsh.'

'It is true. Tomorrow they will take me down to the sea shore. I will be chained to a post at low water and I will be left there to drown in the rising tide.'

'Yet Culhuch is alive. This is not just.'

'He is very close to death, and it was my intention to kill him. If he still breathes it does not reduce my guilt.'

I said angrily,

'Tomorrow they will kill you for personal revenge, no more.'

'They must punish me or there will be no order in the dale. Culhuch must be seen to be invulnerable or, if not, his attacker must be punished swiftly. His mother knows that well.'

I looked into her face and she smiled serenely.

'He is not the Emperor of Rome,' I protested, 'nor even High King of the land. They should not destroy one as fine as you to pay for a petty chief. A money settlement would be more than enough in view of the grief he has brought your family.'

'I have no kin to bring the silver, therefore they will not settle for a fine. I must be punished as a landless carl is punished.'

'I will tell them who your kindred are. Surely they will listen when a presbyter swears that the money will be paid? I cannot let you die without trying this. Moreover Culhuch may not die. I have seen Ælfrid cure terrible head wounds. Do you know what is being done for him?'

'The fracture is being kept clean by washing it with boiled water, in which there is honey, egg white and rosemary. This is done every three hours, day and night. His mother sits at his side and calls his name and rubs his wrists. He is being washed and his mouth cleaned out in the intervals between his treatment.'

'How do you come to know so much?'

'I told them exactly what to do, myself.'

'Why?' I said, confused beyond mending.

'His mother asked me.'

I sat down on the floor and leaned my head on the bench beside her. 'Why should his mother ask you, who nearly killed her son, how he might be cured?'

'Did I not say to you it is a poor warrior who cannot cure the harm he has done? The wound I caused in a fury of revenge will never be fully repaired, but I must do what I can, as she knows. As a reward for this she has promised that I will not be violated tomorrow before they tie me up at low water. She may even keep her word – I cannot be sure, for she believes my maidenhead is a source of my strength.

'After all these years as a virgin I would like to die intact. On the other hand, I am curious as to how it will feel to be deprived of my purity. It is all the same to me.'

'I do not understand you,' I said. 'All I know is that one as wise as you should be saved for the good you can do.'

'You are generous to me, Hw,' she replied. 'But the truth is a torc made of many wires, and it is more twisted than you could realise. The old one knows who my kindred are and refuses to accept a fine. I could escape now and could have done so at any time since I first came to this fortress, but I have chosen not to. You will understand that, for more than once you recommended we should stay captive.'

'I must beg your forgiveness for that. If I had it to do again we would be a hundred miles from here by today and a long life would lie ahead of us.'

'There is nothing to forgive. I took part in the decision. You could not have coerced me if you had tried.'

As if to demonstrate she bent down and opened the link of her shackle. Thus freed, she sat down beside me on the ground and continued,

'The morning I was taken before the meeting of the dalesmen Culhuch's mother came to me and told me all her story. I will tell it to you and perhaps you will see why I cannot do other than follow her design.

Many years ago, when she was still a child, the old one's tribe were clients of my father. For reasons I do not understand, one day he took his protection from them and left them in the hands of invaders. She was taken and raped by their leader, and then they left her in the forest. Soon after that she found she was with child. She and her servants took shelter in the house of swineherds and they survived the winter until the child was born. Then Kigva, for that is her name, was told that she must stay with the leader of the herdsmen and bear his children, for his wife was dead. She had no wish to live as the concubine of a swineherd bringing one child after another into the world until it killed her. She was the daughter of a chief, and her land was the open hillside, not the dark corridors of the forest. There was only one course of action open to her. She fled from her child and the last members of her tribe and went up into the mountains.

When her child was getting near to manhood she returned to the forest. She watched the comings and goings of the swineherds until she knew his daily habits. Then she lay in wait beside the track and met him one day when he was alone. She told him who she was and the true reason why she had left him, for her servants told him she had gone mad. The first day he did not understand and was angry with her for deserting him. He would not speak to her but drove her off as if she were a wolf or a fox. The next day she returned and told him she would give him his name and the name of his father if he would listen to her. He still did not trust her but he bent his head and did not threaten her again. She spoke to him about her sad life and his, and what the world owed them both.

She told him about Usbathaden and his betrayal. She told him about her rape, and that he had a half-brother who had lived as he should have lived, in the great stronghold of a chief. She did not tell him, for she did not know, that the brother had been lost to his parents. But she told him that his father's name was Kilidh, and his brother's name was Kynan. And she sent him to claim his birthright.

When, after many years, Culhuch came to our fortress to kill our father, he was not only seeking to make his name as a warrior. He had come to do his duty as a son and destroy his mother's betrayer. Then Kynan had to suffer from the rage of a brother who had been cheated. And with him, the rest of my family. When Culhuch took Olwen in marriage his only intent was to make her miserable, but it seems he became affection-

228

ate toward her, so his mother intervened. The children my poor sister lost were all taken by their grandmother and left in the forest with the swineherds. Their fate is not known, but as a small comfort Kigva said the swineherds needed the children to swell their numbers. They would not ill-treat the poor innocents but they would keep them close. So Olwen was humiliated and would have finally paid with her life if she had not run away.

Even this did not satisfy Kigva's hunger for revenge. It was said by those who ventured near my father's hall that he was not dead and these rumours found their way here. She harnessed up an ox-cart, for she had never learned to ride, and she went in search of him. Of course she found nothing at the fortress but she followed a trail of rumour and suspicion through the forest to the coast where she came upon the city of her rival's son. There she learned the few weaknesses in his defences, and remembered them well.

In time she came to our palisade and stayed with us for a while. You will recall that I told you of our strange little visitor. When it came to the workings of the human heart my sisters and I were innocents. We guarded our tongues as Kynan had warned us, but we were not careful enough. After weeks of listening and subtle questioning Kigva found out our deepest secrets. She found that we could be weakened by losing our hair, by losing our maidenhead and by hearing a certain kind of keening. She remembered these weaknesses well. That was how my sisters were defeated at Kynan's city and how I was brought down at last.

I do not know how she found these things out. Some of them I did not know myself, for we have had so little to do with those who wish us ill we have never felt the need to study our defences. Kigva, on the other hand, has always needed to defend herself, and is quick to see any weakness in her enemies that she can exploit. We have been like the bull attacked by a terrier. We did not see an attack coming, and when it came we could not see the source. All we could do was shake our heads and scrape the ground.

I should not have vented my rage on Culhuch. He has been

the instrument of his mother's revenge, no more. I will not vent my rage on Kigva, for she is the victim of my father's waywardness. It would be a great injustice on my part to add to the wrongs already done.

Now I am without my fury, my strength is limited to a moment. When I was in the great hall yesterday, facing my accusers, I was tempted for a moment to be like Samson. I could have done it, for when I thought of the misery the woman inflicted on my poor sisters the strength ran through my muscles like fire. They had shackled me to one of the main roof-trees and there was a fire basket near. Kigva had cut my hair and thought that this would be sufficient to keep me weak as a woman. I could have brought the whole house to flame and ruin and burned the dalesmen with me by a shrug of my shoulders. I did not do it, and I am still wondering why.

Since you are my friend you will say that I held back out of compassion and that I could not have brought such a terrible death on all those people. The truth is that I shall never be sure if I did not restrain myself to save my own life. I could escape now to save myself, but I do not because I would leave you almost certainly to die in my place. On the other hand, it may be that I do not feel certain that I will die tomorrow.

But all questions of virtue apart, it is certain that I am tired of this life. After centuries of living on this earth there is little new for me to see. I remember the first time I stood at the foot of an oak tree and looked up into its branches. Everything about it seemed a wonder to me, from the mighty roots spreading so deep into the earth to the tiny, tiny veins on the leaves. Yet every part, from the smallest to the greatest was essential to the tree. I can recall the joy and wonder I felt when I realised this great truth. In my early lives I often saw things for the first time and rejoiced in their beauty and complexity. This can no longer happen to me and the sense of wonder is gone. You must feel pity for one who will never again see anything for the first time. Tomorrow, when the water rises to cover my mouth, at last an experience will be a wonder to me.

After that, if, as you say, I am to go to hell, at least it will be new. Perhaps I will meet my father again at last, and he will tell me why he did those things which have brought men's hatred on us. To this very day I do not know what they are.

Do not be so distressed on my behalf, Hw. It is true I fled in fear from death for many years but now I can accept my mortality. When I die it will be no more than every creature under the sun will do in time. I am happy that now I can call the human race my kindred.

I recovered my breath and said,

'You must not take the threat of hell so lightly, Barve. Once there you will suffer great pain for all of Eternity. No one who knows about it wishes to spend even a moment in that terrible place. All those who have chosen to live outside the church will find no mercy once God has given judgement. I beg you, let me baptise you now.'

She smiled at me.

'Tomorrow I will have baptism, and to spare. You may say what you like at that time, for I will not be able to stop you.

'Now let us pass the time as pleasantly as we may. I have only a few hours left and I do not wish to spend them sleeping.

'Do you have any news of Merthun? He was not at the hearing. I would have been glad to see one face not filled with black hatred.'

I was dismayed by her question. The news of the man's mutilation and probable death were another grief to add to her burden. I decided that the burden was already great enough.

'I have been locked up in the house of the dead,' I replied, 'I hear nothing but the snoring of my companions. If Merthun has left I fear it is something he should have done long since.'

'I am sorry to lose him, but I hope he is safe. His books are still here. Since we may not pass the night with fine wines and silken couches, let us at least beguile the time with the wonders of foreign lands.'

'I would rather that we both spent the time in prayer,' I said, 'but if you wish it you may read while I pray.'

'Pray on, my good friend,' she replied, lightly, 'and I may join you if my terror overcomes me.'

231

A little after the second hour she opened her scrip and her pack and said,

'These are my only possessions, and you are my only heir. I wish you would take them, but you are afraid of them, are you not?'

'I am not afraid of them, but I think it would not be proper for me to own them.'

'Then you must give them to whomever you think fit.'

She held up the brass plates with the round holes in them.

'These plates were made by my sister to calculate the tides on this coast. She also showed me how to use them, and I fear that there is no time to pass on the knowledge to another. If we had learned to trust each other sooner, you would have understood how to use them and the knowledge would be saved.'

She sighed and shook her head.

'I give them to you. Who knows but you may manage to learn their use and they will not be wasted. My comb and burning glass you can use if you wish or give to a bishop to be destroyed. I no longer care about them. The box of family relics you must keep and give into the care of one who will look after them. There is no sorcery here, only long memories. Guard them well.'

I read from her psalter as follows:

Have mercy upon me, O God, according to thy loving kindness; according to the multitude of Your tender mercies blot out my transgressions.

Wash me thoroughly from my iniquity, and cleanse me from my sin.

For I acknowledge my transgressions; and my sin is ever before me.

Against You and only You have I sinned and done evil in Your sight.

Behold I was shaped in iniquity; in sin did my mother conceive me.

Behold, You desire truth in the heart; and in that hidden part shall You make me know wisdom.

232

Create in me a clean heart, O God; and renew the right spirit within me.

Do not cast me from Your presence; nor take Your holy spirit from me.

Deliver me from bloodguiltiness, O God, thou God of my salvation; and my tongue shall sing aloud of Your righteousness.

The sacrifices of God are a broken spirit; a broken and a contrite heart, O God, You will not despise.

They came for us just before dawn. Weighed down with chains, she was put on the back of a mule, and I was pushed on to a horse behind a guard. The old one rode in her cart behind us and though her face was covered again I knew she was watching us closely. As we travelled down through the dale people appeared from the thicket and most of them followed the growing procession to the place where three rivers meet.

They chained her to a post at the low water mark, in a sitting position. They broke her legs so that she could not raise herself above the water. It is a pity that she had strong bones.

I stayed with her until the water covered her head and prayed that the first grace of baptism should be hers. Then, as I had promised her, I returned to the river bank. I felt as if an iron band had been locked round my chest. I feel it now and it will be with me till I die.

We watched in silence until the last strands of her hair were no longer visible. A number of ravens gathered in the trees behind us and flew down into the machair. Still the silent crowd stood on and waited, and waited all the hours until the tide ebbed and her body was returned to us. The guards pulled her out of the water and confirmed that her life had ended.

Then the old woman rushed at me, her veils fallen from her head, crying,

'What has happened? Has she let herself die? What did she tell you? When will she return?'

I shook my head at her. 'She will not return. She has chosen the real death.'

'Do not you be foolish,' shrieked the hag. 'She was as strong as she had ever been. She broke this chain,' and she waved at me the links Barve had broken the night before.

'She chose to be weak. It was her decision to die so that you might keep order in the dale. That was what you wanted, was it not?'

'My mouth said those words, it is true. But what I wanted... I wanted to see...'

I prayed for the strength to remain calm.

'You wanted to see the giant's children suffer.'

'I have done that. But I wanted to see, just once, I wanted to see the power of the giant. I wanted to see it working.'

She started to wail like a child with her mouth hanging open and the tears pouring down her wrinkled face. Her great misery moved me and I put my hand on her shoulder. To my astonishment she took my hand and rained kisses on it crying,

'Help me, Father or I do not know where I shall look. I am weak and ignorant and my son is sick nearly to death. Show me something that will give me the strength to go on living.'

My blood ran cold in my veins. Some demon whispered that Barve's death had brought about the conversion of this woman. I tried to silence the whisper and erase this blasphemy from my mind. It was vain to try, for the old woman knelt at my feet in an attitude of supplication. All the dalesmen and their women were watching, and it was clear from the way they looked at us that they had heard the burden of our talk. One or two of them walked over to the dead woman and raised their hands in prayer. While I stood irresolute, a woman cut a lock of hair off Barve's head. If I did not act soon they would start building a shrine.

I lifted Kigva to her feet. Softly, so that no one else could hear, I said,

'Unhappy woman, you hoped to see a miracle this day. There is none here, and you will look for one in vain. If you wish to see a wonder there is one to be seen in a place not far from here. In the slave's town the woman who slept like one dead has awakened.'

So desperate was the woman and so eager for her miracle that she at once ran off to her cart. Once she had clambered aboard, however, she turned and beckoned to me. Reluctantly I joined her, and we drove off round the headland.

I looked back and saw with relief that the guards were wrapping Barve's body in her cloak without ceremony. A few of the dalesmen had lingered to watch, but most of the crowd were going about their business. We travelled the road I remembered from my first arrival here with Barve. Overhead one of the ravens flew, keeping up with the cart. The old one looked up and saw it and cast a furtive look at me but we both stayed silent.

Memories were wakening at the sights along the road and I said,

'Why did your son hurt Merthun? He was always loyal to him even in his private speech. He should have been with us at the ... execution.' The demon nearly made me say 'sacrifice'.

Kigva was more talkative than I had ever known her. She said,

'I do not know why he betrayed us. He had a good life here and he could have had a better if he had not taken up with a bad woman.'

When I heard this a terrible weariness cloaked my body and my legs could not bear my weight. I sank down and sat in the straw on the bottom of the cart. There was a bundle of soft things on the floor of the cart and I laid my head on it.

At once I was surrounded by a blazing white light. My body was bathed with happiness so intense I could hardly bear it and I tried to speak, to ask that it should be taken from me. Before I could form the words, a voice spoke to me and said,

'Son of man, the light you see has blinded you, but I can tell you what you cannot see. The woman who died is approaching the Presence of the Almighty one. As soon as her body died, her soul was led by the Heavenly Companions to the heart of the Eternal Light. There she was met by the splendid assembly of angels, and now she stands with the college of the Apostles, the throng of glorious Confessors and the jubilant chorous of Virgins. They are welcoming her to their number with songs of praise and delight. Can you hear the music?'

I listened for a moment, but heard only the troubled beating of my heart.

'It is a pity you cannot. Once in a generation a man is born who can hear the music of the crystal spheres. But for all your hope and piety, alas, it is not you.

'The Virgin has joined the Elect and stands, suffused with joy, to wait the coming of her Saviour. Rejoice with her if you can, and weep for her suffering if you must, but remember always that hope of Salvation is humanity's greatest good.'

The light died, the voice fell silent, and I found myself alone and wretched in the dark. I wept for what I could not see and grieved for what I had not heard, but above all this, I begged my Eternal Father for another chance. By and by consciouness left me and I did not waken until the cart stopped at the end of our journey.

Night had fallen and we had come to the slaves' steading. Barve had been right when she said that there was a better road up the dale on this side of the crag. We had not taken when we first arrived because it led to the slaves' town and Merthun had wished to keep his master's secret. It was a secret place no longer. Cressets burned everywhere and the outer gate hung open. The guards who should have been watching had vanished, though there was a light in the guard house. The only person near the gate was a child intent on cutting through the leather of the hinge.

I gathered up my goods, which now included those of Barve, and slid out of the cart. I wondered idly if I would be burdened by any other person's past before my own life ended. My head ached and all I could feel was gratitude that I would soon be able to lay myself down.

Kigva picked up her skirts and hurried in, and I followed as fast as I could. Inside the palisade the gate of every house was flung back and the people were coming and going freely. The guards mingled with the slaves and the slaves mingled with each other and the air was filled with the noise of talk. The centre of all this activity, like the queen's chamber in a hive, was the house of the cripples. There people came and went like bees, now leaving on errands, now coming with provisions and all buzzing loud enough to wake the dead.

At first Kigva ran from one guard to another. Some of them looked abashed when they saw their mistress, but most of them barely recognised her. She did not seem to gain any information for as I plodded towards home and bed she caught up with me crying,

'It has happened just as I was afraid it would. Our laws have been overturned; no man recognises me. I, who stood at my son's right hand and made him the powerful man he is today. Yesterday the dalesmen gave me my place and spoke humbly when I approached them, but today they do not even see me.'

I did not stop to answer her, for I was afraid that, having stopped, I would not be able to move again. I recalled Jeremiah and said as I walked onward,

'You have not harkened unto me in proclaiming liberty, every one to his brother, and every man to his neighbour; behold, I proclaim a liberty for you said the Lord, to the sword, to the pestilence, and to the famine; and I will make you to be removed into all the kingdoms of the earth.'

She trotted beside me muttering, and pulled her veil across her face. It is better not to be recognised at all than to be recognised and passed by. We entered the cripples' house together and found an amazing transformation. Since the day before the whole house had been cleaned and re-ordered. The floor boards were white, the benches were no longer covered with dirty clothes and the tables had been taken down and stacked against the wall. The benches along the walls were filled with quiet, respectful people and they all looked towards the far end of the house. There, in front of the window, sat the sleeper, and she had made a miraculous recovery.

The light of the setting sun shone in through the window and formed a nimbus of light around her head. Her face was hidden in the shadow but I felt that she was smiling. Somehow in that lost place they had found her a chair and she sat upright as if she had never known a day's weakness. As I walked up the house towards her she held out her left hand towards me in welcome. Yet though I walked and walked I got no closer to her, instead she seemed to grow in size until her head was as high as the roof tree. I raised my hand to place it in hers and suddenly I was plunged into darkness.

When I opened my eyes again, it was morning. I was lying propped up on a mound of pillows with Kigva sitting on one side of me and the sleeper on the other. Beyond them stood Merthun and his children and then the rest of the company. I realised that I had missed the hours of the night and tears formed in my eyes. I turned to look for my satchel and the sleeper placed it in my hand. The laces defeated my swollen fingers so she took out my psalter and opened it for me.

'Give me a penance,' I said to the sleeper, 'for I have slept through three of the hours I should have attended.'

'Come now,' she replied, 'you are sick. The Rule may be relaxed for you, I am sure.'

'I must accept what you say,' I answered, and sank back on to my pillows. Kigva handed me a cup of hot green fluid which stank of rotting grass. I retched when I brought it to my mouth.

'Drink,' she said, 'and you will soon feel better. We cannot heal you again but we can make you comfortable.'

'It is not to the point for one such as I to feel comfortable,' I answered and coughed. The sleeper wiped my eyes and mouth with a piece of good linen and I saw pink staining the white. Merthun sighed and shook his head. The sleeper said,

'You must do everything to prolong your life. It is not your place to end it before God has decreed by tormenting your flesh and fretting in your soul. Be calm and trust in the Lord for He has sent you friends to lighten your last days.'

I drank the potion, and that seemed to be a sign for the people to leave. Shortly after that I felt a violent need to go out and two of the children helped me. I lost count of the number of times this happened, but after a while the swelling of my legs and fingers shrank somewhat and my spirits lifted. Kigva left us and I heard her voice outside ordering people around; Merthun left and I heard the voices of his scholars chanting their lessons. A raven staggered along the palisade outside the window. I looked at the sleeper who sat calmly beside me. Her hair had grown so fast it almost covered her head and surrounded her face with a mass of white curls. Her face was beautiful beyond description.

'You are Olwen,' I said, 'Usbathaden's daughter. None but your kin would have recovered from starvation in a few hours.'

'I am,' she replied, 'and you are Hw son of Selyf, presbyter of the people of Rintsnoc. I am sorry I was not with my sisters to greet your father when he came to our hall, but as you know, I was with my husband.'

'From what I have heard, it would have gone better with you if you had been with your sisters.'

'Ah, no. Once I might have agreed with you about that, but not now. I have known much suffering, yet you will confirm, pain is a great teacher.'

A thousand words clamoured in my heart for a chance to reply to this. The only one that found its way to my mouth was,

'Yes.'

I was obliged to go outside once more with the boy. My legs felt better able to carry me so I sent him to join the scholars and returned alone to sit beside Olwen. She was silent for a long time, then said,

'Our concern for your health is not unselfish, Hw. Everyone here has agreed that we have a task for you if you should wish to do it.'

'I am a poor labourer,' I answered, 'and have been for many years. I have never shirked my duty, however, and if you have a task for me I will do it if it does not conflict with the Rule.'

'I will explain and you will judge for yourself.'

When I returned here I came with only one aim – to avenge the death of my kindred. Kigva and Culhuch have caused the death of many people dear to me and an eternity of torment would not satisfy my thirst for revenge.

After I left here I went to see a weirding woman who lives in the north. As soon as she saw me, she told me that the sons

I had borne were dead. Their grandmother took all three children to live in the forest with swineherds. The boys had been
raised in the open moorland were the wind scours the rocks
and the sunlight whitens the grass. In the gloom of the green
forest they grew sick of a lung fever and soon died. The only
comfort I had is that the girl child is well. She was young
enough to grow up used to the forest and loves its strange
ways.

At once I demanded to know where I might find my daughter, but the woman would not tell me. She said,

'The child was so young when she was taken that when you
find her she will not know you. Think about your situation.
You are a woman alone in the world with no home and no
family. What can you offer your child? The two of you will be
beggars and, hardy though she is, the baby needs shelter and
food.'

I answered that I was skilled and strong and that I could
find a way to keep us both. But again the woman answered me
saying,

'Your daughter is more than half human and as vulnerable
as any of them. You may have to leave her side when you go
away to work, and then what will become of her? The word
will travel that you are a weirding woman, and it will be hard
on her. I know too well what I am saying. I had a daughter
once. In the place she is in now your child is loved and cared
for, fed and sheltered. Until you can offer her the same, you
have no right to take her away.'

Her arguments defeated me and I asked her what she recommended. She told me to try and make peace with my
sisters for the sake of my child. She said they would be more
charitable than I could believe, but that I should hurry for they
were in danger and soon must hide themselves where no one
could find them. I travelled at once to my father's hall, but
found it empty. At the time I knew nothing about the sisters
who went to live with Kynan. I believed myself to be alone in
the world and I resolved to use all my power to revenge my
father and children. I believed I had found a way to do so but to
find the key to my power I would have to go to the gates of

death and beyond. While I was preparing for this journey I returned for safety here, where the people are so defeated in spirit that they would say nothing about me.

It was an irony, then, that my arrival had the effect of fanning their little hope to a blaze. I spoke to the slaves of the day they would be free, for it was part of my plan to deprive Culhuch of his property, but also as part of my purification I was eating nothing. The slaves in the house noticed this, and that I lived in spite of my fasting and they began to whisper among themselves that I was divinely moved. They said that I would lead them out of this town to the top of the mountain and there we would set up a wonderful city. Having started the notion their minds worked on it until they believed that from that fortress they would reconquer the whole of Britania and restore the golden age. I was too wrapt in my dreams of revenge to see any of this, and the rumours swelled unchecked.

Culhuch has informers everywhere in this valley, and the slave town is no exception. Soon my old friend Merthun was sent to find out the truth of the matter and for a moment when he first arrived my heart leapt with joy to see him. Sadly he did not recognise me, I was so emaciated, and when I saw this I decided it was for the best and kept silent. I was pleased that I was so divorced from my past.

The darkest days of the year came, and it was time for my journey to begin. I told the slaves that though I might seem to die, I would only be visiting the land of the dead and that they must wait for me. It has happened in the past that the deep sleep is mistaken for death and my kinfolk have awakened in a tomb. As long as I was in my vision none must speak my name and they swore to keep silent. Finally, when I returned I would need them to take care of me until my strength returned and they promised to feed me as I bade them. They were so devoted to me by that time that they would have died, every one of them, to protect me. That is a wonder of the human heart which I will never understand – they will die for a God.

Before I took the road they came to me and said,

'When you return you must tell us the story of your journey.

We have promised to protect your body while you are out of it, and it is only fitting that as your devotees we should do so. But as your are our holy mother you must not keep anything from us. Your adventures in the land of death belong to us as much as to you. We will need them in later times when you are gone from us so that we can tell our children and teach them how to carry on your devotions.'

I was not pleased to find I was the object of worship, but I realised that I and no other had put myself in this position, so I must do as they said. It would have been unjust of me to take their protection and offer nothing in return, so I promised to give them their saga when I returned to my flesh.

Now that you are here they want their saga written down. None of them can read, it is true, but they think that if words are written it makes their power stronger. It is many years since I wrote, and my hands have lost the cunning to do it well. Merthun you have seen.

This is my request – that you will hear the story of my passage into the world of the dead and write it down. I hope that this will not be in conflict with your vows. Believe me, if it were left to me I would prefer by far to keep my history to myself, but I have given my word. You, however, have not and if you refuse I will tell them they have no claim on you.

I thought for a long time before I gave my answer and said,

'It is not true that the slaves have no claim on me. They have cared for me also, and they have been my partners in adversity. That they should claim divinity for you is a blasphemy, of course, but I no longer have the strength to remind people of their duty to God. Indeed, it takes most of my strength to understand my own duties. Tell me your story and I will be your scribe for as long as I can hold a pen.'

Olwen smiled at me but before she could say a word we heard a shout outside. We went to the doorway and saw Kigva beckoning us. Beyond her, in the centre of the township, stood a mound of wood where some women were working. When we appeared they backed away and we could see that the wood was a pyre, and that on top of it lay the fleshly remains of Barve.

'I have prepared her,' shouted Kigva. 'I went down to the sands in my cart and fetched her here for you. These women are skilled in the building of pyres. We will give her a good funeral.'

'She expects to be thanked,' I said, 'when it was she who brought about her death.'

'Who is it on the pyre?' said Olwen.

'It is your sister, Barve,' I replied, surprised. 'Did you not know about her death?'

'I did not know she was in this valley, let alone dead. How did she come to die the bad death here?'

'Kigva will tell you that,' I told her and, suddenly weary, I leaned on the doorpost. Olwen walked to her sister's pyre. I followed reluctantly.

'Kigva,' she said, quietly, 'why is my sister here, and why is she dead?'

'She did not tell us who she was,' the little one answered. 'If we had known we would have given her every welcome due to her. How could we know who she was when she would not give us a sign?'

'Answer my question, Kigva. Why is she dead? Why is the first sight I have had of my sister in all these years the sight of her stiffened corpse?'

'I told you your husband had been wounded. It was she who did it. She had to pay for it. He is your husband – you should seek vengeance for his death also.'

Olwen shook her head like an ox teased by flies.

'Did you not know your sister was here?' I asked.

'I told you all I knew. I went to my father's house and found it empty. The woman told me later that some of them had gone to live with Marighal's husband. I would have gone to beg them to forgive me if I had not become possessed by the idea of revenge for my sons.'

'I wish that you had done so,' I said sighing, 'for then I would have been spared the duty of telling you what I now must.'

'What must you tell me? Say it quickly. A good warrior must kill mercifully.'

'Your sisters lived with Kynan for some years, but raiders came and destroyed his city. Your sisters died in its defence. All but three and Barve herself were killed.'

'Tell me the names of the dead,' said Olwen, her face as pale as her dead sister's.

I drew a breath and almost lied, saying that I did not know, but that would have served no purpose other than to spare me. I said,

'Evir, Gwenlieth, Feidhelm, Derdriu, Ide, Halgerd and Anfol.'

At the sound of each name Olwen seemed to shrink, yet nothing changed except that tears ran down her stony face.

'Seven of them!' she cried, 'How could this happen? They could have stood against a thousand men. Our strength compounds when we fight together and seven of us are invincible.'

'You are not invincible when you are set against sorcery,' I reminded her.

'Who could make sorcery to defeat us?'

Sick at heart I pointed to Kigva.

'She learned the secrets which led to their defeat,' I said. 'Your husband destroyed the remnant of your family.'

Olwen covered her face with her hands.

'It was your father,' cried Kigva. 'He let me and my clan go to our destruction. It was revenge against him I sought. Now my son is dying from your sister's rage and I am left with nothing.'

Sobbing, she threw herself at Olwen's feet and clung to the hem of her gown. The grieving woman uncovered her face and with horror I saw the clean tears of a moment before turn to tears of blood. The short hair on her uncovered head writhed like yellow flames. I blessed myself and sank to my knees with dread.

'Why did I not kill you at that mockery of a trial?' said Olwen. 'I could have done it, then, when you put your destroying hand on Merthun. I watched my friend fall to the ground with pain and I did nothing. I should run to beg his forgiveness, and I am punished for neglecting him.'

244

She leaned down and with one hand lifted Kigva clear off the ground. Higher and higher she lifted her until the little one hung at arm's length. I was sure she was about to hurl her on to the pyre with Barve.

'No,' I cried. 'Do not destroy another, when so many have been destroyed. Your sister died when she knew she could have taken her revenge and saved herself. She did so because she saw what it would be. Revenge brought your family down and you in turn will destroy these people for revenge. What good will that do to you or to the rest of the world? And think of your daughter. She is the heir of all this vengeance. How shall you treat with her? She is your child and the last of your line, but she is also the child of your enemies. What will you do when next you see her? How will you tell her of feuds without end and without mercy?'

Olwen lowered Kigva gently to the ground and looked at me.

'Barve stayed her hand when she might have taken revenge. Is that what you are telling me?'

God forgive me, but my head nodded almost before I could stop it.

'She understood what had happened, and she could still show mercy,' I said.

Olwen looked at Kigva.

'Is this true?'

'She could have killed us all,' the old one answered. 'I do not know why she did not.'

'Culhuch is sick and near to death, but he is her only victim. The night before she died she told me she wished she had not done it.' I repeated what Barve had told me of Kigva's sufferings and, thanks be to God, the bloody tears ceased flowing.

'My sister was generous,' said Olwen and walked over to the bier. All at once crowds of people appeared from behind the walls of the houses and approached us. I said loudly, so that everyone could hear,

'She understood at the last that laying blame is bootless. Life must renew itself, but before it can it must throw off the

245

clogging hatreds of the past.'

'Olwen,' said one of them, 'you have been called the Good. Without our leader we are helpless. We beg you, come and lead us once again and show us how to live.'

'Your sister has destroyed Culhuch,' said another. 'It is only just that you should take his place.'

'You said yourself that in your journey to death-gate you found a new truth,' I reminded her. 'You came here thirsting for revenge, yet your vision dream taught you to hold wrath in check. Have you forgotten so soon what you learned then?'

'I have not forgotten, Hw. What I learned is still true. Only the news of my sisters' deaths broke my restraint. I shall never cease to be in your debt that you recalled me to myself.'

To the crowd now gathered at Barve's pyre she said,

'You will remember what you have heard today till you draw your last breath. By her bright example my sister has shown us all a better way than revenge to right wrongs.

'Do not think I do not know what I am asking from you. I know what it is to hate. There have been times when hate was so strong it has burned in me by night and by day. I have warmed myself at it and found it better than any fire. In the day it has swept through my mind so that I cannot attend to my tasks. At night it has made me writhe in my bed and covered me with sweat as I cursed my enemies. There have been times when hate was the only thing that kept me alive and caring for myself. I know I am asking you to give up a source of much comfort, but I do not do so for my own sake. All our lives will be the richer for it. My sister, Barve, has shown us the way. I do not wish to see her example slighted.

'Fate has decreed that she and I should not see each other's living faces. So be it – the sun and the moon do not share the same sky. All I ask of you now is that you should share my grief and forget the wrong she has done to you. For my part I will throw my grievances on the pyre with her body and burn them both together.

'You may be sure that I will not leave you without a leader. It is true that I long to go searching for the few remaining members of my family, but I know that I am needed here. All I

246

ask of you is that I should find my daughter and bring her here again to live beside me.'

Kigva spoke up,

'Your daughter is also my kin. Let me go and bring her back to you. I know where she is, and I want to make amends.'

'What about your son, my husband? Do you not wish to see him healing?'

'I can do no more for him. Your sister's orders are being followed. Please, let me go. I will not be more than a few days.'

'I cannot stop you,' said Olwen. 'Now there is a last condition I will make for my staying. The slaves must be released, and the cripples must be provided for. I will not see those who suffered with me treated as cattle, or worse.'

The dalesmen agreed readily and to seal the bargain everyone threw a lock of hair on to Barve's pyre. We burned her body then, and I hope we sent her soul to heaven with the smoke. As the ashes collapsed we set off for the fortress with songs and laughter. Merthun and his pupils stayed in the slaves' village and he went about his task with vigour.

I was taken to the fortress on a cart, for I could no longer walk. When we returned we found Culhuch could sit up and eat. He was not yet able to speak many words and his mother said he was still a long road from health, but a smile twitched the corner of her mouth. Alas, the dale is filled with rumours of a miracle. Barve will be venerated before the next new moon. When the moon is full I dare not think what will happen.

And when I think of the full moon, I recall that it is Easter.

CONFESSION

I, Hw, monk and presbyter to the family of Rintsnoc, sinner and wretch, with glad heart seeing death approaching and in the absence of any who will hear my confession, must commit to paper this last record of my offences.

I was born into the religious order whose name has become a byword in the body of the Church for error as much as for stubbornness. Nevertheless ours is the oldest family of Christians in the land and our traditions have the weight of many centuries behind them, though many call us heretics. For years I have struggled to reach a concord with the rest of our brothers in the bosom of Christ, and in my keen pursuit of this end I have often denied truths I was taught to revere from my earliest times. I see now that my only motive for all this was vanity, for it was my wish that, being accepted into the Church of Rome once again, we could enlist the power of the Church in the restoration of our lands. I wished for nothing but to see us restored to a position of esteem. My brother in Christ, Ælfrid, saw this and tried to persuade me to accept that it had pleased God to send us on a separate course. To strive to improve the lot He had apportioned us, he said, is no more than impiety.

I must protest, however, that on many occasions our order has been falsely accused. Our name has been linked with the heresies that came out of Britain and Eirinn many decades after we had established our order. Our founder was trained in the Roman tradition, and his sponsor was Antonius Donatus himself. When the blessed St Cairnech came to this land to eradicate heresy, he saw only the families of the British tradition and followers of Pelagius who uttered dogma against the grace of Christ. We were not of that number, nor did we seek to set ourselves against the authority of Rome over the date we should celebrate the Passion. It is many centuries since we rashly allowed the word of any member to stand as spiritual truth. We believe the blessed martyrs of our faith stand as an example of virtue. Our only divergence from the Church of Rome is in the degree to which some of us are willing to accept the story of the Anointed as literally true. I also acknowledge as error the extent to which we allow free discussion of the nature of God. I have been guilty of this.

I could not say that he was noted as a controversialist. If discussion arose, his aim was always to find the path of orthodoxy. I must confess that sometimes I did fan the flames out of ill-humour, for he provoked me by the narrowness of his vision. I wish there were time to ask his forgiveness, but it is too late.

I have always remembered the first night I ever came to the City of Airemagh. My companions and I had been late taking the road and night fell before we came to the City. We had reconciled ourselves to a night in the forest, and one of the students had climbed a tree to find a safe resting place when he saw the light of a nearby fire. The truth, as we discovered, was that we were no distance at all from the Abbey but upwind of it. The walls were so well-built and so firmly caulked that not a blink of light escaped to tell us of its presence. We gave a great shout and told who we were, and the gate swung wide to let a path of light appear on the ground to lead us to safety. I have always thought of this as a paradigm of God's presence: that as we blunder in the forest, foolishly fearing for our lives, we do not know how close we are to shelter until we cry aloud for it. Then, when we raise our voices in supplication, it will come unstintingly like the light of the Abbey fires to lead us to the greatest City of all.

I had thought that I would be like the ancestors in our order and have the time and the comfort of my last penance before death. I do not think that this will be given to me, for I have found too much doubt in my heart. Miserable offender that I am, I can only give utterance to the thought that has rung through my mind for the last few days and hope that when judgement comes, I will find mercy and recognition for my struggles. As the spring tide bears down on the breakwater and its terrible weight splinters the timbers, so that they give way in anguish to its pressure and the water floods in through the gap, crushing everything that lies in its path with its glassy weight; so it has happened to me that I have been inundated by a revelation. My mind is small and weak and my understanding is limited, my heart is not steadfast. God is too strange and too far away for me to comprehend Him. I would have been better occupied if I had served my fellow man.

Nevertheless, in view of what I will write as my last offering to scholarship, no less than for the honour of my Order, I will make the following testament. There is no god but God, unbegotten and without beginning or end who created all things, and his son Jesus Christ whose existence is co-extensive with God's and who took on the flesh of a man so that He might suffer. By His example of suffering, humiliation and death He has freed us from the necessity of sin into which we were trapped by our ancestors in the flesh. I will not say more on this matter, for my time is short and my strength is flagging.

I here record the vision of the woman Olwen. She dictated the story to me and I wrote only what she said, word for word. She claims it was seen in a true vision, not a dream, for she woke at once when she heard her sister's name spoken. It had seemed to me that she slept, but I cannot be sure. I am not answerable for the content of the vision, and I pray that those who read it will see it only as evidence of how the pagan faiths endure after a thousand years of proselytising. There is so much to do and the millennium is nearly upon us. I pray to be forgiven for lending an ear to such blasphemy and impiety, and for allowing my thoughts to have been re-shaped by what I heard. I tried to resist the inundation, but my strength is not enough. I fear the woman and her family will overpower all. She told me.

In the last part of my life in the valley my poor husband was doing his utmost to humiliate me. I spent hours every day up to my hips in mud and slime, carrying strangers across the ford. At first I loathed what I found there – the smell, the crawling things, the mud squeezing between my toes like lead-coloured excrement – and I became feverish with the horror. I knew it was right that I should be punished, for I was the daughter of an evil man and had deserted my family and chosen to live with my father's killer; my children were dead, and with every day I became surer that I had killed them myself; I had brought disaster on that good man, Merthun, who was now forced to live with me in a loveless union. I was sure I would have deserved it if I had been flogged daily by my tormenters. Since my father had been killed, I knew that my next death would be my final one, and fear of that had driven me to murder. Terror was like grit in every mouthful of food and like poisonous fumes in every breath of air. I was becoming sick with the horror and might even have died, if my dear friend had not given me consolation. He showed me that the slime of the river was part of the process of life – and death – and that I should call the worms 'Brother', not despise them. This gave me a form of hope, for it told me that in death I would be a part of the whole cloth of life.

Nevertheless, when I summoned up the will to escape from the dale the horror had not died, it was merely waiting for the time I should cease my restless travels. When I came back here, I felt all the old blackness arising to swallow me. I had left my child with strangers, for I did not deserve her presence, and I had let myself be raped and thrown into a prison-house for the hopeless. The skin on my right leg had begun to decay and I realised that, in spite of my vigour, I had taken leprosy from one of my companions. I felt as if I had blundered into quicksand and the more I struggled the faster I sank. The only gleam of light in my darkness was the certainty that if I could conquer my unlawful flesh, I would be able to gain my revenge. I undertook the most severe fast and meditated for hours on my wicked past until I could live for days on little more than a sip of water. All at once I had the delightful sensation that the world was slipping away and no longer of any importance to me. At last I was invulnerable and endowed with a strength of will which I had never felt before. For the first time in my life I felt that the sun shone for me and the rest of the world could not harm me, try what it may. I, and no one else, was fit to be my judge.

I wonder how Hw felt when he wrote these words. Alas for his hope that she resembles the fasting saints of olden times. She resembles them in that she has the depression of spirits and the feeling of unworth, but that is as far as it goes. God has nothing to say to one as arrogant as she.

Secure in my faith in myself, I told my companions what to expect and lay down to seek for the little death. I drew myself out of my body and looked for the road into chaos. Drifting upwards, I looked down at our valley, saw the three rivers meeting and since I could see nothing else, went toward them. Along the beach I noticed a road I had not seen before leading to the south. I set my feet on it, thinking that though it was not far from my prison, it would have to suffice. As I walked along, a man with my husband's sign on his tunic came towards me. He told me that the road was very dangerous as it passed through mud and was often flooded. He said,

'It is rocky and nothing grows there. It is only used to move corpses that would defile other roads.'

I looked out to sea and saw a storm coming towards us – a vast dark cloud trailing curtains of rain. I looked back to the road and saw already black waves were crashing over it and gouts of water were being flung into the air. A black pool was forming rapidly on the landward side and the road would soon be no more than a narrow ledge surrounded by water – too dangerous to travel. It was useless to hesitate longer. I reminded myself that when I was in the flesh I had waded through slimy mud.

'It will be much easier to face the filthiness now, when I have no flesh to be soiled,' I said, and boldly stepped on to the causeway. The wind struck at me and nearly blew me into the pool. I dug my feet into the soil and took pleasure in the sensation of mud between my toes, for I was binding myself to the earth and the wind could not snatch me away.

I looked ahead along the causeway and saw a young man in a wide-brimmed hat beckoning me. Beyond him the black clouds were splitting and rays of light shone down on to the rocks at the far end of the causeway. He seemed to be pointing towards them and I knew that the road that led between them was the road to happiness and freedom. I was aware that there were many people sitting on the rocks near me and on those overlooking the causeway, and that these were all watching me closely. If I failed to cross they were waiting to take me back to my prison-house, and I would never escape again until oblivion took me. The young man was beckoning again and I felt a surge of love for him stronger than any I had felt for any human before. He was everything to me, husband, brother and son, and if I could only reach him, he would help me through every adversity.

This young man must be Mercury. The blackness is depression at the start of winter – the realm of the autumn equinox and the south winds when phlegm fills up the body, bones must be covered and night sees the onset of disease.

The road shook like a quagmire. Every time a wave struck it I was thrown about and staggered like a drunken man. As I stumbled from one side to the other, I kept myself on the road by driving my feet into the mud up to the ankles.

The wind dropped and when I looked round, the watchers on the rocks had vanished. Only the swell of the sea sucked at the causeway, which was rapidly disappearing into a mass of black sludge. I tried to move along the road, but I could no longer feel it under my feet. I knelt down and groped in the mess with my fingers for the rocky surface. I found it at last, but the only way I could be sure of keeping to the road was by crawling on my hands and knees. My skirts dragged in the mud and kept pulling me back. My limbs ached with the effort of moving yet I carried on, feeling my way, inch by inch along the rock of the road.

All at once I felt solid ground under my hands. Two strides more and I stood on a surface which did not heave and shift under my feet. I wept with relief as I wiped my hands and feet clean on the rocks, then I looked about me. My veil was gone – blown away long since by the dreadful wind – and my skirt was filthy and torn. The young man in the wide-brimmed hat had vanished, but ahead of me, through the gap in the rocks, I saw light the colour of sunrise. I made for the light, and as I approached the gap I felt warmth bathing my body. I realised then that I had been cold, but I had been so cold for so long that I had ceased to feel the chill. Now I became aware of it and I could almost feel ice melting inside me.

On the rock on the left hand side of the gap there was a large white stone. As I came near, it spoke to me saying,

'If you wish to pass through you must solve a problem.'

'I am ready,' I answered, 'tell me your problem and I will solve it, for I am longing to pass through to the warm land beyond.'

The stone hesitated, then replied,

'Out of the eater came forth meat and out of the strong came forth sweetness.'

'That is an old riddle and too easy to answer,' I said. 'It is the riddle Samson put to the Philistine clan in the Scripture. The answer is a lion that he killed several days before his wedding.'

'Indeed,' said the stone, 'that was a riddle, but it was not a riddle I was setting, I was merely stating the problem. You must learn to listen more carefully.'

In the rocks above me a lion roared.

'Why do you say that lion is a problem to be solved?' I asked, 'Surely it will only be a problem if it comes to attack me? A lion, or any other savage beast roaring in the distance, is no more than that. Hold your peace until real trouble arises if you want men to listen with care.'

With those words I passed through the rocks into the valley beyond. Below me lay a land coloured the yellow of lichen. On the left a range of hills reared up to a green sky, and at the foot ran the road I must take. The sides of these hills seemed to be made of smooth rock or hard sand and all along the bottom of the hills huge eyes were painted in purple paint. Ahead of me a stream meandered through the sands of the valley floor to a distant range of mountains. Half-way along the valley there seemed to be a clump of yellow bushes growing beside the stream, and I thought I could see people sitting in their ochre shadows.

I paused for a moment, wondering which route to take. The road was clearly marked but it wound in and out round the foot of the hills and looked three times as long as the distance straight across. To travel beside the stream directly to the mountains seemed quicker, but I could not be sure how good the footing along the bank might be. Furthermore, the people in the valley might not be friendly towards me. Unable to decide, I sat down on a rock.

All at once, with a mighty crash, the sand behind me erupted. In terror, I turned to face whoever was going to attack me, and saw a man on horseback struggling out of the ground. His horse was white and draped in an embroidered saddle-cloth with tassels at each corner. The man himself was dressed like a Saracen, with a striped turban and long white robes. The hair that I could see under his turban was grey, as was his long moustache and heavy eyebrows, and his skin was tanned. The horseman rode off along the road at a furious pace, and I could follow where he went by the cloud of dust that flew from his horse's feet. I realised that I would follow him eventually, but that I did not have to hurry. The roar of the lion came again and I climbed down the rocks to the bank of the stream.

The water in the stream was very clear, though tinted yellow. I could see every stone on the bottom and, apart from a few purple ones, most of them were the yellow of the surrounding sand. A few wisps of vapour rose from the surface as it flowed slowly and silently onward and it smelled like rotten eggs. I hesitated for a moment, wondering if I could bear the stench, but I realised it was not very strong.

'What harm can a smell do to me?' I asked myself. 'After everything that has happened so far, a smell is nothing.'

Except for some the bushes ahead of me there were no plants, no insects and no animals in sight. The bank of the stream was firm underfoot and I strode along swiftly. I walked for several hours yet I seemed hardly any closer to the stand of bushes. I looked towards the road I had decided to leave and it also seemed long. I traced it as it meandered in and out around the feet of the hills and I was so intent on this I did not look ahead. Suddenly I found I had walked into a bush. The bush was dead and leafless but covered with very long thorns and my hair and shawl caught on them. I struggled for a long time trying to free myself. At last I let go of my shawl and said,

'You can keep it, if you must. The day is warm and I do not need it. But I must ask you to release my hair for it is painful to have it tugged and pulled like this.'

All at once I was free. A voice from the bush said,

'Why did you not ask sooner? I had begun to conclude that you were a beast without the use of speech. You must understand that I do not need your shawl – if you will look closely you will see that I am rich enough to buy myself many such if I so desired. I am keeping it as a token of your passing, no more.'

I looked at the bush and saw that the lifeless branches were made of solid gold. I spoke my thoughts aloud, saying,

'God called to him out of the midst of the bush.'

There was a sound behind me and I turned to find a man in a long ochre garment draped elegantly to reveal one shoulder. He did not appear to wear anything else. His head was shaved bare and his skin shone with a golden sheen. His eyes were like amber beads lit from within.

'Who is God?' he asked.

'"The lord is my rock, and my fortress, and my deliverer; my God, my strength in whom I will trust; my shield and the horn of my salvation; my high tower."'

'Why do you quote from scripture?' he said. 'Do you have nothing to add from your own thoughts?'

'Were I given time to consider my answer, I would.'

'Come with me,' he said, 'and we will give you all the time you may need to find a suitable response.'

'Thanks,' I said, 'I will come, but only if the bush has finished with me.'

'Go with him,' said the bush, 'you have nothing more for me.'

'As you wish,' I answered, angry that I had tired the bush so quickly. The man whispered,

'They like to pretend that they understand what we are saying, but the truth is they cannot follow your meaning for a moment. You might as well recite your genealogy for all they will understand.'

The bushes around us rustled angrily.

The man led me to the middle of the shrubs where a small crowd of people were sitting on the ground beside the stream. There were women as well as men but all of them wore the same clothes and all had the same golden skin and amber eyes. Trapped by the surrounding bushes the smell of the water was stronger, but the people did not appear to notice. Indeed each of them had a drinking vessel of gold which they kept filling from the stream repeatedly. They also had golden plates and bowls of golden fruit, yet while I was there I did not see anyone eat.

This is out of sequence. It is the heat of spring when the winds are from the north. Bitter red bile rises and the body is vigorous – but the hot dryness wins in through the ears and in the afternoon is the greatest danger.

'Welcome to our symposium,' said the one who sat nearest to the stream and seemed to be the leader of the group. 'I am sure you will have much to teach us.'

His companions nodded and smiled agreement.

'Thank you,' I answered, 'you are very gracious, but I must tell you at once that my learning is very slight.'

'Dearest child,' he answered at once, 'modesty is most becoming in one as young as you, but I assure you it is unnecessary. In our little world what counts is not learning, it is wisdom, and this can be attained by the simplest souls.'

I did not point out that I am far from young. The one who

had come to meet me giggled,

'She was quoting the Book of Deuteronomy to the bushes,' he said and went to sit in his place. The group laughed and one of them clapped his hands saying,

'O, excellent! Anything else?'

I opened my mouth to answer but my guide answered for me,

'She also quoted one of the psalms. Say again what you said in answer to the question, "Who is God?"'

'"My shield and the horn of my salvation; my high tower,"' I said quickly.

'How refreshing to hear the old poets after years of rational discourse,' said the leader. 'We really should give them more of our attention.'

'She said she would need time to produce an original answer,' said my guide. They had not asked me to sit down with them and I stood alone and perplexed in the centre of the crowd.

'Can you manage an original answer, dear?' asked one of the women.

'I think I can,' I answered, 'but I would like to know what you mean by original. My teachers did not think to teach us originality. They taught only the work of the past. I would be grateful for your guidance.'

'I understand,' said the leader, 'you have been taught by authority alone. But to quote Augustine of Hippo, "Authority has a nose of wax" and can be pulled into any shape we wish.'

'I think Lycon can help you,' said the woman, and the whole company smiled and settled themselves as people will do when a bard starts to sing. I hoped very much that I would be able to impress them with my discourse. I felt it would be a great privilege to sit down with such wise people and pass the eons in learned discussion. Lycon began,

'First before I expound the most significant statement, I will state that to affirm a truth about one order of nature is to deny it of another; that which is manifest in time and place, matter and form is said to be; only things perceived by the intellect can truly be said to exist since the senses are not to be trusted.

Those things which can be grasped by the sense or the intellect may be said to be, those which escape sense and even intellect may be said not to be.'

The symposium sighed with pleasure. He went on,

'This class of non-beings includes God, the reasons and the essences of things created by him. It can therefore be said that God's more-than-being is the being of all things. It follows from this that God transcends being and since God is superior to all things it is clear that non-being is superior to being.'

The audience clapped their hands and one or two clashed their cups against their plates in approval.

'Lycon, you do that so well,' sighed his neighbour, 'my soul thrills every time I hear you.'

Lycon smiled and nodded gravely in response. With dismay I realised that all amber eyes were now turned towards me. I tried to win myself some time by taking a drink from the stream. No one offered me a cup as I approached the water so I started out to use my cupped hand, yet when my fingers touched the water I found it was unbearably hot. To make my discomfort worse, the leader reached over and filled his cup with a single elegant gesture. I stood up again and faced my audience.

'I am unskilled in this type of discourse,' I began. The oldest man there interrupted me.

'We are sure you will be most enlightening. A new voice is always welcome to our circle. It has been many years since we were blessed with a fresh point of view and we are charmed to find you with us.'

Each member of the symposium had something to say to me on the advantages of a new face and their words of encouragement took quite a long time. I was glad because this gave me a chance to consider what to say. When at last the murmuring died down, I began,

'Lycon has just given us a most elegant proof of God's non-being. If this is the case how are we, poor samples of the inferior categories, to know that He exists?'

The leader broke in saying,

'You have made an excellent start. Lycon has indeed proved

that non-being is the only valid category for God, assuming, of course that any statement about God can be held to be valid.'

This gave rise to another series of interruptions which left me staring at the ground. Suddenly the woman let out a peal of laughter and pointed at me.

'Our visitor finds our interjections discomforting.'

'I do not,' I replied.

'I apologise,' said the leader. 'I should have explained our approach to discussion here. We have been given the whole of eternity to consider the important questions of the Universe. It is possible for us, therefore, to consider each thesis as it arises, to weigh it, to balance it and to give it its true value. This is a lengthy business, as you will appreciate, but it must be done if we are to arrive at an eternal and unshakeable Truth. But I see you are hungry to continue. Please go on. We will consider what you say when you have finished.'

I took up the theme.

'Proof of God's existence is everywhere: in the movements of the world, whose arrangement, beauty and order are signs of Him; in the existence of finite, contingent things which require an infinite artificer and, above all, in the nature and structure of human thought. Reason itself can convince us of His existence as clearly as the sun displays itself before our eyes.'

I looked up at my audience and was alarmed to see contempt in every eye.

'Derivative,' said one.

'Augustine again,' said another.

'Why can she not find us a fresh thesis?'

'We have been so disappointed, so often,' said the older woman, and a golden tear fell from her eye. I sank into the depths of misery and shame. My face reddened as I realised how badly I had failed. This was a humiliation worse than any I had known at my husband's hands and tears started in my eyes. Then a stone bruised my foot and it said,

'If you deny what you know, you are lost.'

The whole company shifted angrily on the ground and the woman's robe slid up to reveal a strange sight. On her feet she appeared to have a mass of gold feathers. Before I had time to consider this the leader said wearily,

'Do you not have anything more to add?'

'I could add a great deal,' I said, 'but I thought you might wish to consider the truth of what I had said, before going on to the next statement.'

'But you did not say anything new,' he protested.

'No more did Lycon. As I recall, his proposition was made over a century ago at the court of Charles the Bald by Johan out of Eirinn, and centuries before that by the followers of Gautama. It is in fact very old.'

'How can you say that?' cried Lycon. 'I devised it myself not many years ago.'

'I do not deny that you have devised it. I am sure you are very clever and that it may be the first time you and your friends have heard it said. Nevertheless, it is not a new thesis.'

'How do you know the thesis was made in ancient times? Were you there to hear it?' he sneered.

'Would I be believed if I told you that I was?'

I was answered by loud but scholarly jeering.

In his agitation Lycon had thrust his foot out from under his robe and I could see it clearly. It consisted completely of a mass of feathers and the only remnant of his foot seemed to be a knob of bone in the middle. I felt it was discourteous to stare so I looked at the road again. The rider was nearly out of sight. I thought, 'Nothing is new under the sun.'

'Why did you offer us Augustine?' asked the leader gently, as if I were a child.

'I like it,' I answered. Every golden face showed disgust.

'LIKE IT?' said my guide. 'That is no sort of criterion to judge eternal Truth.'

I saw that he alone of the group still had the vestige of a foot among the golden feathers.

'It invites me to rejoice,' I answered. 'It tells me that I am a part of the Truth and everything that I can perceive is likewise part of the Truth. Why should I wish for more?'

'Have you no wish to use your mind? Does discourse mean nothing more to you than a source of simple pleasure?'

261

'The pleasure is not simple,' I answered. 'It is profound and subtle and composed of many streams.'

'Do words have no more significance than the sound of the stream, here?'

I could only answer with another quotation,

'"The angels do not learn about God by spoken words, but by the actual presence of the unchanging Truth."'

Everyone turned away from me.

'I can see it is time for me to leave you,' I said, and was ignored, 'but before I go I would like to ask one question.'

'Ask!' said the older woman.

'How are you able to walk without feet?'

'We have no need of feet,' she answered with a sneer. 'We have come so far from the old, human body that we have grown wings where our feet used to be. We no longer need to walk.'

'Can you then fly with these wings?'

'You may take it as a matter of course that if we have wings, we can fly.'

'Have you ever flown?'

'I do not need to fly. I know I could if I so wished.' At that she turned away and gave all her attention to her neighbour. I was dismissed.

I went on my way across the sandy plain to the distant mountains. All at once they grew closer and I hurried panting up the dusty foothills. I heard the roar of the lion once again and the stones I crushed underfoot warned me that I would find danger in the heights. I explained to them that there was no other way open to me and they groaned and let me pass on. As I neared the summit of the pass a pair of lions came bounding towards me from the peak on my right. They were both coloured the bright green of summer leaves and I saw that the sex of the male was inflamed. He roared as they came near me and terror turned my legs to water. I pressed my back to a rock and waited.

The lions stopped in front of me and blocked the road. I tried a question,

'Why are you coloured the colour of leaves? The whole

valley is tawny from the water to the sky, yet you, who should be this hue, are bright green.'

The lion answered,

'We are the guardians of this valley. It is necessary that we should be easily seen.'

'You do so,' I answered, 'but please tell me from whom or what you are guarding it.'

'We guard it from the moon. If her light were to fall here the valley would die.'

'It seems to me that it is already dead,' I answered, and at once wished I had not. Both the lions looked angry at this reply but only the male showed his rage. He shook his green mane so that it rustled like leaves and then he gave out a terrifying roar. The lion's mouth opened wide as he roared and I saw his huge green fangs. The rock I leaned on spoke to me saying,

'Either you will admit him or he will consume you. You must choose now or die.'

'Is there no other route open to me?' I begged. 'Will you not open a passage into your cave and give me another choice?'

'Not on this occasion,' said the rock. 'But ask me again, I may be able to help.'

I studied the lion and made my decision.

'It will go easier on me if I admit him,' I said.

'Do not be sure of that,' said the rock. 'He likes to use his claws when he mates.'

'I would rather take my chances with his claws than with his teeth. They are not dripping with spittle.'

As I knelt down to receive him the lioness came to my head and spoke for the first time saying,

'You have made a sound choice, for I can tell you now, his bite is poisonous. Only be sure when he mates with you that you absorb him all.'

I took heart from hearing her tell me that. I remembered her advice as soon as I felt him touch me and I used my old skills to turn myself into an oven. I thought the fire into my belly glowing red hot; I thought my womb into a cavern built of brick; I turned my lungs into bellows and my nether parts into

263

coals. I was all at once the great furnace in which everything is changed. As he entered me I engulfed him and I heard his roar coming as it were from my belly. With agony in every joint I quickly restored myself to my own shape and the lioness licked my aching limbs.

'Come with me,' she said and led me the rest of the way up the pass.

'Are you not angry with me for destroying your husband?'

'He is not my husband, he is my brother, and you have not destroyed him. He lives on in you and he will be your strength. Now I can be your friend.'

'I am most grateful for your good wishes,' I told her, 'but if you must keep your place in this valley you will not be my friend for very long.'

'Is friendship confined to the services we can do each other? Will not love play a part in our transactions?' said the lioness, and I felt my face redden at this rebuke. She laughed at me gently.

I have often heard women accused of witchcraft tell of mating with strange animals. This is the first time I have found one who conquered her unlawful mate.

'You do not know that I have been with you for many years before today. How may times in the past have you been faced with great trouble?' she asked.

'Many times.'

'And in these times of trouble what have you done?'

'What I have done has depended on the type of trouble. When violence has threatened me, I have used the strength I inherited from my father and driven off my assailant. Other times I may have had to lift great weights or move very swiftly and my father's strength has helped me.'

'Have there not been other troubles?'

'There was a time once, when my younger son fell and struck his head. For many days he lay still as if dead and my husband's followers said that we should bury him. I knew that he was not dead and would not let them touch him. All during that time I stayed awake at his side for fear that they would take him away for burial. I washed his body and sang to him and by and by he woke. The others were filled with joy at first but after a while they whispered that I had used magic to bring him back to life. This was not so. At first I had prayed to the Saviour, it is true, but he was silent. The only power I had was the power to hold on. I do not know the source of that strength.'

'That was one of the times I was with you,' said the lioness. 'You will understand, now. Whenever you have a task ahead of you which needs no sudden access of power to accomplish it, when devotion and persistence are the only ways to succeed, call on me. When a road is long and there is no way to travel it except by placing one heavy foot in front of another, I will be there. When there is no course other than to endure misery, think of me and I will comfort you.

'And now I must leave you for a time.'

I saw that we were on the edge of the next valley. I knelt beside the lioness and pressed my face in her fur. Sorrow at leaving the friend I had just found made my spirits sink. She shook me off and stared at me with emerald eyes.

'Will we meet again?' I said. She nodded and playfully hit me with her paw.

'I will pursue you, if only because I have to find out what has become of my brother,' and with that she turned and loped back through the pass.

I looked out over the next stage on my road. The country I saw now did not seem unusual in any way. The track led down into forest, passed through a number of clearings and appeared on the far away slope heading into the mountains once again. It was spring and the trees and the small fields amongst them were tender green. In the clearing nearest to me there seemed to be a tall building with a wide gate and as I studied it I saw the young man in the wide-brimmed hat entering. My curiosity was roused and I began to hurry down the road.

As I entered the forest I saw that words had been carved on the trees. I tried to read them but they were written in a language I had never seen before. 'I will understand them later,' I told myself and made for the clearing with all haste.

At the clearing I found the tower I had seen from the mountainside. It was built of wood and was not truly a high building, but rather a narrow one. Yet when I stepped inside and looked up, I saw that the tower consisted of very many rooms standing on top of one another. Each level was connected to the other by a ladder which passed through a small hole in the floor. I began to climb the ladders and found that the first levels all had large windows that let in a great deal of light, but at the top there were no windows at all. The last two levels were lit only by the faint light of dips.

The top room had a very low, sloping roof. Even in the centre of the room I could not stand upright. In the dim corner of the room there was a small mattress on the floor. Three people crouched beside it and I could not make out what they were doing there. As I approached they stepped back to let me past. On the bed I saw a slim body, which they had been washing with water from a silver bowl. It was so dark that I could not make out more than that. The young woman who stood closest to me said that it was my brother and that he was dead. I could only answer, 'If it is my brother then he must be dead. My father has no sons.'

The people said that he must be buried very soon, and that it must be out in the open. I did not see how it would be possible to get him out of that room. The hole in the floor was too narrow for anyone to climb down carrying another body. I knew that the task was mine and the thought oppressed me so that all I could do was sit on the floor with my head in my hands. My will was paralysed by the impossible task, and grief and pity for my poor dead brother blinded my eyes with tears. One of the watchers, a young woman, put her arms about my shoulders to comfort me. I looked at her and discovered that she was my daughter as she will be when she approaches womanhood. I bowed my head and wiped away my tears.

One of the men said that he would move the body downstairs for me. I looked up to thank him and recognised Merthun, not as I know him now, but as a youth. He took a board from the floor and bound my brother's remains to it and thus was able to slide him down the ladders. It was not a dignified proceeding but far better than any I could devise and once we were on the ground floor I thanked him with tears in my eyes. I looked out of the door and saw that his grave had been dug – a brown hole in the fresh green of the fields. Beyond the grave ran a wide blue river where I could see men fishing and women washing clothes. I wondered at their callousness but then I reflected that he was not their brother, so there was no cause of grief to them.

'Indeed he is their brother,' said Merthun. 'But they do not mourn for him who is not yet dead.'

'He is dead to me,' I cried. 'I will never see him or speak to him again and that is causing me grief.'

'That is as it should be,' he said, 'but you and he are both what those of human stock call immortal. Therefore they will not truly grieve for either of you, nor will they believe you are dead no matter how much you weep and tear your clothes.

'I must leave you now, but before I go I must warn you that you will meet your brother once more before you leave this dale. When you do, be sure that you treat him properly, or you will be lost for ever.'

My daughter told me that she must go into the world. I agreed with her that it would not be fitting for her to stay with me in the house of the dead and kissed her. We wept for this parting but there was no help for it. Now I was completely alone with my dead brother. I was all at once filled with fear and disgust at being so close to a corpse and had to drive myself to look at the naked body. He now lay in a wooden chest which was just long enough for his corpse but much wider. He was white and hairless and slender. Nothing of the well-muscled warrior showed about him. His hands were soft and white; his neck long and slim; his hair sleek and long and curled. I thought,

'He would not have amounted to much if he had lived,' and I took off my tunic to cover his nakedness.

A few old men had come in and they told me I would have to get into the kist with the body. They were carrying leafy branches from the trees outside and began to cover my brother with them. At first I refused to lie down beside the dead and was horrified to think that I might be buried alive with him. However the old men had said nothing about my own burial, so I thought I might escape. I swallowed my disgust and lay down with the body. It was cold to the touch, but there had not been time for the poisonous vapours to form around it. I sprang out of the kist at once and stood trembling while they carried it out to the grave. I stood in the doorway and watched them covering the kist with earth and heard them singing as they worked. Then they covered the ground with flowers and grass and branches so that none could say where the body was lying.

I left that clearing and found that I had now to carry a huge burden on my back. As I struggled along the woodland track, I saw the letters on the trees again, but I still could not understand the words. I travelled onwards and overtook an old woman bent double under a heap of firewood. When I came up beside her she looked at me sideways and smiled, wrinkling her face and showing her pink gums. She said,

'Ah, it is good to have a travelling companion. Come with me to my hut and we will pass the time of day pleasantly. We can talk about the good days of the past and boast about our grandchildren. I have some sweet butter that I buried last winter and the oatmeal is still good. You could stay for a while if you had a mind to.'

I was furious with rage to think that she had taken me for one as old as herself. I leaned across and slapped her across the head shouting loudly,

'You old fool, do you think I would waste my time in the hut of a landless old hag? I am the daughter of Usbathaden, high lord of the southern march of Alclut.'

The old woman fell into the beech mast beside the road. Her load of firewood fell off and scattered. She knelt on the ground weeping and slime ran from her nose and spittle hung from her lower lip.

'You disgusting creature,' I shrieked, 'why did you take me for one as old as you? My children, if they are alive, are hardly more than babies themselves.'

'Forgive me, mistress,' cried the old one. 'My eyes are not good. I did not see your face clearly. I took you for one as old and poor as I am. I will not trouble you again.'

I looked at the trees around me and at last I could read the words carved there. On one I saw 'PRIDE' on another 'CONCEIT' and once again the smell of rotten eggs filled my nose. The voice of the green lion came from near my heart saying,

'Today you are not old, it is true, but one day, as sure as the sun rises, you will be. Remember that when you look into a rheumy eye and feel contempt.'

'No, mother,' I said, and lifted her to her feet. 'It is you who should forgive me.'

I helped her to gather her firewood again and carried it to her hut in the next clearing. There I stayed for a night and shared her butter and listened to her memories. I slept the night beside her on her sour bed and in the morning I left my shoes with her for I saw that her pattens were broken. As I walked away I read 'CHARITY' and 'PATIENCE' on the trees beside the path. My bundle seemed even heavier that morning as I set off and I wondered how much further I would have to take it, and how much heavier it would get. I heard the sound of a horn in the distance, and an answering note from a point along the road ahead. I walked on and soon met the huntsman.

He was tall and stout and clothed in animal skins. His chest was as deep as a barrel and covered with black hair. His arms were hairy also and as thick as a bull's leg. His face was red and a deep scar ran from his forehead, through his eyebrow, to his jaw. He stood in the path and stared at me so boldly that for the first time I realised that I was wearing only my shift. I dropped my bundle and knelt behind it for modesty. He came up to me then and said,

'What a pretty creature! And all on her own, too. It is not right that one as plump and tasty should be walking the road all alone. If I come with you and protect you from others will you promise to be pleasant to me?'

This can only be the realm of Earth and the summer solstice where ills are received through the eyes. I do not understand the dream here but I can see why Hw was troubled by it.

Rage burnt in my belly then, and I joyfully let it burn until I noticed the word RAGE written on the tree beside me. What was I to do? If I became weak and yielding I would be forced to submit to this man's will. If I used all my strength I would fail in charity. I clasped my hands together on top of my pack and said,

'How will you deal with me? I have no one in the world to care for me and the road I have to travel is long.'

He came towards me, chuckling, and stood on the other side of my pack gazing down at me.

'How shall I deal with you?' he said. 'Well, pretty one, since you are alone in the world, I think I will deal with you just as I please.'

'That was the wrong answer,' I said, and I stood up and pushed him away from me with all my strength. He reeled backwards, his arms flailing and was brought to a halt only by smashing into a tree. He sank to the ground and lay still. I went to him and found that he was still alive, but badly stunned.

'Poor creature,' I thought, 'this is his trial as well as mine.'

Ahead of me down the road I saw a line of smoke rising and I decided that it must come from his home. I picked him up in my arms, carried him there and laid him in his bed. There were no bleeding wounds about his body and his breath came and went lightly and steadily. When I opened his eyelids, however, there was no life in his eyes so I set to and treated him as I had my child when he had been injured in the same way.

As the day faded into twilight his eyes opened and he gave a groan. I was filled with joy, for I had begun to think I might have killed him. There was no sign of a wife to run the house, so I made up the fire and cooked a meal for us both. He was very strong and soon revived enough to eat a little, but then sank back on to the bed with his hands on his head.

'Woman, I think you have finished me,' he said.

'You will be well soon,' I told him. I found some rags which I soaked in water and used to keep his head cool. Sometimes the pain made him weep and all I could do for him was to cradle his head and caress him as if her were a babe. Pity filled me and I saw that even this brutal woodsman was once an infant crying for his mother's breast. In that moment I realised that I could forgive the worst crime if I could see the criminal clearly. But the lion in me said,

'You can say that now, but you still have the strength of your kindred to defend yourself. What if you were weak? Could you still feel so generous?'

In the early hours of the morning the woodsman managed to find sleep. By the time I had made the morning meal, he woke and smiled at me.

'My pain is gone,' he said with delight. 'You have cared for me. How am I to thank you?'

'You do not need to thank me. I caused the pain to start, it is only just that I should do my best to remove it.'

'You did not cause the pain,' he said. 'I had a very unlucky fall and struck my head on a tree. You had nothing to do with it.'

It pleased him to think so and I did not see why I should argue. We finished our meal and I prepared to leave. He came up behind me and crushed me in his arms.

'Will you not stay for a while?' he said.

I decided that whatever happened I would be as weak as any woman.

'I have to leave,' I told him. 'I am searching for my children who were taken from me by my husband's mother.'

'A couple of days will make no difference. Why not stay and rest?'

'If I stay, I do not think I will find much rest.'

He grinned lecherously.

'I will be generous with you,' he said. 'I am a good man. I do what the priest tells me nearly all the time.'

'I do not doubt it,' I said, 'but I must find my children. If I find them, I promise I will come back. Then I will stay with you.'

He pouted but let me go. I ran back along the road to find my burden and as I went I wondered that I had lied to the man, for it is not the way of my family to tell falsehood. We might keep silent or give incomplete answers, but we never lie. Then I saw that as a weak woman I had no other weapon to use against him. If I had not lied he would have forced me, but still the dishonour lay heavy on my soul. I felt it might be better to lie with him as an honest woman than to escape him as a liar.

I picked up my load and grunted at the weight of it. At last I got it on to my back and made off to the next clearing. As I approached it I saw light was flooding out. My burden felt so heavy I began to fear that the bones of my legs would break. Gasping for breath, I advanced step by step into the blinding light with my head bowed, until a voice said, 'Stop.' I looked up and saw in front of me a massive throne of crystal decorated with gold. On the throne sat three men. On the right hand side sat the Father – an old man with a long white beard – who frowned at me grimly. In the middle sat the Moor who had ridden ahead of me in the golden desert and he stared over my head. On the left was my brother, the Son, who had risen from the dead. He was smiling at me.

'You knew we would meet again,' he said.

'What do you want from me?' I asked.

'Babylon the great is fallen, is fallen, and is become the habitation of devils,' said the Father.

'I am yet standing,' I answered, 'and I am the habitation of one devil only.'

'Are you defying me?' said the Father in a voice like thunder.

'You may take it so, if you wish,' I answered. 'You have been abusing me for centuries and your venom is as tedious as it is futile. It was my destiny that for a while I listened to what you said and, poor fool, I believed it. Now a brighter day has begun for me and your lies no longer have any power.'

The Guide said nothing but pulled his many-coloured coat around him tightly. He was also wearing the wide-brimmed hat. The Son shifted in his seat and I looked at him. He was garlanded with oak leaves and wore a short green tunic. His slender white legs were bare and on his feet he wore only thin sandals.

'I have risen from the grave,' he announced. 'Now I have attained perfection and will reign for ever with my Father and his brother. Our Kingdom will last for all of eternity.' He smiled broadly and raised his hand to welcome me. 'You have been chosen as one of the Elect who may live forever and contemplate our Presence.'

'I have lived long,' I said, 'and I have travelled much in this country. In all that time I have never heard such folly.'

The sky behind the throne darkened but I found that my burden was lighter. I decided to speak though the sky itself should fall on me.

'You claim that you have attained perfection,' I said to the Son. 'How can you make such a claim?'

'It is easy for me to make it, for I have conquered death itself. If I were less than perfect I could not have done so. Death is a punishment for imperfection and all humans are imperfect but I am not. I am the Son of the Father, so I could attain perfection and conquer death. Now I will reign forever with my Father.'

I fear he would have prattled on in this manner for much longer if I had not raised my hand to silence him.

'Hear me,' I said, 'and answer. How will it benefit this kingdom to be ruled by a puppet?'

The clouds behind the throne became black but I found I could stand up straight. The three who sat on the throne said nothing. I went on,

'Now that you have attained perfection, you may not change or you will no longer be perfect. Is that correct?'

All three nodded.

'For the Father and the Guide this is as it should be, but for the Son this is doubtful.'

'Be silent, woman,' thundered the Father. 'You may not doubt. Your purpose is to contemplate our perfection.'

'I have told you to be silent,' I said, and addressed the Son.

'You stand before me in the guise of a young man, a youth. Why is this?'

'It is necessary that I should be young. My eternal youthfulness is part of the perfection of this trinity.'

'If that is what you think, then you have misunderstood the nature of youth. You are young now, but if you start to reign for Eternity, in a few decades you will no longer be young. If you reign for a few centuries you will be ancient as is your Father. Therefore you will impair the perfection of your Trinity.'

Tears had started in his eyes. He said,

'What, then is the nature of youth?'

'It is the nature of youth to change, to suffer, to sin and sometimes to die. Only old men are perfect and unchanging in their perfection. If you do not change you will one day merely be old, like your Father and you will be nothing more than his mouthpiece.'

'What shall I do if perfection is denied me?' he cried.

'Join with me,' I said. 'Let me into your life of the mind and I will bring you into the world of the flesh.'

'I will never do that. The mind's punishment is being deprived of the presence of God by the dragging of the flesh.'

'This is childishness. Without the flesh there is no temptation; if there is no temptation there is no trial of steadfastness. The true punishment of the mind is that without flesh it cannot know itself.'

The tears ran down his face as he said,

'You have condemned me to die.'

'True,' I answered, 'but what cannot die cannot live. Only that which knows it dies, knows that it lives.'

The sky was now inky black, but at once the straps of my burden broke and I stood free of it. Without another word I ran towards the distant mountains and the heart of the darkness. As I travelled up the mountain pass, the Guide caught up with me. For the first time he spoke to me and said,

'You are about to enter the last place of trial. Here you will see agonies worse than any you have seen before.'

I looked at the red glow in the sky ahead of me.

'Is this to be a place of punishment?' I asked.

'You may take it so, if you wish.'

'Do you recommend that I should?'

'Punishment is an idea the humans have designed to keep order in their lives,' he said. 'It has no meaning for such as ourselves.'

'If I am human, I will be punished. If I am not, I will be spared.'

For answer he pointed to a wide dish made of gold which lay in our path. The dish spoke and said,

'You will soon know who you are, and who I am.'

I stepped past the bowl and looked down into the valley. It was dimly lit by the red glow of a setting sun and the ground was littered with black rocks. In the middle of the valley stood a fortress built of black stone and surrounded by a low wall. I could see light in only one window. I looked round and found that I was alone. I stepped forward and felt my bare feet scorched by the rocks.

'If I move swiftly I will not be burned,' I told myself and hurried down the mountainside.

Finally we come to the realm of air. The heat and moisture of blood are the strongest influences here and blood is the strongest humour working on us. The wind is from the west and the ill of it is drawn in through the nostrils. There is struggle and diseases can be seen to start in the morning. All this I had of Merthun's books.

The dish called me back and said,

'You do not have to pass this way if you do not wish to. This is a place of special trial.'

'All this journey has been of my own choosing,' I replied. 'Having come so far, it would be foolish to balk here.'

I set off down the slope as fast as I could. By the time I reached the black fortress my feet were burnt and swollen. I looked over the wall and saw that the ground had been planted as a garden with flowers and with pulses. The leaves of the plants were gray instead of green and every flower and every bean was coloured red.

'I am glad I will not be eating here,' I said, and walked to the door of the hall. Here at least the door step was made of a cool stone and I stood on it to take the pain out of my feet for a moment. I was enjoying the sensation when the door was pulled open and a voice said,

'You must hurry in, now. The feast is about to start.'

The passages inside were lit with a dull red glow and I could see to find my way. The stones underfoot were no more than warm and spared my feet from more blistering. All at once I came upon a wide plank door which opened as I approached, flooding the passageway with brilliant amber light. Pain filled my head as my eyes struggled with the brightness and I covered my face for a moment. When I could see once more I made out, through my tears, a long trestle running up the centre of the hall. The wall at the far end of the hall was one vast fire where many, many sides of beef and whole boars were spitted and roasting. A crowd of noisy revellers sat at the table drinking wine and eating great slices of meat which they cut off the hot carcases laid in front of them. No one passed the wine jugs, but everyone snatched the nearest to him and drank from it. There was a good linen cloth laid on the table, but spilt wine and blood from the meat had flooded over it till it was bright red. Nobody noticed that I had arrived.

In the middle of the table I thought I saw two little boys bound back to back, but as I approached I saw that they were only young white calves. They both had garlands of white flowers on their heads and their hoofs had been painted red. I took a seat at the table and the calves turned to look at me. Their mournful gaze fixed on me so firmly that I said,

'Please do not stare so hard. I have not eaten any of your family, nor do I plan to do so.'

To my horror they replied,

'Not so, you are planning to eat many of our kindred.'

'What is this folly?' I cried. 'I have not eaten red meat for many years.'

'Do you not know us?' said the larger of the two. 'You, of all the crowd here should know us. That you do not causes me

276

much sorrow. We are the sons that were stolen from you. We have been kept especially for the day when you would come here.'

'Kept for my arrival. What do you mean?'

'Tonight we are to be slaughtered in your honour.'

'What honour is this?' I asked. 'From the moment I came into the hall no one has spoken to me, let alone shown honour. You must be wrong.'

'There is no doubt,' said Asgrim. 'We are very glad to see you, for now we will find our fate. We have grown weary of living all this time, so young that we could not follow our destiny. If we had been older at the time of our death we would have had penances to perform for our own sins. All we can do now is die for others, but soon we will be released, for here comes the butcher.'

I turned to see where he was looking and saw someone approaching with a short black spear. I could not be sure whether the creature I was looking at was a very small man or a young boy, for his face was hidden by the brim of his wide hat. The butcher went up to the table and slipped underneath it.

'No,' I cried, 'this cannot be. I cannot stand by and watch you being slaughtered.'

'This is not slaughter,' said Asgrim, 'this is sacrifice.'

I saw then that an iron griddle formed the middle span of the table and that the calves had been tied on to it. The manikin appeared under the griddle. He thrust the spear upwards into the bodies of the calves and their blood rushed out and covered him. I laid myself across the table and wept. All around me the feast went on, as noisy and uncaring as before.

I lifted my head to look at the bodies of my sons before they would be taken for roasting. The bodies were gone and in their place there grew a small rose bush. There was only one flower on the bush and as I looked at it it seemed to reach towards me. I cut it off the blossom, stroked its soft red petals, and put my lips to them. The damp golden mat in the middle fascinated me and I drew my finger over it then rubbed it against my cheek. Suddenly the din in the hall stopped. I looked up and saw that there was no one sitting near me. Everyone had drawn away but they were staring at me with hatred in their eyes. I jumped to my feet, holding my rose against me. There was a low doorway on the other side of the hall and I thought that if I could get through it, I might be safe from the malice I felt all around me. I started to run but they were ready for me and I had to leap on to the table. The crowd all reached up to seize me and I saw that their hands were covered with the thorns of roses. One of them took a hold on my shift and I threw myself off the table to escape. My shift tore up the back, but I was near the door now and I ran for it. Other hands gripped the garment and I felt it tearing into ribbons as I plunged through the opening. The last shreds of clothing fell off me but I was free and running through the darkness.

I ran on down a sloping tunnel for a long time. My pursuers were far behind me and I was sure I had escaped when I felt my arm taken in a grip of iron. The other arm was seized also and, shocked, I dropped my rose. I was lifted and felt my back pressed hard against a wall. It came to me, then, that I might try to free myself, but in the darkness I could not be sure how far I was off the ground. I might escape the grip of whatever it was that held me, only to fall and kill myself. I waited to see what would happen. There was a pause, and I heard someone breathing near me. Then I screamed, for a wooden peg was driven into one shoulder, and I continued screaming as a peg was driven into the other. Again a pause and pegs were driven into my knees, then the grip was released and with terrible pain my weight was taken on the pegs.

The first screams had exhausted me but I could hear myself moaning in the dark. Time passed and nothing happened. The slightest movement brought me fourfold agony. I hung there and thought of the green lioness.

'I will be patient and devoted,' I thought, 'but to what will I be devoted?'

I put all my mind on keeping still and for a long time I felt no pain. After a while I noticed a glow in the darkness and I looked down to see that my breasts were gleaming with a faint golden light. As I stared at them my belly and then my limbs started to glow. The light grew stronger as I watched until I shone, blinding yellow, yet darkness still surrounded me. Something was stopping the light from leaving my body like eyelids cover eyes. The pain where the pegs were driven through my body was getting worse, but now I could not find ease in keeping still.

'This must end very soon,' I thought, 'for there is no reason in it.'

The light had spread throughout my body and my face was glowing also. I sensed someone in the darkness ahead of me and I spoke aloud.

'Who is that?' I said. 'Can you take me down from here? The pain is terrible and I am nearly worn out.'

Then I knew that the presence in the darkness was my father. I could feel his eyes looking at my nakedness and for a moment I felt shame.

'Turn your eyes away,' I begged him. 'It is not fitting that you should see me like this.'

'You are only as you should be in this place,' he answered and I knew that he was lusting for me. Suddenly all shame left me and I longed to couple with him. My glowing body ached with the desire for coitus, and again shame struck me to the heart. For a long time I hung there, at one moment racked with lust and in another racked with shame.

Then shame faded and lust died and I drowned in love. Like a tide of honey the joy of love and understanding rose up through me and suffused me from the roots of my hair to the soles of my feet. I found my voice again.

'Father, you are in the wrong place. It is not fitting that you should stand in front of me. You should be standing in the darkness behind me with the others I have met in this world. Go now where you belong and do not plague me and my sisters. We have done with you and found our hope in the world of mankind.'

I heard a mighty rushing of breath and ahead of me the darkness split. My father was a vast black hanging that tore from top to bottom and flew into the darkness at my back. Ahead of me now there was nothing but pure, white light. And the light was bathing me in song. The pain in my limbs was still there, but I could not feel it for the rapture of the light. For a time as short as the blink of an eye and as long as eternity I hung floating in bliss.

At last I heard my sister's name spoken and I returned to the world of men.

At the last the action of Hw's heart was so bad that it did not discharge its heat properly. Heat will have increased in his body and condensed in his lungs to form the fluid which drowned him. I have never heard how to use the willow-bark. I will try it.

The pages enclosed with this were the last that Hw was able to write. He has asked me, Merthun, to complete this before sending it to his brothers in Rintsnoc. The quality of my writing is poor, and I apologise for it, but since I have only lately learned to use this hand I beg indulgence from the reader. The last lines Hw wrote were written with much difficulty, since his fingers were swollen to twice their usual thickness. His legs also were swollen with fluid so that I could lay two of my fingers in them. The skin healed and broke every day and erupted a clear yellow liquor. He slept less and less in the night and could not lie flat for fear of choking. He coughed constantly, and at the end the spittle was mostly pink foam. There was also a constant rattling from his chest like the shingle under a stormy sea, and his eyes streamed with tears when he coughed. I told him that however mightily he had sinned, he was paying a great penance and was sure to go at once to heaven. He was cheerful as he replied,

'The penance is just. I have wronged someone and now I am sharing their last agony. I am drowning, just as they did. I would not have it any other way.'

He would not explain what he meant by this and I fear it is the truth that in the last days he was not clear in his mind. The thought kept troubling him that there were no places for hermits to go. He said,

'Mankind has covered the earth. Soon there will be no rock nor wasteland where we can escape them. We cannot hide. We must make our peace with them.'

This, or something like this, he repeated many times a day. He thanked me for my attentions but said that he wished for me to do him one service only, and that was to tell the world how it had ended here. It was a source of much concern to him that the record should be completed, so here I write it.

Culhuch and Olwen are more besotted with each other than they ever were in the first days they were together. Culhuch has recovered all his faculties, but one. It is as if 'Pig-Run-the-Strength-of-Three-Boars' had never lived. Many of the followers have left to find a harsher leader, where they will feel safe, and I must confess that at times I wonder if we are in danger under the rule of such a mild man. If any come to me saying the same doubts, I tell them that though the master may no longer command the men through harshness, the mistress will command them through love. I am not sure if I believe it but I must watch and wait to see what will become of us. All the Gods will witness that I hope I am right.

Certainly Olwen has the love of every man and woman in this dale. The freed slaves worship her in a way that offends the local presbyter. She has only to set foot out of the fortress for there to be crowds of eager followers standing at the roadside. Culhuch's mother went to fetch the daughter, and now no day passes without a dispute on the beauties of the child and the merits of her mother.

A school has been set up for all the children of the dale no matter who their father might be. The slave children were told they might go to their parents if they wished, and most of them are now waiting to find a boat that will take them home. Some have decided to stay here, and they are so devoted to their mistress that they have formed into a flock who settle at her feet whenever she sits down.

Of all the strange things that have happened here over the last few weeks, the strangest has been the building of the shrine. Olwen's sister, who was killed for wounding Culhuch, has become an object of worship. In the steading where her pyre was laid, and on the beach where she died, the people spend many hours assembling her relics. Anything which might seem to have a slight connection with the woman – a long black hair or a lump of ash – is taken to a site beside the river. There it is placed in a small wooden house.

Mannikins have been seen coming and going in the dale, but I cannot find out anything about them. I know I should tell Hw of this, but I cannot find it in my heart to do so. Olwen knows nothing about it, and when I told Culhuch, he merely smiled. I do not see why I should be troubled.

Hw died soon after Easter day. In his last days of sickness he had to fight for every breath and with such a gurgling and popping in his chest that I said he sounded like a hot kettle. He nodded agreement and we laughed. In spite of his hardships he made a serene and cheerful end. He was very feverish at times, but my willow-bark helped him. I showed him the record of events here enclosed and he smiled approval. It seems strange to me that he insisted his record be complete, since there is no chance of it being read by anyone else. It gave him comfort. I only hope that nothing will happen to give the lie to this account of happiness. It is my experience that fate, or God, or the Gods have their own plan which thwarts us at every bend in the road.

I will stop writing now, before anything can happen to cloud the clear skies. This is what Hw wished, and indeed, for him the story is over. All I can do for him now is write,

Valete.